A NATURAL CURIOSITY

M&S

By Margaret Drabble

FICTION

A Summer Bird-Cage
The Garrick Year
The Millstone
Jerusalem the Golden
The Waterfall
The Needle's Eye
The Realms of Gold
The Ice Age
The Middle Ground
The Radiant Way

OTHER WORKS

Arnold Bennett: A Biography
A Writer's Britain
The Oxford Companion to
English Literature (edited)

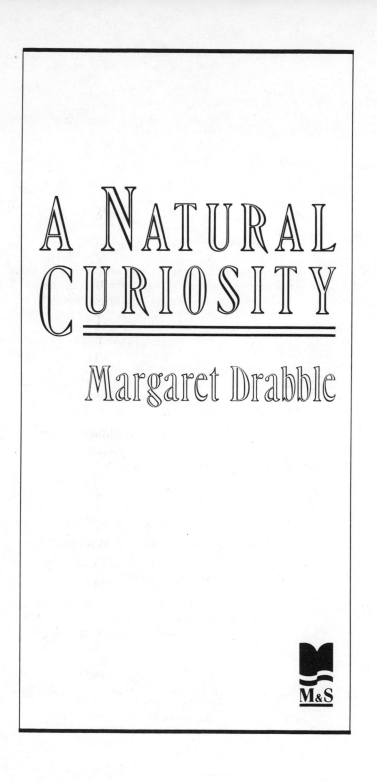

A NATURAL CURIOSITY

Margaret Drabble

M&S

Canadian Cataloguing in Publication Data

Drabble, Margaret, 1939-
A natural curiosity

Canadian ed.
ISBN 0-7710-2865-2

I. Title.

PR6054.R25N38 1989   823'.9'14   C89-094697-3

Printed and bound in the United States of America

First published in 1989 in the United States of America
by Viking Penguin, a division of Penguin Books USA Inc.
and in Great Britain by Penguin Books Ltd.

Published in Canada in 1989 by
McClelland & Stewart Inc.
The Canadian Publishers
481 University Avenue
Toronto, Ontario M5G 2E9

AUTHOR'S NOTE

A Natural Curiosity is a sequel to *The Radiant Way*, and picks up some of the characters and stories, while adding others. I had not intended to write a sequel, but felt that the earlier novel was in some way unfinished, that it had asked questions it had not answered, and introduced people who had hardly been allowed to speak. At the moment of writing this, I intend to write a third but very different volume, which will follow the adventures of Stephen Cox in Kampuchea.

Margaret Drabble
London, 1988

A Natural Curiosity

A low pale lemon grey sun hung over the winter moor. It swam, haloed, in the grey mist. The road climbed gently into obscurity. Dimly on either side appeared straw-grey tufts of long grasses, pale reeds, patches of dwindling, lingering snow. Grey shades, yellow shades, a soft damp white light. Alix Bowen gazed ahead, exalted. She was on her way to see her murderer. Her heart sang, in the cold landscape, as she drove towards the flat summit of the moor.

Alix Bowen goes to see her murderer quite regularly. This will be her first visit for a month, her Christmas gift, her New Year's gift. Some of her friends disapprove of what could now, Alix realizes, be described as an obsession, but most of them are too polite to comment. Her husband Brian says nothing to deter her. He smiles indulgently, anxiously, as he listens to her stories. If he thinks her interest excessive, or unnatural (which it is, and he must), he does not say so.

Alix's old friend Liz Headleand is less restrained. 'You're barmy, Alix,' Liz would comment, from time to time, over the phone, as Alix reports her murderer's latest intimations, her own most recent speculations. But then, Alix tells herself, Liz is probably jealous. Liz, a professional psychotherapist, probably thinks it quite wrong that an amateur meddler like Alix should have acquired such easy and privileged access to so notorious a criminal. Liz had missed her own chance to befriend the murderer. She, like Alix, had been in the same building with him, had been more or less held hostage by the police on his behalf: if Liz had thought quicker then, had acted quicker then, he could by now have been Liz's murderer, and Liz herself could be driving to visit him across this lonely moor.

The murderer had come Alix's way, without much intervention on her part. He had followed her, as it were. He and Alix were inextricably, mystically linked. Well, that was one way of looking at it. It was not Alix's, whatever her friends might suspect. But it *was* rather odd, reflected Alix, as she drove along through the mist at a steady fifty miles an hour, that he should have turned up here, more or less on her doorstep. She had moved north from London a couple of years ago, and he had followed her, though less voluntarily. It took Alix under an hour to drive from her north Northam suburban home to reach the desolate top-security prison which now housed Paul Whitmore. Not exactly her doorstep, but near enough: in the old days, when she had worked in London, it had taken her at least an hour and a half to drive across the city to work, whereas here, up here in the north, you could be out of town in ten minutes, in the depths of the landscape in twenty, and safely arrived at the iron gates of Porston Prison in fifty. If that's where you wanted to be.

'O come, O come, Ema-a-anuel, Redeem thy captive I-i-israel, That into exile dre-e-ear is gone, Far from the sight of Go-o-od's dear son,' sang Alix, cheerfully, as the white mist parted for her. She had the illusion of moving in a small patch of light, her own small pocket of clarity. She took it with her, it moved with her. The pale sun loomed. The horizons were invisible, but Alix knew they were there, would be there, and that she herself would see them again. The sleeping place of the sun, near the freezing of the sea. As the Ancients put it. And the sun indeed seems to slumber, up here in its dim haze, in its cold thrall.

Alix had brought a book as a Christmas present for her murderer. A new, illustrated book about Roman Britain and the resistance of the Brigantes. She had been browsing in it the night before, captivated by tales of Client Queen Cartimandua's deals with the Romans, by the stubborn resistance of her divorced husband Venutius. Colourful stuff, and colourfully narrated. It would make a good television mini-series, the story of Cartimandua. The treacherous Celtic queen, gold-torqued, magnificent, betraying her people for the civilization and comforts of the Romans: the rejected consort, hiding out in the snow with his bands of warriors. North and South, the Two Nations. One could make it topical, surely — a hint in the portrayal of Cartimandua of the Prime Minister, duplicitous Britannia, striking deals with a powerful America, abandoning the ancient culture of her own folk? Those stiff hair styles would surely lend themselves well to allusion, to analogue.

Alix had become intrigued, excited, the night before, and had got out her battered old purple Penguin Tacitus to look up the story, and yes, there it was, most aptly prefigured. 'And so Agricola trained the sons of chiefs in the liberal arts ... the wearing of our national dress came into favour ... and so, little by little, the Britons were led on to the amenities that make vice agreeable: arcades, baths, and sumptuous banquets. They called such novelties "civilization", when they were in reality only a feature of their enslavement.'

She read this passage aloud to Brian, who nodded agreement: Coca-Cola, McDonald's, blue jeans, jacuzzis ... yes, that was surely what Tacitus had in mind. But, continued Brian, mildly, he didn't suppose that the Brigantes and the Iceni and the Silures were very nice people, really, either. Hadn't they burned people alive in wicker cages? Hadn't they consulted the gods by inspecting the twisting human entrails of their tortured and sacrificed victims?

'A bit like P. Whitmore, you mean?' said Alix.

'Well, yes. Not unlike P. Whitmore.'

'I think those are just atrocity stories,' said Alix. 'Roman

3

propaganda against the native population. Recent research seems to indicate that maybe the ancient Britons weren't even very war-like. They were just peaceful farmers. That's the newest theory.'

'Really? And the figure of 60,000 Romans put to the sword by Boudicca is just a historical figment too, is it?'

'I don't know,' said Alix. 'I think that's a different period. And anyway, how can they possibly have known? How can they have counted?'

She paused, reflecting that P. Whitmore said he could not quite remember how many of the inhabitants of North Kensington he had killed. Brian, who could read her mind, said, 'And P. Whitmore, is *he* atrocious?'

'Well, that's what I'm trying to work out,' Alix had said, closing the Tacitus, getting up to put on the kettle.

Yes. P. Whitmore was very interested in the ancient Britons, and knew quite a lot about prehistory. Indeed, Alix wondered if the book she had bought him was perhaps a little too easy for him, a little too popular in tone? But it *was* new, and covered the new excavations by Ian Kettle at Eastwold, and had new speculations about the relationship of the Parisi and the Brigantes. And some very attractive photographs of Celtic mirrors and shields. And an authoritative introduction by an important professor, a real professor.

'If it's not too easy for me, surely it can't be too easy for him?' asked Alix, doubtfully, returning with a pot of coffee.

'Don't be absurd, my darling,' said Brian. 'He's lucky to get any book at all. *I* think it's a perfectly acceptable book. I'd be quite pleased if somebody gave me such a nice book. I think you've done him proud.'

And so, really, did Alix.

So why is Alix Bowen in such a good mood, as she drives across the top of Houndsback Moor?

Alix Bowen is in a good mood partly because her protégé, Paul Whitmore, is offering her intellectual and psychological stimulus of an unusually invigorating nature. He has come to her by chance, but it is almost as if she had invented him, as an illustration of whatever it is she wishes to discover about human nature. At the age of fifty, Alix had come to recognize that for some reason as yet obscure to her, she, an exceptionally law-abiding and mild-mannered and conscientious citizen, has always been peculiarly interested in prisons, discipline, conviction, violence and the criminal mentality. Is it perhaps *because* she is so 'nice' that she is so intrigued? Does her interest express her other darker ever-repressed self? Will that repressed self break out one day wildly or can it remain for ever latent, as, apparently, can the aggressive nature of *Onychomys leucogaster*, the stocky stubborn mouse of Utah (see study by L. D. Clark)? It is getting a little late for it to break out now. She is already fifty-one, inexorably heading for fifty-two. Or maybe it is precisely *because* she definitively *lacks* this element in her psyche that she is drawn towards it, and has spent so much of her adult life teaching in prisons and studying the deviant behaviour of female offenders? As though in a search for her own wholeness? Or in search of a refutation of the concept of original sin?

Alix does not know. But she does realize that in P. Whitmore she has stumbled upon an uncannily appropriate subject of inquiry. He fits her queries geometrically. He is like a theorem. When she has measured him, she will know the answer to herself and to the whole matter. The Nature of Man. Original Sin. Evil and Good. It is all to be studied, there, in captive P. Whitmore, towards whom she now drives, bearing her propitiatory copy of *The Queen, the Rebel and Rome: A Study of the Resistance of the Brigantes AD 40–AD 79*. It is not entirely coincidental that Porston Prison is sited in the heartland of the ancient territory of the Brigantes. The interest of Paul Whitmore and Alix Bowen in the

Brigantes has been much stimulated by the location of the prison and by the recent Yorkshire Television programme on the finds of Ian Kettle's dig. Had the prison been in Newport, or Colchester, other aspects of the historical past might well have captured their attention, other tribes might have solicited their sympathy: but then, of course, they would not have been together to be so captivated.

Paul Whitmore is serving a life sentence. He was convicted of the murder of four women and one man, although he claims to have killed at least one more. The last of the corpses was that of an old friend and professional acquaintance of Alix's, a young woman called Jilly Fox, whose severed head was discovered in Alix's car in a shabby street in North Kensington. Paul Whitmore was in the habit of decapitating his victims. He did not know why, or so he told Alix, but Alix was in the process of working it out.

Paul Whitmore had become something of a folk monster, because of the sensational nature of his crimes. His personality, however, did little to stimulate that sensation. He was a dull-voiced, monotonous, studious young man, not a flamboyant monster. The Horror of Harrow Road (for such had been his sobriquet) proved something of a disappointment, to those in search of *La Bête Humaine.* Even the women's lobby found him rather dull. There was not much to get at, in Paul Whitmore. No obvious hatred of women, no Ripper-like despising of prostitutes. The crimes had not been sexual, or not obviously so. Members of the anti-racism lobby had slightly more to build on, as most of the victims (although not Jilly Fox) had been black, but they had not managed to build much, for even they conceded that maybe the victims had been black for geographical reasons, because Paul Whitmore happened to live at the wrong end of Ladbroke Grove. They suggested that the police might have been more active had the victims been white, pointed out that it was only after the peculiarly noticeable murder of the white Jilly

Fox that P. Whitmore had been apprehended, but these arguments did not carry much conviction, even to themselves.
P. Whitmore remained unclaimed, unwanted.

Alix Bowen had kept quiet about her association with him, her
claiming of him. She did not fancy poisonous letters from either
lobby, or from the general public, which would, *en masse*, though
not human soul by human soul, have liked to see the Horror
hung, drawn and quartered and mouldering on Tower Bridge,
rather than visited by Alix Bowen bearing an illustrated book on
Roman Britain costing £9.95.

She talked about him to Brian, and to her friend Liz Headleand,
and to her employer, the ancient poet Howard Beaver, the Grand
Old Man of Yorkshire letters. The ancient poet was way beyond
all moral judgement, and was possessed, in the last evenings of
his life, with what Alix considered an admirably lively curiosity
about Paul Whitmore.

The ancient poet would listen, fascinated, as Alix described
what she had learned of Paul's childhood and background. The
father was a butcher, the mother a hairdresser, in a small town in
the north Midlands. When the mother ran off with a lorry driver,
Paul had been taken into care for a while, and then returned to
his father. He had been taken on a school outing at the age of
eleven to see the Bog Man of Buller. He had become obsessed
by death and human sacrifice. He had devoured books on the
Druids and Stonehenge, on the Celts and the Romans, on the old
gods. History had been his favourite subject, although he had
also, less dangerously, enjoyed botany. He had no doubt seemed
a docile pupil, with a good future ahead. A quiet boy, who liked
to avoid the playground's rough and tumble, who liked to keep
his nose in a book.

Beaver too had been, was interested in ancient Britain. He had
even written a poem about the Bog Man of Buller. He was very
interested in Paul Whitmore's interests.

7

He made Alix find the poem, read it aloud to her, noisily. It was an uncollected piece, originally published in *Collusion*. 'You can read it to your murderer, if you like,' he offered, helpfully, provocatively.

'No thank you,' said Alix, primly. 'I don't think he'd like it. He's not into Modernism. He likes Swinburne.'

Reading Swinburne, alone, in his lonely flat. Dusky ladies, delicious tortures, Our Lady of Pain.

Paul did not, in fact, read Swinburne, but he might have done, reflected Alix. As she invented P. Whitmore.

The ancient poet found the whole subject very entertaining.

A poet and a murderer. Odd company I now keep, thought Alix to herself jubilantly as she traversed the sodden high flatland, beneath a winter sky.

Ancient crimes arise to declare themselves, to invite detection. Graves weep blood, sinners return to the fatal scene, the primal crime. And Alix Bowen once again finds herself in front of Paul Whitmore, in the visiting room, with its strange huge view. This Victorian building is so designed that once inside, once through the clanging gates and the turning of the keys, one cannot see the walls and watch-towers that surround it. There is an illusion of freedom, of space, of being islanded upon the moor. Not imprisoned, but stranded, with all perspectives opening, helplessly, widely, impersonally, meaninglessly, for ever.

Alix is entranced and appalled by this view, but looks down from it to Paul Whitmore, who is inspecting Alix's gift.

'Thank you very much,' he says, politely.

'It's really quite interesting,' says Alix. 'In fact, I think I may get myself a copy too.'

Paul Whitmore leafed through the pages, pausing at a photograph of a Parisi chariot burial. A skeleton lay between two great preserved iron wheels, which retained traces of wooden spokes.

'There's an exhibition of British archaeology on at the British Museum,' said Alix. 'A friend sent me a catalogue. I must try to get down to see it.'

Paul was reading the captions. 'A woman,' he said. 'A tribal queen, it says. They say she was buried with a side of pork on top of her. And an iron mirror.'

'A side of *pork*?' echoed Alix. 'I missed that bit. Show me.'

He handed the book back to her. She stared.

'I can't see a side of pork,' she said.

'I suppose it rotted,' said Paul Whitmore.

'Then how did they know it was there?' asked Alix. Foolishly. Paul looked at her in friendly contempt, and they both laughed.

'I don't know much about archaeological techniques,' said Alix, in apology.

'I had a letter from my Dad,' said Paul. 'He says he's shut up the shop. My fault, he says.'

Alix did not want to imply that it was not, so said nothing.

'He blames me,' continued Paul, experimentally.

'He must be getting on a bit anyway,' said Alix, as a diversionary tactic, as a semi-excuse. One of these days, Alix fears, Paul will ask her to go and visit his father. She half hopes he will, half fears it. Paul's father had been pursued by and interviewed by the press at the time of the trial, but had not said much. Would he have more to say now?

'Fifty-eight, he is,' said Paul.

A silence fell, during which Alix reflected that she was getting on a bit too and that, though it did not seem so to her, it must seem so to others, including Paul, who was young enough to be her son.

Paul abandoned the subject of his father, turned another page, and lit on a picture of a coin portraying the vanquished Britannia, elegantly perched. From the next page, the Colchester sphinx with a human head in her forepaws gazed bare-breasted at them.

Riddles, mysteries. How to read them? *Was* there any way of reading them? Was this mild amateur scholar victim, villain or accident? The sphinx's nose was battered, but her wings were powerfully built, undamaged.

Alix could tell that Paul was pleased with the book, and this gave her pleasure. Though why she should try so hard to please a convicted multi-murderer is a riddle, a mystery.

Ancient crimes. Clive and Susie Enderby contemplated them over a glass of sherry. Separately, together, a whole assortment of them. They were both in a state of mild shock, though neither would have admitted it. The new year had begun badly. This evening, Susie had put on her new mustard-coloured layered co-ordinates, to cheer herself up, but they hadn't made her feel all that cheerful. She kept glancing at herself in the carefully angled mirror over the fake marble mantelshelf, to keep up morale. And this was supposed to be a good year, a prosperous year, with Enderby & Enderby in its glittering new premises in Dean Street and Clive in the running to become the youngest ever President of the Chamber of Commerce. A pity it had started off on such an odd note. They should never have gone to Janice's. It was Janice's fault. But the mustard was a good shade. And a good dry silky rustly texture too. She stroked her own sleeve. Amber. Amber would look good on the mustard. The false gas fire glowed.

Domestic tranquillity. The children were playing upstairs, already in their nightclothes, model children. The table was laid in the dining-room, with cloth and candles, for a rare quiet meal together. Susie had looked forward to this evening, had hoped that it might be a small occasion for celebration, for self-congratulation, for closeness. Not that she had consciously thought that she and Clive were growing apart, no, but he was so busy these days, so preoccupied – as indeed he was now, but at least it was by something that she knew about, something that she understood. Susie did not understand Regional Development Grants and European Investment Strategies and Incentive Zones, but she understood all too well what had happened the night before, at Janice's, and could feel herself, despite herself, drawn towards dragging it up again. Clive couldn't just go on sitting there, saying nothing, sipping his sherry. And why was he having a sherry anyway? He usually had a gin and tonic. Was it meant to be some kind of comment or something?

The silence was irritable, painful. It was all Janice's fault.

'What an evening,' said Susie, at last, irresistibly. 'I'm never going to try to make you go to Janice's again.'

'No need to assume responsibility,' said Clive. 'She's my sister-in-law, not yours.'

'But I was at school with her,' said Susie.

'That's hardly *your* fault,' said dynamic thirty-eight-year-old Clive Enderby, with a shade of his usual briskness.

'Though as a matter of fact,' said Susie, ominously changing position in the corner of the settee, 'though as a matter of *fact*, I don't quite see *why* we were all so upset. By what Janice said. After all, it was probably true.'

Clive gazed at his bouncy chestnut-haired wife in alarm. She couldn't want to talk about it, could she? He couldn't face it. No, he couldn't face it. There are some things one just can't talk about. Janice had cheated. She had broken the rules. Was every wife in Hansborough, Breasborough and Northam, was every wife in Yorkshire, about to start cheating too?

Susie smiled, edgily.

'Actually, *I* blame Edward,' she said.

'I don't see why we have to blame anyone,' said Clive. 'It's not Edward's fault that he's married to a neurotic bitch on the verge of a nervous breakdown.'

'How do you know it isn't?' asked Susie.

11

Feminism had reached South Yorkshire with a vengeance, in the 1980s. Or at least that is one interpretation of the scene at Edward Enderby's on New Year's Day, and of Susie's reaction to that scene.

I suppose, thought Clive, we may live to find it funny. But it hadn't been funny at the time. And Susie was right, the whole thing was probably Edward's fault. Edward had always been a bully, with a sadistic sense of humour: where he got it from, his younger brother Clive couldn't imagine. Early ill health, perhaps. Quick-tempered Edward, always ready to put people down. Thin, even gaunt, now, in his early forties. Pushing and pushing. Teasing beyond the limit. Ambition disappointed. He'd always taken it out on Clive, but Clive, so brightly prosperous, had learned to fight back amiably, without hurting, without being hurt. Why quarrel with one's one-and-only brother? That had been Clive's attitude.

But last night had been over the top. Right over the top. Drink, was it? Edward never seemed to drink much, to be drunk, but you could never tell. He'd started at the beginning of dinner, teasing Susie about her new hair colour, teasing Clive about his posh new premises, asking uncomfortable questions of Derek and Alice Newton about their son who'd dropped out of the sixth form at King Henry's, embarking on a whole run of risky jokes about AIDS. Janice had looked uncomfortable through a lot of this, though whether that was because she didn't like the chat, or because her mind was elsewhere, you couldn't really tell. She was a very nervous hostess, was Janice, a bit of a perfectionist who managed to make everyone feel slightly uncomfortable as she dished up not-quite-perfect meals. She kept apologizing because the beef was a little overdone. They all assured her they liked it overdone. And anyway, in Clive's view it wasn't over-done at all, it was practically raw, so what was the woman talking about? Not that he minded, he liked it red, himself, he really didn't like it overdone. He caught Susie's eye and smiled, as he tucked in. He hated cringing and apologies. He liked people to be sure of themselves. Like Susie.

It was over the second helpings of beef (second helpings they all felt obliged to accept) that Edward really got going. Reminiscing about meals of the past, cooked by their mother. Not a very good topic, in Clive's view, as the Newtons were new to the district and had never met the colourful quaint old Mrs Enderby, but less dangerous, it proved, than reminiscences about Janice's early days of cooking. 'And you'd never believe this, from this *excellent* meal we've just eaten tonight,' said Edward Enderby, smiling a little manically, gesticulating with the carving knife, 'but Janice, when I first met her, was an *atrocious* cook. *Atrocious.* Couldn't boil an egg, could you, darling?' Janice stared at her husband with loathing, while the others politely laughed. 'You remember that first chicken you cooked, when my mother came round? Left the giblets inside in a little plastic bag, didn't you? Cooked the little plastic bag and all? Didn't you, my darling?'

'That wasn't for your mother,' said Janice, in a reasonably equable tone. 'I remember it well. It was for Kate and Bill Amies. It *was* embarrassing.'

So far, so good. They all sat round and munched the red flesh.

'No, no,' said Edward, his grey eyes glinting, 'it was definitely for my mother. I remember it well.'

'No,' said Janice, firmly, but with a note of slight (and to Clive quite understandable) distress creeping into her manner. 'No, it wasn't for your mother, it was for Kate and Bill Amies. I remember it well.'

'A little of the gravy?' asked Clive, desperately, passing the new fashionable Christmas present *gras et maigre* sauce-boat along the table to Janice. It ran with thin red blood. No gras, no alleviating emollient gras.

'No, no, for my *mother*,' repeated Edward. 'We did laugh. Yes, you've learned a thing or two since then, Janice. You've learned a thing or two about cooking since then.'

'It was Kate and Bill, and we'd only been married a fortnight,' said Janice. 'It was the first time we ever had anyone round.'

'My mother,' said Edward, helping himself to another roast potato. 'Yes, you've improved since those days.' And he laughed, heartily, from his thin asthmatic chest.

'Yes, we'd only been married a fortnight,' said Janice, staring straight across the table at Edward. 'I didn't know much about cooking. And as I remember, you didn't know much about fucking, in those days. We weren't much good, either of us. At cooking or fucking.'

Edward's face was, Clive had to admit to himself, a study. He turned dark red (which for so pale and grey a man was astonishing) and a vein stood up terribly in his forehead.

One didn't use words like fucking, over dinner, like that, in 1987, in Yorkshire, in the presence of strangers. It wasn't done. Or certainly not done to use such a word seriously. As Janice Enderby had done.

A terrible silence fell over the gravy. Susie coughed, nervously. Edward twitched. The Newtons looked at their plates. The unspeakable had been said. Three sexual initiations, three wedding nights, three honeymoons, played themselves in mental images for the three couples around the table. Clive and Susie guessed that their memories were the least disagreeable, as they were the ones to find their tongues first.

'Well, we all learn as we get older,' said Susie, platitudinously but boldly: and, simultaneously, Clive volunteered 'Well, I know I shouldn't say so, but *I* think Janice's beef is much better than Ma's ever was, she always overcooked it, and her Yorkshire puddings were like soggy dollops of wet cement.'

'I *like* soggy Yorkshire,' said Alice, gamely, and the conversation staggered on. But Janice and Edward said nothing more all evening. They had done one another in, they had murdered one another.

If looks could kill. Sticks and stones will break your bones, but words will never hurt you.

And now Clive and Susie Enderby sipped their sherry, in the safety of their own home, looking back over the evening before, on the first ominous night of the New Year, contemplating their own marriage and its chances of survival.

Fucking and cooking. Division of labour.

Susie had kept her side of this primitive bargain: Clive wondered, a little uneasily, if he had kept his. The unease of the 1980s. She hadn't seemed to fancy it much, after the birth of Vicky, but whose fault was that?

These thoughts were uncomfortable: surely it was dinner time? He glanced at his watch ostentatiously, but Susie didn't seem to notice. He guessed that she was going over it all, apportioning blame, beginning to blame him as well as Edward, blaming all Enderbys, blaming men in general and Enderbys in particular, abstracted by resentment as she sat neatly there in her mustard silk.

But Susie's mind had moved on. Susie was remembering, with a flutter of panic that she was sure was even now tinting her well-made-up complexion, an encounter on New Year's Eve, at the Chamber of Commerce dance. An embarrassing encounter, a revival of yet more ancient crimes, and crimes worse (or so it had seemed to her) than cooked giblets in plastic bags, worse than insults over the roast beef. Crimes that she had repressed, disowned, forgotten, until they rose to confront her in the person of Fanny Scott Colvin, whose name she had never ever been able to forget. And there, appallingly, on New Year's Eve, in the Victoria Hotel, in a black sequined evening dress with great shoulders like wings, like black angel's wings, stood Fanny Scott Colvin, whom Susie had not seen for twenty years, with whom she had, mercifully, and, she hoped, for ever, lost touch at the age of twelve. She would never have recognized her, never have glimpsed in her that red-haired schoolgirl, but Fanny came swooping up to Susie, and claimed ancient friendship. 'Susie!' she shrieked, as though sure of her welcome, 'It's Susie Bates, isn't it? Don't you remember me? Fanny Scott Colvin I was then, and Fanny Kettle now! How *are* you, Susie? After all these years and years and years?'

And Susie had stood there shocked, amazed that this woman could stand there claiming acquaintance, as though nothing had ever passed between them, as though they were adults in an adult world. Guilt over her association with Fanny Scott Colvin had nearly killed Susie Enderby née Bates, and yet there Fanny stood, calling herself Fanny Kettle, invoking old times, as though they had been times of innocence, of childhood innocence, in the school playground, in the bicycle shed, upstairs in the twin bedroom, in the secret dell.

Two evenings of revelations. Susie thoughtfully stroked the sleeve of her silk blouse. Guilt. No, not guilt. Shame. Yes, that was it, shame. Shame, like a dark stain, pouring through her body, flooding her cheeks. And Fanny Kettle had seemed to feel none of it. 'We must have tea, coffee, lunch, you must come and see me now I'm a neighbour again!' declared Fanny Kettle, her red hair blazing, her prominent eyes bulging, her neck extended like a fighting swan's, and Susie had smiled, coldly, drenched in ancient shame.

Clive Enderby coughed. 'Would you like another sherry, darling?' he inquired. Susie looked at her gold Tissot watch. 'Heavens, it's late. Sorry,' said Susie, in a voice that spoke from miles away, a choked small diminished voice. Yes, she's blaming me, acknowledged Clive Enderby. Fucking and cooking. What a disastrous evening. Would they ever live it down?

*

Janice Enderby lay on the large double bed, moaning and gurgling and thrashing her head backwards and forwards on the hot pillow. 'Help *me*,' she moaned, '*help* me, *help* me, can't you *help* me, *help* me.' On and on, a monotonous keening. A sour perfumed psychotic smell rose from the crumpled sheets. Edward Enderby sat and watched helplessly. 'Never mind, never mind,' he said, from time to time, ineffectually. His sharp grey pointed face was peaked with misery. 'I'm *sorry*, I'm *sorry*, I'm *sorry*, help me, *help* me, *help* me,' moaned Janice.

A bad start to the new year, said the sardonic corner of Edward Enderby's consciousness, as the rest of it kept dumb vigil. Yes, a bad start. But at least there's no one to hear it through the wall. Now we're detached. Detached misery. Semi-detached misery had been hell.

Paul Whitmore was composing a letter about his prison diet, addressed to the prison governor. He had asked Alix's advice, and she had recommended this course of action. 'Be polite,' she had urged. 'There's nothing to gain by being rude.'

Paul Whitmore was a vegetarian. He was not satisfied with the variety of diet offered. He would like more fresh vegetables and something other than lettuce and tomatoes in his salad. Eating meat is bad for the mind and body, and leads to aggression. So, laboriously, he informs the Governor. Eating meat is against Paul's principles.

Paul Whitmore spells it out, as he conjures memories of sides of beef hanging from hooks, of pigs' heads grinning, of trays of kidneys and livers and lights. These memories fuse suddenly with the image of a woman, sitting in a chair, gazing at herself in a mirror. Her hair stands out from her head in a shining halo of stiff silver spikes, some six inches long. A fevered smell of burning fills the room.

Paul Whitmore shakes his head, dully, like an animal on which a fly has settled, and the images separate and dissolve. Doggedly, he continues his letter to the Governor.

'Last week,' he writes, laboriously, 'I had potatoes with tinned peas, twice . . .' Paul Whitmore leads a sedate, solitary life in prison, protected from his fellows by Rule 43.

Alix Bowen, driving home towards her husband Brian and her son Sam, bottles for the Bottle Bank clinking merrily in her car boot, is glad she does not have to look forward to a supper of tinned peas. Tinned peas had been one of the torments of her childhood. They are one of the few foodstuffs she still finds repulsive. Repulsive pulse. She does not blame P. Whitmore for finding them unpalatable, but then, if he's so fussy about what he eats, he shouldn't have put himself in a position where he can't pick and choose, should he? Refrain from Murder and Eat what you Want.

It is dark now, and she cannot see the white landscape. The river running through the little town above the prison had been fringed with slabs of ice. How the Romans must have hated it, up here. P. Whitmore's book claimed that they imported vast quantities of wine, olives, figs, mulberries, raisins and a pickled fish sauce made of mashed sprats, pepper, lovage, caraway, honey and vinegar. But these luxuries probably hadn't reached them up here, the legionaries pitted against the Brigantes probably had to make do with barley and lentils and cabbage and lard. The tinned peas of yesteryear. Or was that view of the diet of Roman legions out of date now? Hadn't somebody recently proved that the Roman legions, even in the far north, ate quite a lot of meat? A dim memory of an article in *The TLS* flutters in Alix's mind. Is nothing safe, is all knowledge to be revised, will not the dead lie quietly with their stomachs full of cabbage, do we have to chop them up and anatomize them again and again and again?

All sorts of delicacies had reached Northam and Brigantia since Alix's wartime cabbage childhood. Now one could buy fresh coriander, cumin, mangoes, Chinese leaves, and more than one variety of mushroom. Despite the decay of the manufacturing industries, despite the slump.

Alix ponders privation. She wonders if P. Whitmore expects her to slip him condoms full of heroin, which she gathers are all the rage amongst the criminal population these days, or whether he has decided she's a dead loss as far as that kind of thing goes, and good only for bars of chocolate and books. P. Whitmore does not seem interested in drugs, though he had in his time been a heavy drinker. Vodka and peppermint had pepped him up on his night sorties.

Alix wouldn't know heroin if she saw it. Once, years ago, when her elder son Nicholas had just left home, she discovered while clearing out his bedroom a carefully secreted old Maxwell House coffee jar containing some strange white powdered substance. She had stared at it with suspicion. What was it? Was it illegal? She did not trust Nicholas at all. She sniffed it, and finally, greatly daring, put her finger in and conveyed a speck to her tongue.

Detergent. Unmistakable detergent. Daz, or perhaps Persil.

How *deeply* law-abiding I have been, thinks Alix to herself, as she drives homewards towards baked potatoes and, she hopes, a nicely roasted guinea fowl, with some spinach purée from the freezer. And, as she drives, pondering her willingness, nay eagerness, to see the upsetting P. Whitmore, a new lump of memory detaches itself from the frozen forgotten backward stretches, and bumps downstream into the light. As a child, as a nice, timid obsequious law-abiding deputy headmaster's daughter, she had been haunted by the idea that one day she would find herself in the dock *accused of a terrible crime which she had not committed.* For years, this notion had haunted her, for years she had prepared her defence, her moving pleas for acquittal, her heart-rending reproaches upon conviction. Why? What on earth had all that been about? Alix smiled to herself at the absurdity of her childhood fantasies. What on earth had caused them? Had her mother unjustly blamed her for eating a slice of cake? Had her sister unjustly blamed her for losing her French Grammar? Had she been found masturbating?

Heroic courtroom dramas she had staged in her head. Innocent Alix Doddridge, a mere waif of a girl, accused of — of what? Murder, infanticide, treason? Alix could hardly recall. Nor could she now remember whether the essence of these daydreams was that she *felt* innocent or *felt* guilty. She suspected that she must have felt guilty, or the fantasies would not have been so elaborate, indeed would not have arisen at all.

Paul Whitmore did not feel guilty, although he admitted guilt. Alix felt guilty when she was not, and knew she was not.

Alix added this perception to the conundrum, drew this new line into her equation.

Paul Whitmore was not getting much psychiatric help at Porston. The chap that he saw once a week sounded a fool. Alix had, by and large, a perhaps exaggerated respect for the psychiatric profession, fostered by her friendship with Liz Headleand and Liz Headleand's first husband Edgar Lintot, both people possessed, in Alix's view, of compassion and common sense. This chap up at Porston, from P.W.'s account, did not seem to have much of either. Though that doesn't mean he's not a professional. Maybe he knows what he's doing, after all, thinks Alix Bowen.

But she doubts it.

Alix sees herself in the dock, pleading her case. She is convicted, perhaps, of participating in the Human Condition. Is that it?

Alix gnaws on, like the stubborn Utah mouse.

Nature and nurture. She would like to acquit Mankind, and if she can acquit P. Whitmore, then she can acquit absolutely anybody. Anybody and everybody. Nurture and nature. Alix cannot help believing in the nurture argument, as the nature argument is so *unfair*.

Why on earth should Paul Whitmore have been born a murderer?

Or made one, come to that?

Alix feels it is very, very unfair.

The one thing she cannot believe is that Paul Whitmore, of his own free (God-given?) will, *chose* to hack the heads off various young women by and near the Harrow Road, and *chose* thus to end up eating tinned peas in Porston Prison. She is sorry, but that she simply cannot believe. And that is my last word on this subject for tonight, she says aloud to the empty passenger seat of her car, as she enters the yellow fluorescent glare of the suburbs of Northam, and sees the steep hillside of home.

'Rat a tat *tat*, Who is *that*, Only grandma's pussy*cat*,' chants Alix's friend Liz Headleand, to the step-granddaughter bouncing on her knee. The baby laughs, obligingly, but Liz has forgotten the rest of the rhyme. It is a long time since she bounced a baby on her knee. 'Rat a tat *tat*,' she repeats. The baby does not seem to mind repetition. Liz is delighted to have a step-grandchild. It is about time. Jonathan, her stepson, the father of this child, is into his thirties. Liz had begun to think that none of her stepchildren or children would ever reproduce. Something had put them off family life and babies — her own behaviour, their father's behaviour, the overcrowding of Britain, the violence of city life, the nuclear threat, the decline of Empire? Any or all of these things could have done it. But Jonathan and his silly wife Xanthe had overcome these hesitations, or else the Life Force had overcome them independently: either way, there bounced and

21

wriggled young Cornelia Headleand, triumphant, in her fancy little smocked and embroidered dress.

Xanthe does dress the child oddly, Liz thinks. But then, Xanthe dresses oddly herself. All bows and ribbons and bits of glitter on her stockings. Liz thought all that kind of thing had gone out decades ago, but she supposes it could have gone in and gone out again several times while she wasn't looking. Do other people *really* wear these funny balloony puffed up Bo-Peep very short skirts? Liz has never seen them around anywhere. Liz thinks Xanthe is a bit batty. Yes, that's the word for her. Batty. Those bright eyes, those shiny dark-red lips, those very white teeth, that strange vacant giggle. Liz prefers the toothless young Cornelia. But recognizes that probably Xanthe Headleand is quite the thing. In whatever circle it is that she and Jonathan move in.

She's not very good with the baby, Liz thinks. Doesn't know how to keep her happy, holds her awkwardly, looks nervous when she cries. At home, Xanthe has a nanny for the baby. I mustn't interfere, says Liz to herself, as she marvels at the child's soft blooming skin. No wonder mothers want to devour their babies with kisses, feel the urge to gobble them all up. Cannibal mothers.

Liz had been, just before Christmas, to the archaeology exhibition at the British Museum, 'New Views of the Past', and had stared, along with all the other morbid sightseers, at the strangely preserved, smooth, brown, plump, patterned immortal skin of Lindow Man. Bard or Druid, victim or sacrifice. Ageless, timeless, rescued from the bog.

Liz is withering, the veins stand up on the back of her hands, and she is even developing dark freckly spots. She is putting on weight, but she is also withering. It is an interesting process, and she watches it with an amused fascination.

The baby bounces. She is soft, seductive, delicious. She smells of milk and biscuit and sweet breath.

At the far end of the room, sitting together on the window

seat, Jonathan and his brother Alan are in conference. Liz's tabby cat lies on the rug before the fireplace. A great gold-rimmed jug of yellow chrysanthemums, curved overbred formal globes, stands in the fireplace. Their acrid perfume mingles with the smell of baby, with Alan's Gauloise, with the sweeter scent from a small cut-glass vase of freesias, with the general smell of dust and room and home and cat and London. The lights are warm and low. A charming domestic scene.

But the conference is serious. Jonathan and Alan speak in low, worried voices. The men of the family. They are discussing their father Charles, who has, they think, gone mad. Alan runs his fingers through his hair, Jonathan leans forward intently, gesticulating wildly as he speaks. Alan shrugs. Alan is laid back. Mostly.

Liz cannot hear what they are saying. The baby is getting tired, soon she will summon Xanthe to take her away.

Liz is not so worried about her ex-husband Charles Headleand. She has spent enough of her life worrying about him, because of him. He can look after himself. Or if he can't, well, that's too bad.

The baby struggles, and makes herself into an angry, tired shapeless shape. Liz joggles her, soothes her, rests her over her shoulder, sings gently in a dull undertone. Cornelia wriggles, settles, wriggles, sucks her thumb.

Liz has always been good with babies. She is glad she has not lost the knack.

Liz's thoughts move to her friend Alix Bowen, who had telephoned earlier that week to say she might come up to London soon. She feels vaguely aggrieved with Alix, and cannot think why. Is it something to do, as Alix supposes, with the murderer, in whom Alix takes such a proprietorial interest? Liz sometimes feels like saying that some of her patients are just as mad and just as interesting as Alix's murderer, and that if she were to tell all . . . Yes, there may be an element of that, but it is also likely that Liz resents Alix's having moved out of reach — and resents the fact that, having moved, Alix seems quite happy, and even occasionally delivers herself of comparisons between Northam and London in which London comes out badly. Sour grapes, of course, Liz says to herself, but nevertheless it is irritating. Liz has been deserted by both her close women friends, both her friends of college days, whom she used to see regularly, on whom she relied for gossip and support and provocation, for reading lists and shared memories. Alix had gone north, and the third of what was once a triumvirate, art historian Esther Breuer, had gone to live in Bologna. Liz has been left alone, holding the fort of London single-handed.

The baby settles, slumps, nestles, and begins to breathe evenly and deeply. Damn, she's gone to sleep, says Liz to herself: I should have got Xanthe to take her away, now I'm lumbered.

Liz ponders the subject of infantile sexuality. The oral phase. Cornelia has an engaging way of sucking not her thumb but her knuckle.

Although Liz does not yet know it, 1987 is to be the Year of Child Sex Abuse. For some years now the subject has been arousing interest and controversy amongst the professionals, but in 1987 it will catch the press and the popular imagination like a fever. 1987 will be a psychotic year, the year of abnormality, of Abuse, of the Condom. Perhaps it is already possible to detect the early symptoms.

And as if in anticipation, Liz sits there rocking her step-granddaughter and wondering what normality is. Is this it? This comfortable bourgeois room, with flowers?

If one reads ancient texts — the Bible, the Koran, Sophocles, the Veda — is one not sometimes led to suspect that the whole of human history is nothing but a history of deepening psychosis? That something went wrong at the beginning of human nature, of human nurture, that humanity mistook itself fatally, for ever?

False revelations, hoax riddles, grinning sphinxes from prehistory. Murder, arson, pillage, savagery.

The baby sleeps and sucks, her pearly dewy eyelids a pale veined blue.

A pity one can't reinvent the whole thing from infancy, thinks Liz, and get it right. A world without violence, murder, aggression. Some of her calling believed that if you brought babies up properly, if you loved them and fed them and weaned them correctly, there would be no more Paul Whitmores, no more Hitlers or Pol Pots, no more wars: Liz does not believe this. She thinks this is simplistic. The whole thing has got quite out of hand. It is irreversible. Abnormality is in-built, by now.

Alix, up in Northam, returning again to Tacitus, reaches the same conclusion. Tacitus strikes her as sane. Now what does she mean by this? He is reporting mass historic madnesses that make Paul Whitmore's aberrations seem trivial. Yet he himself is sane. On the other hand, if you define sanity, if you define normality, so narrowly that only one or two exceptional people can ever achieve it, what does that signify?

The baby's little temples beat. Her little life is fragile, hardly yet incarnate. Her skull is soft, frail, open.

Charles Headleand has been reading the Koran. He is reading the Koran because he plans to go to the Middle East to rescue his old enemy, cameraman Dirk Davis, from the clutches of a bunch of terrorists, who have been holding him hostage for over two years. The Koran has driven the Iranians mad. Who would have predicted, back in the 1970s, the tide of Islamic fundamentalism that has swept the land masses of the East, that threatens even the secular monolith of the Soviet Union? Charles certainly did not, although he knows he ought to have done, because he has always been gripped by News, by day-to-day News, has always been a privileged receiver and passionate

25

disseminator of News. But he had not foreseen the rebirth of Islam, the rise of the Ayatollah, the war between Iraq and Iran, the boy soldiers clutching the Koran, the Turkish women returning despite menaces to the veil, the murmuring in the Soviet colonies, the floggings and the amputations of Pakistan. What is it all about?

He has discussed this with various Middle East experts of his acquaintance, with Hugo Mainwaring the journalist, with Harry Painter the historian, and with a varied collection of television reporters from various countries, some of whom had once worked for Charles's own company, Global International Network (a company now, incidentally, in severe financial difficulties). He has discussed it with experts in famine relief, with members of the International Red Cross, with employees of Amnesty International. Some of them, he suspects, had not foreseen all this either, although some of them (himself, most of the time, included) lay claim to hindsight, cast backwards premonitions that they had never truly felt, or had felt late, late, late.

He had even discussed Islam with one believer, a friend from college days, a gentle-mannered woman married to the American-born WASP director of a multinational conglomerate. She was bringing her children up in the faith. Why? He had wanted to know why? She had explained that the extremists, the fundamentalists, were as far from her conception of the true Islam as Seventh Day Adventists or Mormons or American Bible Belt faith-healers were from the Church of England. How can that be, he had wanted to know, as Ishrat smiled gently and poured him another cup of tea. He had not been able to comprehend her replies. They are fanatics, said Ishrat, but that need not make me an unbeliever.

It was his ex-wife Liz Headleand who suggested that he should pursue his inquiries by reading the Koran. Frankly, this notion had not occurred to him, nor had it been put to him by any of the experts on Middle Eastern affairs. But, in the grip of obsession, he had humbly taken himself to the nearest bookshop, the Owl in Kentish Town, and purchased a Penguin Classic: *The Koran*, translated with notes by N. J. Dawood, first published in 1956, many times reprinted. He attempted to open his mind, he attempted to make his way through it: Charles was not used to reading, he was accustomed to news flashes and teletext bulletins and telex reports and memoranda. He found the Koran heavy going, and was more than slightly put off to learn that the chapters of the version he was reading had been rearranged, their traditional sequence abandoned. The original editors of this sacred text had, apparently, arranged its chapters not chronologically but in order of length, 'the longest coming first and the shortest last'. He complained about this narrative anarchy over the phone to Liz: Liz, not having read the Koran herself, was intrigued by this revelation. 'You mean you can read them in any order, like the chapters of an experimental novel?' she asked. 'Like that novel in a box, by whoever it was in the sixties?'

Charles, who had never read an experimental novel, and very few traditional ones, cut the conversation short. 'How can you understand the minds of people who don't respect *sequence*?' he wanted to know.

'I'm sure there must be *some* kind of sequence,' said Liz, vaguely. 'Why don't you read on, and see if one emerges?'

Charles read on, but not very far. He managed to find one or two pleasant passages about rich brocades and sherbet and fountains and young boys as fair as virgin pearls, but he found a great deal more about unbelievers and wrongdoers and the Hour of Doom and the Curse of Allah and thunderbolts and pitch and scalding water and the Pit of Hell. 'Will they not ponder on the Koran? Are there locks upon their hearts?' Charles decided that there was a lock upon his heart: was it because he had been seduced by Satan, as the Koran suggested? Surely not.

He even found himself thinking of the New Testament with some affection, and went so far as to open it, drunkenly, one night, to see what it had to say to him. He stabbed at his old school Bible with his finger, looking for a message. He lit on Matthew 6:25. 'Behold the fowls of the air, for they sow not, neither do they reap, nor gather into barns; yet your heavenly Father feedeth them . . . Consider the lilies of the field, how they grow; they toil not, neither do they spin: And yet I say unto you, That even Solomon in all his glory was not arrayed like one of these.'

The words glowed with a hesitant, radiant beauty, a beauty of remembered faith. Was there not something about God caring even for the sparrows? About each hair of our head being numbered? Inspired stuff, divine stuff, said Charles to himself, hunting for the text, but failing to find it. 'Christ,' thought Charles, at midnight, 'the Koran has converted me back to Christianity.'

The effect of the New Testament did not last. Charles was not a reader, but a man of action. He had persuaded himself that the amateur video of the death of kidnapped Dirk Davis, which had been thrown over the embassy wall in Baldai, was a fake, and had been given enough hope by reported sightings and messages to build on this persuasion an elaborate structure of explanation. He was abetted in this by Dirk Davis's wife. Dirk Davis's wife also refused to believe that Dirk was dead. She and Charles encouraged one another, in speculation, in fantasy.

Dirk Davis's wife was not quite what one might expect, from her brief grieving public appearances: but then Charles knew enough about television duplicity not to be surprised by the real Carla. Wives and widows are never quite what one might expect: what we see is a strange public construction of what we think we would like to see, what the news presenter decides would be suitable for us to see. We are all partly aware of this, and Charles knows it more than most. Nevertheless, the gulf between the public Mrs Davis and the real Carla was unusually wide. The public Mrs Davis was a woman of, say, fifty, dressed plainly and soberly in black, with a bruised, pale face, huge dark pained saucered eyes, long straggly black, limp, grief-unkempt hair, and a husky, pleading whisper of a voice: a woman of sorrows, a victim, worn down by prolonged misery and hopeless vigil. The real Carla was an animated, hard-drinking, loquacious, vitriolic, dangerous creature, aggressive, witty and only occasionally tearful: life had dealt her some hard blows, and Dirk's disappearance was not the first of them, but she was a fighter, and would not surrender.

Carla Davis lived in Kentish Town, under half a mile from Charles Headleand's flat.

Is Carla manipulating Charles, or is it the other way round? Is it *folie à deux*? Is Carla trying to send Charles off to his death, because she blames him for Dirk Davis's death?

These are the questions that Jonathan and Alan Headleand ask themselves. They are of the opinion that the video of Dirk Davis's death is genuine. Jonathan has reached this conclusion after many inspections of the tape, professional inspections (for he has followed in his father's footsteps and now makes TV documentaries), Alan after two viewings through half-closed eyes, a barrier of fingers, and a natural blindness when confronted with the unacceptable. Jonathan ascribes Charles Headleand's obsession to the financial problems of Global International and Charles's loss of status. Alan thinks it is more closely linked to sex and the *Zeitgeist*, to the need for self-assertion and machismo so common in middle-aged men.

Charles and his third wife, Lady Henrietta, are now divorced. Charles lives on his own in Kentish Town. The divorce was expensive. Charles spends evenings drinking with Carla Davis in Carla's dark terrace house, with Carla's odd assortment of lodgers and teenage drop-outs. Some of these look a little like terrorists themselves, North London terrorists. Carla, witch-like, presides. She has an entourage. She is queen of a small dark world. She has a certain style. She hates Liz Headland, who lives spaciously, in the light, in St John's Wood: who has seduced and corrupted Charles Headland's three sons, and drawn them into her own orbit.

Charles plots to go to Baldai to track down Dirk Davis. Carla eggs him on. Liz is neutral. Jonathan and Alan are concerned, because they are the responsible members of the family. Aaron, the irresponsible son, rather admires his father's late recklessness. Sally and Stella, the youngest, daughters of both Charles and Liz, do not know what to think. They have their own problems, both of them, and anyway nobody cares what they think. So why bother to think anything? This is Sally's line. She is not interested in the ridiculous male world of plots and bombs and fanatics and hostages and warfare. She fights on another battlefront, and belongs to another plot, another story.

Stella weighs twelve stones, hates university, is very unhappy, does not get on with either Liz or Charles, and with some justification thinks herself neglected, the neglected runt of the family. She will be neglected by this narrative too, for thus is the injustice of life compounded. But it has to be said that none of the Headland children will get much of an appearance here. They will serve only as occasional chorus. There are too many of them to be treated individually. And anyway, Charles himself is only a small subplot. This is not the Headland saga. You do not have to retain these names, these relationships.

But nevertheless, Liz rocks her step-granddaughter Cornelia in her arms, as she sits in the cane-backed rocking chair in which she nursed her own babies. Alan and Jonathan plot against their father's plots. The eagle clock ticks on the mantelshelf. Liz thinks Dirk Davis is a heap of crumbling bones.

*

It is a Friday lunch time in late January, and Tony Kettle and Sam Bowen are taking a short-cut through the Botanical Gardens. They are on their way to a talk at the old grammar school. They both attend a sixth form college downtown, and have struck up a friendship, as they are both new boys in Northam. Tony is newer here than Sam, but he has not travelled so far. Sam is from London, from Wandsworth, and spent his early years of second- ary education in a mixed, noisy neighbourhood comprehensive. Tony Kettle spent those years in a quiet dull old-fashioned school in a small market town in the flat wastes near the Humber.

Tony and Sam have compared notes, over the past three months. On Northam, on the sixth form college, on their own past experiences of school, and, very circumspectly, very in- directly, on their parents and on the factors that have brought their parents to Northam.

They are talking, now, about racism, prompted by an incident reported at school that morning by Ramesh Bannerjee. Ramesh claimed that a pair of pig's trotters had been suspended from his next-door neighbour's front door knob, and an abusive message had been scribbled on the door. PAKI SWINE, it had declared, in yellow aerosol. Tony and Sam are not sure whether to believe this story. Ramesh seemed to enjoy relating it so much that his relish made them suspicious. They like Ramesh, and respect him as an advocate for his cause, but sometimes think he goes too far. 'I mean, in Brixton we heard a lot of stories,' said Sam, 'but you wouldn't think, on the Hilldrop Estate, would you?'

'It'll be a pig's head next,' said Tony.

'There *was* a case of a pig's head, in Bromley,' said Sam. 'Nailed to the gatepost.'

'And what about that kid in Manchester?' asked Tony.

They walk on, in silence, for a while. The papers that week had been full of reports of a thirteen-year-old schoolboy, knifed to death in a school playground, amidst racial taunts.

31

Tony Kettle remembers the street life of the little town of Ogham. Dull, dull, dull. Faded pink-tinted advertisements of out-of-date fashions piled haphazardly in the window of a small shop selling knitting wool. An estate agent, a grocer, a newsagent, a video library. The old medieval market cross and the little bridge, where a bored sullen knot of teenagers would gather of a summer evening, in the empty rural wastes. Boredom. God, Tony Kettle knew what it was to be bored. Boredom could drive you out of your mind, could make a knife in the chest seem a soft option.

He kicks a stone.

'Things are worse in Manchester,' volunteers Sam. 'More blacks. There's a very small black population in Northam. Comparatively.'

Sam knows this because he often hears his parents discuss these matters. The Kettle parents do not discuss them. Tony expresses scepticism. There seem to be a hell of a lot of blacks in Northam, Tony says, not that he has anything against them, but there are, I mean, even in the sixth form college there are a few, and that's not even a proper sample. Sam expresses scorn, worldly wisdom, implies that Kettle, from the sticks, doesn't know a thing. He describes, luridly, some of the goings-on at his old school in Wandsworth. 'You're from the backwater, the backwood,' says Sam. Tony Kettle nods as they skirt the over-grown ancient bear pit, where once captive bears paced back and forth, back and forth, for the entertainment of the citizens of Northam. It still has a hint of the Colosseum, a dangerous whiff of barbarity. 'Yes,' says Tony, 'there wasn't much going on in Ogham.'

They emerge into the well-kept stretch of gardens, the land-scaped areas, leaving the back path and the bear pit. Under the vast swollen bole of a large labelled rare tree, a fine specimen of tulip tree, *Liriodendron tulipifera*, cluster many brave little clumps of snowdrops, raising their heads, their green leaves, from the pale cold tender yellow-green grass of January. Their little white heads assemble. A promise of spring. Tony Kettle and Sam Bowen pay them no attention at all. They do not even see them. They are too old and too young to see trees and snowdrops. Tony Kettle kicks another stone.

Alix Bowen has picked a little wineglass full of snowdrops from her own back garden and placed them on her desk. They cheer her, they comfort her. Alix Bowen believes that her son Sam Bowen is at heart a country boy, a snowdrop lover, a pond examiner, a springer spaniel enthusiast. This is her image of him. She would be surprised to learn that he is no longer much interested in springer spaniels or botany, and that something in him hankers after the violent delights of Wandsworth.

Sam and Tony are on their way to listen to an address from a visiting dignitary of the Wildlife in Britain Fund.

The dignitary, when he arrives upon the platform, is not very dignified. He is one of the new style campaigners, a jolly young bearded forty-year-old with an indeterminate accent and a stock of quips. He speaks of the destruction of the countryside, of the Green Belt, of the threat to the landscape from Britain's agricultural policy and the EEC. He gives a little history, he shows slides. He conveys a lot of information, but he conveys it so informally, so chattily, that many of his listeners are not aware that it is being conveyed at all. Old Mr Spriggs, Geography teacher of the old style, on the verge of retirement, listens with mingled admiration and irritation. Is this the way to do it, then? Jokes, a little bad language to season the discourse, a lot of amiable smiling and a big Guernsey sweater? Mr Spriggs does not know. He is glad he is leaving the battlefield of educational ideology. He has had enough. Will any of this bright and breezy talk stick? Mr Spriggs doubts it.

The bearded dignitary concludes. It is up to them, the next

generation, to cherish the heritage of Britain. He announces the plans for the nationwide Wildlife Competition he is here to launch. The prize money is generous, the judges are glamorous. 'We really want *your* ideas,' he assures the audience. '*You* can *help* us.' He beams sincerity and *bonhomie*. He does not solicit questions, as he is running out of time and has to be in Leeds by six for another meeting. He leaps down from the platform with conspicuous agility, and, as he departs, distributes free ballpoint pens and little badges bearing symbols of badgers and birds and buttercups, along with copies of the competition leaflet.

He does not distribute them very democratically, as he has not enough to go around, but nevertheless Tony Kettle manages to acquire a ballpoint.

When that evening Tony, in the middle of his supper of sausages and baked beans, tries to take down a telephone message for his often-absent, much-telephoned mother, he finds his Wildlife Pen does not work. He presses hard, trying to indent the paper deeply enough to be able to read it by impress alone, but the name and number he has been asked to convey to Fanny Kettle never reach their destination. Fanny Kettle never rings back. One of her many ghostly victim-admirers will wait for ever in vain, reprieved by chance from the lethal attentions of Fanny Kettle.

'My God,' says Carla Davis, opening the front door to Charles Headleand in Kentish Town, 'whatever has happened to you?'

Charles stands there, his face covered with elastoplast. Strips cover his forehead, his nose. His eyes stare out as from a visor.

'I was mugged,' says Charles. Morosely, grudgingly. He is not best pleased, one can tell.

Carla, I am sorry to say, laughs. Mysteriously, this response brings a smile to what is left of Charles's features.

'Come in, come in,' she says, although she is in fact blocking his entry, as he stands there in the narrow London hallway. He pushes past her, hangs his coat on the row of hooks, amidst an untidy array of raincoats, scarves, cardigans, anoraks, overcoats, plastic bags.

In the dark drawing-room, she inspects him more closely. What one can see of his face is yellow blue with bruising.

She pours him a stiff Scotch, adds a splash of water, without asking him what he wants.

Charles explains that he was mugged while jogging in Regent's Park. This makes Carla laugh some more. She has always been amused by Charles's jogging habits. 'Who *wants* to live longer?' asks Carla, self-destructive Carla, rhetorically, from time to time.

Nevertheless, she listens with interest as Charles explains the detail of his encounter with the two muggers, at six on the preceding evening, interrupting only to wonder why anyone should want to mug a jogger who clearly hadn't got thousands of pounds of cash stashed in his track suit pocket.

'It was just by the rose garden, on the Inner Circle. Outside Regent's College,' said Charles, as though this somehow made matters worse.

He had been hit across the face by a heavy object – a metal bar, a wooden club, he hadn't been able to tell which. Fortunately he hadn't fallen, had been able to stagger on, then had run towards Regent's College, streaming blood, and had crashed wildly in as though for sanctuary. The porter had been alarmed by his apparition and so had Charles's old friend Melvyn Stacey, who was just on his way in to give a lecture on the Thai–Kampuchean border on behalf of the International Committee of the Red Cross. Assembled agency do-gooders and governmental procrastinators had had to wait for their address while Melvyn listened to Charles's outpourings of rage against thugs and vandals, while Melvyn dabbed at the spatters of Charles's blood that had somehow communicated themselves to Melvyn's best grey lecture suit, while Melvyn convinced Charles that he couldn't possibly drive himself home but would have to go to St Andrew's casualty department in an ambulance.

'And when I got back from the hospital,' said Charles to Carla, 'they'd locked the gates, and I had to leave the car in the college car park overnight, and as I don't have a permit they had the cheek to fine me £15 for unauthorized parking. Bloody inhuman, if you ask me, and now they'll be on the look-out for me whenever I use the park again.'

'That'll teach you to go jogging,' said Carla, sipping her Scotch.

'If I hadn't been a jogger, I'd never have been fit enough to run away. I might have been dead in the gutter by the rose garden,' said Charles.

'If you hadn't been a jogger, you wouldn't have been mugged in the first place,' said Carla.

His nose had been broken and pushed sideways across his face. Would it go back to where it had come from, Carla wanted to know? God alone knows, said Charles, who was cheering up under the stimulating influence of Carla and Scotch.

He did not divulge to Carla his mixed feelings about Regent's Park, which had somehow broken out in this broken nose. Once he had lived a short walk from Regent's Park, with his second wife Liz Headleand: once he had lived in a grand eighteenth-century house in Harley Street: once he had been able to take a turn beneath the red horse-chestnuts while the potatoes boiled. Now, thanks to the legitimate claims on his estate of his second wife, the extravagance of his third wife, the demands of his five offspring, and the insolvency of his business, he was obliged to live in a flat in Kentish Town, drive his car to Regent's Park to jog, and park illicitly in the grounds of Regent's College. Regent's Park represents all that is gracious in London living, all that Charles had lost, all that need never have been forfeited had he lived more prudently. Outer circle, inner circle, little bridges, roses, ducks, tennis courts, avenues of trees, urns with wall-flowers, pink blossom in spring. Charles is not much interested in flowers, but he has, partly through Liz's influence, become accustomed to them, both indoors and out. His own flat, where he lives alone, is flowerless. Sometimes he buys himself a bunch of daffodils and shoves them in a jug, but they never look convincing.

Carla has dried flowers. Honesty, sea lavender, all a little dusty. She rarely indulges in the freshly cut variety.

However, Charles continues, some good has come out of his misfortune. This unexpected, bloodstained renewal of acquaintance with Melvyn Stacey may bear fruit. Melvyn had rung Charles that morning at nine, to ask after his nose, and Charles had managed to engage his interest in the plight of Dirk Davis, languishing forgotten in Baldai. The International Red Cross was one of the only channels through which one could get a visa to Baldai these days. Journalists were unwelcome in Baldai. Charles had raised the subject at once, in what seemed uniquely favourable circumstances, and he and Melvyn were to meet for lunch the following week.

'Well done,' said Carla. Her large eyes swim with pain, with anger, with subjection. She and Charles stare at one another, the bruised and the broken-nosed. They stare and stare, attempting to read what they see. Aggressors and victims. Once, years ago, Charles Headleand and Dirk Davis had come to blows, in a car-park in East Acton, on Bonfire Night. Over a union dispute. Blood then had flowed also, and silence had followed. The silence of the seventies, of the eighties.

'Anyway,' said Charles, 'at least they didn't break my teeth. They cost a fortune, my front teeth. I've spent a fortune on these teeth.'

He bares them at Carla, in what passes for a smile.

*

37

Shirley Harper finally plucked up her courage and made an appointment to see Clive Enderby, solicitor and executor of her mother's will. It was not the will that worried her, but her husband's business. She could tell Cliff was in trouble: his little empire of wing mirrors and picnic sets was rusting, unassembled, as the bills poured in. What if he went bankrupt? Where would that leave her? She had consulted her sister Liz Headleand, with whom she was not on intimate terms, but for whose financial sense she had some respect: Liz claimed to know nothing about money at all, but she always seemed to land on her feet, and Shirley thought that must mean something. One did not live comfortably in a handsome freehold house in St John's Wood by chance, thought Shirley. Liz had suggested Clive Enderby. 'And while you're at it,' she had said, 'you can ask him about probate on Mother's estate. It can't still be dragging on, can it? It sounds to me as though you could do with the money.'

The scheme had seemed sound to Shirley, but it was nevertheless with a heavy heart that she made her way to Hansborough to keep her appointment. Enderby & Enderby had moved to new premises. They had abandoned the poky but rather charming little early-nineteenth-century house in Dilke Street, with its pretty little stained-glass windows where swans floated amidst water lilies. They had moved uphill and up-market to an office in a fine new building, deep carpeted, air-conditioned. It was smart, functional, unwhimsical, for the quainter fancies of Post-modernism had not yet hit Hansborough: in fact, its modernity was already a little old-fashioned, but Shirley did not recognize this, and neither, yet, did Clive Enderby, who rather liked its grey steel and sheet-glass and large windows.

These large windows survey one of the most spectacular views of dereliction in twentieth-century Britain. From the fifth floor, where Clive sits, one can see all the way from Hansborough to Northam, across the waste land of demolition. It is a beautiful view. Clive Enderby has plans for it. He regrets the failure of the Enterprise Zone Scheme, of the Rate Reduction Incentive, of the scores of variants of YOPS and TOPS and Restarts and Job-bangs and Youth-boosts and Community Programmes that have tried, piecemeal, to rescue the area, but he is not surprised by their failure. Messy, confused, contradictory, piddling little schemes, doomed to disaster. Clive has his own Master Plan, his own Operation Pegasus. He can foresee that whatever happens at the next election (and he confidently predicts a handsome Tory victory) something will have to be done about dereliction and the inner cities, and Clive means to make sure that Hansbor-ough will be in a position to get what is going. From this rubble will arise the winged white horse of new industry: the lion will lie down with the lamb, and the right-wing Chamber of Com-merce will work hand in hand with the left-wing Council. The right hand shall know what the left hand is doing, in Clive Enderby's scenario, and a glittering new high-tech industry, clean and sparkling, will arise from the ashes to employ the redundant hordes and to dazzle the envious soft hearts of the lascivious south and the less forward-looking dumps of Tyneside and the Black Country, of Liverpool and South Wales. It is a vision of a fabulous rebirth. Clive Enderby, in his own way, is a dreamer.

But his dream is in the future, and will not much help the struggling small businessman in trouble. Shirley now sits before Clive Enderby, with her back to the view, and listens patiently as he explains about her mother's will. He assures her that every-thing is in order, that the house in Abercorn Avenue is sold, and that cheques will be on their way to Shirley and her sister Dr Headleand in a month or two at most.

'These things always take time,' he says. 'You did receive the interim statement I sent you, didn't you?'

Shirley nods.

'I'm afraid we've been a little held up in our regular work by the removal,' he says, conversationally, as she continues to say nothing. 'It was shifting the papers that was the problem. Mountains of stuff, going back to my grandfather's day. You can't throw it all away without looking, though, can you? Some of it probably has historical interest, if you go in for that kind of thing. You know, local history. Archives. But most of it went into the shredder, I'm afraid.'

'It was the same with the stuff at my mother's house,' says Shirley, with an attempt at interest, at politeness. 'The things people hoard. We burned boxes full of paper.'

'Really?' Clive looks at her with sudden acuteness.

'Boxes,' repeats Shirley, dully. The very thought makes her feel tired.

'Lucky she kept the will in a sensible place,' says Clive, slightly probing.

'Yes, very lucky,' says Shirley, bored.

Clive explains to her the capacities of his new shredding machine, but she does not listen. Gradually she works the conversation round to Cliff's ailing business, to her own liabilities as a director.

'I was so worried,' she says, blushing slightly, 'that I went round to the Information Centre at the public library. And they gave me this leaflet. And frankly, it worried me even more.'

She hands over the leaflet. It is entitled 'Implications of the Insolvency Act 1986 and the Company Directors Disqualification Act 1986'.

'I mean,' says Shirley, 'what about our house? And all my personal assets? Can they be included in the company assets? I'm a non-executive director, I know, but look, it says the Acts make no distinction between executive and non-executive. I don't know what it all means. To be frank with you I don't even know what the word "executive" means. I don't know where I stand. At all.'

'Hmm,' murmurs Clive Enderby, playing for time. He asks for the name of Cliff's own solicitors, for the company's name and registration number, for the names of its other directors. He scribbles them down on a piece of paper and looks knowing. Then he tries to explain to her the distinction between wrongful trading and fraudulent trading, but she is not listening, she cannot follow, she takes in only one word in ten. He explains that he cannot offer useful advice in the absence of more detailed information about the company's liabilities. He encourages her to call a meeting with the other directors.

'But Cliff is my *husband*,' says Shirley. 'How can I call a *meeting* with my *husband*? He won't speak about these things, anyway. He's very depressed At least, *I* think he's depressed. He won't admit it. But he is.'

'Perhaps you should get him to see his doctor,' says Clive, brightly, eager to shift responsibility for the Harpers' financial and marital problems on to another profession. After all, they aren't even his clients. They are small fry, little victims of recession, tiddlers.

Clive watches Shirley closely, as she promises to speak to Dr Peckham. He's not surprised that she can't follow her husband's affairs, but frankly he *is* rather surprised that neither she nor her clever sister Liz has spotted the intriguing anomaly in their mother's financial statements. He had noted it at once, and it had led him to an interesting revelation. Now, of course, he does not know whether or not to share it. It is, arguably, of no importance, better left sleeping. Neither Shirley nor Liz has shown the slightest suspicion.

'Give my regards to your sister,' he says, as he ushers Shirley to the lift.

Perhaps women never read account sheets, financial reports. Women are interested only in the bottom line, and they can't always find that. Women will sign anything — hire-purchase agreements, life insurance policies, applications for shares, joint mortgages with defaulting husbands — and they never read the small print, as Clive knows all too well. And even if they try to read it, as Shirley has just demonstrated, they do not understand it.

They shake hands, outside the gleaming lift. Shirley voices her thanks, but the interview has left her more worried than before.

And Clive too, trying to put her from his mind, feels a certain unease. The images of Janice and Susie swim, unsummoned, towards him. Wives, women, marriage. The voicing of dissatisfactions. The crumbling of loyalties. The breaking of bonds. Where will it end? He opens a desk drawer by his left elbow, and stares at a new brown legal envelope in which lies a rather grubby document, a Deed of Covenant dated 23 December 1934. Should he have handed it over? He shuts the drawer, and lets it lie there, inert.

Alix Bowen stops her two-finger typing of a draft of a letter to one of old Beaver's one-time correspondents and looks up to gaze at her snowdrops. They jostle in the wineglass on their thin stems. She lifts the face of one of them, gazes inquiringly into its intricate green and yellow and white, and lets it fall back. With a sigh, the whole wineglassful rearranges itself, with inimitable, once-only grace, to create a new pattern. The flowers shiver and quake into stillness. They cannot fall wrongly. They cannot make themselves into a false shape.

'If you do happen to have kept any of Howard's letters,' Alix types, 'we would be so grateful for photocopies of them. As I am sure you will appreciate, they would be of great value to any future biographer, and there may be the possibility of a volume of *Collected Letters* at some point in the future.' She crosses out 'in the future' as tautologous, crosses out the 'future' in front of 'biographer' on the same grounds, and then puts it back in again, as the sentence looks a little too bare, a little too definite, without it. There is no certainty that there will be a biography, no certainty that Beaver's recent renaissance of reputation will last, although he clearly believes it will. It is Alix's task to set his papers in order, a task with which Beaver himself co-operates only intermittently. A Herculean task, for the disorder is considerable. But Beaver seems to like Alix, and does not mind her rooting around in his upper rooms.

Alix does not know whether or not she likes Beaver. 'Liking' does not seem to be relevant to what she thinks about him, feels for him. Indeed, the word is not wholly applicable to Beaver's feeling for Alix either. She is useful to him, in more ways than the way in which she is paid to be useful. She is company, she is a welcome irritant, she shops for him sometimes, she sometimes does his washing up.

He is a dreadful mess, is Beaver. An egg-stained, tobacco-stained, shabby, shapeless mess. A *memento mori*. Alix, who does not find the company of old people easy, is frequently disgusted by him. He eats noisily, slopping and slurping his food, and blows his nose violently, and spits in the sink. Coarse, fleshly, decaying.

Grammar-school educated, university educated, the son of a miner, once destined for a life as a schoolmaster, read Classics, waylaid for some years by poetry. A brilliant mind, he must have had, reflects Alix. There is little evidence of that brilliant mind now, for Beaver has engineered and capitalized upon his return to popularity by cultivating a deliberate boorishness, an aggressive provincialism. Alix is the only person to whom he speaks of literary matters, and even with her he sometimes relapses into a gross mockery of the mind, a philistine, snook-cocking, infantile savagery. Alix cannot tell whether it is all a pose, whether he thinks that this is how a working-class northern intellectual ought to behave, or whether he has relapsed into behaving like this because he finds it more comfortable, and no longer cares. Is he copy or archetype? She cannot tell.

43

His career has been curious, enough to drive anyone into eccentricity. After a year or two of schoolmastering in Wakefield, he had taken off for London and lived the life of a literary hanger-on, working in publishers' offices, writing reviews when permitted, scrounging review copies, copy-editing, borrowing money, publishing the odd poem. He had then vanished to Paris for a couple of years in the late twenties, where he claimed to have got to know the American expatriate literary community and to have worked as assistant editor on *transition* — although Alix finds this period of his life suspiciously ill documented, and his knowledge of French is now rudimentary and rusty in the extreme. (But he may be joking, that awful accent may be a fake, a stage prop, like that custard-stained check waistcoat and that cloth cap.) He had returned to England, and had become, in the thirties, briefly, successful. References to him and his work during this period were easy to uncover in the little magazines, in the review pages, in the now published letters and diaries of his then eminent contemporaries. 'Met Howard at the Roebuck.' 'Saw Beaver walking along the Embankment with Rose Feaver.' 'Discussed Pound with Howard Beaver.'

And then, after this fragile notoriety, he had vanished. He had vanished utterly, into obscurity. He had returned north, and taken an office job with a company that published technical journals and children's comics. He had married his old school friend Bertha Sykes, and had children, and grown old. He had missed out on the vogue of provincialism that had swept Britain during the 1950s. He now claimed that he had not even known that it had existed. Kitchen sinks, Angry Young Men, no, he had never heard of them. He lived in the past, in the past of the 1920s that had been his own twenties, in the distant past of Greece and Rome and Ancient Britain.

Now he has been rediscovered, a living fossil. He has been televised, recorded, reprinted, honoured. He is seen as a sort of missing link in literary evolution, a coelacanth hauled up from the depths of a cultural Continental shelf.

Or is he, as Alix sometimes wonders, Piltdown Man? A hoax?

Well, he can't be a *complete* hoax, because somebody must have written his poems, and by all accounts that somebody seems to have been him. It seems unlikely that this crusty old relic could have produced such work, but somebody must have done, and it must have been either him or the person that used to live inside him. Alix sometimes peers at him to see if she can see any sign of that delicate, shy and vanishing spirit, but Howard Beaver, in his robust eighties, glares defiantly back, his red-rimmed bloodshot eyes mocking her curiosity, her disbelief.

Alix types on. 'We would very much appreciate any help you can give us,' she continues.

Beaver wants to edit his own past, to make sure that an authorized version survives him. Alix is slightly surprised that he should care about his posthumous reputation. It depresses her, to find vanity lurking in such a hulk. But she collaborates, because she is paid to do so. And because she is curious. And because she is, by now, involved. Beaver needs her, although he would never admit it. His rudeness, as she occasionally admits to herself, is in part an admission of that need.

Susie Enderby is appalled to find herself sitting in Fanny Kettle's drawing-room. She cannot think how it has happened. She has been drawn here like an innocent bird by a hypnotic snake. Fanny Kettle's protuberant, lascivious eyes stare at Susie Enderby.

Fanny is wearing green, dark green, in a shade traditionally favoured by those of her colouring, and she looks at once archaic and avant-garde. Her shoulders are padded, huge, soaring, as they had been at the evening of the Chamber of Commerce ball: her waist appears tiny, her legs are long and her long clinging skirt is carefully arranged to reveal a stretch of hard brown nylon shin. Susie, who takes a pride in her appearance and considers herself one of the best-dressed young professional wives of the region, suddenly feels herself to be a little dull, a little stocky. Fanny pours herself another cup of tea, her long fingers and crimson nails hovering over silver pot, china cup and saucer, sugar tongs. After all, it *is* only tea time, says Susie to herself, bracingly: nothing awful ever happens at tea time.

Fanny has been describing the reasons for her reappearance in Northam, after years of exile in the flat fens of the East Riding. She shudders with horror as she recalls the desolation. 'I can't tell you,' she says, 'how lonely it was, how isolated, how cut off from all social life of any sort ... if you didn't make an effort, you could speak to *nobody*, nobody at all, for *weeks on end*. Well, *days* on end. If it hadn't been for my little trips abroad, my little trips to London, I'd have gone mad, quite mad.'

Susie wants to ask why on earth Fanny and her husband Ian had spent so long in such an out-of-the-way region, but she does not want to betray her ignorance. Fanny seems to expect Susie to know all about Ian Kettle's work. She talks about him as though he were famous. As Susie has never heard of Ian Kettle, she has to tread warily, Gradually she pieces together the information that he has been on television, but is not a television personality: that he was vaguely connected with York University, and is now vaguely connected with the University of Northam: that he is, perhaps ... yes, this must be it, and now it somehow begins to come back to Susie, as though she had known it all along, that's right, he is some kind of archaeologist, who has spent years excavating burials in the wet dull flat eastern bits of the county ...

'Of course, our house was rather grand, and that was a consolation,' says Fanny. 'We had house parties. Quite *famous* parties.'

Susie does not know whether to believe this or not, and slightly hopes it is not true. How could one have famous house parties in that damp wilderness?

'Ian's people are called the Parisi. I always thought that was a *hint,*' said Fanny. 'Parisian parties. You know.' She insinuates.

Susie does not know. She has no idea what Fanny is talking about. Ian's people? Parisian parties?

'Yes, the house was good, but it was *too* far out . . .' Fanny sighs, looks round her new residence, which is a detached Victorian granite building high on the ridge by the university, in a suburb once fashionable, now slightly 'mixed'. It is an area dominated by the great architectural fantasies of the fabulously wealthy nineteenth-century iron masters and by houses like this, the solid comfortable spacious houses of the solidly prosperous. 'Now *this* house,' says Fanny, 'has some party potential, I'd say. Wouldn't you?'

Susie nods, smiles. She is out of her depth. She herself sometimes gives little dinner parties for six or eight, and a cocktail party once or twice a year. She considers herself, by Northam standards, a successful hostess. But is she? What new scale has Fanny Kettle introduced?

Fanny Kettle has a son of nearly seventeen. Susie expresses disbelief. 'Yes, I can hardly believe it myself, such a big boy now . . . of course I married very young, with all the usual conse- quences . . . only twenty, I was.' Fanny Kettle laughs. 'I'm afraid poor Ian has found me rather a *handful,*' she says, and laughs again, with display of teeth and rather gaunt neck.

Susie feels sorry for Ian Kettle. She thinks she has no recollec- tion of him, from their one meeting – or was he perhaps that shadowy figure lurking at Fanny's elbow?

Fanny inquires, formally, after Susie's own children, without displaying much interest: Susie says she has two, William, aged eight, and Vicky, aged six. 'How sensible you have been,' says

Fanny, as though sense were a commodity she mildly despised. 'To wait, to have them a little later, when one can afford more help . . .'

'Yes,' says Susie, conscious that she has been emerging dully, uncompetitively from this interchange. 'Yes, we *are* very fortunate, we're very well placed now, and I have this excellent' — she hesitates over terminology — 'this excellent *girl* . . . a trained girl, you know — who lives in. So life is very agreeable.'

'And you're quite free, then? To do what you want?'

Fanny stares at Susie with her shockingly personal, investigative, unmannerly stare. Susie feels herself blushing, hopes her make-up will conceal the colour in her cheeks.

'Yes,' says Susie, firmly, primly (why does Fanny make her sound so smug, so prim, so suburban?), 'yes, I do speech therapy at the clinic where I used to work, two half-days a week . . . and apart from that, yes, I am quite free.'

Free. The word hovers in the room, over the very slightly tarnished silver teapot, over the three-piece suite, over the coffee-table and the occasional tables, over the silk-fringed shades of the standard lamps. Free. An uneasy word, an uneasy concept, a confession, a concession. What has Susie surrendered? Something, she knows. Fanny has noted, has recorded, will exploit. Despite herself, Susie feels a faint tremor of excitement, a physical thrill, a stirring of the flesh. Fanny continues to chatter on, about her parties at Eastwold Grange, about her weekends in Paris, about her plans for future parties, about the complaisance of poor Ian . . . Susie does not know what to believe, does not know what is fact and what is fantasy, succumbs to a mild gin and tonic, refuses a second ('I have to drive back'; 'Ah, next time you *must* have a proper drink and go home in a taxi!'), and as she drives back through the waste land that links Northam and Hansborough, images of a strange, sinister, isolated Grange float into her mind, a Grange with brightly lit windows moated in mist. Laughter echoes into the surrounding emptiness, laughter on stairs and in bedrooms. Carnival, abandon, licence. Susie is outside, out on the flat grey mist-spangled lawn, looking in. Fanny, within, lies back on a brocaded settee, in a silken dress that parts to show the lace of her underskirt. Her head is thrown back. It is cold outside. Susie shivers and turns up the fan on her car heater, as she drives home to a solitary supper. Clive is out at a meeting, and the girl will have fed the children, will be waiting to go out with her boyfriend. Susie will eat eggs on toast in front of the television. Fanny's ringed hand with its crimson nails reaches for a glass, and a high-heeled shoe drops from her thin hard ankle. A hand — an unattached, disembodied hand — reaches for Fanny's lean thigh, beneath the silk.

Tony Kettle returns from an evening at the Bowens to find his mother lying snoring on the living-room settee. Her head is thrown back, and she snores, deeply, evenly, rhythmically. The television is still on, but it is soundless. The remote-control gadget has dropped from Fanny's fingers and lies on the Persian rug by an empty bottle of Bulgarian Mountain Cabernet, an empty wineglass, an empty packet of cigarettes, an orange plastic cigarette lighter, and a stub-filled triangular Craven-A mock-antique ashtray. It is twenty to ten. Tony gazes at his mother with an indeterminate expression which accurately reflects his indeterminate feelings, then watches for a while the muted but loquacious participants in an incestuous BBC Answerback free-for-all about the alleged obscenity of a recent drama series. Tony does not know whether to creep quietly upstairs, like a prudent coward, or whether to attempt to wake his mother and persuade her to go to bed too. His father is away at a conference, so it doesn't really matter if she lies there all night, or until (which is more probable) she rouses herself in the small hours, makes herself a cup of tea, and then puts herself to bed.

He wanders into the kitchen to think things over. He has had a pleasant evening with his friend Sam and Sam's parents. Tony had not met Alix and Brian Bowen before. Alix did not seem the kind of mother that one would find lying asleep on a settee with an empty bottle of wine, but she was by no means unalarming: her wild grey hair, her piercing blue eyes, her intent concentration on everything one said, her large gestures, her sudden exclamations over forgotten parsley sauce, all these things had been slightly disconcerting. She seemed of a different generation from Tony's mother, but Tony was used to that: most mothers belonged to an older generation than his own freakish darling. Most mothers, in Northam as in Ogham, seemed more reliable, more capable, more regular, more *dull* than Fanny Kettle. But Alix had not been dull: she had been full of talk, full of questions, full of enthusiasms. She had been particularly interested and indeed well informed about Tony's father's recent dig. She knew about chariot burials and Romans.

Sam Bowen claimed that she was obsessed by a murderer in Porston Prison, and Tony Kettle had waited eagerly for evidence of this, but none had emerged.

Instead, Alix over the fish pie had talked of the finds at Wetwang, the burials at Eastwold. She was fascinated to learn that the Kettles had actually lived at Eastwold, practically on the site, as it were. She wanted to know what it was like living at Eastwold Grange, how he had found the social life of Ogham, whether she ought to go and visit the ruins of Ogham Abbey. She expressed a polite desire to meet the Kettle parents.

Tony had drunk a glass of white wine with his supper. There wasn't any pudding.

'I'm afraid I never make puddings,' said Alix, as though this deficiency had newly occurred to her. 'I don't know why, but I never do.'

Brian Bowen, Sam's father, had showed less interest in archaeology, but equal interest in Tony's impressions of social life in East and South Yorkshire. Brian worked, Tony gathered, for the Education Department of Northam City Council. He wanted to know what Tony thought about sixth form colleges, how many kids had gone on to do A-Levels at Ogham, that kind of thing.

'Your parents didn't think of boarding-school?' he asked, at one point.

'I wouldn't go,' said Tony. 'They suggested it, but I would stay at home.' He laughed, a little uncomfortable at being the centre of so much attention. 'Really boring it was, but I would stay.' He paused, took another sip of wine, continued boldly, 'But they took me around, you know. I didn't spend all my youth in the sticks, as Sam likes to think. I went around with my mother. To London. And Paris. And Venice. Places like that.'

'How nice,' said Alix; thinking, what an odd boy, what can his parents have been up to?

Tony Kettle, standing irresolute an hour later in the vast high-ceilinged kitchen of the new Kettle residence, wonders the same thing. And wonders if Brian and Alix are *normal* parents, or whether there are no such creatures as normal parents? And if there were, would he want them for his own? He shrugs. He doubts it. He will take life as it is. What choice is there, after all?

He returns to the living-room, quietly removes the glass, the bottle and the ashtray, and slowly, sneakily, from the far end of the room, increases the volume of sound on the television. His mother stirs, mumbles, suddenly sits bolt upright, as Tony backs out of the door and makes his escape up the stairs.

Attractive danger. Natural curiosity. Unnatural curiosity. Charles Headleand cannot resist pursuing a visa for Baldai, Alix Bowen cannot resist travelling to see her murderer across the lonely moor, Susie Enderby cannot resist returning to take tea with Fanny Kettle, Janice Enderby cannot resist inviting people to dinner and Liz Headleand will not be able to resist an invitation to appear in a contentious debate on television. Their friend Stephen Cox has been unable to resist one of the challenges of the century, the secretive Pol Pot, hiding in his lair, at the end of the Shining Path.

Cliff Harper's approach to the cliff edge of danger is less voluntary. He does not have an illusion of freedom. He has been struggling for years to prevent himself from reaching this precipice. He lies awake at night, adding up columns of figures, counting his creditors. He lacks the gift of self-deception, the Micawber touch which might have got him out of this mess. His partner Jim Bakewell blames him for lack of confidence. 'You've got to think positive,' Jim is — or was — fond of saying.

Cliff thinks that is all beside the point. Figures are what count, not faith.

His relationship with Jim deteriorates, almost as dramatically as the non-contractual relationship between Jim's wife Yvonne and Cliff's wife Shirley has done. These two women cannot stand one another. The origins of their mutual dislike are lost in history, though there is some remembered legend about a rejected piece of lemon meringue pie. It is known that Yvonne thinks Shirley gets 'above herself', 'thinks a lot of herself', 'thinks she's too good for this world'. 'Who does she think she is?' is the phrase that springs most frequently to Yvonne's lips, when speaking of Shirley. Shirley, for her part, cannot forget or forgive a remark Yvonne once made about Shirley's mother and the virtual seclusion in which Shirley's mother chose to live. Cliff and Jim, for years, attempted to mediate, and then to keep the women apart, but rancour persisted, and has now flooded into their own friendship. 'What did I tell you?' is now Yvonne's refrain.

Jim resigns as fellow-director, tries to get his money out. There is no money. There is talk of liquidation of assets, of consulting an insolvency practitioner. Jim argues (rightly) that insolvency practitioners come very expensive and that the company's accounts will not rise to one. Cliff muddles on. He cannot sleep, he cannot eat, he loses weight. He worries, secretly, about his health, and furtively consults medical dictionaries in the Information Centre at the public library. They terrify him, as leaflets on insolvency in that same library terrify Shirley. Things drag on, good money is borrowed and thrown after bad, money leaks and oozes away, staff are laid off, the Customs and Excise query Cliff's V A T returns, he cannot work out how to deregister.

He does not discuss these matters with Shirley. He has become morose and surly, impossible to live with. He punishes her for his sense of impending failure. He torments her. She wonders if she can stand it much longer. He is a changed man, he is not the man she thought she married. She can see no way out. A kind of dull despair settles in her: this is it, this is the end. But there is no end.

Meanwhile, she cooks Cliff's breakfast, and cooks his supper: she cleans his house, pays his household bills, washes his clothes, cleans his bath, buys his soap and lavatory paper. The house ticks over, Shirley ticks over, Shirley-and-Cliff tick over. They watch television together, they sleep in the same bed, occasionally they even go out for a meal together.

It all seems a little unreal, but then, the country at large seems a little unreal too. It is hard to tell if it is ticking over or not. Are we bankrupt or are we prosperous? Have we squandered our resources and drained the North Sea gold, or is the economy booming and the balance of payments healthier than it has been for decades? Are our hospitals crumbling and our streets full of litter, or have we triumphantly reduced the Public Sector Borrowing Requirement? Are there nearly four million unemployed with unemployment rising daily, especially in the north, or are the unemployment figures sinking daily, especially in the north? Has spending on the National Health Service since 1979 gone down by 5 per cent, as the Opposition claims, or up by 24 per cent, as the government claims? Each day brings new figures, new analysis, new comment, new interpretations, newly false oppositions of factors that cannot properly be compared: for the nation has fallen in love with statistics, although it cannot decide what they mean. A few eyewitnesses continue to describe what they see, as they travel by tube, walk the streets, wait in bus shelters, queue in doctors' waiting-rooms, serve on juries, and clutch their wire baskets at the supermarket check-out, but others accuse them of telling atrocity stories, of indulging in a pornography of squalor.

Brian Bowen has learned nothing from the last few years. He stands where he did. He is an unreconstructed socialist. He has not learned doubt. Alix has learned doubt, but not Brian. Brian is less reconstructed than his friend Blinkhorn of Northam City Council, a man of the New Hard Pragmatic Middle Left. He is far less reconstructed than his older and closer friend, Otto Werner, economist, who has left for Washington, as part of the Brain Drain. Brian is way, way out of date. He is so far out of date that sometimes he thinks the revolution may, in its revolving, turn again to his own aged and honourable position. Meanwhile, he organizes evening classes and worries over balance sheets and interviews teachers and sets up courses and seminars, and even finds time to do a little teaching himself. And out there, amongst the people, he fancies he finds some unreconstructed socialists like himself. One of them, a middle-aged catering manageress, is so unreconstructed that she thinks the correct term is 'unreconstituted', and firmly declares herself on any suitable occasion to be just that – unreconstituted – proudly, as though she were a wholesome piece of prime beef or fresh fish, not a knitted turkey roll or a soya hamburger.

The truth is that Brian, since coming up to Northam, his home town, has felt happier, less isolated, in his unreconstructed state. He is not, here, driven to extremes of position, as he had been in London. The political atmosphere here seems more decent, more realistic, less febrile and opinionated than the atmosphere in London. This is partly because the left here has more roots, more confidence, more sense of tradition. Northam has a left-wing council and a vast majority of Labour Members of Parliament, so Brian here does not have to feel like a pariah or a crazed dreamer. He does not have to fight every inch of the way, every day, as he did in the Adult Education College in south London that jumped at the chance of making him redundant. True, Northam has a reputation for being extremist, for being of the 'loony left', but anybody who lives there knows that this reputation is greatly exaggerated. Northam is a solid provincial town, staggering now from the recession, but not yet on its knees. Perry Blinkhorn and Clive Enderby may not yet be on speaking terms, and may feel culturally condemned to despise one another, but they come from the same stock, they speak with the same accent, they share some of the same hopes, and they have more in common with one another than either have with the yuppies and city slickers and get-rich-quick boys of a south which they distrust. Brian fits in here. He settles back into the familiar city that bore him, and which he struggled so hard to leave.

And Alix, far more uprooted than he, far less a northerner, far less in tune with Northam's brand of socialism — she does not seem too out of place, too unhappy, either. She has made new friends, she has found herself a job, she keeps up her criminal connections, and she too loves the landscape. She does not miss London as she had feared she might.

Sometimes Brian finds himself remembering (or reconstructing, perhaps?) some remarks made by Alix when there had seemed to be a probability that Brian's new job might take him not from London to Northam but from London to Gloseley, an unattractive

Midlands town famed chiefly for its nuclear missile station and its attendant Peace Women. Alix had said that if they went to Gloseley, she could join the women over their camp-fires. But, Brian had protested, you don't even think you believe in unilateral disarmament. No, said Alix, I don't suppose I do, now, but I could become an outcast, and if I became an outcast by joining those women, then I would begin to believe what they believe. That's how it would go. I would sit by the fire, and that would bring belief.

Fitting in, believing, consensus, outcasts. Yes, he could see clearly an Alix who would crouch by a fire warming her hands on a mug of soup, her fingers dirty, her grey hair wild, her eyes glittering, her mind slowly filling with belief, as her body took on the posture of a witch. She would knit little Peace Emblems and tie them fluttering to the barbed wire: she would murmur incantations in ghostly gay company. It was perfectly plausible, this version of Alix, in a way it was what she had been bred to be, by her school, by her parents, by generations of radical intellectual nonconformists. She had been bred to be a protestor, a marcher, a martyr, a woman of faith. She had met her first husband, who had died long before Brian met her, on a protest march. In the face of such destiny, the details of conviction, of opinion, did not matter: it was the posture of protest that gave one shape, belief, faith. If one is born and bred to a role of outcast protestor, then one must adopt it, in order to conform.

But Alix had not adopted it. Reason had been too strong for her; reason followed, fatally, by doubt. She had become deviant. And she had detached herself from politics, in disillusion; she had taken up psychotics and long country walks instead.

Well, she had not quite detached herself from politics. She cannot wean herself away altogether. She cannot help looking for a way forward, for a new consensus that will unite her and Brian and Perry Blinkhorn and Otto Werner and their absent friend Stephen Cox, Stephen, the most extreme of all. She has been reading a book called *How Britain Votes*, which describes the emergence of a new semi-professional class of Perry Blink-horns and catering manageresses and nursery schoolteachers and social workers, which suggests that higher education in practice as well as in theory leads to a liberalization of attitude on such matters as capital punishment. Clutching at straws, at men of straw. For does not everything else she reads suggest that we are moving towards a new intolerance, a new negation of 'progress', a culture where education is openly used not to liberalize and unite, but to segregate and divide?

Alix and Brian agree to differ, for their hearts are united. They may differ about means, but their vision of a just society is the same. Their marriage has been through some rough times lately, but they seem to have survived them. Unlike some of the couples in this narrative, they do not seem at the moment to be heading for marital disaster.

Shirley Harper has no interest in politics at all. At the last election, she did not even vote. Cliff Harper, small businessman, small employer and member of the petty bourgeoisie, is, as *How Britain Votes* would predict, of the die-hard right-wing. He is slightly acquainted, through Shirley's sister Liz, through his sister-in-law Dora, with Brian and Alix, but they do not, cannot like one another or trust one another. Alix, who extends sympathy and interest to criminals and murderers, finds it very hard to listen with patience to the views of a Cliff Harper. This is one of her more serious limitations, a limitation of which she is, seriously, unaware.

Alix enjoys danger, but Brian, like Cliff, does not. Brian does not need it, does not see the point of it, wishes that people could get along without it. He gets impatient when rescue teams are called out in appalling conditions by parties of stranded walkers in the Lake District. He secretly sympathizes with judges who are held up to derision for saying that young girls in mini-skirts shouldn't ask for trouble by hitching lifts from strangers at midnight. Brian cannot see why people have to climb Everest or cross the Atlantic single-handed in coracles. He cannot see why his friend Stephen Cox has gone off to Democratic Kampuchea when he could have stayed at home writing novels in his bachelor flat in Primrose Hill. And as for Charles Headland's plans – well, Brian thinks they are ridiculous, embarrassingly ridiculous. But then, he had somewhat harsh views of the generally admired conduct of the long-vanished kidnapped envoy of the Archbishop of Canterbury, Terry Waite. Why can't people accept the limitations of the human condition, instead of trying to *show off* all the time? Brian is not a risk-taker. Or so he thinks. He does not admire heroism, would never himself aspire to act heroically. Or so he thinks.

Ancient crimes, ancient victims. Over supper, in St John's Wood, Alix and Liz Headland laugh heartily, with abandon, as they recall the scene in the British Museum archaeology exhibition, by the glass coffin where the upper half of Lindow Man sleeps everlastingly. 'So nice,' says Alix, almost choking over her lentil soup, 'so absolutely *sweet*, such a – such a *little* boy!'

'And oh *dear*, that *marvellous* old lady, though I don't know why I call her old, she wasn't all *that* much older than us,' agrees Liz, dabbing her eyes with her rose-sprigged napkin: happy to see Alix, happy to remember the day's adventures, still amused by the little seven-year-old, grey-uniformed, pink-braided boy who had piped up so sweetly, so piercingly, so unselfconsciously in his treble, gazing at the miraculously preserved, multiply wounded, overslaughtered sacrificial corpse, the corpse of a victim who had been bashed on the head, stabbed in the chest and garrotted, whose throat had been cut, and who had been left to lie for two millennia in a boggy pool. 'Gosh,' the little boy had announced, to his schoolmates, to his teacher, to Alix and Liz and two Japanese tourists and the old lady in a felt hat. 'Gosh, isn't he lucky, to have ended up here!'

Liz, Alix and the old lady had all smiled: the old lady had spoken up. 'Not very lucky *up to that point*, young man!' she had admonished him, pointing to the writings on the wall announcing the probable sequence of events that had led to his death and his body's recovery. The schoolfriends had laughed, Alix and Liz had laughed, and the little boy himself had smiled broadly, unabashed, his freckled face with its gap tooth and small nose open as a flower, open as a book that all might read, open as innocence. He knew what he meant. And of course, as Alix and Liz agreed over their lentil soup, they knew what he meant too, there *was* something rather wonderful, rather lucky even, about such defiance of time, about Lindow Man's role as a link and a messenger from the underworld, about such arbitrary, quirkish, museum-venerated fame.

'I wonder if people would *pay* to be put in museums after their death?' ponders Alix.

'Well, the Egyptians did, in a sense,' says Liz. 'And the Chinese. And the holy saints of the Catholic Church that hang around under altars in Italy.'

'The saints didn't *pay*,' says Alix, reprovingly. 'They were preserved by sanctity.'

'Sorry,' says Liz.

Liz and Alix have had a good afternoon. Alix is pleased to have caught up with the exhibition before it closes and wonders if she has not become more conscientious about attending cultural events in London now that she does not live so near them. She has come down on the Rapide Coach and is spending the night with Liz. They have a lot to talk about.

They discuss Bog People in general, the poems of Seamus Heaney, the Bog Man of Buller, P. V. Glob, the excavations of

Ian Kettle, P. Whitmore's interest in corpses and Ancient Britain, and Alix's notion that the story of Queen Cartimandua of the Brigantes should be adapted for television.

'Why don't you write it yourself?' asks Liz.

'I'm too busy. And anyway, I can't write.'

'Get Beaver to write it. It's his period.'

'Oh, he's well past it.'

They discuss Beaver, briefly. Beaver claims to have an ex-mistress living in elderly seclusion on the shores of Lake Maggiore.

'You should get him to send you to visit her,' suggests Liz. 'In some pleasant month. Like May. Or June.'

'He says she's the subject of his Novara sequence,' says Alix. 'But she disputes this. At length, and illegibly.'

The conversation moves to their friend Esther Breuer, who now lives in Bologna, and who has it would seem dropped from their lives as from this volume. They do not hear from her often. She has been translated into another world. They miss her, but not perhaps as much as they thought they would. Maybe she will come back, maybe not. She is living with an Italian Etruscan scholar, Elena Volpe, sister of Esther's dead admirer, Professor Claudio Volpe. Esther had lived for years, unknowingly, in a flat in the same building as P. Whitmore, in North Kensington, at the wrong end of Ladbroke Grove, and his arrest had in part led to her departure. The house in which Esther and P. Whitmore lived has now been demolished, and a row of what Liz says must be Small Industrial Units has been erected on the site. They will, according to Liz, never be occupied, and already look derelict. 'The area is too much for them,' reports Liz to Alix. 'They haven't a hope, they died before they began.'

Liz and Alix drop the subject of Esther, as she has dropped them, and move on to Charles and Carla Davis (a subject new to Alix, who has not seen Charles for a year or two). They allude to the long silence of their friend Stephen Cox, who is somewhere in Kampuchea, and is said to be writing a play about Pol Pot.

'Are they quite *mad*, these men, to want to go to such disagreeable places?' asks Liz, rhetorically.

They speak of Liz's step-grandchild Cornelia, and Alix expresses regret that her older son Nicholas and his consort Ilse have not yet had a baby. They have made do, so far, with one of Liz's tabby cat's kittens, which has already had kittens of its own.

Then they move, with slightly sinking spirits, to the financial problems of Liz's sister Shirley and her husband Cliff Harper.

'I told her to get independent advice,' said Liz. 'I don't know why she doesn't just leave him. He's making her life a misery. Why not quit? The children have all left home, why doesn't she just clear off?'

'People don't just leave their husbands, up in Northam,' says Alix.

'Don't they? I thought that had all changed.'

'Swift and Hodgkin argue that the divorce rate is 20 per cent higher among the professional and semi-professional classes and the petty bourgeoisie in the south than it is in the north and the north-east,' says Alix.

'Really? And what do Swift and Hodgkin have to say about Scotland?'

'They don't cover Scotland,' says Alix.

They both laugh, although they agree it is not a laughing matter. But, as Liz points out, she is not her sister's keeper, and anyway she doesn't understand business. 'I thought of asking Charles to give her some advice,' says Liz, 'but frankly, Charles is in a terrible mess himself. He owes money all over the place. It's on a grander scale than Cliff's mess, so I don't suppose he'll ever have to pay up, but it does rather make one distrust his judgement.'

Alix says that her opinion on such matters is not worth

having, and that moreover she has a feeling that Shirley doesn't really like her. 'She doesn't really like me, either,' says Liz. 'In fact, that's probably why she doesn't like you.'

They abandon Shirley as a lost cause, and move on to grander themes: prison visiting, insanity, Foucault, Lacan, the oddity of French intellectuals, the grandeur of Freud, the audacity of Bernard Shaw, the death penalty and social attitudes towards.

'I mean, really,' asks Liz, mellowed by a plateful of Toulouse sausage and swede-and-potato mash, 'really, do you think P. Whitmore ought to be alive or dead? Do you think there's any *point* in keeping P. Whitmore alive?' She stirs the green salad.

'I don't know,' says Alix, slowly. 'I suppose one can argue that he's a kind of – a kind of living experiment. A kind of Lindow Man in a glass coffin. That we can learn from him if we can learn how to. I suppose that's what I think.'

'Shaw would have had him polished off. Painlessly, of course,' repeats Liz, who has already made this point earlier in the conversation.

'As no use to society, I suppose?' says Alix. 'As a meaningless sport of nature, like a dog with two heads? Well, yes, I can see that.'

'And he, what does he think? All those American murderers seem to long to end up on Death Row. They are after the publicity. Hundreds and hundreds of them. Or so we are told.'

'I don't think P. Whitmore wants to be hanged,' says Alix. 'No, I don't really think he wants that. He wouldn't be so interested in the Romans and so worried about his tinned peas if that's what he wanted. Would he? But then, *I* think, I have to think, that he wants to understand what he did. And he probably doesn't at all, I'm simply projecting on to him *my* desire to understand what he did. In some way . . . it sounds absurd, but I don't think he's all that *interested* in what he did. As though it's not quite real to him. You know what I mean? Is there a name for that?'

'Plenty,' says Liz, the expert. 'But they don't explain much.'

'No,' says Alix. 'It's circular, really. Naming and observing, observing and naming. One can never tell what it's really like, inside his head. Any more than one can tell what it's like inside the head of those guys who bumped off poor Dirk Davis.'

'Or inside the head of Charles Headland, come to that,' says Liz.

'I wonder,' says Alix, speculatively, 'if we know what it is like in one another's head? You and me? After knowing one another — how long is it — for thirty years and more?'

'We could only know if we found out that we *didn't* know,' says Liz. 'If one or the other of us did something really surprising. Really out of character, or that would *seem* to be out of character to the other person.'

'Like that defector Esther, you mean? Whom we both thought we knew so well, until she suddenly vanished?'

'I sometimes wonder about the children. I mean, I'd say it was impossible that Jonathan or Aaron or Alan could turn out to be a murderer. Or Sally or Stella either, not to be sexist about it. But then, one wouldn't know, would one? Because it wouldn't be obvious. So it would come as a shock. If one found such a thing out.'

'Oh, I don't know. I imagine if anyone had been in close touch with P. Whitmore, they might have known. It was because nobody *was* in touch with him that nobody found him out.'

'Well,' says Liz, 'I think I do know *you* quite well. I know that you aren't a murderer, and I can predict, for instance' — she pauses, watching, as Alix turns over the leaves in the salad bowl — 'I can predict that you are about to reject the bits of fennel in favour of the lettuce and watercress.'

'I've always hated fennel,' says Alix, pleasantly. 'In fact, I don't like anything with that aniseed flavour, really, it's about the only flavour I don't much like. I can't understand how people can drink Pernod.'

'People are mysterious,' says Liz, somewhat guiltily pondering the reason why she has put fennel in the salad at all, when she knew quite well Alix wouldn't touch it. To test her? To annoy her? To attempt to dominate?

'Tell me again,' she says, 'what P. Whitmore said about the tinned peas.'

The next morning Alix got up early and caught a bus down to Baker Street and Madame Tussaud's. She did not mention this outing to Liz, who was already seeing a patient when she left. She felt slightly furtive about it anyway, slightly ridiculous, at her age, queuing with an ill-assorted crew of down-market foreign tourists and oddly ill-complexioned provincials. Did she look as out of place as she felt, she wondered, would she be arrested for wrongful curiosity? And she was indeed stopped, at the top of the stairs, by a young woman with a market survey, wanting to know, amongst other things, if and when Alix had last been to visit the waxworks.

'Oh, I don't know,' said Alix, 'About forty years ago, I suppose. With my mother.'

And she wandered on into the dark exhibition, recalling her mother's reluctance to indulge Alix and her sister in this outing, remembering their pleadings and cajolings and whinings, their eventual success. They hadn't been able to understand why their mother, who had seemed keen to let them visit the British Museum and the Natural History Museum and Kew Gardens and the Zoo, should have tried to draw the line at something they considered equally educational. Nearly everyone at school had been to Madame Tussaud's, they said, why couldn't they?

Gazing, now, at the exhibits, Alix could see all too clearly why their mother had thought it unsuitable. Gloomy, morbid, grisly. Horrible history. Guy Fawkes, Mary Queen of Scots about to have her head cut off, Henry VIII with a tableau of his ill-fated wives, the infant cavalier of Yeames's 'When Did You Last See Your Father?' Right-wing History. Martyrs' Memorials. Alix moved on, through modern times, where she recognized Princess Di and Boris Becker and the Beatles, but was at a loss to identify many other personalities from the ephemeral world of entertainment; she was amused to see Ken Livingstone, and wondered whether Perry Blinkhorn would ever make it into wax.

She had come, of course, to see the Chamber of Horrors, but could hardly make herself descend the fake-dungeon stairs. She had been frightened by it as a child, just as her mother had said she would be. Her mother, having given in, had washed her hands of them: 'Well, if you must look, you must look,' she had said, and Alix and her sister had gazed uncomfortably at tread-mills and tortures. It seemed now, forty years on, perhaps slightly less gruesome – but oh dear yes, there were the authentic casts of the severed heads of Louis and Marie Antoinette, there was Marat in his bath. Well, one could hardly call Paul Whitmore all *that* peculiar in his interests, could one? Yesterday in the British Museum a cluster of perfectly respectable people had gathered to stare at Lindow Man, and here an only marginally less respectable lot were goggling at Marat and a replica of Garry Gillmore in the electric chair. A natural curiosity?

Paul also had been here when he was ten, or so he had told Alix.

Alix walked through quite briskly, but not so briskly that she did not, in the last section, come to a standstill face to face with an effigy of her friend P. Whitmore. There he was, the Horror of Harrow Road. It seemed rude to stare at him, but she did. He shone with a waxy pallor, and looked slightly smaller than he did in real life, though she supposed he couldn't be. They must get the measurements right, surely? He didn't look quite – well, real? He was dressed in a grey suit, and stood to attention, alert, helpful, like a shop assistant. Oh dear, thought Alix. She did not know whether to laugh or cry. Poor dummy. There he stood.

She looks at him, he does not look at her. She is reminded of
the day when she went to watch his trial. Then, as now, she had
felt furtive, guilty, ashamed. She had not been called as a
witness, although this had at one stage seemed a possibility, and
she had avoided the early days of the hearing. But at the end of
the second week she had found herself drawn there, to the Old
Bailey, by an attraction more powerful than her natural distaste.
In vain did she say to herself, as she stood in the queue waiting
to enter the public gallery, that this was her civic right, that she
had a right if not a duty to enter a court of justice to see justice
being done: in vain did she say to herself that her interest, unlike
that of those around her, was prompted by something more
legitimate than mere idle sightseeing or muckraking, money-
making curiosity. She had continued to feel uncomfortable, embarrassed, conspicuous, as she sat on the back row of the gallery, as
unobtrusively as possible, her eyes modestly lowered for much
of the proceedings, occupying as little space as possible, clutching
her bag and her shopping basket.

She had chosen, unwittingly, a dull day, not a day of lurid
revelations. There had been interminable cross-questioning of a
witness who had had a drink in a pub by the canal on the night
that one of the victims had been murdered, and who had spoken
to Paul at approximately 10.25 – or was it more like 10.35? – for
some minutes about a newly released horror movie. There was a
long slow rigmarole about fingerprints and a carnival float on a
waste lot. Time was spent clearing the court while matters of law
were discussed. Time was spent refilling the court to proceed.
Alix had watched the judge in his wig and half-moon glasses,
making notes, twiddling his thumbs, occasionally almost yawn-
ing: she had watched the bewigged counsel, one of them high-
coloured, large-nosed, scrubbed, choleric, the other pale as soap.
She had watched the faces of the jury, the twelve random
citizens, and had tried to read their faces: a handsome neatly

66

suited Turkish lad, a white youth with cropped hair and a scar blaring across one cheek, a perky girl with tufty black Gothic hair and a red necklace, a woman with a soft weary managerial face, a raw-boned man with an open shirt and a gold medallion at his throat, a cashmere-cardiganed Sloane Ranger with smooth blonde hair . . . And she had watched, covertly, Paul. There he had sat, in the dock, impassively, this monster, unmoving, unmoved, expressionless, listening to the catalogue of his crimes, the slowly unfolding drama of his massacres.

And it had been high drama, however slow the pace, however silent the protagonist. His very silence spoke. Alix, then as now, found herself wanting to ask the unaskable. 'But why? Why? How did it happen to you? Why and how?' The court was not interested in 'why' and its interest in 'how' ended where Alix's began, but nevertheless the raw material was there. She had been transfixed. She had wanted to return the next day, and the next, like an addict, but luckily work prevented her. But she had felt, from that one long day, a bond, a connection, a continuation of that curious relation begun so obliquely on the night that the police had surrounded the house where Paul Whitmore and Esther Breuer lived. She had felt an obligation.

The wax figure of the Horror stared at Alix from his subterranean chamber in the Hall of Fame. Yes, her mother had been right to consider such sights unsuitable for schoolgirls. But society condoned rather than condemned her curiosity; her mother was revealed as a woman of unnaturally high principle. Mrs Thatcher had posed upstairs for her image here, and so had Bob Geldof, and Kenneth Kaunda and Marie Antoinette (twice, in her case, alive and dead). They'd all condoned it. Alix wandered on, up, towards the daylight. The Hall of Fame, the Chamber of Horrors. Snigger, snigger, have your photo taken with the famous, with J. R. or Red Ken or Marilyn. Oranges and Lemons, say the Bells of St Clement's. Here comes a chopper to chop off your head. Oh God, the gruesome panic of those party games, the little clutching fingers, the human trap . . . and here, at last, was Baker Street, sanity, traffic, human faces, newspapers, pigeons, double-decker buses in a splendid convoy, tourists, touts, ice-cream vans, gift shops, bureaux de change, roasting chestnuts – for a moment, Alix wildly loved the 1980s.

Paul Whitmore is carefully copying in fine pencil the famous outlines of the bronze horse mask found at Stanwick. Probably a chariot ornament, the text tells him. The sad blind horse face stares in curved Celtic lines. Paul is a poor draughtsman, he is dissatisfied with his handiwork, he rubs it out and begins again. Bronze, dull bronze, buried, now bright again. The last stand of Venutius. The triumph of the Romans. It has square pierced ears, the bronze mask, holes by which it had once been attached to long-rotted wood. In his mother's salon, Mrs Murphy had pierced the ears of the young women of Toxetter.

He rubs out, begins again, discards. The enigmatic horse stares. Heads had hung in rows from hooks. Pigs' heads. Not horses' heads. The British do not eat horse. They do not even feed horse to their dogs and cats. Horse is totem, taboo, sacred. But there had been jokes about horsemeat, unkind jokes in the little town. Horsemeat. Whoresmeat. Somebody had made such a pun. He hadn't known what it had meant, had make the mistake of asking his father, over tea. Had been clipped over the ear, shut out of the house, while they screamed and ranted at one another. Near the end, that had been.

He turns the pages of Alix's book. There is a bronze mask boss from the River Thames at Wandsworth. Alix Bowen had lived in Wandsworth, she tells him. Sometimes she describes her life there. She describes the house that is now let to a visiting professor from Australia. She describes the neighbourhood, the shops, compares notes with North Kensington, where Paul Whitmore and Esther Breuer had lived.

Paul Whitmore does not know the region where he is now imprisoned: he knows it only through books. He knows London, where he earned the sobriquet of 'The Horror of Harrow Road', and he knows the small town in the north Midlands, of the hairdressing salon and the butcher's shop, where he was known as Piggy Paul the Porker (although he is not and never has been fat). He has drifted in other places (a few months in Manchester, a year in Stoke-on-Trent), but he has become a Londoner, a drifting Londoner, a lost Londoner. Now he is nowhere, in limbo, in a coffin. He does not know Northam. He has never been there. It is to him a fictitious city, a city of the mind. Alix describes it to him sometimes. He cannot visualize it well. He knows nobody else who lives in it. Alix is his sole personal source of information about Northam and Leeds.

He turns the pages of the book, to the paragraphs on Celtic ritual and the impact of the Romans on the Old Religion. A wooden rubbed armless old god from Ralaghan, County Cavan, stares at him expressively, reproachfully, balefully. He reads: 'A grove there was, untouched by men's hands from ancient times, whose interlacing boughs enclosed a space of darkness and cold shade, and banished the sunlight from above ... gods were worshipped there with savage rites, the altars were heaped with hideous offerings and every tree was sprinkled with human gore ... The images of the gods, grim and rude, were uncouth blocks, formed of felled tree trunks ... The people never resorted thither to worship at close quarters but left the place to the gods.' A quotation from Lucan, the poet. Not Lucan, the murderer.

Paul Whitmore has made of himself a hideous offering. Here he is, offered up. But no one can see him. He is absent, obscure. No light reaches him. No one looks at him, save his fellow-prisoners, the prison officers and the blue eyes of Alix Bowen. Is this what he had wanted? He does not know. He knows there had been a need for sacrifice, for appeasement. The gods had wanted a sacrifice. But of what nature? Had it been accepted? One does not worship at close quarters. It is not safe to go too near the sacred grove.

As he sits there, chewing the end of a pencil, the people of Britain are still in the process of making him up, of inventing him. He had offered himself up to their imagination, as he had offered up his victims. What will they make of him, of them? Will they fail him, themselves? Sometimes he thinks that Alix Bowen will be able to invent him, that her story will make sense, that it will persuade the newspapers and the courts and the people. Sometimes he thinks she is incapable of doing anything of the sort.

Paul Whitmore would like to ask Alix Bowen to try to contact his mother. He has not heard from his mother since she ran away, fifteen years ago. He knows that in similar cases parents have been retraced, interrogated, their memoirs have been purchased for vast sums by the tabloids.

So far, he has not dared to suggest this course of action to Alix. He does not quite know how to bring the subject up. It is a little delicate. He is hoping that she might think of the idea for herself. On her next visit, perhaps, he will drop another hint. By months, her visits are measured. He will wait for the next moon.

It is early March, and daffodils bloom in London window boxes. A faint false spring deceives the buds, and trees turn bronze, pink, lime green. Liz Headleand is lunching with her old friend and enemy Ivan Warner, as she does once or twice a year. They gossip. On Ivan's part, at least, seriously, professionally. Ivan is a gossip columnist. He likes to pick Liz's brains. He is always hoping that Liz will present him with a psychiatric scoop. As one of her specialities has been the problems associated with the reuniting of adopted children with their true parents, maybe she will one day find for him an abandoned princeling, a reclaimed cabinet minister, a film star's rejected babe, a tycoon's incestuous marriage with his own daughter? The plot possibilities in Liz's line of business are endless, he reminds her, as he plies her with Pinot Chardonnay and admires the little pastry fish swimming in the saffron sauce of her ivory sole.

'No,' says Liz, 'nothing. Nothing exciting at all. Sorry.'

She smiles at him, amiably. It is only a game. He knows she will not tell. Her heart softens to Ivan, over the years. She used to think him a dangerous little man, but time has mellowed him or strengthened her, she is not sure which, and she no longer half fears him. She indulges him. And he her.

'I *had* heard,' said Ivan, in that inimitably suggestive way of his, 'that we were to be honoured with the sight of you on television? Can this be true, I asked myself? I *had* thought you didn't approve of the television.'

'Who told you?' asked Liz, disconcerted despite herself.

'I can't remember,' said Ivan.

'Well,' said Liz. 'I did agree to be on this panel thing. That's all.'

'I wonder why?' insinuates Ivan.

'I don't know *why*,' says Liz. 'I mean, why not?' But she also wonders why. She admires, yet again, his sense of her weak spots, her Achilles' heel.

'It's just not your style, that's all,' says Ivan.

'No, I suppose not,' says Liz. 'But they were very pressing. And I thought it was time *somebody* talked some sense.'

'So we shall have the pleasure of seeing you talking sense?'

'I hope so,' says Liz, briskly, staring hard at his inquiring small black well-hidden eyes.

'Well,' says Ivan, 'you're a brave woman.'

'But of course,' says Liz.

'I didn't know you knew Christopher?' says Ivan, gently probing, cutting in half a green bean with the edge of his flat fork.

Liz's mind races. Christopher? Does she know a Christopher? Ah, yes, she has got it. Christopher What's-his-name, newly appointed Director of Programmes for PPS. What *is* his name? A false trail. An utterly false trail. So *that's* why Ivan was interested in her TV appearance.

'Oh, *Christopher*,' she says. 'Of course I know Christopher. I've know him for *years*.'

Ivan can tell he has drawn a blank. He loses interest in the pursuit, switches track, starts again.

'And your ex?' he inquires. 'How's old Charles?'

'Oh, *Charles*,' says Liz. 'He's mad, poor darling.'

'I heard he broke his nose?'

'Mugged,' says Liz. 'Nothing personal. Just mugged.'

'And how's his business?'

Liz shrugged. 'Oh, I don't know. I don't understand such stuff. He seems to have switched his interests to some kind of Euronews project. It's all to do with satellites. I'm sure you know more about it than I do.'

Liz has no intention of mentioning the Baldai fantasy to Ivan: it would not even amuse him, it is too bizarre, too foreign. She allows him to rattle on for a while about Charles's ex-wife Lady Henrietta, one of whose children has been involved in a drugs scandal. A small, dull drugs scandal. Liz cannot take much interest in it, can feel only a very limited degree of *Schadenfreude*, as she can think with only a limited degree of complacency of her own family. They may not go in for quite such vacuous pursuits as the upper classes, but they cause her anxiety, neverthe-less, in their separate ways, and there seems little point in triumphing over Lady Henrietta's bad management. She refuses to be drawn into bitching about Henrietta.

Ivan moves from Lady Henrietta to Robert Oxenholme, Minis-ter of Sponsorship for the Arts, by a transition that seems more natural to him than it does to Liz, for Liz has forgotten that these two characters are vaguely related, that their names are part of the meaningless genealogical reticulation of Hestercombes, Oxenholmes and Stocklinches. Liz is more interested in Robert, for he is a friend of her friend Esther, and it is this connection that Ivan wishes to probe.

'Well,' says Liz, 'the last I heard, they were writing a book together. On some minor Bolognese or Ferraran figure. But I don't suppose they'll ever finish it.'

'Why not?'

'Esther never finishes anything. And Robert's too busy.'

'Why doesn't Esther finish anything?'

Liz considers. 'I don't know,' she says. 'I've often wondered. She lacks ambition. Not confidence, but ambition. I don't think she sees the point. Of trying to make a lasting mark.'

'It seems odd, perhaps. When her profession is to study the lasting marks of others?'

Liz smiles.

'And you, Liz, how lasting will your mark be? Do you ever wonder?'

Liz stares at Ivan, who squats before her, neckless, toadlike, but, like a toad, somehow enchanting.

'In my job,' she says, 'one doesn't expect to make a *lasting* mark. One's patients recover, recirculate, suffer less. That is all.'

'And yet,' says Ivan, 'some would say your profession is full of megalomaniacs who long to live for ever, and who impose their views on others with an autocratic zeal, and who are quite happy to kill off all dissent in order that their own names should shine more brightly in the halls of fame?'

'You're only speaking of a small percentage. Of the stars. I grant that many of them are megalomaniacs. But there are a lot of quiet toilers in the vineyard. Like myself.'

'I've never seen you as a quiet toiler.'

'That's because you never see me at work, you only ever see

me at play. Eating a nice lunch, like this. Wasting time in the company of timewasters like yourself.'

'*I* think of you as a more – forceful figure. A bit more of a star than you suggest! Surely?'

'That's very kind of you. But to be a star, one has to ...' She hesitates. She is not sure if she wants this conversation, is not quite sure how Ivan led her into it.

'Yes?' he prompts.

'To publish. To have one's own theory. To defend one's own theory. To be – in a word – original.'

'And you think you are not?'

'I know I am not. I am a pluralist. I take from here and there, I use other people's bits and pieces. I use what seems useful. This seems to me pragmatic. It's a good way to care for patients, but it's not a good way to make oneself famous.'

'But you have published, I thought?'

'Only papers. Articles. Like Esther, I've never got round to writing a whole book.'

'But you could, now, presumably? Now you have time, and the family are all grown?'

'Ivan, what *is* this? Why are you being so peculiarly mephistophelean? My life is perfectly busy, thank you, without any further ambitions. Why can't I just carry on as I am?'

'Why not indeed?'

A little plate of dark red salad arrives at Liz's left hand. She rearranges it with her fork, and chews a bitter leaf.

'Fame is the spur,' she says, after a while, 'that the clear spirit doth raise, the last infirmity of noble minds ... A very honest statement that, on Milton's part, I've always thought. But for some reason Esther and I don't seem to suffer from it. No doubt because we are nice, modest, unassuming women. We don't need to see our names in print every week. As you do.'

'Well, yes, I do, I admit it,' says Ivan. 'It's like a disease with me.'

'An infirmity.'

'Yes. An infirmity.'

'Actually,' says Liz, 'what I *do* suffer from is curiosity. I want to know *what really happened*.'

'When?'

'At the beginning. When human nature began. At the beginning of human time. And I know I'll never know. But I can't stop looking. It's very frustrating. When occasionally it comes over me that I'll never know, I can't quite believe it. Surely, one day, I will find out?'

'We don't even know what happened in our own lives. Let alone the life of the species.'

'No. I know that's true. But I can't help waiting for the revelation.'

'When you've had it, will you publish it?'

Liz laughs. 'No, no, it will be the end of the world, there will be no more publishing and delivering of lectures,' she says.

'You are in an apocalyptic vein, suddenly.'

'It is your fault, Ivan. You encourage me.'

'So apocalyptic are you that you are failing to see what is sitting in front of your own nose. You say you suffer from insatiable curiosity, but you let me ask all the questions. Ask me a question, Liz.'

Liz looks at him, sharply. Is he teasing her? Is it a trick?

'What question shall I ask you, Ivan?'

'No, no, you are the clever one, you are the diviner. You must guess.'

'Not the answer, but the question?'

'That's correct. You must guess the question.'

Liz, comically exercised by guilt and conscience (for it is true that she never asks Ivan about himself, always lets him make the running), peers at him, as though hoping to read his face, his mind. He smiles back, shrugs his shoulders, crinkles his eyes at her, taps his chin with his thumb, and raises his glass.

'Well,' says Liz, 'you're looking very pleased with yourself. So I guess something good has happened to you. Have you got a new job? No? Have you been promoted? No? Ah, I know what it must be — are you in love?'

Ivan nods, encouragingly.

'Yes? But there's more to it than that? Are you getting *married*?'

'Yes,' says Ivan. He is beaming satisfaction at her, and of course, now she sees that this must be why he has been so amiable, so benevolent, so well disposed, he has been hugging this secret all the way through lunch, waiting to astonish her with it. And she is astonished.

'Good Lord, Ivan, how amazing! I thought you never would, I thought you were the only real bachelor left in London! Congratulations! Am I allowed to ask the name of the other party, or do I have to wait for the official announcement?'

'If you read the serious information in gossip columns, as everybody else does, you'd know it already. So I might as well tell you. I'm going to marry Alicia Barnard.'

'Good heavens. Are you really? Good Lord!'

Liz is silenced by this coup, silenced and delighted. No wonder Ivan is looking so smug. Alicia Barnard is not only a beauty, she is also a distinguished classical guitarist of impeccable provenance and reputation — how can it be that Ivan has persuaded her to *marry* him?

'Congratulations,' repeats Liz, rallying. 'That *is* romantic. What a happy story! What wonderful news!'

'The story,' says Ivan, twiddling with the stem of his wineglass, and quite unable to stop smiling, 'is called Beauty and the Beast.'

'Oh Ivan, I hope you'll both be *very very* happy. Tell me about her. Tell me what she's like. Tell me how it happened.'

And Ivan tells, and Liz listens, making up for lost time and shameful indifference and incuriosity, learning what all London knows already, that Ivan and the red-haired Alicia have been courting for eighteen months, that they have been spotted at concerts and cited at functions and photographed at receptions and caught dining in small smart restaurants, that they have been on holiday together in Tuscany and shopping together in Harrods and have bought a small house together in Berkshire. Ivan relates all this with a helpless innocence, with a naïve delight that brings tears to the eyes of Liz. Love has transformed him. The arbitrary, accidental goddess has smiled on Ivan, and he has become another person, a nicer person. In his fifties, he has become a new man. They call for a cognac with their coffee, to celebrate.

'I was a stage-door Johnny, I admit it,' says Ivan, blotched and glowing with pride. 'I just hung around. I waited. I drove her around. I made myself useful. And she let me. She liked it. She got to like it. And then one thing led to another. And here I am, an almost married man. Do you think I'll be able to manage it? I've never really lived with anyone before. Or not for long. And neither has she. Amazing, isn't it? She's very shy, you know. She's a very *nice person.*'

'I'm sure she is,' says Liz, faintly. It is almost too much for her, this late flood of hope and innocence. She wishes Ivan and his Alicia well, yes, of course she does, but how can she, at her age, have any faith in their vision of married bliss in a small house in Berkshire? Unless they are freaks, who have escaped the human condition altogether, one can be certain that grief, boredom, infidelity or disillusion await Mr and Mrs Ivan Warner, will creep up upon them more familiarly, more insidiously, than love itself did ... Liz shakes her head, drains her glass, looks bright again. Maybe Ivan has been *so horrible* in the first fifty years of his life that he has already paid his debts to human nature, and can now be free, like the frog prince, to sit by his fireside and listen to music and gaze across his lawn?

'Goodbye, Ivan,' says Liz, on the dirty Soho street, where old newspapers, cardboard boxes, cauliflower stalks, empty bottles and plastic bags of prawn shells heap and rustle and sigh and stink in the March breeze. 'Goodbye, Ivan, good luck!'

The last, perhaps, of her little lunches with Ivan, she thinks, as a taxi bears her back to St John's Wood and work. Or the last until he and Alicia quarrel, and he needs a shoulder ... but enough, enough of these gloomy thoughts, she tells herself, as she tries to compose her mind to receive her next patient, who is suffering from severe depression which he thinks was caused by the sudden death of his wife. As perhaps it was, perhaps it was: but whatever caused it, it is with him now, sitting on him heavily, as he puts it, like a heavy beast. Can Liz charm it, can she turn it into a little frog, can she make it hop lightly away? He hopes so, she hopes so. They work together to seduce the heavy beast. The wife stays dead, she will not come back to life and sew and dance and sing. She is ash in a north London garden, where a few crocuses outlive her and her planting of them.

Janice Enderby is preparing food for another dinner party. She has rashly invited Alison Peacock, the director of Northam's Theatre-in-the-Round, and Tony Troughton, local radio reporter and his wife, and a couple of staff from the school where her husband Edward teaches. She asked them without properly consulting Edward, and he was not wholly pleased to be told. He knows she will get in a state about it, and take it out on him later. He knows that something will go wrong. It always does. It goes wrong because she tries too hard. In vain does he urge her not to make such efforts, in vain does he try to persuade her that everyone is quite happy just with a plateful of spaghetti or shepherd's pie. Janice has pretensions, and they make her and everybody else very uncomfortable.

At the moment she is making chicken liver pâté, with butter, sherry, juniper berries and minced bay leaf. Round it goes, in the liquidizer, reducing itself to a warm smooth pale-brown paste. She takes the lid off the machine, sniffs the contents. The smell, warm, is nauseating, although she knows it will taste all right cold. The texture too is nauseating. She splatters it out into a bowl, flattens it. It steams, odiously. It looks like a mound of shit. Janice shudders with distaste.

She runs the hot water over the complicated interior structure of the blender, directing the rubber swizzle tap into its innards. The tap pulses, hotly, in her fingers. It pulses and throbs like a live thing.

Janice feels quite faint with disgust. She decides to make herself a cup of instant coffee, opens a new jar, has to break the paper ring that seals the contents. She tears it, clumsily, with her finger, she violates it. The smell of coffee granules rises at her, rank like a tomcat.

She slices a red cabbage. Its red and white veins open, its crisp pretty involuted guts stare back at her. Her fingers are stained red, and so is the butcher's block. She has killed the cabbage.

Prunes, then, she stones, to add to her braised cabbage and her dish of quail. The prunes are like small turds, small sticky turds. She had been given prunes, as a child, when suffering from constipation. Prunes and syrup of figs. But how had her mother *known* she was suffering from constipation? She had never complained of it. Her mother did not watch her, day and night. Nevertheless, once a week or so, 'Oh, Janice *is* out of sorts, she *is* a grumpy little girl today. Prunes and syrup of figs for Janice tonight!' It had seemed a violation then, and seems one now, as Janice, unforgivingly, looks back.

The body is a trap, a trick, a betrayer. One should keep one's own body secret, private, concealed. Not let them poke about in one's entrails. Not let them have power.

Edward had seemed a bodiless person, a disembodied person. But it had not been so.

Janice knows she is neurotic, hysteric, on the verge of some classifiable disorder. She wonders what it is. She has a lump in her breast, but has no intention of telling anyone about it. Sometimes she finds herself almost hoping that it may be fatal. If she were to die, she wouldn't have to go on worrying, would she, about what else it is that is wrong?

She slices an onion, and weeps. She layers the earthenware pot with cabbage, prunes, apples, cranberry jelly, onion, she sticks in cloves and pours over it raspberry vinegar, which has reached the north of England, as fish sauce reached the outposts of the Roman Empire. She puts it in a slow oven, and gets the quails from the freezer.

Little birds, frozen in a row. Some people are squeamish about little birds. Janice, who is squeamish about a cabbage, does not feel too strongly about little birds. They do not much resemble any part of the human body.

Rabbits are another matter. The quail farm, where Janice buys the quails, sells frozen rabbits. But they remind her of dead, skinned, red, sad babies. No, she could not cook a rabbit.

One could be a vegetarian, of course. Like Alix Bowen's murderer. Janice had thought of asking the Bowens to dinner, but had hesitated – she does not really know them, she has met them only once, at the Northern Schools Drama Festival, she had no excuse for inviting them. But she had had a conversation with Alix, as they sat next to one another on hard institutional seats, waiting for the curtain to rise on High Cross Comprehensive's winning production of Doctor Faustus. A proper conversation. Alix had asked Janice what she did, and Janice had said that she had once been an actress (which was more or less true) and that now she worked part-time at the Regional Arts Office (which was not *very* true), and that her husband Edward (that 'skinny chap over there waving his arms about') was Head of English and Drama at High Cross, and the director of this ambitious production that they were about to behold. Alix in turn had divulged that she had herself been an English teacher and had taught female offenders in a psychiatric prison in London, and that she recognized Edward's name because she had heard he was trying to set up a Drama Group at Porston Prison, where Alix visited. 'Ah,' said Janice, 'you're the person who goes to see that murderer.' Alix admitted that she was, and answered a few stock questions about P. Whitmore. She then pointed out Brian, who was also up front, talking to a group of civic dignitaries and the Mayor, and claimed him as her husband and the Head of Educational Projects of Northam Council. 'Your husband ought to meet my husband,' said Alix. 'I'm sure he'd be interested in the prison drama group.'

But it hadn't got any further than that, because the curtain had gone up, and pleasantries had to be abandoned. Janice, who had seen the production before, was of course worried about all the things that might go wrong — Edward had been complaining that the stage was too shallow for the set, and that the lighting man was a fool and wouldn't let Edward's own lighting trainee protégé explain the schedule to him properly — and she was also apprehensive that Alix would be bored out of her mind. But Alix had settled into a dutiful attention, which seemed to intensify into real interest. And it *was* a good production, even though it was Edward's: the modern-dress balletic chorus moved beautifully, the Helen of Troy apparition got a round of applause, and the Faustus and the Mephistopheles were excellent. Edward had chosen it for them, and they had done him proud. Two sixth formers, friends, rivals, passionate amateur actors, desperate to get into R A D A or L A M D A or the Central, both immensely talented, in Edward's view — sophisticated, delicate, perfect timing. The boy who played Faustus was an Indian, a doctor's son, tall, lank, elegant, melancholy with a strange deep husky catch to his voice: the Mephistopheles was big, broad, physically assertive, red haired, potato featured, compelling. 'I've cast them *against* the grain,' Edward had explained to Janice, a hundred times, until she had said all right, I've got that, let's talk about something else, shall we? — but it had worked, and they worked together, with a sinister intimacy, a suggestion of erotic collusion. Brilliant, thought, as Marlowe's mighty lines rolled on.

'Brilliant!' said Alix, turning to Janice at the end, her hands hot with clapping, her cheeks pink with excitement. 'Quite, quite brilliant! What talented boys — and what a wonderful production. Your husband must be very proud!'

The audience had clapped on, and the young men had smiled and bowed. Beautiful, they both were, in their different styles. Eighteen years old. The world before them. Utterly confident, utterly assured. They bowed, on a civic stage in Sheffield, as though they were already stars. The theatre tempted them, they would sell their souls to it. The hot bright lights shone on them.

And so they had shone, once, on Edward Enderby. He too had been stagestruck, he too had dreamed of applause, of the footlights, of green rooms and dressing-rooms and good luck telegrams and dazzling notices in the press. He had been ruined by delusions of glory. He had refused to go into the family firm, as his younger brother Clive was to do: he had insisted on going to drama school, had thrown himself into wild hopes, had worked and worked — and to what avail? He had had a few jobs, here and there, odd jobs. And was now a teacher of drama. Still stagestruck, still besotted, still convinced that he could dazzle the nation, given the chance.

Yes, that was the odd thing about Edward, reflected Janice, as she cracked eggs for the lemon mousse. He really hadn't accepted that he wasn't a star. Inside himself, he really thought he was. He thought he was better than Albert Finney and Peter O'Toole and Ian McKellen and Derek Jacobi and Tom Conti and all those other talentless actors who had so mysteriously made it to the top. Edward really thought he could do it better given a chance.

And once, he had been good. Oh yes. She had seen him shine. At drama college, where she first met him, when he could have been little older than those two boys, Shokat and Stuart. She had seen him give his Prospero and it had been — yes, magical. Magical. Against all the odds. A twenty-year-old playing an old man. A twenty-year-old with the remnants of a Yorkshire accent playing the Duke of Milan. Not a part much coveted by the young, a dull part, a prosy, unshowy, sexless part. But Edward had inhabited it, had made it his own. He had been dark, frightening, powerful: Miranda and Ferdinand, Ariel and Caliban, Alonso and Sebastian had been shadows, puppets. His puppets. He had shone, he had stolen the play's thunder. The college had admired, theatrical agents had admired and solicited, his contemporaries had applauded wildly — and Edward had been ruined.

He still believed he had that power. That he could step out of banishment, out of retirement, wave his wand and hold the stage.

She hopes those two boys make it.

She stares at the bowl of egg white. It is globby like mucus. A thin trail of unborn chicken lies in it, like a trace of nosebleed and snot.

Janice is menstruating. It is the third day. She has had an IUD fitted and her periods now are heavy, bloody, dark, rusty. She has to wear pads as well as tampons. She is afraid that she will mark her clothes. She is afraid that she may smell.

She starts to whip the egg whites, and they begin to transform themselves into something less revolting.

She wishes she had invited Alix Bowen. Alix Bowen's murderer is a vegetarian. The red cabbage had split like a skull.

Janice shudders. Thinking about these things has made her feel quite ill. She knows she cannot afford to feel too ill. She has to carry on, for Edward's sake, for the sake of the children.

She whips the egg whites until they froth and stiffen and peak. Some evil is oozing from her into them, through the metal beaters, through the plastic handle. Dangerously, furiously, she whips. The kitchen is a dangerous place. It is full of horrible animations, appalling suggestions. It is not a charnel house, no, no, Paul Whitmore is wrong there. It breeds, it incubates, it brings forth young.

Clive Enderby sat alone in his sitting-room in Hansborough, watching Liz Headleand on television. It was not the kind of programme he usually watched, but he found himself compelled to stay tuned. She interested him, and not only through the chance geographical connection, through the natural curiosity aroused by the sight of a Northam girl made good. Clive's connection with her was more intimate. He did not know her well, but he knew more about her than many people did, and indeed he knows more about her than she knows, or can know, herself. To him, by chance, had come the delicate task of revealing to her the circumstances of her father's suicide, of telling her how he had hanged himself, years ago, when she was a little girl, before Clive was born. They were connected.

Liz was taking part in a panel discussion on sex and the young. The other participants were a politician, a retired head-master-turned-pundit, and a woman from some family-planning organization. One of the starting points of the discussion was the much publicized case of the suicide of a fifteen-year-old boy. The parents of his fourteen-year-old girlfriend had dragged him out of bed in the middle of the night and set the law on him.

He had been accused of unlawful intercourse. He had thrown himself under a train. Everybody had piously deplored this outcome, but only Liz used the occasion to speak up for the abolition of the age of consent.

There she sat, dressed in a cream and yellow flowing robe, a handsome middle-aged matron, knowingly uttering atrocities. With a calm smile, and a mildly but not enthusiastically animated manner, and a battery of statistics. Her performance disturbed the live studio audience, the other panel members, and Clive Enderby. He listened, at first idly, then intently, to her immodest proposals.

Yes, she was in favour of abolishing the age of consent, she said. She couldn't see the point of it. Sex had been progressively criminalized, she said, rattling off dates and acts and by-laws, invoking Home Office working parties, policy advisory committees, the National Council for One-Parent Families, the Criminal Law Revision Committee. What harm had that boy and his girlfriend been doing? They had been obeying nature's law, not man's. In other times, in other societies, they would have been committing no offence. The offence is man-made, said Liz Headleand, let us unmake it. That boy was hounded to his death by our inability to think clearly, said Liz Headleand, smiling like an oracle, like a sibyl, in her faintly Grecian garb.

Brave words, unfashionable, unwise words, in these days of AIDS-induced terror, in these days of mounting paranoia about child sex abuse and child sex abuse detection.

What you are recommending is a pederast's charter, the keen-faced hornrim-spectacled young politician had protested, to loud applause. He appealed to parental rights and the sanctity of family life. Unmoved, Liz had said that she didn't think it was desirable to use the law to settle family disputes, and that the boy and girl in question were both underage and had been sleeping together by mutual consent for several months. Now one was dead and the other was no doubt damaged for life. I don't see what this case has to to do with pederasty, she said. Or with paedophilia. It's more a Romeo and Juliet case, if you ask me.

'But you can't deny,' said the politician, 'that the removal of legal constraint would open the floodgates?'

Liz appeared amused, quizzical, interested.

'You mean you think everyone is longing to have sex with the underaged, and that only the law prevents it?' she asked.

The politician did not answer, but proceeded to cite instances of abused children, of sex offences against children, of prostituted children, of slaughtered children.

'But I don't think you're being very logical,' said Liz. 'I'm not recommending that we decriminalize murder, or assault, or kidnapping, you know.'

Her air of patient detachment goaded and irritated the politician and the audience. The discussions rambled on from cliché to outrage to cliché. An elderly gentleman in the audience mentioned the decline of the Roman Empire. A woman in a lively pink blouse, with a curiously salacious manner, blamed sex education in schools for an increase in teenage pregnancies. Television talk, the pub talk of the public. Liz appeared to be genuinely interested by the oddity of some of the views expressed, and returned, perhaps unfortunately, to one of her original queries: 'Do you really think,' she inquired, innocently, this time of the retired headmaster, 'that the desire of adults for sexual contact with children is so widespread and so strong that only the most severe social and legal sanctions can control it?' While he hesitated, she pursued: 'And if this is so, does it ever occur to you that this desire itself could be less abnormal than you believe it to be? And possibly less harmful?'

Now, Clive could tell, she really had gone too far, she had broken a taboo, she had said the unspeakable. The studio simmered and bubbled and spluttered. Nobody listened, as Liz expressed her sympathy with the headmaster, her appreciation of the onerous responsibility of his career, of his difficulties in controlling the staff, perpetually lusting illegally after the pupils, and the pupils, perpetually lusting illegally after one another. 'It is a strange world you conjure up for us,' said Liz, 'a world which I find it hard to recognize from my own observations ...'

But nobody was listening. Liz was a witch, an unnatural monster. Liz smiled on, as they rounded upon her, one after another.

Clive Enderby, watching this curious performance, wondered: is she trying to commit professional suicide? Is that her *aim*? If she goes on like this she will be struck off. You can't expect people to be rational about a topic like that.

Even the chairman seemed to think things had got out of hand, and tried to make one or two efforts to bring Liz back into the fold of orthodoxy. 'But surely you don't mean ... surely you're not trying to suggest ...' he proffered, helpfully. But Liz persisted. Yes, she did mean, yes, she did want to suggest. Moreover, she said, she assumed she had been invited to take part in this discussion in order to make these suggestions, however much antagonism they might arouse, so she was hardly likely to back down now. When asked if her views represented those of her profession as a whole, Liz, for the first time, hesitated and then continued: 'No, I wouldn't say so, these views are my own. Some share them, some do not. But may I say that I haven't really been expressing *views*. The rest of you have been doing that. I have been asking questions and making suggestions. And your response to those questions has been most illuminating.'

So, not professional suicide. But still, risky stuff. Unpopular, probably untenable. Clive, who knew next to nothing about psychoanalytic theory, was fascinated. As Liz vanished from the screen, he remembered her behaviour at the time of her mother's death, when she and Shirley had been to visit him in Dilke Street. He remembered her mixture of curiosity and carelessness, of interest and indifference, as she confronted some of the squalid details of her own past. They were probably less squalid than she had feared, for she had greeted them almost with relief. 'So *that's* what it was all about,' she had said, as though it was nothing – and yet how could it be nothing?

It came to Clive Enderby that what he had been watching on television that night was not a cool, objective, detached contribution to a debate, but an act of elaborate professional and personal self-justification, a baroque attempt on Liz's part to justify her own genesis, her own history. And some of the facts, Clive suspected, she had misinterpreted. She was building on false premises.

Fascinating. I am out of my depth, thought Clive Enderby, and poured himself a whisky and soda, and switched over to the golf.

Liz's extended family had watched her television performance in a different spirit from Clive Enderby's, and with varying degrees of irritation or approval. Her eldest stepson Jonathan and his wife Xanthe, sitting before their pleasant log fire in their cottage in Suffolk, had not been amused.

'Christ,' Jonathan had groaned, more in sorrow than in anger, 'someone should tell her the permissive society's dead and buried, you just can't *talk* like that these days, it's embarrassing, it's ridiculous, it's so bloody old-fashioned, whatever can she be thinking of?'

'Mmm?' said Xanthe, who was not listening either to Liz or to Jonathan.

'Any minute now,' said Jonathan, 'she'll start singing the praises of the swinging sixties and going on about the moral backlash, I mean, you just can't *say* that kind of thing these days, or not on this kind of programme – whatever got into her, to start appearing on telly like this? She never used to, in the old days, she always said it was a waste of time and a professional misjudgement, and my God how right she was!'

'I think she looks rather good,' said Xanthe. 'Is that a Zoe Bittersweet dress, do you think?'

'And at her age,' repeated Jonathan, taking a disconsolate swig of claret.

'Or it could be from Hannah's in Baker Street,' mused Xanthe, trying to pretend not to hear her baby daughter's voice raising itself above the television's ceaseless commentary.

Jonathan threw another log on the fire. 'Please God, let her not start on infantile sexuality, not now,' he implored, as the sparks flew upward.

Stepson Aaron was more indulgent, as his non-aligned attitude to life permitted him to be. He sat back in his battered old armchair in his flat above a junk shop in Chalk Farm and smiled in appreciation as the expressions of her co-panellists grew more outraged, more self-righteous, more disbelieving. The crosser they got, he noted, the more serenely Liz smiled. 'That's the spirit, Liz,' he said, aloud, approvingly, to his empty room. He would ring her, in the morning, to congratulate her upon her stand.

Stepson Alan up in Manchester missed the programme altogether. He never knew it was on, and was never to know: oblique references to it continued to bewilder him for some weeks. Alan watched quite a lot of television, but being a true intellectual his favourite programmes were soccer, snooker, a cartoon about subversive mice and a sit-com about the rag trade. He hated chats and debates on the box. He did enough chatting and debating, with his students and his friends.

*

Daughter Sally watched, loyally, with her friend Jo in their flat in Streatham. They were both slightly bored by it, but did not say so. They were eating a Chinese takeaway as they watched. Their minds were not on Liz and her arguments. Their minds were on other things. They were both well over the age of consent.

Daughter Stella watched, and was perturbed. Like Jonathan, she had had enough of her parents making fools of themselves, but unlike Jonathan she had also had enough of England. Watching the extraordinary mixture of whining vote-beseeching, arse-licking vulgarity, demotic stupidity, intellectual pretension, moral confusion and entertainment-packaged pseudo-seriousness, she groaned within her twelve stones of self-dislike, disliking Liz and her live studio audience even more than she disliked herself. But in some way, deep down, she felt the stirrings of hope. The dislike was about to come to a head, to burst, and she would be purged, free again, light as air again, she would take off, for another continent, another world.

Ex-husband Charles, watching alone in Kentish Town, was also perturbed – not so much by what Liz said, which was old hat to him, as by the fact that she was there on TV saying it at all. Her disrespect for his medium had been so consistent, so sustained. Why had it now crumbled? What weakness in her was showing itself in this belated consent? Did she need attention, notoriety? Surely not. She was diminished by her concession. The medium had been too powerful for her, it had sucked her up and into its great dusty bag full of rubbish. Charles loathed discussion programmes. He liked Hard News.

Carla Davis watched Liz Headleand's programme with a mixture of rage and satisfaction. Like Charles, Carla Davis is a news addict. She was addicted long before Dirk's disappearance, although that had condoned and intensified her passion. As a bored home-worker (she worked as a freelance editor, usually on dullish reference books) she had often switched on the news in hope of a catastrophe to divert her from the tedium of her task. Sometimes she was rewarded by a plane crash or a Beirut bomb or a hijacking, but not often enough. As she listened to the same round of repeated or minimally updated reports of union negotia-tions, of President Reagan's operations and ill health, of assess-ments of the prospects of the Tory Party at the next election, she had often had a wild desire for a completely different lot of news. Completely and utterly different. She sometimes fantasized about a day which would begin normally enough, with a dullish selection of items on the *Today* programme on Radio 4 at 7.30 a.m., items which would reappear in identical or slightly updated form throughout the morning until the noon news, but which would vanish utterly from *The World at One.* The nation would switch on *The World at One,* and find a completely NEW LOT of news! Ten new items. All wholly new. A New World, with New News, New Made. Change history. Begin again, at lunch time.

This fantasy chimes in well with some of Charles's ambitions. It is one of the foundations of their alliance.

Carla Davis watched Liz Headleand in a cream dress comment-ing on a non-news story that will be forgotten in no time. A non-story. Who cares that a grubby little fifteen-year-old fucker from Formby had bumped himself off because his girlfriend's parents had set the law on him? Who cares? It is a non-story. Liz digs her own grave to Carla's delight, and makes a complete fool of herself. Carla thinks she herself has a much better television personality than Liz Headleand. Much more cleverly calculated. Why, Liz has aroused the antagonism of the viewers and the other participants. Carla knows this to be a mistake. On tele-vision, one should play for sympathy. One should present oneself favourably. Carla has a deep instinct for this. Liz, apparently, not. So reflected Carla Davis as she watched the woman whom she regarded as a rival, as a threat.

Alix and Brian Bowen failed to see their old friend on television. They were too busy that evening watching the local news which carried a distressing story about a Northam boy who had been killed in a school playground by a crossbow bolt. One of Brian's colleagues had put out a statement regretting that such a thing could have happened on Council property. Too cruel anywhere, had been Alix's reaction to that, and she had rung Brian in his office when she heard this announcement on the news at lunch time. She never rang Brian in his office, not being a meddlesome wife, but this was too much. 'For God's sake, Brian,' she said, agitated, 'how *could* he had said something so stupid, so insensitive? Can't you get them to put out another statement? It will do the Council terrible damage, if they go on repeating *that* all day.'

Brian had indicated that he couldn't speak then, that he would do what he could. But nevertheless, all day, relentlessly, on every news bulletin, local and national, this crass remark had been recycled and broadcast, and when Brian came home in the evening he and Alix sat miserably watching *News from Northam*, in which Stan Ackroyd said it straight to the eager camera. 'He's not a bad chap,' said Brian, apologetically, 'he's just a bit slow, he's not good with the press, he's a nice man, really, he was trying to say the right thing.'

Stan Ackroyd disappeared, mercifully, from the screen, and another face appeared, a plump smooth pale face, above a bow tie. It spoke knowledgeably about the dangers of crossbows. 'Until we outlaw the crossbow,' said this face, 'we risk these terrible accidents daily.'

'I don't suppose it *was* an accident,' said Alix, glumly. 'He probably shot him on purpose. Have you ever seen a crossbow, Sam?'

Sam shook his head. 'They don't have them, in our place,' he said. 'Or not yet, anyway.'

'Well, they'll be on their way,' said Alix. 'Tell me what they look like, when you've seen one. And what people want them for.'

'Retaliation, probably,' said Sam, and told them about Ramesh Bannerjee's reports of pigs' trotters suspended from Muslim doorknobs.

'Oh God, how *disgusting* people are,' said Alix. 'And to think we left London to get away from the violence.'

'That's not why we left at all,' said Brian, reasonably.

'You know what I mean,' said Alix.

'If you wanted to get away from violence, you'd have to go and live in an anchorage,' said Sam, surprisingly.

'An anchorage?' queries Alix.

'You know. One of those places where anchorites live. Where they wall themselves up. There was one at Ogham, Tony says. Twenty years inside, she did.'

'Did she ever come out?'

'I don't know. I think she died in there.'

'Well, I *suppose* she was safe from violence in there,' said Alix. 'But it's rather an extreme solution. Almost defeats its own end. Like that poor chap in the Post Office in Earlsfield Road who died of a heart attack behind his grill because nobody could get through the security to give him the kiss of life. There they all were, lined up, doctors, ambulance, fire brigade, and they couldn't get through to him quick enough. So he died in there, safe with all the Post Office savings accounts, and sheets of stamps, and pension books, and ten-pound notes. Quite safe, and quite dead. In his cage.'

'Who told you that one?' asks Brian, who has not heard it before.

'The man in the Earlsfield garage. I said to him, I'm just leaving the car there while I pop into the Post Office to buy some stamps, and he said don't do that, it's all locked up, the old man's snuffed it. And then he told me how.'

'The Post Office anchorite,' said Sam. 'A tale of our times.'

'I'm sure they're not called anchorages,' said Alix. 'You've confused me.'

'I don't see why they shouldn't be,' said Sam, and reached for the dictionary. 'Yes, here we are. Anchorage, a place inhabited by a recluse, hermit or anchorite. From the Greek, *anakhoreo*, to retire.'

'How very *odd*,' said Alix, puzzled. 'I was sure they were something to do with harbours, not hermits.'

'Same thing,' says Brian, who has noticed that Sam is teasing his mother. 'You know, it's like in that Hopkins poem, "*I have desired to go where springs not fail . . . where the green swell is in the havens dumb, and out of the swing of the sea*", or something along those lines. The nun, the anchorite. *Heaven-Haven*, is that its title?'

'How very *odd*,' repeats Alix, as false, ill-derived, delusive yet somehow persuasive images of nuns and green harbours fill her mind. Peaceful images, far from the savage playground and the crossbow.

Cliff and Shirley Harper also watched a bit of local news, took in the crossbow story, then flipped channels to discover quite by accident Liz talking about teenage sex and suicide. They settled to watch in silence. Shirley could not tell whether Cliff was listening or not. She herself was listening with only half her attention. The sight of Liz annoyed her. What had she got to be so pleased with herself about? But everybody else on the programme annoyed her too. Talk, talk, talk. Fools the lot of them.

Romeo and Juliet, childhood sweethearts, death on the railway line. She and Cliff had been childhood sweethearts. They hadn't had sexual intercourse before the age of consent, not quite, but they'd done everything they could think of, short of penetration. Heavy petting, it was disgustingly called, in the fifties. Seventeen, just seventeen, Shirley had been, when she had opened her legs for Cliff in a field of long grass and shiny buttercups and pollen-laden cow parsley. She had opened her legs and pulled him into her. And they had married young, and had three children, and now those three children had grown up and left them. Celia, the clever one, was studying Ancient History at Oxford, and although she still had a bedroom at home she rarely visited it now. Shirley didn't blame her. There wasn't much going on at Blackridge Green. Celia had escaped, she had flown high beyond the reach of bolts and arrows. She had no sweetheart, Shirley suspected. She worked, and worked.

Cliff muttered to himself. Shirley switched channels, to get rid of Liz and the end of Liz's programme, and discovered yet another programme about sex; an AIDS warning, complete with a giant plastic penis, some uneasy jokes and an array of brightly coloured condoms. A mad world we live in, thought Shirley. She and Cliff were like strangers now. Nothing interesting, thought Shirley, will ever happen to me again.

A week later, in mid-March, Cliff Harper committed suicide. Shirley found him in the car in the garage, lying back on the reclined driver's seat, with a piece of tubing leading from the exhaust and in through the small back window. Carbon monoxide poisoning. Shirley stood her distance, her hand still on the remote-control button that worked the automatic roll-up door. It was nine o'clock in the morning. She had gone to the garage to look for her secateurs.

Should she advance, see if he was really dead? She knew he was. She edged forward. He was lying back, his mouth open, his eyes open and sunk back, his face a soapy blue-yellow. The key was in the ignition. Gingerly, delicately, she tried the door. It was locked. She peered inside. The passenger door was locked too. He had locked himself in, had done it properly.

A cold sweat stood on her forehead, her heart beat loudly. Maybe the garage was still full of gas? She backed away. How long had he been there? How could one tell? He had left for Manchester the night before, had said he was spending the night in Manchester. Had he driven back in the night and done this thing? Or had he never left for Manchester at all? Had he been lying there dying while she was watching the last episode of *The Crystal Ball*? Would she not have heard the car engine?

He was sealed into the car as into a tomb. It did not occur to her that she had a key to the car in her desk. She never drove Cliff's car, it was too wilful for her, it frightened her, she hated its power steering. Cliff had been very proud of it.

She found herself backing out of the garage, glancing nervously around to see if she was overlooked. She pressed the button and the door rolled down like a crematorium shutter. Untouched, Cliff lay there in his double sepulchre. She had not even touched his hand.

She went back into the house, stood in her kitchen, put the kettle on. She supposed she ought to call a doctor, an ambulance, the police. But did none of these things. She made herself a cup of tea. Why hurry? There was nothing to hurry about. A lot of horrible things would begin to happen quite soon, whatever she did. She was quite angry with Cliff.

She could pretend she hadn't found him, she could have one last dull normal day. It was a fluke that she'd gone to look for her secateurs. She'd been intending to use them to chop up some picture wire with which she was attempting to mend the handle of the cloakroom lavatory. If she hadn't had this sudden fit of do-it-yourself, of not waiting for Cliff, Cliff could have lain there all day. She never went near the garage in a normal day's routine: her own car was parked outside on the short driveway. If Cliff had fixed the lav when she'd asked him, she would never have found him.

This sentiment seemed so like the sort of thing her mother-in-law would have thought and said that Shirley was quite taken aback.

Had Cliff left a note? She hadn't seen anything in the car, but then, she hadn't looked. Shirley had never seen a dead person before. She had declined the undertaker's invitation to view her mother.

Did Cliff's death mean that his financial situation was even more dire than he'd let on? Or did it simply mean that he was even more depressed than she'd thought?

She didn't look forward to finding out. She drank her hot tea.

Perhaps she'd never find out. She could commit suicide too. A joint suicide. Childhood sweethearts. A pact. She could swallow pills, or put a plastic bag over her head, or jump off a high building.

She shuddered at the thought of the high building. Cliff had chosen the best way, the decent modern way. There wasn't room in the garage for another car.

But really, thought Shirley, washing up her cup and saucer, really, I don't much *want* to commit suicide.

She unstacked the dishwasher, wiped down the stainless steel sink, sat down again at the kitchen-table, picked up the newspaper, read a few items. Cross-Channel ferry disaster. President Reagan. Interest and mortgage rates.

She was still angry. How dare he land her in such a mess? Whatever was she supposed to do now?

Shirley's father, of whom she had no recollections at all, had also committed suicide, shortly after her birth. Or so she rather recently had been told. He had been charged with the offence of indecent exposure, and had committed suicide shortly after his acquittal. Had hung himself, or so Clive Enderby said, in a disused warehouse on Jubilee Road.

Well, said Shirley to herself, aloud, this is ridiculous. She thought of ringing Celia, or her son Barry, or her sister Liz, or her brother-in-law Steve. But recoiled from such a prospect as much as she recoiled from the high building.

She began to feel strange, airy, irresponsible. She went up to the bedroom that she and Cliff had shared for fourteen years, for more than half their married life. She pulled a small suitcase out from under the bed, dusted it. She opened drawers, opened the wardrobe, took out at random tights, pants, skirts, jerseys, blouses. She packed a sponge bag. She went downstairs.

She opened another little drawer and took out two rings, a necklace, a bracelet and some brooches; opened her desk, found her passport, put it in her handbag. So Cliff had left no message, had left without a message. Two can play at that game, said Shirley to herself. She walked out of the house, locked the door.

She got into her car, switched on the engine, and drove off, waving as she passed Joan Halliwell on the corner walking her Airedale. She drove down to the shopping mall, parked, got out, bought herself a pound of apples. She drove on, to the next suburb, where she parked again. She approached the cashpoint of the Midland Bank on the corner, waited politely for her turn, inserted her card, requested and read the balance. £495 in her current account. She hesitated. Then she pressed the digits. The machine squeaked responsively. She collected her card, collected her money, put them in her bag, got back in the car. She counted her credit cards. American Express, Access, Gold Standard, Midland, Midland Gold. Cliff had been liberal with credit cards.

She put the bag on the passenger's seat, hesitated once more, then drove away, towards the M 1.

*

98

'What do you mean, *vanished*?' said Alix to Liz.

'Vanished,' repeated Liz, her voice over the telephone hitting a note of unseemly but probably hysterical mirth. 'Vanished. Not a sign of her.'

'And Cliff was *dead* in the *garage*?' repeated Alix, stupidly.

'So they tell me. Been dead for days, they tell me.'

'And Shirley . . .?'

'Not a sign of her.'

'But Cliff . . . hadn't been *murdered*, had he?'

'No, no, of course not — well, at least I *assume* of course not — hey, wait a minute, are you suggesting that my sister Shirley murdered him? You've got murder on the brain. You move in murderous circles, Alix.' Liz laughed, wildly. 'No, it's a nice idea, but I don't think Shirley did murder him, I think he committed suicide, and she ran off. Though whether she ran off before or after he killed himself I don't know. All I know is what they told me.'

'Just now?'

'Well, not long ago. About two hours ago. I've been ringing you for hours.'

'Sorry,' said Alix, guiltily. 'I was out. At Beaver's. Working.'

'Anyway, I don't know *what* to do,' said Liz. 'They thought she might have come here. But she hasn't. I had Cliff's brother Steve on the phone. He's in a shocking state. He seemed very angry with me, for some reason, as though it were all my fault. Which it can hardly be, can it?'

'So nobody knows what happened, is that it? Why he killed himself, when he killed himself, why she disappeared, when she disappeared?'

'I don't think it's a crime to disappear,' said Liz. 'But I suppose it may be. It's suspicious, anyway. Definitely suspicious. Disappearing is suspicious. I suppose I'll have to come up to Northam to see what's what. Have you ever had the misfortune to meet

99

Shirley's mother-in-law? She's a classic. You would hardly credit. I'm sure everyone knows *why* Cliff did it, it's because his business has gone bust, but you'd think he'd have done something a bit more subtle.'

'Perhaps he was too upset to think clearly,' ventured the charitable Alix.

Liz snorted. 'Ha,' said Liz.

'You can come and stay with me, if you like,' said Alix. 'The house is quite comfortable now, I've had central heating put in the spare room.'

'I don't know,' said Liz. 'I don't like to be in the way. Maybe I'll stay in that hotel. I'd better get on to that chap Enderby, I suppose. I'll give him a buzz and find out whether it's a crime *not* to aid and abet one's husband's suicide. I wonder if the law is clear on this point. Apparently her car has vanished, but nobody knows when it went. Nobody noticed. Nobody notices anything in that dead-alive little pelmeted suburb. You could rot for months. I'm amazed they *ever* found him. Will you be around tomorrow evening, if I decide I do have to come up?'

'I've got to go to prison in the afternoon,' said Alix. 'I'm off to see P. Whitmore. But yes, I'll be in in the evening. Brian's out, teaching his evening class on the Victorian novel. But Sam and I will be in. We'll make you some supper. And do stay, why spend money on a hotel?'

'I like spending money,' said Liz. 'It cheers me up.'

Alix laughed.

'Oh God,' said Liz, 'what a nuisance my family are. If it's not one, it's another.' But she didn't sound too put out. It would take more than a suicide and a vanishing trick to upset Liz Headleand.

Alix drove across the wet moor. The car was peaceful, quiet, for the bottle-bank bottles in the boot were muffled by the Oxfam-intended cast-off garments. It was cold, but there was a hint of warmth in the air, and the light had a golden misty tinge. Spring-time, the turning of the year, the sweet of the year. Alix intensely enjoyed her solitary drives, her occasional solitary walks. Sometimes she thought she enjoyed them *too much.* The buried romantic dreamer of her childhood was coming to life again in her, in these northern lights and levels. A battle was being waged in her between the romantic and the statistical, the solitary and the sociological. Her good angel and her bad angel. But which was which?

She passed the turning to Ogham Abbey, and thought of the immured anchorite in her twenty-year seclusion, staring at the sky through a high window, denying herself the beauties of the natural world, denying herself the snowdrops and the coltsfoot, the violets and the moss, indulging herself only in clouds. And then thought of the more gregarious Fanny Kettle, Tony Kettle's strange mother, whom she had met the week before at a reception at the Holroyd Gallery. Fanny and Alix had bumped into one another first in the solid polished antique Ladies' Room, as they took off their coats, Alix divesting herself of an old blue raincoat, and Fanny Kettle of something that might have been a mink. But Fanny Kettle had been incongruously encumbered by a shopping trolley full of groceries which rather cramped her style. They had eyed one another, cautiously, in the mirror, as, side by side, they touched up their complexions – Alix dabbing a little powder fiercely on her nose, Fanny paying more elaborate attention to eyelashes and lips. They had half smiled at one another, as women do in such accidental proximity. Then, five minutes later, out in the high Victorian hall, a monument to past civic pride, they had been formally introduced, and had claimed contact through their sons. Sipping a glass of white wine, they had discussed the education of their sons, and the social potential of Northam. Fanny got on to the subject of parties in no time.

'You must come round,' she said to Alix, pressingly, 'I'm trying to organize a big house-warming party, you must come, and bring your husband and that nice boy of yours.'

Alix smiled, a little forbiddingly, and said that Brian was not much of a party-goer, and was only here tonight in the course of duty.

'But one mustn't be cramped by *them*,' cried Fanny, with spirit, reaching deftly with practised timing for another glass from a passing tray. 'Husbands *always* hate parties. Come alone, if he won't come. We're entitled to our own amusements, aren't we?'

Alix smiled again, not very encouragingly. Fanny Kettle struck her as vulgar. Intriguing, but vulgar. Ian Kettle had not been on view at the Art Gallery. It was not clear why Fanny Kettle had been invited.

The party had been in aid of an exhibition to celebrate the centenary of the death of Northam's one well-known nineteenth-century artist, Simon Blessed, whose vast canvases of moorland scenes and shooting parties had once been much prized by the wealthy manufacturers of the neighbourhood. He had fallen out of favour, inevitably, but had been to some extent rehabilitated, largely through gossip about his private life, which had leaked out gradually over the decades in biographies of his con-temporaries, in footnotes, in little monographs: Blessed, to out-ward appearances a pillar of respectability, had in fact been a man of the greatest private eccentricity, a good-natured and philanthropic homosexual who seemed to have been more in touch with his own impulses than most of the eminent Victorians. A new *Life*, published this week, would tell all. There, in the gal-lery, had been its author, a self-effacing, bearded young gentle-man aged, in Alix's eyes, about twenty-two. Alix had spoken to him, briefly, politely, beneath a massive scene of feathered slaughter. 'You should look at the smaller canvases,' he had said, 'they're quite different, they tell another story altogether.' And she had meant to do so, but had not found time, in the throng, with all the people that she now seemed to know in Northam clustering and chattering around her and at her.

The new Northam had taken Simon Blessed back to its bosom, now he had proved to be both kind and deviant: looking around at the varied guests, Alix had thought that Northam had a good heart. One would not guess this from the national press, but here, in this civic gathering, one could not but warm to Northam's style. The assembly was comically mixed: dumpy little women with soft Yorkshire voices and sharp opinions, tall county women with loud braying voices and mild opinions, soberly suited professors, young men in rainbow silk tie-dyed shirts, a weather-beaten girl in dungarees who lived in a bender at the Gloseley US nuclear base, a bearded Shavian gentleman with a baby in a rucksack on his back, the mayor with his chain of office, the Chief Executive of TV North, and brooding intensely over the scene, an exotic white-faced androgynous creature dressed in sequined black, with long black hair and bold blue lips and jet jewellery. 'He calls himself the Black Orchid,' local broadcaster Tony Troughton had told Alix, 'but nobody knows who he really is.' Tony had brought along his six-year-old son, a delight-ful lad who entertained himself at knee level by making strange quiet comforting farmyard noises at two outer-space, plastic monsters which he was clutching in his little hands. 'They're frightened, you see,' he told Alix, 'by all these people.' Alix had moved on to speak to Perry Blinkhorn himself, the great man, and had complimented him on the richness of the gathering: Perry had taken this seriously, had considered it, had said that yes, *it* was a good crowd, yes, he was glad the gallery could put on an event like this and that the trustees had at last allowed wine to be served in the main hall, yes, he was glad that Blessed was getting a good show, but where was it all going to end, were we going to discover that *everyone* is really homosexual? 'I mean,' said Perry, puzzled, 'I'm in favour of Gay Rights and all that, I mean in my position I *have* to be, but I do sometimes wonder. What do you think, Alix? Do you think we're all bisexual? I can't really believe that, whatever people say.'

'I don't know,' Alix had said, touched by the unusual sound of honest doubt.

'People say it's my religious background, that I'm full of prejudice,' said Perry. 'And maybe I am.'

'I think it's a pity he had to paint all these dead animals,' said Alix, 'when he probably wanted to paint live young men.'

'I take your point,' said Perry, and turned to shake the hand of a ninety-year-old lady with a moustache and a walking stick who was claiming his attention. 'Perry, Perry, you *naughty* boy,' she was saying, as Alix wandered off to rescue Brian from the headmaster of St Anthony's Infants.

Yes, an odd scene, but a harmless one: tolerance, efforts at tolerance, inclusion rather than exclusion. Some might think it undignified, but surely they could not label it lunatic, fanatic?

Thirteen miles to Ogham Abbey, the signpost had announced. Thirteen miles across the flatness. The Kettles had lived out that way, amongst the chariot burials. One day, thought Alix, I will turn off, on my way to see P. Whitmore, and visit the ancient ruins and the small dull town.

Her mind turned to Paul Whitmore. He had written to her, enclosing a V O and saying that he had urgent matters to discuss with her. He had mentioned in his letter Alix's old friend Esther Breuer, had said that he had a message for Esther. This had surprised Alix, who had rung Esther in Bologna in a fit of sudden anxiety and was reassured but not surprised to find that Esther had no idea what Paul Whitmore could possibly be on about. 'I never exchanged a word with him, or hardly a word, in all those years,' she said, emphatically. 'And I certainly haven't heard from him since. Well, I wouldn't be likely to, would I?' Alix and Esther had quickly abandoned the subject of P.W., and had exchanged other news: about the book Esther was supposed to be writing, about Beaver and his papers, about Beaver's ex-mistress in Pallanza. 'Come to Italy in the spring and see her and me,' Esther had suggested. 'Please do, Alix. It would do you good.'

'I don't need *good* done to me, thanks,' said Alix, a little briskly, resenting the suggestion that Northam, Beaver and prison-visiting might lack goodness. 'But I would *like* to come. If I have time.'

'Ha!' said Esther. 'Time!'

When she arrived at Porston, Alix discovered that Paul Whitmore's message for Esther concerned Esther's potted palm. It was clearly in code: or was it?

'I had this dream, you see,' said Paul, 'about that potted palm she used to keep in the window of the red room. Do you remember it?'

'Of course I remember it,' said Alix. 'She had it for years.'

'I had this dream, it was on her doorstep, it was crying out. "Take me in, little sister, take me in, little sister," it cried.'

'Goodness,' said Alix.

'And when I woke up, I realized what it meant,' said Paul.

Alix listened, leaned forward, for revelation.

'What it *meant*,' said Paul, 'was that she should never have put it out. They need to be indoors, those plants. It died, when she put it out on the front steps.'

'But I think she put it out because it was dying anyway,' said Alix. 'She decided to sort of – finish it off.'

'But that's the whole *point*,' said Paul. 'It wasn't really dying. They always look like that. Half dead. It suddenly came to me, when I woke up. That's their *natural* look. When they look as though they are dying, they are really living. And that's why it cried out, little sister, take me in. You tell your friend she needn't have killed it. It was doing OK, that plant. Tell her not to do it again.'

105

He spoke with urgency, as though much hung on Alix's response. She faltered.

'Of course I'll tell her,' said Alix, 'though there doesn't seem to be much point in telling her now. After all, it's dead by now, poor thing. Well dead.'

She recalled that Esther had said that Paul had expressed concern about the palm. It had been one of the few remarks that this silent young man had addressed to her, over their years of living under the same roof.

'But she might get another,' said Paul. 'She might do it again.'

'Yes, I suppose so,' said Alix. 'I don't know if she's got any pot plants at the moment. She's gone to live in Italy, I haven't seen the place where she lives now.'

The conversation had become absurd, grotesque. Into Alix's mind swam, involuntarily, the macabre details of a recent murder case in Leeds: a dentist and his wife, who had murdered their adopted Brazilian daughter (who knows why, or how?), had chopped her up into tiny pieces and buried her in a hundred different places — in the garden, under the floorboards, and, most horribly, in plant pots around the house. They had lived with bits of her buried beneath rubber plants and cheese plants and a winter-flowering jasmine. Alix wished she had not remembered these details, and hoped that Paul could not read her mind.

But he had moved on to other thoughts.

'My mother had a palm,' he suddenly said, as it were, inconsequentially.

'Yes?' said Alix.

'That's why I know about palms,' said Paul. 'Hers was in the salon. It lived for years. But it was always going brown round the edges. She used to trim off the brown bits. It didn't seem to mind. She had it for years.'

Alix waited.

'I don't know where she went, my mother,' said Paul, innocently. He looked directly at Alix. It was an effort for him to do so. Usually he stared at the plastic-topped table, at the chipped ashtray.

'Fifteen years ago, you say,' said Alix, picking up threads from older conversations.

'When I was fifteen,' he agreed.

Alix paused. She could see no option.

'And you haven't heard from her since?' she asked, stalling.

'No,' he said. He looked at her again, then looked away. Pain and defeat and misery oozed out of him.

'I used to hear you laughing,' he said, suddenly. 'I used to hear you and your friends laughing, downstairs. I used to wonder why you were laughing. I liked to hear you. I was always alone, you see. So I liked to hear you all laugh.'

Alix stood condemned. What could she do, what recompense could she make, for this past laughter? For this harmless gaiety?

'Well,' said Alix, 'I wonder if I can help? You'd better give me some idea of where to begin to look.'

'Extraordinary,' said Liz. 'That wretched palm. Deflection tactics. Quite subtle, really. I suppose it died when she ran off with the lorry driver?'

'I suppose so. I didn't ask.'

'And she never surfaced again? None of those investigative journalists managed to dig her up during the trial?'

'No. Nobody.'

'"Little sister, little sister",' Liz repeated. 'I wonder if he read fairy tales, as a little boy?'

'I didn't ask,' said Alix.

'I suppose it's more likely that he read fairy stories than that he read Isabella and the Pot of Basil,' said Liz. 'Whose head was it that Isabella kept? Her brother's?'

'No, her lover's. Her brothers murdered him. In a forest.'

'What for?'

'What do you mean, what *for*? People didn't need a reason for murdering people. In those days. Any more than P. Whitmore did.'

'Sorry,' said Liz.

'Anyway,' said Alix, 'he's right about palms. Horticulturally speaking. I looked them up in my houseplant book when we got back. They do go brown round the edges. Naturally. It's what they do.'

Liz wasn't interested in palms, as palms. 'Amazing,' Liz continued, 'the intelligence of dreams. The way quite stupid or unimaginative people can dream dreams of a stunning complexity. People who wouldn't recognize a symbol in their waking lives, even if they fell over one.'

'But I'm not quite sure what it's a symbol *of*,' said Alix. 'It's obviously something to do with his mother, but what?'

'Who knows? Defective nurture? The castrating shears?'

'I never worked out what the beheading thing was about, either. You said *that* was castration complex, but I don't quite see why.'

'And will you try to find his mother for him?'

'I suppose I'll have to. I sort of said I would.' She paused. 'And what about you and Shirley, Liz? Will you try to find *her*?'

Liz hesitated, took off her glasses, polished them on her sleeve, and put them back on again.

'Well, to tell you the truth, I'm not all that keen on finding Shirley. What a mess she'd have to come back to. But I suppose she'll have to come back. And face the music.'

'And you still haven't been able to contact Celia?'

'Well, you know what it's like in Oxford, they're not on the phone, you leave messages at the porter's lodge, nobody seems to have seen her for days. But that doesn't mean anything. She's probably sitting quietly in the Bodleian, with a pile of books. You can't page the whole of Oxford.'

'But the boys have been contacted?'

'Apparently. Steve spoke to Bob in Australia. Didn't let on about Shirley, just said his father had had an accident. And they've got black sheep Barry back from Newcastle.'

'It's a bit worrying, about Celia.'

'Oh, I don't know. She's a cold fish, Celia. She'll survive.'

'So what happens next?'

'I'm going to Clive Enderby again in the morning. He seems quite bright.'

Alix poured another cup of coffee, stirred it.

'And what do *you* think has happened to Shirley?'

Liz laughed, heartlessly, miserably, perplexed.

'God knows. Maybe she's dead too. They're trying to trace her Mini. Apparently she took £400 out of her Midland Bank current account at a cashpoint in Ecclestone three days ago. So perhaps she's just bolted.'

'For a new life?'

'A new life, at her age?'

They both contemplated this cold prospect.

'Out of a *cash*point?' said Alix, eventually. 'How come? I can only ever get £50 out of mine. And it won't always let me have that.'

'She must have had one of those supercards,' said Liz, 'It's just the sort of thing she and Cliff would have had.' (Liz, of course, had one herself.) 'Well, well. I'd never have expected such a thing of Shirley. Though I suppose she was a bit of a rebel, in the old days. But I thought she'd settled down.'

'And what about Cliff? Would you have expected such a thing of Cliff?'

Liz shrugged her shoulders. 'I knew he was depressed. But he belongs more to your realm than mine, don't you think? He's become a statistic. A victim of the economy. Another failed-small-business suicide. There are hundreds of them a week, probably.'

'No, not a *week*, surely.'

'Well, you know what I mean. You can feed him into the counter-attack. Write off to the Employment Institute and present it with Cliff as a small statistic. Poor old Cliff.'

Sadness fell in the pleasant, muddled drawing-room. They nursed their coffee-cups. They could hear Sam on the telephone, upstairs. He had asked permission, like a polite boy, to ring his half-brother Nick.

'Your primroses are lovely,' said Liz, gazing for comfort at the wineglass of yellow deep-cored open reaching faces.

Alix brightened. 'Do you know what I found, yesterday, at the end of the garden under the chestnut tree? A little clump of tiny tiny cyclamen. I hadn't the heart to pick them. They are too beautiful.'

They fell silent, contemplating the primroses, summoning the cyclamen.

Alix did not admit that she had fallen to her knees by the miracle of the cyclamen, and spoken to them. She does not want Liz to know she has gone mad.

Liz Headland paced up and down Clive Enderby's office. Paced energetically, demonstratively. Clive Enderby watched her with admiration and apprehension. She paused, gestured largely, walked on, speaking the while.

'My guess,' said Liz, 'is that they had some kind of final row, some kind of show-down, and that Shirley walked off, or rather *drove* off, and that Cliff went and filled himself full of carbon monoxide as a result. You say she was here consulting you about her legal position? I imagine she'd just had enough, she just blew up and walked out. In which case, she won't even know he's dead. How could she? It's hardly national news.'

'And you've no idea where she might have gone?'

'How should *I* know? We weren't very close. She wouldn't have come to *me*. Why should she?'

'And were there friends she might have gone to?'

'I don't know if Shirley *had* any friends. No, I've no idea where she is. And while we're on the subject – which we're not, but maybe we should be – I gather she came to see you a month or so ago to ask about the money from my mother's will?'

'Yes, that's right.'

Clive, at his desk, watched Liz intently.

'And you told her a cheque would be on the way?'

'That's correct.'

'But it's not come through yet. Or at least, I haven't had my bit, so I assume she hasn't had hers. The will left everything to us equally, I believe?'

'That's correct.'

'But the money will be on its way – would have been on its way – soon?'

'Oh yes. That's quite correct.'

Impatiently, Liz paused, stared, suddenly sat.

'And would it be indelicate of me to ask how much it would be?' She glowered at him, commandingly, then continued, without pausing for an answer, 'Because it's odd, isn't it, that Shirley should have left now, without the money?'

Clive Enderby was looking through a file on his desk. His colour was slightly heightened. His collar was very white, his light suit was very grey.

'The house,' he said, 'was sold for £21,000. Your sister approved the sale.'

'Really? Is that all? Can you really buy a three-bedroomed house in a desirable suburb for £21,000? You can't get a bed-sit for that in London. Not even in the nastiest parts of London.'

Clive coughed. 'I think it was quite a good price,' he said. 'Your sister seemed to think so too. I know that house prices have been soaring down south, but they've actually been dropping round here. And the suburb is no longer quite so desirable. And the house was — somewhat neglected.'

Liz smiled. 'Yes, it was a dump,' she agreed. 'And you say Shirley knew the house had been sold? So she's walked out on ten thousand, or whatever's left of it when we've paid your fees? Was there any more? Did the furniture bring in anything?'

Clive shook his head. 'We had to pay the house clearers to take it away,' he said.

'So that was it,' said Liz. 'Ten thou. Give or take a few hundred. I wonder what happened to that silver wine cooler. I don't suppose my mother had anything in the bank, had she?'

'I sent you a statement,' said Clive. 'With all the details. Well, an interim statement.'

'Did you? Oh yes, so you did.'

She relapsed into silence, then fumbled in her bag, found a packet of cigarettes, lit up, laid the dead match in a black and silver ashtray.

They looked at one another. Behind Liz glittered the devastation. Clive wondered whether or not to speak, whether or not to produce the final explanatory document from the drawer at his elbow. Was this the moment? Her incuriosity astonished him. Had she never looked at her mother's bank statements? Had she never asked herself about her mother's income? He had photocopied clues and sent them to her, but they seemed to have aroused no suspicions. Perhaps it was better so.

He changed tack.

'So you've no idea,' repeated Clive, 'of where your sister might be?'

Liz shrugged her shoulders.

'Look,' she said. 'I've told you. We weren't a very close family. I haven't seen much of Shirley for — oh, for years. She resented me. She thought I got off lightly, not having to look after Mother. She would never have confided in me.'

'But she did ring you, about her husband's business?'

'Well, yes. But that wasn't usual. I was surprised to hear from her.'

'It did just occur to me,' said Clive, apologetically, 'that it was possible that her husband might have . . . attacked her, in some way?'

Liz looked puzzled, then caught on.

'Murdered her, you mean?' said Liz, nodding energetically. 'Done away with her?'

'Well, yes,' said Clive. 'But the police say there's been a sighting of her since the established time of death. But then, as you point out, she might never have gone near the garage. The police aren't very bright, in these parts.'

Liz shook her head. 'No,' she said. 'Cliff would never have killed anyone. He wasn't that kind of chap.' She laughed, a little wildly. 'No,' she went on. 'It's much more likely that it was the other way round. She vanished, he kills himself. Though that's not *very* likely either.'

'Well, there must be some more or less likely explanation,' said Clive. 'I'm sure it will all sort itself out in the end. Would you like a drink?'

'I rather think I would,' said Liz. And Clive opened the little office refrigerator.

Over the gin and tonic, they talk about Northam, about the Town Council, about the privatization of British Steel, about house prices. And while they talk, Clive watches Liz and wonders. As she is about to drain her glass, he suddenly says to her, 'I admired your performance on television, a couple of weeks ago. Very brave, I thought it.'

Liz starts, stares, goes into a different mode. She suddenly speaks to him in a different kind of voice, in a different register, as equal to equal. Clive, who is not an insensitive man, notices this, notches it up in his memory. 'Really?' she says.

'Yes,' he says. 'I thought you made your case very well.'

'Well, that's more than most people did, and very kind of you to say so,' said Liz. 'I got a lot of flak over that programme. You wouldn't believe the kind of thing people write. Well, perhaps you would. Being a lawyer. You'd think I'd personally tried to rape their own personal infants. People are odd. Deranged, a lot of them, without knowing it.'

'It's a disturbing subject,' said Clive.

'Yes. But they must have been pretty disturbed beforehand, to write such violent letters. It can't have been just the sight of me on telly that tipped them over the edge.'

She smiled, boldly, but not wholly comfortably.

'It's the sanctity of the family,' said Clive Enderby. 'People don't like to hear it attacked. Or to think they are hearing it attacked.'

'People talk a lot of nonsense these days about the sanctity of the family,' said Liz. 'I don't know why. If they'd seen some of the cases I'd seen, they wouldn't think it so sacred. The things people do to one another, in the name of family. Somebody has to speak up against it. For the sake of the outcasts.'

'But you yourself have a large family,' said Clive, responding to a vibration of distress in her voice. Offering comfort, requesting explanation?

'Yes,' said Liz, softening. 'Yes, a large family. Three stepchildren, two children, and now a granddaughter. She's lovely, my granddaughter. Mine is the new extended family, the new model. We thought we'd do it better, my generation. But I don't suppose we have.' She paused, continued, in a sudden spurt of intimacy. 'I wanted a large family, because mine was so small. So *silent*. And we had no relatives, Shirley and I. None. There must have been some, but our mother hid them all. No father, no aunts, no grandparents, nothing. Oh yes, I wanted a family, I married for family. And I love my children, all of them. But do they love me? No, they judge me, they resent me, they think I have crippled their lives, they think I am making fools of them and of myself.'

114

'Now that cannot be quite true,' said Clive.

'No, of course it isn't true, it's an exaggeration, of course they love me. But you know what I mean.' The gin and tonic, on an empty stomach, had gone to her head, the memory of her mother had momentarily demented her. 'And you, Mr Enderby, how many children do you have?'

'Two,' he said. 'And do call me Clive.'

'Two. And how old are they?'

'Eight and six. A boy and a girl. William and Victoria.'

'A model family.'

'Yes, a model family. And we live in a four-bedroomed house with a double garage and an au pair girl attached. And my wife works part-time. Mr and Mrs Average Professional Couple.'

'There's no such thing as the average professional couple,' said Liz.

'No,' said Clive, echoing Liz, 'maybe not. But you know what I mean.'

They gazed at one another, appraisingly. Clive smiled, Liz smiled. They had spoken to one another, in human voices, across a great divide, and both were surprised that this had been possible. They contemplated the nature of that communication, of that surprise. It was tinged with sex on both sides. Clive put it to himself that he fancied Liz. Liz fancied Clive, though she did not put it to herself so clearly or so crudely. There he was, a young man still in his thirties, looking at her with admiration, and expressing that admiration. It has been a long time since she had solicited or been aware of receiving such attention. She responded to his interest with interest. A small excitement, pleasurable, containable, stimulating, like a mild sweet breeze, stirs the carefully regulated office air. As Clive helped Liz into her grey cashmere coat, he smelled her odour, she smelled his. He patted her shoulder, as she settled the coat fabric, and she felt the weight of his hand. He touched her arm as he opened the door for her. He stood by the lift, his hand on the button, and smiled at her. When they shook hands on parting, both hands lingered slightly, warmly, in a friendly professional clasp. A little warmth flickered and glowed between them, a small animal bodily knowledge. Cliff Harper was dead and Shirley Harper had vanished, but Clive and Liz (as they now called one another) were alive.

Celia Harper lies prone on her bed in her room in north Oxford, wrapped in a rug against the cold, with a woollen hat on her head and a scarf around her neck. She has run out of fifty-pence pieces for the meter and cannot be bothered to go out in search of more. She is too absorbed to move, despite a sore throat and an incipient chill. Surrounded by books she lies. Books in many languages. The bed of Babel. Greek, Latin, Russian. Open before her lie volumes of the poems of Joseph Brodsky, in both Russian and English, on top of an open Homer. 'Letters to a Roman Friend'. 'Odysseus to Telemachus'. She has been picking her way through them patiently, finding odd words she recognizes in the Russian text. Now she is reading Tacitus. The murder of Galba. She reads of the death of Piso, dragged from the Temple of Vesta and slaughtered by Sulpicius Florus and Statius Murcus. She reads that Otho studied Piso's severed head 'with peculiar malevolence, as if his eyes could never drink their fill'. She can read Latin quickly, thanks to her excellent classical education at Northam Girls' High School. She races on, through the dreadful annals, fortifying herself on nibbles of Kendal Mint Cake.

Neglected on the floor lie two letters delivered by hand from college, at the request of the porter. One is from her brother Barry, the other from her uncle Steve. They ask her to get in touch because her father is ill. The phrasing in each is slightly different but the import the same. Celia pays no attention to them. She feels safe, safely out of touch. The cold dull breath of home cannot touch her here. Home, where nothing ever ever happened, where tedium reigned supreme. If they really want her, they will have to come and get her. She does not believe that her father is ill. They are just annoyed with her, she speciously reasons, because she forgot his birthday. She is glad there is no telephone in the flat, for if there were, they would surely be nagging at her. She can't afford to let them get at her. They will slow her down, rust her up, paralyse her. She banishes them, exiles them from her attention. She will read Tacitus until 5.30, then allow herself half an hour more of Brodsky, then a little Aeschylus, and then she will bicycle into hall for her supper. After that, who knows, she may go to a film at the Film Society with Anna and Pat. This is the real world, the world she has created for herself. She does not wish to be pulled out of it by her father's illness. She eats another square of mint cake. These days, she eats and eats, and stays as thin as a pre-puberty child. She eats and eats and reads and reads. She is devoured by greed. She devours.

Shirley Harper walks along the beach, gazing at the distant headland and the sea. She remembers this little bay. It is called happiness. She takes off her shoes, rolls down her tights, steps delicately on the cold ridged wet sand. Lug worms. Razor shells. Her naked instep aches with imprinted memory.

Steve Harper sits at the kitchen-table with his head in his hands. His wife Dora is ironing pillowcases. The kitchen is filled with the soothing smell of hot wet cotton, but Steve is not soothed. Dora is crying, quietly, stoically, her plain kind broad friendly face blotchy with misery. She grieves for her husband. She worries about Shirley. She worries about Celia. She cannot forgive Cliff. She refuses to see her mother-in-law. She is sorry for old Mrs Harper, but she cannot bring herself to see her. Mrs Harper does nothing but complain. Even now, in these sad days,

Mrs Harper blames Shirley, blames Cliff's partner Jim, blames the boys, blames Celia, blames Oxford, blames Cliff. Given half a chance, she would blame Dora. Moan, moan, moan. No, Dora cannot bear it. Somebody else will have to comfort Mrs Harper for the death of her son.

Shirley settles her boarding-house bill, surprised by how little her out-of-season night had cost. True, the bed had been narrow, the room tiny, but it had been a bed, in a bedroom. With a washbowl, although no soap. And a small electric fire. She had slept little. Images of childhood had drifted through her drowsing. A loneliness, an oppression, a desire to escape, a craving for the normal. She had failed to find the normal. She had been marked out. Marked from birth. In a little terraced house on a desolate seafront she lay listening to the waves, in utter solitude. Nobody knew where she was. Nobody but this landlady, to whom she now offers a ten-pound note, from whom she now waits for change. The landlady is loud-voiced, stout, falsely jolly, chatty. She seems the most normal person in the world. But who knows, thinks Shirley, who knows what oddities, what longings, what past crimes, this large mobile acrylic-cardiganed bosom may conceal? Human nature, since Cliff's death, has gone soft and shapeless, has melted into an amorphous mass, an unpredictable uncorseted lump of matter. Shirley cannot tell where it will break out next. What lumps, what growths, what abnormalities, what liquifyings, what solidifyings? The bosom heaves with laughter at its own joke. It is a wild morning, and the sea crashes against the sea wall.

Alix Bowen, sitting in Beaver's attic sorting out a box of papers, wonders where Shirley has gone to, and whether she herself will ever find Paul Whitmore's mother. People don't disappear, she tells herself. Even Beaver's famed disappearance had been only figurative, for during it all sorts of people had known perfectly well where he was and who he was. His colleagues, his wife, his children, his parents, his bank manager, his friends from the pub, his neighbours, his barber. Even his not very enthusiastic publishers.

She wonders about Stephen Cox, and Cambodia. In Cambodia, people disappeared. But not in Britain, in the late twentieth century.

Beaver's papers are wonderfully inconsequential, defiantly lacking in chronology. A Final Notice dated 12 December 1978 from the Electricity Board in glowing red, demanding £24.89, is clipped to a handwritten letter from Faber & Faber dated 5 June 1939, explaining the absence of royalties. A vicious anonymous review from *The TLS* of a volume by Geoffrey Grigson with the note 'I wrote this' is paper-clipped to a restaurant bill, dated 1932, from Bertorelli's for £2 2s. 6d. What appears to be a fragment of a poem is written on the back of a draft of a letter to *The Times*, noting that Our Queen has been forced to take part, surely against her will, in the rubber-stamping of the execution of a young man in Jamaica. 'I protest, on Her Majesty's behalf, and on behalf of a country that has wisely seen fit to abolish capital punishment, against this indignity committed in her name,' declares a Beaver of the late 1960s. Alix wonders if he ever finished the letter, ever sent it, ever had it published? Would a biographer have to follow up such clues? What a nightmare, thinks Alix. Occasionally Beaver hints that it would be convenient if Alix herself were to become his recording angel. She finds the idea faintly obscene.

I have become a detective, thinks Alix, as she wonders how to file what appears to be a pile of old reports from Hansborough Secondary School. They have so far been lovingly preserved, as though Beaver had been proud of his classroom prowess. Number of Pupils in Form, 23, Place in Form, 1. Occasionally he was beaten into a humiliating second place by a character called

Maud Hand, but most of the time he was on top. His childhood sweetheart (later his wife), Bertha Sykes, hovered supportingly in the middle ranks. Maud must have been a thorn in Beaver's flesh. Alix wondered what had happened to her. Dare she raise her name, one day, over lunch, as a diversion from the ex-mistresses and the ill-used, lamented Bertha?

Class places, examination marks, marks for everything. Naked competition. At the bottom of each page, in red print, it was stated that 'On the withdrawal of a pupil from school, a term's notice, in writing, addressed to the Headmaster or to the Clerk, is required. In default, a term's fees are payable.' How had they paid, what had they paid *with*, these sons and daughters of South Yorkshire miners? Alix had been under the illusion that education, in the 1920s, had been free. She knows she knows nothing.

Alix opens another little bundle. It is full of references for the young Beaver, hopeful and frequently disappointed applicant for teaching posts in schools up and down the country. Some of the references strike Alix as inattentive or lukewarm. There is one from that great classical scholar, Hubert Hawkins. On it, an older Beaver has scribbled, 'Couldn't remember me from Adam, could he?'

There is something mournful about the bundle. Alix drops it, and for light relief picks up a dusty but much more recent box of slides. She has a slide viewer to hand (Bertha had been a keen and hopeless photographer), and she starts to peer at coloured images of the fifties and sixties. They are all jumbled up: scenes of Swiss mountains alternate with Hadrian's Wall, Rome is mixed up with the Rhine, and a wholesome array of Scandinavian barns is enlivened by a good (museum-bought) shot of the Bog Man of Tollund, smiling his sweet smile of everlasting anguish, of enigmatic resignation. There is a sequence of ill-shot views of the sea, showing bits of boat rail and sloping deck and occasionally a small distant object on the horizon − a rock, a lighthouse? − and slipped amongst them a view of a formal Italian garden with statuary and white peacocks and a fountain and a distant lake. She continues through the box, and is rewarded by a shot of Bertha Beaver sitting on a beach in a deck-chair in a plastic rainhood, by a shot of the broad backside of Beaver as he leans to stroke a dog of which only the tail and a quarter of the rump are visible. And here is Beaver standing in a garden, wearing a ridiculous scarlet and black furred robe and a medieval hat, and here is a snap of a tortoiseshell cat. And who are these figures, sitting in the sun and wrinkling up their eyes against the light? That is Bertha, her legs planted wide apart, her skirt rucked up to let the sun get at her knees, and that is Beaver, dark-glassed, in a Panama hat, and that, surely, is Robert Graves? Today, when Alix descends from her attic to join him for lunch (cold baked beans, tomatoes, salami, many slices of white bread, and a banana – his choice), Beaver wants to talk about the woman in Pallanza, on the shores of Lake Maggiore, the woman who is the queen of his Novara sequence. Alix says she has found no snaps or slides of her.

'She didn't like having her picture taken,' says Beaver. 'A captivating creature. But my God she was plain.'

'Then why was she captivating?' asks Alix, spreading her bread with a novel highly coloured polyunsaturated spread: Beaver, in his eighties, has suddenly stopped eating butter because of its cholesterol content.

'Her conversation,' says Beaver. 'She could talk. And talk and talk and talk.'

'Sounds awful, to me,' says Alix, who is permitted liberties, is encouraged to take liberties.

'She was awful,' says Beaver. 'But she was rich.'

'So it wasn't her talk,' says Alix. 'It was her money.'

'They make a stunning combination,' says Beaver. They both laugh. Then he falls a little silent, as he chews on his salami and

121

then vigorously with his buckled fingernail extracts a bit of rind from his surprisingly fierce teeth, and lays it, spittle-covered, on the plastic tablecloth.

'Bertha,' he says, reflectively, 'Bertha, she was neither rich nor talkative nor pretty. You never met my Bertha.'

'No,' says Alix.

'Bertha was the love of my life,' says Beaver, mournfully, sentimentally, spearing another slice of salami. He sighs, chews, sighs. Alix says nothing, rather loudly. This too is her liberty.

'Well, never mind,' says Beaver, reaching for his banana. 'Let's talk about something cheerful. Tell me some more about your murderer.'

Clive Enderby is on the phone to his brother Edward. 'But I thought Janice knew Shirley Harper quite well,' he insists. Edward repeats his denial: Janice and Shirley were acquainted, their daughters had been at the same school, they had greeted one another at school concerts and Parents' Evenings, but that was about it, there was no more to it than that.

'There's absolutely no trace of her,' says Clive. 'She's vanished off the face of the earth. Nobody seems to have any idea where she might have gone to. No living relatives apart from her sister, no friends.'

'Maybe she's run off with a man?' suggests Edward.

Clive had not thought of this possibility, but it strikes him as implausible.

'No, no,' he says, 'she's not that kind of woman.'

'How do you know what kind of woman she was? How does anybody know what kind of woman anybody is?' asks Edward.

Edward laughs, not happily.

Clive is silent. His gaze wanders round his lounge and settles on the mantelpiece. There reposes a large white gilt-edged invitation card. IAN AND FANNY KETTLE. AT HOME. HOUSE-WARMING PARTY. 7.30 ONWARDS, it reads.

Clive's wife Susie seems to have become quite friendly with Fanny Kettle.

'Anyway,' he says to his brother Edward, 'if Janice does think of anything, any kind of clue, tell her to let me know.'

'I've told you,' repeated Edward irritably, 'she hardly knew the woman.'

Everyone seems eager to disown Shirley Harper. Even her own daughter Celia, who has finally been traced, does not have any suggestions as to her whereabouts, and appears peculiarly unmoved by the domestic tragedy that has struck her family. Shock, assumes the Dean of her Oxford college, who does not know her: shock, assumes uncle Steve, who does not know her very well. There seems little point in tearing Celia away from her studies, so she stays on in Oxford. Liz tries to get in touch with her on the phone, fails, is obliged to leave a message for Celia asking her to contact Liz if she needs to. Celia does not get in touch. The Warden of the college, an acquaintance of Liz's, does, however, make contact: he rings Liz and expresses anxiety on his ward's behalf and bumbles on about feeling himself to be *in loco parentis*. Liz thinks this is decent of the old boy, and somewhat surprising. At the end of his bumbling he mentions to Liz as though in passing that his own son has been going through a few little difficulties not unconnected with hard drugs, and could Liz possibly suggest the name of a sympathetic psychiatrist: Liz ceases to be surprised, and helpfully suggests names.

Shirley sits in a multi-storey car-park in Luton. She thinks of Cliff, slumped in the driver's seat. He seems quite unreal to her. Much of her past life seems quite unreal to her. She walks round Luton, has a cup of tea in a department store, collects her car, and drives on, down the M1, towards the south.

*

Alix Bowen is alarmed to receive an immediate reply to her letter to Paul Whitmore's father. Yes, he will see her. Oh dear. Her heart sinks. This time I've gone too far, she says to herself. She had no desire whatsoever to see Paul's father, to try to trace Paul's mother. How has she got herself into this position? It is one thing to rummage around in Beaver's past, amongst old school reports and old photographs and scraps of manuscript and dead bills, trying to create order out of paper. People are another matter. Live people. She should never have followed up Paul Whitmore. She should have let him rot in his box. She is not even being paid to visit him, as she was paid to teach English Literature to his final victim, Jilly Fox. Despite all her protests, she has ended up, effectively, as Paul Whitmore's unpaid, untrained social worker. Is this wrong, is it immoral, is it prurient, is it foolish, will it end badly? She is an amateur, rushing in where angels might fear to tread. She wishes she dare consult Liz more openly. But she dares not. She is afraid Liz will tick her off, as she has done in the past, for taking on tasks for which she is not qualified.

And yet something in her knows that she is, despite all, doing the *right thing.* And maybe it will not be too bad? At least it will be 'interesting', she tells herself.

But this is only a justification. She is going to see Paul Whitmore's father because she believes it is the *right thing.* The phrase repeats itself in her head, as she bends in Beaver's attic over yet another box of holiday slides. *The right thing.* A watery little unobserved smile hovers on her lips. Ah, the poverty of moral language, the poverty of discourse, the thin vagueness of words. Instinct, intuition, utility. Here sits Alix Bowen, in her fifties, battling with these concepts afresh, as though she were a girl still, as though nothing had ever been settled and sorted. As though there were still everything to play for.

All things out of abstraction sail, mouths Alix to herself. Is it a line of a poem? All things out of abstraction sail, and all their swelling canvas wear.

Downstairs sits the poet Beaver, watching the racing on TV. Out of that old carcase had sprung images. Berries, oak apples, mistletoe, emmer wheat and einkorn barley. And rhetoric.

Does he, in his Indian summer, in his Lapland winter of rude health, recall his bronchial childhood, his mother's fears of the pit? Alix nurses in her lap a letter from old Beaver's mother. How has this letter survived? Has he cherished it? It is written to Howard Beaver in hospital, in Northam Children's Isolation Hospital. It is dated 1912. 'Dear Howard, I hope you are improving, I will be along as soon as they let me, I think of you night and day. Be a good boy. Your ever loving mother.' What had it been? Influenza? Diphtheria? Scarlet fever? He had been a delicate child, little Howard, seventy-odd years ago, asthmatic, bronchial, chesty, like most children from the dirty industrial north. Infant mortality, child mortality, had been high here, in the early years of the century.

Despite herself, yet again, Alix weeps. She is a hopeless sentimentalist. It is that phrase, 'your ever loving mother', that has done the trick this time. Her heart turns to her sons, whom she loves beyond all words, beyond all rhetoric, beyond all images and all imagining. They no longer need her love. Her love is a smothering cushion to them. Nicholas in Sussex, landlord in his farmhouse, inheritor of lands, painter of increasingly large canvases, lover of Ilse Nemorova. Sam at his sixth form college, studying biology, mathematics, chemistry, physics. She is their ever loving mother, but so what?

And, as a matter of fact, reflects Alix, drying her automatic tears, to tell the truth, she does not *really* think all that much about Nicholas, these days. She thinks far more frequently about Paul Whitmore. What does *that* mean?

*

Alix has become a detective, but Shirley has become a criminal. She is on the run.

She tries to remember tricks from the who-done-its she used to like in the old days, before she gave up reading. Faked suicides, bundles of clothes left on the beach, abandoned cars? It is too cold to fake a drowning. In March, nobody would commit suicide by drowning, not off the North Yorkshire coast. So Shirley decided, as she stared at the level grey sea at Robin Hood's Bay, where once, on an outing with her friend June and her family, she had been happy.

At the back of her mind, she has a vague plan. She herself does not know what it is, but it is forming itself, in the obscurity. It has no shape, no features, it has merely a mood, a colouring, like a forgotten dream. It pulls her southwards, down the M1, south, towards the south coast, with her passport in her pocket.

The solitude is intense. She has not spoken to anybody except shopkeepers and boarding-house owners since discovering Cliff. She feels an unperson. But something in her does not dislike this sensation.

She is nearing London. Roads beckon her in all directions. The North, the South, the East, the West. Blue motorway signs, with large white lettering. The big M. She is in a slight daze. She has not been eating much. Something called the London Orbital, the M25, announces itself. Indecisively, she joins it.

No Services on the Motorway, she is told. Places peel off: Potters Bar, the Dartford Tunnel, Sevenoaks, Gatwick, the South, Heathrow. She is travelling at a steady sixty, and seems unable either to slow down or to accelerate. Shall she go on for ever, round and round, until she runs out of petrol? Inertia appears to have her in its grip, the inertia of movement. Maybe she is hallucinating? She knows she should not be driving, that she is a danger to herself and others, but the mechanism offers no exit, and on she goes, round the full circuit of the one hundred and seventeen miles of the Orbital, on a conveyor belt, on a treadmill. She sees a sign to the North, to the M1, beckoning her back to Cliff and the garage. She ignores it, and drives on. She passes flashing lights, a concertina of cars in the slow lane, roadworks. She recalls a news item of a woman her own age who had earlier this month driven the wrong way down the fast lane of the M4. She had ended up in a psychiatric hospital. Shirley's eyes blur slightly, she resolves that she will leave the fated circle at the next exit, but for some reason does not. For some reason, for no reason, she is making her way back and on towards the Dartford Tunnel.

The Dartford Tunnel, which is new to Shirley, does not impress her. She had been expecting something grander, more modern. She is now making for the M2 and Dover. The word 'Dover' has written itself upon her mind. Kent and Canterbury, the Pilgrim's Way.

A strange blue-green light is shining: she glimpses a vast landscape of cement-green-grey glittering water, quaking, ruffling, in a high invisible wind. Cooling towers, pit heads, industrial vistas, and then rural England, little stunted dwarfed orchards of apples and cherries, crabbed little trees, caravans, white soil, grey soil, polythene-glistening fields under plastic. The mini-garden of England. It looks poisoned, ashen, ruined by fertilizer, insecticide. The colours are glacial. The Ice Age, the last of England. A few flakes of snow fall from a clear sky.

She will have to stop soon, for petrol, for the lav, for coffee. The Little Chef, the Happy Eater, the Roadside Diner. Will she be *able* to stop? Her foot seems to be stuck to the accelerator, as in some Grimm fairy story. She must make an effort. She slows down. Little deceleration signs take her in, she is sucked into a car-park. She stops.

She sits for a moment at the wheel, shaking. She looks at herself in the driving mirror. Her cheeks are flatteringly pinked, deceptively normal, but beneath the rouge she looks and feels a very odd colour.

She staggers out of the car, stiff-kneed, into a raw wet wind. The service station appears not to be finished. Mounds of pitch lie around the edges of the car-park, bordered by slices of cracked tarmac, buckled in heaps. Hoardings implore her to Buy Her Ferry Ticket Now, or to indulge herself in Low Tar Cigarettes. It is bitterly cold. She staggers, bowed, clutching her coat round her, towards the building, pushes at the door, finds the Ladies' Room. It is squalid, there is no lavatory paper, the dispenser soap smells of hospitals or prisons, and the water in the taps is so rationed that it is impossible to get one's hands under the jet for long enough to rinse them. Shirley sprays herself with a little Anaïs Anaïs. She still has her creature comforts about her. She powders her nose. Then thinks she will buy herself a bite to eat.

The restaurant is surrounded by a waist-high moving conveyor belt, moving as relentlessly as the London Orbital, bearing dirty plates, cans, glasses, cups and saucers, discarded paper rubbish, smears of ketchup. She gazes at the menu, then at the food. It is disgusting. Glass compartments full of salads. Wilting lettuce leaves, dried-out mounds of cottage cheese, thin grey gelid ham, yellow-grey chicken. It is hard to tell which are the plaster models, which the Real Thing. Shirley shudders, moves to the hot foods, recoils from the heavy smell of grease, from the pots of gristle brew and dark gravy and wet cabbage, wanders back desperately to the salads, sickens, turns to the sandwiches, in despair takes a plate covered in cling-film, knowing it to be a mistake, but what else is there? She gets a pot of coffee, sits down, gazes round her.

The room is full of waifs, witches, grotesques. Shirley has never seen such a miserable collection of people, such a gallery of unfortunates. What has gone wrong? Is this some outing for the disadvantaged, the disabled? No, it is Britain, round about Budget Day, March 1987. Shirley is appalled. An immensely obese woman spoons scarlet jelly from a cardboard dish. Two thin tall lanky youths devour a mountain of chips and swill from cans of Coca-Cola. A young couple with a baby, pale like convicts, glare into space as the baby wails and wails. An old man on crutches picks uneaten chips and crusts from the dirty plates on the passing conveyor belt. A young red-haired scruffy Irish girl with a back pack is in loud dispute with a pale-faced, fat, crumple-suited member of the management: she is about to be thrown out. A grim-faced middle-aged couple is engaged in bitter marital discussion about the route ahead. A four-foot dwarf weaves her way bravely between the plastic tables carrying a tray loaded with highly coloured cakes. Is this the prosperous south, the land of the microchip? Everybody looks half dead, ill from the ill wind. Their faces are white, pink, grey, chapped, washed-out, ill nourished, unhealthy, sickly, sickening. Shirley takes a bite of one of her sandwiches. It is dry, grey, it tastes of nothing. Shirley does not know whether she feels sorry for these tramps, these refugees, these motorway wanderers, or whether she feels she has nothing to do with them at all. Is she still part of the human race? Is this the human race, or are these shadows, ghosts, lingering afterthoughts? This cannot be what is meant.

I am delirious, thinks Shirley. This is a dream, and these are apparitions. Perhaps, thinks Shirley, I died back there on the motorway. She takes a gulp of coffee. Surprisingly, it tastes of coffee.

The plump managerial lout is manhandling the pale Irish girl. He is pushing her towards the exit. She resists, but half-heartedly. Nobody pays any attention. She is not shouting. She is hardly even mumbling.

Shirley shudders, drinks her coffee, stares through the high glass window at the flow of traffic beneath. Wet flakes of snow swirl in the wind.

Up in north Staffordshire, the weather is better. If Alix had not been so dreading her appointment with Bill Whitmore, she would have been enjoying the drive. It is cross country, and Sam and Brian have worked out a route for her. It is open on the passenger's seat: their nice clear writing and red arrows are reassuring. The heavy industry of South Yorkshire and the north Midlands gives way to that strange mix of town and country, that no-man's-land which she thinks of as Lawrence landscape. And this in turn, as she reaches the land that lies just south of the Peak, becomes deeply rural, agricultural, Green England. The sun is shining brilliantly on scattered snow drifts, on green fields, on sparkling brooks, on mossy tree trunks, on a herd of muddy white prehistoric cattle, on the grey stone walls of a little ruin. She winds down the car window, and smells the fresh cold sap of spring.

It is only ten miles now to the small town where Paul Whitmore spent his childhood, where his father owned a but-cher's shop, where his mother permed and fashioned hair. Alix has written to William Whitmore, requesting an interview, and has received a reply. He will see her. That is all he said. Dear Mrs Bowen, Thanks for your letter. The day you suggest will suit. Sincerely. She plans to arrive at tea time, a harmless time that will involve no fuss, no hospitality, but which will give him an opportunity to put the kettle on to distract himself, if he is that kind of man, if he is so inclined. It is now only three; she will drive on to Toxetter, park, have a walk round. Look for clues.

She has never been here before. She parks in front of what she at first takes to be a disused cinema, but then registers as, indeed, a cinema. Everything here looks slightly disused. The films (three a week, all American) are current, indeed almost new, far too new for Alix, but the posters announcing them look tatty, already out of date. A handsome large old red brick building flanking the cinema forecourt is falling to pieces: its rafters are exposed, its windows gape, but housed in its centre, in two rooms saved from time, is something that describes itself as 'The Pets Parlour'. Alix walks down the street, past tiny little shop windows, towards what she senses to be the town centre: shops selling knitting wools, bicycle parts, baby clothes, some with their windows covered with a strange orange-yellow shiny transparent cellophane. A barber's has three objects in its window: a photograph of a young man with a Brylcreemed hairstyle from the fifties, faded (through lack of yellow filter?) to a dangerous hard pale blue-pink; a pre-AIDS Durex advertisement; and a vast marmalade cat. Alix pauses, stares at the cat, says Hello, Puss. The cat blinks and smirks, safe behind its window, in the spring sun.

And here is a pedestrian precinct, with fish and chip shops, shops selling birthday cards and gifts. The Maltings, Tudor Fayre, the refurbished Old Saddler's Yard offer unconvincing, indeed psychotic, attempts to combine modernity and fake antiquity. Standing alone, set slightly back from the muddle, is another handsome red brick house, with a conservatory, with bay windows, a garden with crocuses, a clump of fine purple-green hellebore. Next to it, another muddle of an ancient building, part of it now housing the Manpower Services Commission, and part of it, in a strange hut-like plywood annexe, the branch library. Another wool shop, called the Beehive. A lady's hairdresser (subtitled Unisex) called Tangles. A television rental shop, and on the roof of its outside lavatory in the back yard a dish receiver. And then, suddenly, clustered together, almost cheek by jowl, an extraordinary density of butchers. Never has Alix, in one small town, seen so many butchers' shops. How can they all survive? Could one small town ever eat so much meat? Yards and yards of meat, red, glistening, display themselves.

Chunks of braising steak, trays of kidneys, hundreds of chump chops, layers of liver, great circles of rolled beef, wave upon wave of overlapping sirloin and rump. There are also puddings, tripes, pies, pasties. But red meat dominates, red red meat, crazily decked and adorned with unexpected oranges and cherries. There are oranges and cherries everywhere, they are not signs of single originality but of mass dementia. A whole beach of bright red mince, six feet wide, rippled in a silver tray, is stuck with orange slices and plastic greenery. Meat sculpture.

Alix is amazed. She had not realized that this part of England was so full of meat. No wonder Paul Whitmore is a vegetarian.

She has reached the town centre, with its building societies and its weathered market cross. Is this place derelict or prosperous? She cannot tell. How does it vote? She cannot tell.

It is four o'clock.

Reluctantly, she retraces her steps, past shops that seem almost friendly now in their familiarity. She dawdles, lingers. She can see the shop, a two-storey building. Upstairs, the closed salon. The windows are boarded. The butcher's below is also closed. Its window carries a notice saying 'Closed through Circumstances Beyond My Controll'. There are empty steel trays, an insect-death-ray machine, a garland of plaster sausages, and two plaster pigs in butcher's aprons, which have fallen over on to their sides. She pauses, peers through. She sees a great wooden slab, stained and impregnated by decades of old blood. The floor is covered still in sawdust shavings. Death of man and animal.

The doorbell to the flat, Paul had told her, was down the side alley. She opens the wooden gate, nervously presses the bell. She is hoping Paul's father will not answer, that he will have changed his mind, that he will refuse to see her. But she hears coughing, shuffling, as somebody descends the stairs, peers through the frosted panes of glass, fiddles with the latch. The door opens, and there is William Whitmore.

132

They shake hands, and Alix follows him upstairs to the sitting-room. He says he will make her a cup of tea, and disappears into the kitchen. Alix looks around her, at a room of unexceptional ordinariness. Flowered carpet, shabby flowered loose-covered three-piece suite, gas fire, television set on a small metal-legged table, useless brass coal-scuttle, some brass and copper ornaments, a few framed family photographs on the mantelpiece, a sunburst clock that ticks. In the corner there is a grandfather clock that does not tick. The only feature of interest is a palm in a pot. Alix wonders if it could be the same palm, the palm that Paul knew as a boy, the palm that will live and die for ever.

Bill Whitmore returns with a tray, settles himself, pours. They speak of the weather, of the approach of spring, of the pleasant sunshine, of the nip in the air.

He is, like Paul, slightly below average height, slightly built, perhaps becoming a little bowed and shrunken. His hair is grey-brown, short, neat, combed fiercely back and flattened down. He is wearing grey trousers, a blue shirt, a maroon tie, a grey cardigan, soft shoes which are not quite bedroom slippers. A pink, clean face, and National Health glasses of the same model as Brian's. He sags, slightly, as though some spring had given. But is trim, orderly, he has not let himself go. There is something in the fussy manner in which he marshals sugar, biscuits, tea-spoons, that indicates the habits of one who has lived long alone, of one who tries to maintain proprieties against some odds.

Alix's chair sags too, unevenly. She sits cautiously, tensely.

They continue to speak of the weather.

Alix clears her throat.

'Mr Whitmore,' she says, 'did you know I'd been seeing your son Paul? Does he write to you at all?'

He heaves a terrible sigh, and says nothing.

'He wanted me to . . . make contact,' she says.

'Are you from the prison?' he asks.

'No. No. I'm just a friend.'

She pauses to let this sink in, then continues. 'There's no point in explaining how I got to know Paul, I used to teach in a prison in London, then when my husband was moved up here, well, I sort of took to visiting him.'

He did not look at her. He stares at the tea leaves in the bottom of his gold-rimmed rose-patterned real china cup.

'Are you religious?' he asks eventually.

Alix pauses, hesitates, unsure how to answer this on any level, even to herself.

'No,' she finally ventures, in a tone that has a faint hint of interrogation. Then what is your motive, his prolonged silence seems to imply. She sips her tea. She does not know the answer.

He clears his throat.

'I had to shut up shop,' he says.

'Yes,' says Alix. 'Paul told me he thought you had.'

'But I'm not moving,' said Bill Whitmore. 'They'll not get me to move.'

'Why should you move?' agreed Alix, who could think of many reasons.

'If I'd been going to move, I'd have moved earlier. All those years ago.'

Alix puts down her tea-cup. This seems promising. She leans slightly forward, attentively. He says nothing.

'Yes?' she prompts.

He sighs, heavily.

'Paul wanted me to ask' — she hesitates, then comes out with it — 'after his mother. He wondered if you knew where she is.'

The little man slumps deeper into his chair, stares intently at the poor flowered carpet. Alix wants to run away, to run out of the stuffy little room and down the stairs and out, down the street, back to her car, and off, off across England. But she sits it out.

'Some questions,' says Bill Whitmore, 'are best left unasked.'

'He did want to know,' whispers Alix, softly.

The old man makes a sound like a snort or a groan, and suddenly begins to speak, in a low, urgent, bitter flow. 'He may well ask,' he says, 'he may well ask. Does he think she'll welcome him with open arms, after what he's done? She had no time for him even when he was a good lad, and he *was* a good lad, he was a quiet, good lad, wouldn't hurt a fly, a quiet boy, was Paul, no harm in him, wouldn't hurt a fly, couldn't help me in the shop, *oh* no, far too squeamish to help in the shop, always hanging around his mother's apron strings, but she wouldn't have him, no, she'd no time for him, too busy she was with her ladies and her gentlemen, too busy, and does he think she'll have any time for him now? She never wanted a boy, no, it was always a girl she'd wanted ... oh, she'll be wishing he'd never been born, she'll be cursing the day he was born, she'll be cursing the day she ever met me, even then she used to curse him and me, and what does he think she'll think now, the prodigal son, no, she'll be pretending we never existed, she'll have wiped us out and forgotten us, she'll be riding high and pretending she never knew nought, *"Oh, what horrible murders,"* she'll be saying, how could anyone, must be a monster, yes, that's what she'll be saying, she never cared for Paul nor me, she tormented the lad, she teased him and tormented him, and he hung around after her as though she was God's gift, but she wouldn't have it, get off, she'd say, get off my back, shoo, scram, out from under my feet ... no, she couldn't be doing with him ...'

As he rambled on, Alix listened, intently desperate to catch the story beneath the story: whenever the old man tried to mimic his wife's voice he put on a strange, falsetto, fake-posh accent, was that a clue? High and mighty, she was now, for all that she was little better than a paid servant, Bill Whitmore continued. Clearly he knew exactly where she was, and what she was doing: but would he tell? Would he tell?

Alix let him run down, into a sort of mumbling silence.

'From what you say,' she suggested, diffidently 'she *never* seemed to care for him much, is that right? Not even when he was a little boy, a baby?'

'Unnatural, she was,' said Mr Whitmore. 'Unnatural. I used to tell her, it's not right. She never wanted a boy. Well rid of her, we were. No,' he repeated, with emphasis, 'she never wanted a boy.'

His eyes wander towards the framed photographs on the mantelpiece, but Alix's eyes do not follow them. She is too busy trying to piece together the story she thinks she is hearing.

'And when she left,' said Alix, 'Paul was taken into care, is that right? And then he came back here to live with you for a while, is that right?'

'He had to go,' said the old man. 'He had to go. I couldn't cope. I was ill.'

'Weren't there grandparents, aunts, relatives?'

He shook his head. 'No good, they were. A bad lot, her family. I was warned off her. I should have listened. I should have had more sense.'

'Were they from these parts?'

'No, they were from Derby.'

He relapsed into silence. Then repeated 'Derby', as though that explained all. Alix did not dare to ask him about his own family: he looked too crushed, too crumpled. She felt a terrible sorrow for him, as he sat there in his old armchair. She wondered if she dared pursue anything, whether she should try to talk to him about Paul, whether she should go away and try to come back another time.

'Are *you* religious?' she tries, as a diversion. He looks up, surprised, even smiles a small tight sad smile.

'Nay,' he says, 'nay, not so as you'd notice. My family was. Chapel going, they were. But I never held with that stuff. All this with Paul, though, all this trouble — well, it makes you wonder.'

She wondered what theological position he was pondering, as he sat there in his soft shoes. She knew what he meant, though, like him, could not work out why he meant it.

'Songs of Praise I like,' he offered. 'The old tunes.'

'Yes, so do I,' said Alix, not wholly dishonestly.

'Well, I suppose it's good of you, to go and see the boy. I suppose I should thank you,' he says, in what seems to be a preliminary to closing the meeting. Alix is torn between a desire to run for it, and a desire to stick it out just a sentence or two longer, a question or two more.

'He needs somebody,' says Alix. 'And I don't mind.' She wonders whether to say that she finds Paul interesting, or whether this is too insulting a reflection to offer to this ruined man.

'Well, I do thank you,' he says, with some dignity. 'Yes, I do.'

Alix seizes her opportunity.

'And his mother?' she says. 'You think there's no hope? No point? I somehow feel it would mean so much to Paul. If she — if you both — could bring yourselves — well, to forgive him, I suppose I mean.'

'Forgive? Forgive? What's the point of that? I don't blame the boy.' He pauses, on this amazing statement. 'It's *her* I blame,' he concludes. '*Her.*'

'Yes,' says Alix.

He looks at Alix sharply, hesitates, speaks. 'I'll tell you where she is,' he says. 'I'll tell you. That's what you want to know, isn't it? Yes? I thought so. I'll tell you what you want. She's in Hartley Bridge. Yes, Hartley Bridge. Over your way. You'll find her easy enough. I'll get you the address.'

Slowly, he rises to his feet, shuffles across the room: prematurely aged, a life collapsed in upon itself. He rummages in a

137

drawer, produces a scrap of paper, and writes upon it, laboriously, copying from a notebook. 'Hartley Court, Hartley Bridge, North Yorkshire,' he writes, and hands it to her. 'That's her,' he says. 'That'll find her.'

As an afterthought, he writes her name. 'Angela Malkin,' he writes, and hands the paper back.

'That's her,' he says. 'That's what she calls herself now. She'll disown us, that's for certain. She won't want to be hearing from us.'

He seems to be attracted, now, by the idea of Alix and his wife in confrontation: Alix, the avenging angel with unwelcome news?

'Has she remarried?' asks Alix, cautiously.

'Nay,' he says. 'We've never been divorced. Still my wife in law, she is. But Malkin's not the man she ran off with, if that's what you're thinking. Nay, he didn't last long. She's been with this one a good few years now.'

'Thank you very much,' says Alix, carefully stowing the paper in her handbag. He seemed to have cheered up, to be relishing the prospect of further news of Angela.

'It's a queer place, where you'll find her,' he says, with a glint in his eye.

'Queer?' echoes Alix, nervously. It has already occurred to her that Hartley Bridge is probably less than thirty miles from Porston Prison, that Paul and his mother, unknown to Paul, are within an hour's drive of one another. Bill Whitmore has not pointed this out, but something in his manner tells Alix that he is conscious that she is conscious of this.

'Yes, queer,' Bill Whitmore confirms, with satisfaction. Alix does not wish to inquire further. Suddenly she has had enough and more than she can take. She cannot wait to flee from Toxetter. When she gets downstairs, she runs past the meat shops, with wings on her feet.

Shirley is wandering around Marks & Spencer in Dover. Up and down the aisles she goes, backwards and forwards, staring at pale pink acrylic jerseys, at rows of white cotton blouses, and pale duck-egg blue polyester cardigans, at socks and shoes and pot plants and soap and bath salts, a galaxy of choice, a domestic paradise, a consumer dream in pastel spring shades, fern green, coral pink, forget-me-not blue, primrose yellow, oyster beige, and white, white, white: does it comfort, does it appal? She has come in here for comfort, for the familiar, for the solace of shopping, she knows she blends into the surroundings here, she is undetectable, invisible, a normal housewife, mother of three, nobody will know she is delinquent, on the run. Primrose, forget-me-not, lavender, honeysuckle, cornflower. Dying flowers, imperishable dyes. Up and down she goes. Shall she stop, effect a purchase? Or pace on, and on, and on? She finds herself returning again and again to the lingerie, and finally comes to a halt by the nightdresses. She fingers the material. White, patterned damasked nylon, with thin yellow ribbons. Pretty. Pretty, she supposes. Will the act of purchasing rescue her? After the brutality of the motorway café Marks & Spencer is calming, assuaging, clean, sane. She handles various garments, holds them against herself for size. £16.50, the nightdress that she fancies. She takes it to the counter, to the PAY HERE signal. Unlike her sister Liz, Shirley has kept her figure well. Liz, reflects Shirley with wonder and triumph, must need at least a size fourteen by now. The woman at the till smiles at Shirley. She is middle aged, in her fifties, grey haired, motherly. She approves Shirley's purchase. She folds it with care. 'Very pretty, the new season's nighties,' she says, and Shirley smiles and nods. She understands this kind of conversation. She takes her carrier bag, smiling. She has achieved a purchase, she is a successful shopper, she had made a decision, she has a carrier bag as witness.

She drifts on, through the well-swept, well-lit, air-conditioned aisles, and out, out of the hospital, hostel, asylum of Marks &

Spencer, into the raw wind, the biting cold. Where is she going, what is she doing? The sky is leaden, bruised, pewter dark. She walks through a churchyard. A young man with long bedraggled hair is playing a guitar, busking. Before him lies his guitar case, an old jersey, a cap. The cap contains two tenpenny pieces. He is playing a piece by James Taylor: 'Oh I've seen fire and I've seen rain, I've seen sunny days that I thought would never end,' he mourns to the shoppers of Dover. It sounds vaguely familiar to Shirley: was it a piece her sons had once thumped through the house on their amplifiers? Cliff had been hard on the boys, had over-restrained them, and they had deserted him in their hearts and left him, had grown up, grown away, and left their parents. The young man's hair is in greasy ringlets, of a dull tarnished brown-gold: his dark face gleams lightly from dirt and weather, his throat is bare to the cold, his wrists protrude from the short sleeves of his denim jacket. He does not look at Shirley as she pauses before him: he is gazing into nowhere, as he strums his guitar, and a bitter smell of coal and cold sweat emanates from him. He does not glance or pause as she throws a fifty-pence piece into his cap. He plays on, and Shirley, as homeless as he, drifts on, clutching her Identity Bag, her pretty white nightdress with its cheap yellow ribbons and cheap knot roses at the yoke.

Clive Enderby sits alone, watching the local television news, and thinking about Liz and Shirley. Is Shirley perhaps, like Cliff Harper, dead? Had Cliff murdered her? The police do not think so, as they are not dragging lakes and digging up the Harper back garden, but Clive cannot quite get the idea out of his mind. He wishes he had never had it.

No, it is more likely that she has done herself in. Like her father before her. Bad blood, the Ablewhites. Do these things run in families?

Those girls had been brought up very oddly. The social

services might have got called in, these days. Their childhood ruined by shabby little secrets.

Secrets, pigeon-holes, little plots. As a solicitor, Clive Enderby is aware that there are far more family secrets in the world than most people know of — well, if they knew of them, they wouldn't be secrets, would they? People don't want to think about these things. So they don't. People want to believe in an ordered, regular world, of faithful married couples, legitimate children, normal sex, legal behaviour, decent continuity, and they will go to almost any lengths to preserve this faith. Any suggestion that 'real life' is otherwise tends to be greeted as 'melodramatic' or 'implausible'.

Solicitors know better. The police know better. Social workers know better. Doctors, especially since the emergence of AIDS, know better. The subplots fester, break out, infect strangers. Dark blotches spread. Life is more like an old-fashioned, melo-dramatic novel than we care to know. Clive knows more about the Ablewhite girls than they know about themselves.

The local television news comes to an end. The police are appealing for witnesses to a mugging in the underpass leading from Northam Bus Station to Northam Railway Station. Mug-gings are rare in Northam. They are still news.

Where is Susie?

Where is Shirley?

Clive Enderby shivers, gets up, adjusts the central heating. It is a cold night, a cold spring.

Shirley has stepped out of plausibility, into the unknown. She had boldly driven her little car on to a cross-Channel ferry, and is sitting in the bar drinking a Dubonnet with lemon and ice. The ferry is almost deserted: a recent and appalling tragedy with as yet unnumbered dead has brought a deathly chill to this watery transit, and Stygian gloom pervades the smoky grey air. Shirley sits neatly, precisely, her legs crossed. Is she glad that she is not lying crushed and swollen at the bottom of the North Sea? It would be hard to say. Has she yet taken stock of the absurdity of her own flight, or begun to feel sorrow for her husband Cliff, whom she had once loved, and to whom this narrative has so far been less than generous? Again, it would be hard to say, hard to tell from her demeanour. And she herself could not say. Her mind is on other things. It is at the moment preoccupied with an awareness that she is being closely watched by a man at an adjacent table, who is pretending to read a book, but who is, in fact, eyeing Shirley in a manner that she would, when younger, have confidently identified as a prelude to an attempted pick-up. In the midst of death, we are in life.

Covertly, she inspects him. He is presentable, indeed to her eyes attractive. Late forties, early fifties, a regular traveller, bored, wanting diversion, she guesses. Businessman, executive? Perhaps slightly too casually, a little too shabbily dressed. Media, civil service, teacher of some sort? May be. These thoughts, for Shirley, were almost subconscious: a sizing up, not a placing. Grey curly hair, a large nose, a broad, good-humoured face, permanently tanned, a little overweight, dark-rimmed glasses, sitting comfortably. A touch of Mr Punch, a benign Mr Punch. She tries to read the title of his book, but cannot quite make it out. It is a large paperback with a bold but plain emerald-green cover. Non-fiction.

Shirley recrosses her legs. She knows that when she has finished her Dubonnet, he will carefully time the draining of his own glass and offer her another as he passes her table to the bar. She will accept.

She is interested to discover that this kind of thing is still going on, in the outside world. A cross-Channel ferry hardly seems at this moment in the century, the most romantic of meeting places; indeed, given recent circumstances, there is something ghastly, doomed, menacing in the venue. But this is not, in Shirley's view, inappropriate. Shirley takes another sip of her diminishing Dubonnet and waits.

Charles Headleand has acquired, through the good offices of his friend Melvyn Stacey, a visa, of a sort, to visit Baldai. He stares at it, suspiciously, inspecting its small print. Melvyn had been depressing about conditions in Baldai. 'Journalists and reporters distinctly not welcome, from this part of the world,' said Melvyn. 'What does it say on your passport? Better get it changed.'

'It says company director,' said Charles, slightly hurt: for he was not a reporter. He was (or had been) an employer of reporters.

'Oh well, that'll do,' said Melvyn, 'that's a phrase that covers a multitude of crimes.'

Melvyn gave him a few names and addresses. Melvyn was of the view that Dirk Davis was dead, and was sure that Charles was going to get himself kidnapped. 'Don't expect me to come and get you out, my friend,' he said, jovially, shaking Charles's hand forcefully. 'On your own head be it. You have been warned. And there are no consular facilities of any sort, got it? Only poor young Bicester who looks after the plumbing. It's becoming a new kind of game of dominoes, this hostage business, and I've no intention of being next in line.'

Secretly, Melvyn thought it would be poetic justice if Charles Headleand got himself kidnapped. Charles and his like had been responsible for this new hostage industry: their indiscriminating passion for live news of any sort, the nastier the better, had put all sorts of unhealthy ideas into people's heads.

'I shan't expect a rescue,' said Charles. 'I know how to look after myself.'

But now, the papers in his hand, he hesitated. He found himself curiously reluctant to ring his fellow-conspirator, Carla

Davis. He found himself suddenly wondering if Dirk *was* still alive, after all this time: was it not a little unlikely? He walked up and down his sitting-room, pondering fretfully. The room was cluttered with the debris of various snacks: the young man who did his cleaning had, yet again, failed to turn up. Charles was beginning to wonder whether he should move into a service flat, if he could afford it. The notion of Carla's dark muddle, which he had been intending to visit, suddenly lacked charm. He thought of Liz, in her sunny house, and sat down and rang her, on impulse. Liz, he said, I've got my visa, for Baldai. Oh good, she said, vaguely, as though not quite listening. Yes, he said, with what he hoped was serious emphasis, I'll be inquiring about flights tomorrow. That's splendid, she said, again without due attention; and then, as though she had just taken in what he had said, she changed tone, and addressed him.

'But Charles,' she said, 'the boys will be furious. They think you're mad. Have you told them?'

'Not yet. Do *you* think I'm mad?'

'Not really. Not more mad than most people. We're all mad . . . Why don't you come to supper, before you go, and tell me all about it?'

'All right,' said Charles, not ungraciously. They arranged an evening.

'Don't tell the boys,' said Charles, as he rang off. 'I'd rather tell the boys myself. And don't ask them to supper, will you? I've had enough of being ticked off by those whippersnappers.'

Fanny Kettle was drawing up lists. A first round of invitations had already gone out, and she had received one or two refusals, as well as several acceptances, and had now reached the stage of second choices. Some were so grand that there was not much point in asking them, which is why she had not asked them in the first place, but now, emboldened by a couple of gins, she

144

inscribes envelopes. 'The Marquis of Stocklinch,' she writes. 'His Grace the Duke of Devonshire.' Well, she had *met* them, after all, had shaken their hands and chatted them up at a university charity banquet: why not invite them? Nothing venture, nothing win. Recklessly, she added the name of that sour disdainful mandarin, Sir Martin Daintry, Professor of Romance Languages: why not? He had prestige, unpleasant and (in Ian's view) outdated though he was. She chewed the end of her felt-tip pen. Who else? That young couple in the English Department, the Bells, they had looked quite promising. Down they go. And what about Perry Blinkhorn, from the Town Hall? In some curious way, over the past year, Perry Blinkhorn has become respectable, even fashionable: the press has stopped describing him as 'loony', has started to quote him as a moderate, a man of ideas, as a possible straw in the wind of a new future. Should she invite him? Ian does not like him, but then Ian lives in the past (albeit the fashionable up-to-date past), not in the future. Fanny ponders Perry Blinkhorn. Perry Blinkhorn is not her type. He lacks style, he is earnest, and his hair looks as though he cuts it himself with the kitchen scissors: his accent is irredeemably Yorkshire, and she suspects him of Low Church leanings. But he may be a coming man. She wonders if he ever has a drink? He does not look like a drinking man, but he clearly does not object to wine being poured in the Town Hall. Maybe it would be interesting, to see what happened to Perry Blinkhorn if he got a drink or two inside him? She smiles to herself and down goes his name.

The thought of Blinkhorn leads her to Alix and Brian Bowen, whom she has not yet invited, although she seems to remember that she mentioned her party to Alix at the do at the Holroyd Gallery. Perhaps she'd better ask them. Are the Bowens smart, or not? She does not know. Alix dresses very badly, but she is a good talker, and Brian has published novels and is kind to the elderly. One needs such people to pad a party. And after all,

Tony and Sam are friends. Yes, down go the names of Alix and Brian. And what about Beaver, Howard Beaver, the most famous son of Northam? Is he past party-going? Well, why not ask him anyway? It does no harm to ask. She has never met Beaver, but that does not deter her. Down he goes.

Susie Enderby lies on her bed, her eyes closed, listening to *Cosi fan tutte* and wondering what to wear for Fanny Kettle's party. She hopes that Clive will agree to go with her. She thinks she hopes that Clive will agree to go with her. Clive has been behaving oddly for this last few days, an oddity she connects with the disappearance of that Harper woman. But then, she, Susie Enderby, has been behaving oddly herself, in a way that is quite out of character, or quite out of the character she had thought she had settled into in her adult life.

She has been seduced by Fanny Kettle. No, not in *that* way, no, nothing of *that* sort, for she and Fanny, even in the worst childhood naughtiness, had always been resolutely, nay, excessively hetero-sexual, in their fantasies, in their experiments. But she had been seduced, by Fanny, back into these memories. Fanny seems not at all ashamed of them, and it is her lack of shame that has seduced Susie. Fanny seems to think that sexual promiscuity is both natural and normal. Susie does not know what to think, is lost, slightly, as she lies there on her bed. She moans, slightly, as Ferrando besieges Fiordiligi with an impetuous torrent of syll-ables, a surging outpouring of rapid rhyme. She moans, and touches her own body. She touches, wonderingly, her breasts, her thighs. She does not touch her own cunt. She dare not. She dare not even think its name.

'Io ardo, e l'ardor mio non è più effetto d'un amor virtuoso: è smania, affanno, rimorso, pentimento, leggerezza, perfidia e tradimento!' laments the half-guilty Fiordiligi, as she breaks into her penitent aria. 'Remorse, regret, frivolity, perfidy, treachery!' All foreknown, all foreseen, all familiar.

146

Susie breathes lightly, a shallow light breathing. It is mid-afternoon. The children will soon be home from school, collected by the Swiss au pair girl. They will be wanting tea, chat, games, talk about their homework. A restlessness runs though Susie's well-preserved, under-used thirty-seven-year-old body. Her skin is smooth, taut, silk. She feels she might softly explode, as she lies there in her champagne silk underwear and her light oyster-grey wrap. She knows she is beautiful, desirable, desiring. She is wasting away. She will buy some new beads, some new pink coral beads, for her new grey-brown pink silk dress. Her hair is now tinted a soft pink-brown, a grey-brown-strawberry-pink. She will wear the new beads to Fanny's party.

The telephone by her bed rings. Susie shuts her eyes and listens to its ringing. She does not answer. She holds her breath. It stops. Fiordiligi sings on. *'Per pietà, perdona, perdona, per pietà!'*

The children will be home in ten minutes. Heavily, with immense effort, Susie swings her mind round to worrying about her children, who seem to inhabit a different universe from the one occupied by Fanny Kettle. The thought of them disturbs, oppresses her. Her very existence seems to be a troubling betrayal of them, of their eager little faces, their gapped teeth, their freckles, their scabbed knees, their satchels full of projects on dinosaurs and wildlife and Roman Britain, their squabbles, their pleading for a pony of their own. They are far too little to have a pony, Clive says, rightly: they will have to make do with a couple of hamsters and a kitten. Susie once briefly had a pony. A little strawberry roan, called Lightfoot. She had been stabled at a farm out towards Gonersall.

'Barbara! Ingrata!' shouts the deceived Ferrando.

Last time she had been to Fanny Kettle's for a drink, Fanny had engaged her in the most appalling conversation about AIDS. How had it happened, how had she, respectable house-wife, mother of two, and part-time speech therapist, permitted it?

There had seemed to be no resisting, no turning back. 'What *I* don't like to think about,' Fanny had said, balancing a tumbler full of gin and tonic on her plump upholstered chair arm, and wriggling her bracelets on her thin wrist, 'is the idea that the virus sort of *hangs around* for years, I mean, I don't mind being a little careful *now*, but what about all those episodes six years ago, seven years ago? Before we knew *anything*? One might have caught *anything*, in those days.' Fanny giggles, changes tack slightly. 'Do you remember those cholera graves, outside the churchyard wall, that we used to walk past on the way back from school? And how everybody said they were still full of cholera, and that if you went near them it might leak out, and how they didn't dare move them to widen the street because cholera germs never never die? Do you remember?'

Susie nodded: yes, she remembered those schoolgirl superstitions. But Fanny was not content with the harmless, distant past. She returned to more recent alarms.

'I mean, that Frenchman who picked me up in the Gatwick Hilton, now I think about it, he could have been *anyone*, he could have been *anywhere*. One can't tell with the French, can one? Or at least maybe *you* can, but *I* can't.' Susie listened, wide-eyed. Fanny reminisces, relentlessly. 'Though now I think about it, *he* was the one who was so obsessed with hygiene. Insisted on us both getting into the bath together and *scrubbing* ourselves before we got on with it. *I* thought he was just kinky about baths with strange women, but maybe he knew something I don't know? He can't have done, can he? It was' – she counts on her fingers – 'at *least* seven years ago. *Nobody* knew about AIDS then, did they?'

Susie is lost, shocked, has no idea and yet has every idea of what Fanny is talking about.

'No,' concludes Fanny, to her own satisfaction, 'I'm fairly sure he was just kinky. He had a suitcase full of porno magazines.

Fairly mild stuff, but all to do with water, now I think about it. Bathroom scenes, showers and swimming pools and that kind of thing.' Fanny sighs, for the good old days. 'I feel sorry for young people,' she says. 'They're going to have a hard time, eroticizing the condom. Don't you think?'

Susie had not known what to think, for her own sexual experience (as surely Fanny must divine?) had been confined to a few harmless pre-marital flirtations, a doomed romance with an inept young medical student with whom she had slept perhaps half a dozen times and who had left her for a radiologist, and marriage to Clive Enderby. Since marriage she had been faithful to Clive, and had never been much tempted to be otherwise: the nearest she had got to temptation had been a lunch-time meeting or two in the hospital canteen with Stewart Folger from neurology, who had seemed to like to get next to her in the queue with his tray and to make occasional plaintive and pointed references to his wife, who had run off with an ophthalmic surgeon. Not much risk of catching AIDS from Stewart Folger, Susie reflected. Fanny seems to suggest that everyone in Northam and Hansborough was at risk, whereas Susie was quite convinced that the kind of behaviour Fanny seemed to think normal was aberrant, deviant, almost pathological.

Or was it?

'Hai vinto!' cried the conquered Fiordiligi. 'You have prevailed!' she sobbed, as she flung herself into the arms of the triumphant but betrayed Ferrando. Cosi fan tutte. Cosi fan tutte, tutti.

Susie hears the door open, hears children's voices downstairs. Guiltily, in a hurry, she banishes her dubious oyster-coloured consumer romance fantasies, strips off her wrap, struggles into her camel skirt and beige cashmere sweater (which don't quite go with her new hair, but never mind, all the better for that), runs a comb through her new hair, puts an everyday expression on her face, and runs lightly down the stairs to greet William, Vicky, and the bad-tempered Danielle. 'Hello, darlings,' she cries, and kisses the little ones. Danielle glowers, crossly. Susie puts the kettle on for tea, chatters brightly as Vicky unpacks her felt-tip drawings of the day and displays a painted egg box, as William complains about a character called Ollie Cox, and shows her his sketch of an Iron Age Celtic chariot, as Danielle grudgingly gets out the Marmite and the honey. Susie feels flustered, at a loss. 'Look, Mummy,' says Vicky, unrolling a tattered scroll, 'look, here's a picture of you and Daddy!' Two stick figures in bright green, with huge inane smiles, stand square and large on the page. They are holding hands, after a fashion. One has short hair sticking straight up, the other has orange curls and a short triangular miniskirt. They are strangely recognizable. 'Lovely, darling,' says Susie, faintly cheered, as she slices a Marmite sandwich into fingers, and reminds herself that it is only two months, two weeks and three days until Danielle's departure.

'To Paris?' says the middle-aged travelling man. Shirley nods. She has declined a second Dubonnet, on the grounds that she is or will be driving, but has accepted an orange juice, and allowed him to join her at her table, where he sips his second drink.

'I haven't been to Paris for years,' she confides, misleadingly: implying that she once visited France frequently, and for some casual reason has allowed this habit to lapse. Well, perhaps the implication is not all that misleading, for in the prosperous old days she and Cliff had taken several package weekend breaks in Paris, had stayed a few days there once or twice with the children on their way to summer holidays in Spain or the South of France. Shirley is not totally unacquainted with Paris. She recalls, fleetingly, visiting a nightclub with Cliff. Cliff had tried to get her to argue with the waiter and the bob-tailed semi-nude hostess about the price of drinks. 'Go on, you speak French,' he had said, when his own efforts at protest had been shrugged off.

'Yes, but not *much*,' Shirley had said, remembering a few phrases from Battersby Grammar O-Level, 'and anyway, not that *kind* of French.'

'Go on, Shirl,' Cliff had insisted, and Shirley had been forced to try phrases like '*Monsieur, sur le menu il dit vingt francs et vous avez dit cent francs.*' The waiter, not to Shirley's surprise, had continued to pretend to be bewildered, and after a lot more huffing and puffing Cliff had been forced to pay up. But he had felt guilty about this little display of unreasonable anger, and as the cancan dancers lifted their legs and showed their scarlet skirts he had taken Shirley's hand and squeezed it in apology. Shirley had enjoyed the seedy splendour, the bright lights, the steep views over Paris, the street thronging with people in the warm night air, the hot friendly breath of the Métro, the displays of oysters and *langoustines* and lemons and sea urchins and prickly erotic monsters of the deep. Was that perhaps the night that Celia, the austere Celia, had been conceived?

'I suppose Paris must have changed quite a lot in the past few years,' Shirley says, mildly, to her new companion. 'Do you know it well?'

'Quite well,' he nods, reflectively, modestly, a man of the world. 'Quite well.'

'And do you come this way often?'

He shrugs. 'Usually I fly,' he says. 'But this time I had to bring the car. To pick up some stuff. From my ex's apartment.' A rueful little smile disguises a more sombre note. Shirley thinks, Aha, I guessed right. He too is in trouble. Obviously. Why else would we be talking to one another? She is in a dilemma. She does not know whether to continue the conversation or not. She smells danger, involvement, confidences. Is this what she wants, what she has come to seek? She cannot be sure. Yet.

'Do you think they will ever really build the Channel Tunnel?' she asks, politely, harmlessly. 'Would you like to be able to drive to France? *Will* we be able to drive, when they finish it, or will it just be for trains?'

They discuss the Channel Tunnel. Cliff had been very keen on the Channel Tunnel. He thought it was go-ahead. Shirley shares with her new friend her unfavourable impressions of the motorway facilities, and of the as yet unserviced M25. She is talked into acknowledging that she comes from South Yorkshire.

Is he a detective, planted there to apprehend her and take her home against her will? No, surely not. He wants to talk about his ex. Ex-wife? Ex-girlfriend? Shall she let him? It would be safer, surely, than saying more about herself. Delicately, she probes.

Ah, but here is real pain, real, banal, everyday pain. A cross-Channel love affair, solid for ten years, now in ruins, and worse than ruins, for her new friend is now discovering that some of those ten years have been far from solid, have been marked by hidden treachery. His woman, he hints, had been carrying on behind his back for most of those years. He blames himself for having been so gullible, for having accepted the way things were, for having been decent, loyal, trusting. These are not the words he uses about himself, but this is what he implies, what she receives. He has been the faithful party, the victim. And now he is on his way to pick up his books, his shoes, his clothes, his birthday presents to and from her, his specially designed armchair.

'It's for my back,' he explains. 'It's made to measure. I have a bad back. I hope to God it fits in the car.'

He laughs, lightened by confession. She likes him.

'Yes,' he says, 'it's the end of the affair. She's moved out already. Won't even see me. Not that I want to see her. Ever. She's gone off to live in the Marais. I forget, did you say you knew Paris well?'

Shirley, smiling, shakes her head. Not well, she says, not well.

And are you, perhaps, on a little holiday, he inquires? A spring break? He is only being polite.

Yes she agrees, a little holiday.

And will she visit the new gallery at the Musée d'Orsay? All Paris talks of it, visits it, queues for it, he assures her.

Yes, she says, she probably will. She has not heard of the Musée d'Orsay.

And is she spending her holiday alone? Escaping, perhaps, for a little peace and quiet from her family obligations? Or will she be meeting friends in Paris, staying with friends?

Shirley's head begins to thrum and throb. The note of polite, civilized sympathy and interest in his voice assaults her defences. She feels a little faint. She shuts her eyes for a moment. The boat is heaving and lurching.

'Are you feeling all right?' he asks, anxiously. 'It *is* a little on the rough side today, isn't it?'

His tone is impeccable. Courteous, restrained, unintrusive.

'I'm fine,' she says. 'I'm fine.' And then she hears herself go on to say, 'My husband died this week. I've run away. Yes, that's what I've done, I've run away.'

Her eyes are still shut. The ferry creaks and slaps its way on. He hesitates, then she feels his hand upon her hand.

'Oh. I *say*, my dear, I *say*,' he says, 'I *am* so sorry. I *say*, poor thing, I say.'

Tears stand in her eyes, her lip trembles. She stiffens it. His voice is so acceptable, so miraculously acceptable. Who would have believed it possible? A human being is speaking to her. She has been locked into solitude for years, for a decade at least. Now, somebody speaks, a stranger speaks. He does not rise and reject her, he does not run away in shock. He pats her hand and says, 'Oh, oh dear, poor *thing.*'

She opens her eyes and smiles, bravely. He is leaning towards her, full of concern. 'There, there,' he says, and pats her hand, then withdraws, in case he should cause offence by too much solicitude.

They sit there like that for a minute or two, in silence. He offers, again, to get her a drink — a soft drink, a glass of water? She shakes her head.

And where is she staying in Paris, he wants to know? She shakes her head. She admits that she has no idea.

'I left — on impulse,' she says. 'I had to get away.'

The ferry is nearing Calais. The gulls cry.

'But will you be all right, on your own?' he wants to know, as announcements are made about the rejoining of cars and the not switching on of engines.

'Oh yes,' says Shirley bravely, but when she rises to her feet she is shaking violently. Her teeth chatter, she is suddenly, mortally cold. Her legs will hardly support her. Surely, at this stage, he will summon a doctor, summon the police and desert her? She should never have admitted a moment of human weakness, it has destroyed her.

He takes her elbow. 'Look,' he says, 'you're not fit to drive. You're not well.'

'I'm fine,' she says, as she stands there trembling. She takes a deep breath, calms herself by force. 'I'm fine,' she repeats, and starts to move calmly towards the door, towards the stairs to Car Deck B. He follows her. He follows her to the door of her little red Mini, watches anxiously as she unlocks it and climbs in. She sits there and rests her head for a moment on the wheel. The truth is that she has no idea how she will ever get the car off the ferry, her knees are shaking, her heart is pounding, her head is buzzing, and however would she in this condition manage to drive to anywhere on the right-hand side of the road? It was a miracle that she got up the gangplank onto the ferry at all. She will never get off. She sits upright, smiles again. He is still there, hovering.

'Look,' he says, 'let me help.'

She cannot believe her ears.

'Let me help,' he repeats. He can read her mind.

'Look,' he says, 'you get in my car, and I'll drive you off, then come back for yours. Then we'll think about it.'

She begins to cry, noiselessly, and bows her head again over the wheel. He takes her elbow, helps her to her feet, takes the car keys from her, lets her into his own car, into the passenger seat of a spacious, elderly, slightly battered grey Citroën. 'Just sit there,' he tells her, and she sits obediently, as he vanishes, then returns. 'They say they'll drive it off for you,' he says. 'Is that all right?'

She nods.

'I've told him to follow me,' he says. 'Is that all right?'

She nods again, and sits there as the ferry docks, as the bow doors swing open, as he starts up the engine. 'I told them you'd been taken ill,' he said, with a hint of returning humour, growing intimacy. 'They were very understanding,' he said. She smiles acknowledgement, but dares not speak. 'This kind of thing probably happens all the time,' he says. The car moves forwards, she turns round, sees her own red Mini with a uniformed seaman at the wheel. The seaman waves encouragement, starts up after them.

They reach dry land, park. Money changes hands. Her new friend is good at such things. Everybody smiles, including Shirley. The seaman departs.

'And now,' he says, 'what now?'

'I don't know,' says Shirley. All sorts of possibilities are passing through her head. She does not know what to say, what not to say.

'I wanted to disappear,' she says, forlornly, in the hiatus.

He shows no sign of losing patience with her. He sits and waits for more.

'They don't know where I am,' she offers.

'You can leave your car here, and come to Paris with me,' he offers in return.

155

'But they'll find the car,' she says. 'I should never have brought the car. I nearly left it in Luton. I ought to have left it in Luton.'

'We'll leave it,' he says. 'In the supermarket car-park. Could you drive, do you think, just a few minutes? You could follow me.'

She nods.

'We'll get your things out first,' he says. They get out, into the fresh cold air, into a light rain, into the darkening afternoon. The cold revives her. They transfer her suitcases, her raincoat, her plastic bags to the boot of the Citroën. She has become a hostage.

'All right,' she says, and gets back into the driver's seat of her Mini.

'Just follow me,' he calls. 'And drive on the right, remember!'

She follows him, slowly, carefully until they arrive in a large, roughly surfaced, almost deserted supermarket car-park on the fringes of town. It is PARKING GRATUIT. Free Parking. How did he know it was here, Shirley asks herself? Shirley parks her car with its nose in a corner, next to a small rusted van which looks as though it has been there for some time. She gets out. Her friend gets out. It is very cold now. He puts his arm round her shoulders, in a friendly, comforting gesture. They stand there, for a moment. He squeezes her far shoulder, lightly, slightly.

'All right?' he asks.

'All right,' she agrees. He opens his car door for her. She gets in, docile, passive, bold, and sits down, leans back, stretches out her legs.

'You see,' he says, with an air of patience, of reason, 'you can't just set off into the night, with no booking, and no idea where you're going. When you're not feeling well. Can you?'

Shirley thinks. 'Well,' she says, after a while, 'I suppose I could have done. If I hadn't met you.'

He turns the key in the ignition.

'But you did meet me. Or rather, I met you. It was my idea, remember.' He moves off, gently. The car's suspension is very good, it rises softly up, then inches smoothly over the bumpy waste site, gathers slow speed on the tarmac, accelerates as he sets off towards Paris. She does not even look back, towards her abandoned loyal faithful decent red Mini.

'You can spend the night in my apartment. No strings attached, of course. But at least spend the night there quietly, and think things over.' He pauses, continues. 'It will do me good, to have someone to look after. Take my mind off my own worries.'

'You are too good,' she says.

'No,' he says. 'I'm just pretending to be, for a change. People tell me I'm not very good at all.'

She gazes out at the dark mistletoed landscape of northern France.

'But you can trust me,' he adds, as an afterthought. 'I'm quite a safe driver.'

She laughs at this.

'My name is Shirley,' she says.

'And mine is Robert,' he says.

They drive on, into the darkness. As they go, Shirley tells him something (not too much) about her flight. She leaves some details vague, purposefully vague. He listens, sympathetically, quietly, with the odd exclamation of commiseration. 'Poor thing,' he says, from time to time, 'you poor thing.' Then he tells her the story of Amélie and her infidelity. He had considered Amélie a permanence, a consort until death, a lover confirmed by distance, he tells Shirley: a perpetual romance. Amélie worked in Paris, he was taken by business affairs regularly almost weekly to Paris. He has suspected nothing. Yes, he had had a wife in England, years ago, but she had divorced him over Amélie and remarried. Quite happily, he thought. He had trusted Amélie. 'It was by accident that I discovered,' he said. 'I arrived unexpectedly. The only time in ten years. The phone was out of order. I wish I had never found out.'

Shirley says that maybe things will alter, improve. He shakes his head. No, it is over, he says.

She tells him of her clever daughter Celia, of her two difficult truant boys.

He tells her of his son Lucas, who is now a computer programmer, and of his son Edward, who is physically handicapped.

Their stories interweave, join, separate, and join again. He drives, as he had claimed, well. It is a strange sensation, to be in the care of a man, to be with a man who takes responsibility. Shirley reflects that for years now, she had been living with Cliff as with a stranger, had been taking care of him as though he were a stranger, had been dreading, foreseeing, from a distance, the inevitable collapse. Robert is companionable, easy. They talk, fall silent, talk again. Eventually she falls asleep, and when she wakes they are in an unfamiliar Paris, making their way through broad, then narrower streets, until they turn down a one-way road, slow down, and turn through an archway. Robert gets out, unlocks an iron gate, and drives through into a small cobbled courtyard.

'Here we are,' he says.

Shirley looks around, rubs her eyes. Is she dreaming? Is she hallucinating? It is a little French courtyard, ancient, rustic. She knows they are in a heavily built-up area, she can sense that they are not far from the centre, not far from the Paris that everybody knows, but this is a corner out of time. There are flower pots and, to the right, a long obliquely angled three-storeyed building with shutters and little iron balconies. A small tree grows in the middle of the irregular long triangle of yard. Grass sprouts from the cobbles: a little house, a cottage, faces them, separate from the long larger building, tucked away perched, stranded, a little house all on its own. Robert parks the car in front of this little doll's house, this little garden pavilion. He gets out, goes back to shut the iron gate, comes to open her door. She gets out and stands in the cold Paris night. The air smells of France.

A few steps, a little iron staircase, lead up to the front door. She follows him. The heavy door, unlocked by an impressive tangle of antiquated keys, opens straight into the tiny living-room. He switches on the light.

'Well, this is it,' says Robert: meaning that only this floor is his, that whatever goes on upstairs is nothing to do with him. And there are no stairs. There are three doors, opening off this central chamber. This is it.

The apartment is half stripped, as perhaps he had half expected. She senses his distress, as he looks around. The pot plants are dead or dying. A packing case stands in a corner. The ornately papered dark walls show pale patches, where paintings have been removed. Other paintings stand on the floor, their faces to the skirting board. The small round dining-table has two en-velopes upon it. 'Robert,' one says, in a firm large script. The other says, more waveringly, 'M. Holland'. Robert stands there jangling the keys, weighing them in his hand, and sighs. The apartment is warm: the heating is on. He stands. Shirley wonders whether to speak. But he speaks first.

'Well, at least she hasn't taken the lampshades,' he says, and Shirley looks up and round. She sees that the lampshades are pretty, patterned, brown and red and orange flowered, art nou-veau. The room must have been cosy, intimate, a little brown-red nest. It is still cosy, even in its half-dismantled state. Shirley decides to say so.

'What a lovely room,' she risks, on its threshold. Robert is roused back to concern, chivalry. 'Yes, it's a good corner,' he says, as he puts down Shirley's bags (he has none) and waves to the couch. 'Sit down,' he says, 'sit down,' and he reaches for his letters, opens them, glances at them, throws them back on the table. She does not sit.

'Well,' he says, 'we'd better see what she's left. Would you like a drink? I could do with a drink. I wonder if there's anything to eat?'

He opens one of the three doors, which reveals a tiny kitchen, into which he disappears. She hears him rummaging through cupboards. Shirley looks round, inspecting more closely the remnants of a ten-year intimacy, wondering which is the bedroom, wondering about beds. The couch, upholstered in shiny repellent striped fabric, has wooden scrolled ends and is as hard as a rock. The rooms must all be tiny, she supposes.

Robert returns with a couple of glasses and a couple of bottles. He offers a choice of Pernod and whisky. She chooses Pernod, because there is more of it, and she thinks it might be milder. He has the same. He tops it up, reassuringly, with water.

'Well,' he says, sitting in his specially designed armchair, 'our health.'

The Pernod is strong stuff, she realizes, halfway through her glass.

It is eight o'clock. They talk about Amélie's desertion, and about the concierge, Madame Lambert, author of the second of Robert's letters. 'She's on my side, of course,' says Robert, 'she wanted to let me know she wouldn't let Amélie take down the curtains. Made her put them back up again, she says.'

They decide to go out for a bit to eat. 'There's nothing much here,' says Robert. 'A couple of eggs and an old crust and a tin of anchovies. We'll go down to the corner. Have another drink?'

There is only the one bedroom. When Robert opens the door, he discovers to his irritation that the bed is unmade. 'Perhaps she's taken all the sheets,' he speculates, morosely, as he looks in the wardrobe, in a drawer under the bed. The room is more or less filled by the large double bed. He finds sheets, in a brown laundry parcel under a folded blanket. There is a note on them, from Amélie. 'I think these are mine, but you can borrow them,' she has written.

'My God,' groans Robert. 'What a woman. Relentless. She might at least have made the bed up.'

Shirley stands in the doorway. There is nowhere else to stand. She has by now discovered the bathroom, which leads, also, directly from the small square sitting-room.

'Let me help,' says Shirley. 'It's easier with two.'

This quasi-proverb, this commonplace, seems to soothe Robert. Together, they make up the bed. The sheets, Shirley notes, are pretty, a pale faded blue pattern, with a deep *broderie anglaise* border, and the pillowcases are lace-edged. They are carefully, professionally ironed. But not new. Nothing here is new. There is a pathos in the old age of the sheets.

They tuck in the blankets, pull over the pale-blue counterpane.

'Supper, now,' says Robert, and they put on their coats and go down the street, past butchers, grocers and greengrocers to an unsmart brasserie on the corner, where Robert is greeted as an old friend. 'Robert, Robert,' customers and management cry, in French, and shake his hand: masculine solidarity is at work, Shirley reflects, vaguely, as she sinks on to her bench, but she is almost past reflection, she can no longer quite take in where she is or what she is doing. She gazes round semi-dazed, at the strange tortoiseshell-coloured glass panelling of the walls, at the tiled floor, at a plant in a hanging basket, at two middle-aged men leaning on a pinball machine, at an old man in a crumpled shirt and a straying tie drinking a bowl of soup, at a young man in a cloth cap eating a plate of ham and reading a book, at three bearded men in animated conversation over beer, at a middle-aged woman sitting alone eating a great dish of what looks like stuffed cabbage. A wooden napkin ring sits by her plate. She is a regular. Robert orders a steak and frites, Shirley orders an omelette and frites. The young waiter brings bread in a silver-tin basket, a paper cloth for the Formica-topped table, an earthenware jug of wine, and a salad in a glass bowl, and oil and vinegar in a cruet. He wishes them *bon apétit*. They eat, they drink.

Robert introduces Shirley to one or two of the clientele, as they pause by Robert's table, or call across the room. *'Je vous présente mon amie Shirley, elle est en visite d'Angleterre,'* he cries. Shirley nods and smiles. Her French is not up to replying to courtesies, but nobody seems to mind. The evening wears on. Robert tells her about Amélie's new-old lover, who is something to do with a bank. Shirley tries to explain about Cliff's financial troubles and her own uncertain position as shadow director of his company. She asks Robert why Cliff hadn't left her a suicide note. After all these years, says Shirley. Maybe you didn't look hard enough, says Robert. She has by now revealed the nature of Cliff's death, but she has not revealed that she did not wait to speak to the police. She allows Robert to think that her running away was less impulsive, less mystifying than in fact it was. She does not want him to turn her over to Interpol. But she finds herself somewhat surprisingly telling him all about the sterilization she had undergone a few years ago, and how (unaccountably) it had depressed her. He is sympathetic, concerned. He tells her of his ex-wife's troubles with high blood pressure and the pill, her worries about their handicapped son. They order cheese, and more wine.

It is late now, and a drunken Englishman enters the bar and greets Robert as a long-lost friend. He talks and talks, but Shirley cannot follow. The talk is of something called TEFAL, which Shirley assumes at first is a consumer product, a trade name, as most of the talk is financial, but she gradually realizes that TEFAL is something to do with the teaching of English, and that both Robert and this newcomer are involved in it. They talk of tapes and audio-visual aids. The English language, she learns, is a marketable product, it seems it sells better than the wing

mirrors and picnic kits of Taiwanese steel that have ruined Cliff
Harper and his partner Jim Bakewell. Shirley yawns, accepts
another coffee. Her head swims. The talk lurches from visual aids
to AIDS and the drunken Englishman declares that the slowly
acquired morality of nations is in sudden eclipse, and that the
poets and novelists of the future would have to change their
tune about sex pretty sharply. Not so, not so, argues Robert,
AIDS is merely another manifestation of the dangers of sexuality, dangers which have always existed, risk is part and always
has been part of the game, physical risk, emotional risk, says
Robert, and had anyone read Goethe's *Roman Elegies*, which are
obsessed both with sexual passion and with venereal disease?

> *Zwei gefährliche Schlangen, vom Chore der Dichter gescholten,*
> *Grausend nennt sie die Welt Jahre die tausende schön,*
> *Python dich unter dich Lernaischer Drache!*

he intones, to the incomprehending but interested stares of
Shirley, the Englishman, and other drinkers and diners: wonderful
poet, says Robert, to himself almost, quite unperturbed by the
lack of more animated response, for clearly Goethe's *Roman
Elegies* do not pass for currency with anyone within hearing. 'The
longing for the south, the flight from the north,' says Robert.
'Oh, how happy I feel in Rome, when I think of the dull old grey
days of the dark leaden north, that's what Goethe wrote.' Rome,
Paris, the same kind of thing. Flight from the grey pall.

'Yes, quite,' says the drunken Englishman, who has lost the
thread more than Shirley (who sort of thinks she follows it). The
Englishman says goodnight, and wanders off uncertainly into the
brightly lit darkness.

The café shows signs of shutting down. Robert calls for the bill.
Robert and Shirley walk arm in arm down the narrow little street
to the archway and the iron gate and the courtyard. They let

themselves in with the large bunch of keys. It seems that they have been living here, together, for a very long time. Shirley tries to have a bath, but cannot control the antique gas jet or the snake-like vicious shower attachments, so satisfies herself with a cold wash. Shivering, she puts on the new nightdress she had providentially purchased, a hundred years ago, in the Marks & Spencer of Dover. Robert is already in bed. She joins him. He puts his arms around her, kisses her, holds her. He is very broad, very warm. He strokes her hair and kisses her on the face, the lips, the throat. She takes off her new nightdress, and he enters her, very slowly and firmly and heavily. He makes love to her for what seems like hours. He seems completely untroubled by the process. Shirley is too tired to work out what is happening, but her body responds for her, it warms up and melts and receives him. She is passive, at peace. They do not speak, until after some time he murmurs in her hot, wet ear, 'More?' and she says, 'Yes, more,' and he goes on and on, without excitement, with a kind of swelling reassuring persistence. Her body has not felt so comfortable for years. She dissolves and cries out. 'Yes, yes,' he says, and comes into her, fully, generously, completely. They lie there, half asleep. They fade into contentment, into sleep. She turns over, he puts his arm around her breasts, holds her against him. They drift away between the pale-blue faded sheets.

Maybe, in the morning, when they face one another over what little coffee Amélie has left them, he will discover that she is a temporarily unbalanced small-minded suburban housewife, consumed with embarrassment and shame: maybe she will discover that he is a middle-aged bore and a philandering neurotic who has treated the women in his life with a callousness that deserves their desertion. Maybe. Meanwhile, let them lie there, for the night, safe in one another's arms. It is not impossible, that they should lie there. Not quite impossible.

*

Alix waits for a reply from Angela Whitmore Malkin, brooding on the image of her summoned up by Bill Whitmore's indirect discourse. For some reason, Alix is convinced that Angela is a very nasty bit of work. She has little to go on, but she has a smell of her, an instinct. The Bad Mother. Have I been brainwashed by Bowlby? wonders Alix, as she examines her suspicions. The Bad Mother. The Runaway Mother. Can she be blamed for everything? Can she be blamed for the disaster of P. Whitmore and the deaths of his random victims?

She does not think she will get an answer from Angela. Investigative journalists have tried already to dig up Paul's mother, to buy her story, but they have failed, so it is not likely that she will respond to Alix. She has gone to earth, deliberately. But Alix has the advantage of an address. Of knowing that she is alive, and lives at Hartley Bridge. She knows that she will go and look for her, invited or not. Angela is uncannily, irresistibly close.

Meanwhile, in pursuit of other scapegoats, other prime motives, of the primal crimes, she continues to read her Tacitus, even branches out with a little Lucan.

Lucan's *Pharsalia*. Her Latin is a little rusty, for all that she studied it with interest for six years and took an A in her A-Levels, all those decades ago. The Ancient Britons, the Romans. If Paul Whitmore had not become obsessed by them, would his mania have taken another form? Is some innocent secondary schoolteacher in north Staffordshire as implicated in his decapitations as the evil Angela and the butcher's shop? Alix would like to ask Liz about these questions, but has not quite formulated them, even to herself. But she does sit up with a start when, one evening, she is idly and sleepily watching a television programme about Celtic religion and hears the sentence, 'As the cross is to Christianity, so the severed head to the Celtic religion.' She jerks her eyes open, sees museum shots of a few primitive stone *têtes coupées*, one of them originally from Toxetter. This can only be a coincidence: Paul has never mentioned anything to do with such aspects of his interest in the past. Severed heads. One or two journalists, after Paul's trial, had tried to make some sense of the symbolism of this obsession, and one had even quoted Iris Murdoch's contribution on the theme, but nobody had come up with Celtic ritual.

The soul resided in the head, according to the Celts.

Alix finds the passage in the *Pharsalia* which describes Caesar's desecration of the sacred grove of Massilia. Her copy of Lucan's work is on loan from the Literary and Philosophical Library of Northam; it is in two volumes, bound in blue canvas, and contains both the Latin text and the English version in heroic couplets by Nicholas Rowe, Esq. It is dated 1812. It was last taken out in 1981. Alix wonders who else had been reading Lucan, so recently.

> Black Springs with pitchy Streams divide the Ground,
> And Bubbling tumble with a sullen Sound.
> Old Images of Forms misshapen stand,
> Rude and unknowing of the Artist's Hand;
> With hoary Filth begrim'd, each ghastly Head
> Strikes the astonsh'd Gazer's Soul with Dread
>
> . . . *simulacraque maesta deorum*
> *Arte carent caesisque extant informia truncis.*

Yes. She reads on. Caesar sentences the grove to fall by the axe, in order to facilitate his siege of the pro-Pompey Forum of Massilia: she does not quite grasp what the sacred grove has to do with Caesar's battle plans, but quite understands why his soldiers are afraid to chop down the trees and images. Caesar seizes an axe and strikes the first blow:

Deep sunk within a violated Oak
The wounding edge, and thus the Warrior spoke.
Now, let no doubting Hand the Task decline;
Cut you the Wood, and let the Guilt be mine.

The men follow his example, unwillingly, chopping down oak and ash and holm and alder, and the trees, crashing, 'display/Their dark Recesses to the Golden Day'.

The Gauls watch, some groaning, others assured of the coming vengeance of the gods.

The golden day.

Does one admire Caesar for hacking down superstition, for letting in the daylight? Alix thinks that she remembers that Lucan, writing under Nero, was a supporter of Pompey, and portrayed Caesar as a bloodthirsty ogre, so can one trust his account of this episode in the grove? Is it perhaps a subtle atrocity story? Nero compelled Lucan, at the age of twenty-five, to commit suicide. Lucan chose the warm bath, the severed veins.

The golden day. Maybe the teaching of the classics teaches us monstrosities rather than balance, wisdom, stoicism, reason.

Alix wishes Stephen Cox were still in England, so she could ask him about these things. Stephen is interested in atrocity stories. But Stephen has vanished from the map of the known world.

What level of intention *can* Paul Whitmore have had, when he murdered total strangers? Old Images of Forms ... Rude and unknowing of the Artist's Hand. *Informia.*

Alix wonders if she should ring Liz anyway, wonders if there is any news about Shirley. There has been no news of Shirley for ten days.

She reads on. Lucan's epic is full of writhing serpents, severed limbs, foaming priestesses, rattling rocks, sulphurous portents, monstrous births and spouting blood. Ornate, psychotic stuff. How is he rated, now, as a poet? Alix cannot even construe the sentence about 'Old Images of Forms' — what forms? She re-members that Celia Harper is reading some classical degree or other at Oxford. Celia would know. But are such things worth knowing?

Alix sighs, shuts her book. She will write, once more, to the evil Angela, and if Angela does not reply, well, she will telephone. She has to know the answer. Whatever it may be.

Liz and Charles Headleand are finishing their cheese and salad in St John's Wood. Charles is about to fly off to Baldai, although now his departure has become a reality to him he has begun to share the common view of the fate of Dirk Davis. 'All right,' he concedes to Liz, 'it's just a psychological need on my part, I recognize that, I just feel I've got to make one last effort.'

'You didn't even like the man,' says Liz.

'No. But that's not the point.'

'I did like him, once,' says Liz. 'Do you remember the old days when he used to come and have supper with us in Harley Street with the crew? He used to be fun, in the old days.'

'He was always too fucking big for his boots,' says Charles. 'An aggressive kind of chap, even in those days. A born trouble-maker.'

'Yes, dear,' says Liz, in a parody of wifely submission. They both laugh.

'I read a piece in one of today's papers,' says Liz, 'about the kind of money that videotape editors and television technicians and electricians are getting for overtime. It says someone from one of the breakfast television stations put in a claim for £90,000 for covering the volcano story in Sicily at the end of last year. And that equally exaggerated claims are being made over the Zeebrugge ferry disaster. Is this all true, or are these just atrocity stories?'

'They're true enough,' says Charles. 'I blame Dirk Davis. The

ACTT is a monster. It's time this government did something about it.'

'And I blame you,' says Liz, pleasantly. 'People like you, with your passion for atrocities. I can't see why people need to gaze at sinking ships and burning mountains.'

'Can't you? Wasn't it you who dragged me up the slopes of Etna once, on a so-called holiday?'

Liz stops, considers. She remembers Etna with pleasure. And Vesuvius also suddenly arises before her in classic form, smoking decoratively. It too had charmed centuries of visitors. Goethe had clambered up it, Tischbein had painted it. She had received a postcard-painting of it from an ex-patient on holiday only the week before. It still attracts. The ashen bodies of Pompeii, like Lindow Man, still attract.

'Touché,' says Liz. She is always open to argument from historical precedent.

'Anyway,' says Liz, 'for God's sake take care. I don't want to be turned into a television widow. Not even a divorced television widow. It's not my style.'

The allusion to tragedy queen Carla goes down rather well, she thinks. Maybe Charles is going off her, at last? But if he is, what is that to her?

They have already discussed the enigma of Shirley's continuing disappearance. Liz has confessed that she is beginning to worry. Maybe Shirley is dead. There has been no trace of her or of her red Mini, although the police have been making inquiries. Liz takes up this thread again.

'Maybe something really awful *has* happened to her,' she says. 'Or maybe she knows something we don't know, and has run away from?'

'Don't you class Cliff's suicide as something really awful?'

'Well, yes, awful for Cliff, I suppose.'

She drains her wineglass.

169

'Anyway,' she says, 'you see how important it is for *you* not to vanish. Think how embarrassing it would be for me, to lose both a sister and an ex-husband, all in the same month. It would look as though I'd planned it.'

'That's a very self-centred way of looking at it.'

'Yes, it is, isn't it? Well, there's nothing new in being self-centred.'

She hesitates, continues.

'I've always had it at the back of my mind, I suppose, that I was somehow responsible for my father's death. Do you think I could have been?'

Charles stares at her.

'You? How can you have been? You were only an infant. What an odd idea.'

'Odd ideas aren't always false ideas.'

'Well, I think that's crazy. Just crazy.'

'So do I, really. But I think that's what I used to think, when I was little. That somehow my mother blamed me. And that therefore I was guilty.'

'Well, really, Liz,' says Charles, quite warmly, 'I think that's quite potty. I know what a lunatic your mother was, but I don't think even she can have blamed a four-year-old for her husband's behaviour. I don't like to hear you talking such rubbish. I've always thought you were remarkably sane, coming from a household like that. Amazingly sane. Don't start cracking up now, for God's sake, or what will the rest of us have to look forward to? I was always impressed by the way you and Shirley kept your heads screwed on . . .'

His voice trails away, as he realizes what he has said.

'Yes, there you are,' says Liz. 'That's what I mean. Shirley's lost her head. It seems. Me next, perhaps?'

'No, no,' says Charles, bracingly. '*Me* next. I'm the next in line, not you. You can stay sane, to pick up the pieces.'

170

Liz smiles, sighs, shakes her head, and begins to move, as though to rise to make coffee. Charles arrests her, with a hand on her arm.

'You know, Liz,' he says, astonishingly, 'I've often wondered what really happened to your mother. Did it ever occur to you that something might have happened in her life *before* she married your father?'

Liz's eyes widen.

'What *do* you mean?'

'Oh, I don't know, some early sexual trauma, some escapade. Some seduction. I mean, it's odd that she was so utterly without a history. She must have been concealing something.'

'Well, yes,' said Liz. 'But I'd assumed it was him. Our father.'

'I don't know,' said Charles. 'I sometimes think there was more to it than that.'

'What on earth makes you think that?'

'Oh, I don't know. Something she said. Once. Ages ago.'

'Really, Charles.' Liz tries to summon up the light-grey questioning eyes of Clive Enderby. She laughs. 'A mystery. You may be right. A different kind of mystery. Yes, that's quite possible.'

'Anyway,' said Charles, backtracking. 'There's no point in looking into these things too closely. We might not like what we find.'

'You are ill placed to take that line,' says Liz.

'Well, yes,' says Charles.

'You know,' says Liz, 'I keep thinking about my friend Stephen Cox. Did you ever meet Stephen? I can't remember. You did? He went off to Cambodia, you know. And nobody knows what he's up to. He used to send postcards, but now he doesn't write. There's no news. Do you think he's dead?' She laughs again, miserably. 'Maybe when you're tired of looking for Dirk, you could go and look for Stephen. He was a good friend, Stephen.'

'What made him go off to Cambodia in the first place?'

171

'Oh, I don't know. Curiosity, he said. He was a traveller by nature. A political traveller. He said he was going to write a play about Pol Pot. But he's been gone nearly two years now. It can't take two years to research a *play*, can it?'

She falls silent, muses. 'The fatal curiosity. That's what he said it was. I think it's the title of something, but I can't remember what. It's a good title, isn't it?'

'He went to see what had happened?'

Liz shrugs her shoulders, plays with a crumb of bread, repeats the phrase. 'The fatal curiosity. Yes. That's the phrase he used. Perhaps it will be the title of his play. Or his novel. Or his memoirs. Or whatever is left. If anything is left.'

'But why Cambodia?'

'Oh, I don't know. I think he wanted to see if the atrocity stories were true. To see for himself.' Liz looks at Charles. '*You* should understand. Isn't that why you are off, yourself?'

Stephen Cox is still alive, although none of the characters in this novel know it. Liz, in bed, having said goodbye to Charles, thinks of him, and of their last meeting. They had dined together, here, in this house, and had discussed truth, facts and the nature of curiosity. Maybe, Stephen had said, there is no history. Nobody but God can record how many died. And as there is no God, there is no history.

Liz lies in bed, wondering if it is right to try to unravel mysteries, whether it is right to try to count the unnumbered dead.

Stephen had been interested in Pol Pot because he represented the apotheosis of the demented intellectual. As Saloth Sar he had studied at the Sorbonne, and failed his finals. Or so Stephen said. Stephen said that Pol Pot's wife, who was also Ieng Sary's sister, had been the first Khmer woman to obtain the baccalaureat, and that some other woman in the group had studied English

172

literature at the Sorbonne. Imagine, Stephen had said. Imagine them, discussing *The Mill on the Floss*. Or *Cranford*. Or even *Macbeth*, Liz had said. But neither he nor Liz had been able to imagine. And that was why he had departed.

Charles Headleand has got as far as the Gatwick Hilton. He is sitting on a king-size bed, by himself, in his maroon cotton pyjamas and his grey towelling dressing-gown, playing with the remote control of his television. He summons up arcane messages, for he is a wizard with such machines, and they will tell him matters which they divulge only to the elect. He is now informed that Obolensky and Trubetskoy are playing chess in Bratislava, that a dam has burst in the Upper Volta, that an Iron Age burial has been excavated near Bristol. He calculates (with the aid of another little machine from his pocket) that on the day's trading in the Stock Exchange he has lost on his shares in Britvest and gained on his shares in Comicot. He learns that the French poet René Longuenesse has died aged seventy-two in Toulouse, and that the exhibition of the works of Simon Blessed now in Northam is to be shown in Manchester later in the year.

He is drinking a miniature whisky from the drink dispensing machine in the bathroom. It is his second. He has chickened out of saying goodbye to Carla. He cannot face Carla. His evening with Liz has undone the spell of Carla. He knows now that Liz is right, that Dirk Davis is dead. Charles is feeling unwell. He hates travelling. He is still brooding on the bare parting words of his eldest son Jonathan, who had said, over the phone from his yuppy Suffolk cottage, 'Well, Dad, don't expect the kind of coverage they gave Terry Waite, will you? You're not in the Archbishop's envoy league yet, you know.' Aaron had been more sympathetic, and had asked his father to send him a postcard. Alan had sounded quite upset, and had gone so far as to say, 'Don't get yourself killed, Dad, will you?' The girls, Liz's girls, his girls, had been as heartless as Jonathan, though in less media-conscious style. They had implied they thought he was irresponsible.

And maybe I am, thought Charles, sitting heavily on his bed. He flicked up a few flight departures on the screen: Ulan Bator, Kathmandu, Madrid, Dalaman. Where the hell was Dalaman? A holiday place, not a news place, or he'd have heard of it. His own flight took off at six in the morning. Charles hated flying. He hated the whole business – the queues, the claustrophobia, the take-off, the sound of the wheels retracting, the bullying music, the seat belts, the staff's psychotic switching from servility to contemptuous indifference. It was bad enough, setting off to somewhere reasonable, like Paris or New York or Los Angeles. But Baldai – no, crazy.

Charles pottered into the bathroom and prised another whisky out of its slot. He was getting drunk, waiting for a room-service order of cheeseburger and French fries and beer. This isn't the kind of food he likes, but it's the kind of food he eats in airport hotels. If he'd brought Carla with him for a farewell dinner, they could have eaten downstairs in the restaurant and had a proper meal with real meat and wine. He knew Carla had wanted to make a big deal of his departure, a publicity stunt, with cameras and the press. He'd slipped away, without telling her quite when. Is this a bad omen? It occurs to Charles that he needn't go at all. He could just sit here for a week. Lying low. And return home, quietly, saying 'mission accomplished'.

The cheeseburger arrives. He tips the waiter and sits down on the bed again to munch. He watches a bit of an American New York Jewish comedy, a few minutes of a black-and-white left-wing heroic peasant film set in Turkey, a soccer goal, and a nature programme about the wildlife of the River Barle on Exmoor. The camera work of this last section is excellent. The water flows, the fish waver in the stream, and a fisherman in dark green who might or might not be Michael Hordern or Ted Hughes stands thigh-deep in the distance. We see lyrical examinations of moss and fern and lichen, and hear a woman's voice speak knowledgeably of undisturbed woodland. The camera dwells lovingly on a magnified close-up of a tree trunk, at the strange calligraphy of nature and time, then pulls back to show the whole great ancient oak by the running water, encrusted, fringed, dripping with creepers, sprouting exotic ferns like orchids from its generous branches. It is stag-crested, but will live for many years more, and it is host to a multitude of life, the woman explains. The colours of ferns and lichens and mosses astonish with their richness, their clear and subtle profundity: gamboge, ochre, deep rust red, silver grey, velvet orange, luminous green, dark olive, emerald, goblin scarlet. The camera moves to a bird, a dipper, standing on a stone and flirting its wings, then pans downstream to the packhorse bridge of Tarr Steps, which strides across the Barle with broad crooked feet like a prehistoric reptile's. Everything is composed by time and man and nature into a knot, a vortex, a pact of harmony.

Charles switches off the sound, and superimposes upon the picture some instant Global News. Over the flowing river appear newly calculated statistics of crime and violence in the inner cities, and predictable telespeak protestations of imminent action from the Home Secretary. Charles watches this combination with satisfaction. It is artistic. He has made it. It occurs to Charles that we do not really need a Home Secretary any more: we could just programme a machine to issue statements, and another machine to issue equally predictable Opposition statements.

The river is subtle, supple, infinitely varied. No two days in time, no two minutes in time of its long, long history have ever been, will ever be repeated. Its patterns flicker, alter, flow, and each moment is unique.

Charles drinks his beer, finishes his cold French fries, belches, gets himself another whisky to settle his stomach. The evening wears on. The walls of the room are pastel, the bed is pastel quilted, the prints are bland. A mild, repetitive geometry prevails.

Charles can no longer pay attention to one source of information at a time. He is Modern Man, programmed to take in several story lines, several plots at once. He cannot quite unravel them, but he cannot do without the conflicting impulses, the disparate stimuli. Perhaps he hopes the alcohol will simplify them, will stick them together and fuse them all into one consecutive narrative. The narrative of his own life, of his place in the history and geography of the world.

By one in the morning he has had enough of the machinery and of the reassuring décor, and is forced to contemplate his fate. Muslim extremists, the Koran, hostages, armaments. He knows fuck all about it.

All the programmes he's seen, all the reports he's read, have explained nothing. They are all biased, inevitably misinformed. How can one know what's going on in the mind of another culture? Perhaps his contact, the abandoned young diplomat Nigel Bicester, will explain Baldai to him. Perhaps not.

Charles prepares for bed, stumbling around a little in the unfamiliar room, barking his shins on unfamiliar corners. He settles, then reaches into the drawer of his bedside table for the Gideon Bible. Yes, it is there. Charles has resolved, once more, to play the *sortes Vergilianae*. They had done him proud last time. He shuts his eyes, lets the page fall open, and stabs. He does not cheat, although he hopes that if any travellers have ever before picked up this book, they will have given it a merciful bias towards the New Testament.

And it appears that they have. Fate, Chance or Custom has chosen him a fine text. Charles stares at it in wonder. Mark 8: 34, 35. 'Whosoever will come after me, let him deny himself, and take up his cross, and follow me. For whosoever will save his life shall lose it: but whosoever shall lose his life for my sake and the gospel's, the same shall save it.'

These words had been covered by his broad stab of his middle finger. But Charles reads on. Legitimately, he considers.

For what shall it profit a man, if he shall gain the whole world, and lose his own soul?

Or what shall a man give, in exchange for his soul?

Whosoever therefore shall be ashamed of me and of my words in this adulterous and sinful generation; of him also shall the Son of man be ashamed, when he cometh in the glory of his Father with the holy angels.

Charles stares, ponders. This does seem meant for him. He is, after all, supremely, of the adulterous and sinful generation. He acknowledges this, across the centuries. 'What shall a man give, in exchange for his soul?' Thoughtfully, Charles stumbles out of bed, clutching the Bible. He packs it in his hand luggage. Is it a crime, to steal a hotel Bible? Surely not. His need is greater. Maybe, he thinks, as he collapses between the sheets, there is even some absolving message in the volume, for those Bible thieves compelled by the spirit to read on. He will look, in the morning. He is too tired to look now. His eyes shut. Within seconds, he is asleep.

At two in the morning, the hotel fire alarm begins to shriek and wail. Charles wakes, from dreams of fish and rivers. He lies there, listening to the alarm. He can hear doors banging, along the corridor. He decides it is a false alarm. If there were a real fire, there would be more noise. Calmly he goes back to sleep.

Shirley Harper and Robert Holland are standing, arm in arm, in the foresting *fin de siècle* statuary of the Musée d'Orsay. Lithe bronze boys gambol above their heads, placid white marble

matrons pluck classical musical instruments before them, voluptuous asp-bitten nudes writhe and recline to the left of them,
stone lions prowl to the right of them. Shirley is leaning slightly
upon Robert, partly through devotion, partly through shock. The
recent shock to her system has been intense. After ten years of
intermittent love-making and several years of none, she has
rediscovered the body which she had thought for ever lost, her
own body, in which she now hazily, drooping, staggering,
stands. It is more of a surprise to her than Robert's. Indeed,
Robert's solid, fleshly, comfortable self seems in a way no more
than a projection of her own body, of her own desires. This does
not mean that he is not important to her, for he is: he is a
miracle, an intervention, a salvation, she is obsessed by his
presence. But only in so far as it relates to her, serves her,
delivers her. There he is, a solid person, more solid than bronze
or marble or travertine. She leans on him. She needs him, for her
own purposes.

She does not really see the statues, the paintings, the vast
well-displayed canvas of decadent Rome, the huge arched ceiling
of solid rosettes, the walkways, the Parisian crowds. She sees and
does not see. She has never frequented galleries and museums, it
is surely too late to learn now. She is here because Robert
wished to come here. She has no wishes of her own. She drifts. It
is Thursday evening, the museum's late night. She has spent the
day, while Robert was at work, pottering around the neighbourhood, looking at the cafés, the bundles of brown rags in the
gutters, the crawling spined crabs of the fishmonger, the arrays
of vegetables, the children on their way to and from school. It is
a homely district: the fifteenth *arrondissement*, Robert tells her,
but that does not mean much to her. It could be anywhere,
north, south, east or west.

She has had an unsatisfactory but friendly encounter with
Madame Lambert, the concierge, who wears a flowered apron

such as women used to wear in Northam once, in Shirley's girlhood. She has tried to take a bath, and failed, for even by daylight the attachments are serpentine, unmanageable, the bath too narrow even for her slim hips. She has glimpsed, from afar, the Eiffel Tower. And now she is in the Musée d'Orsay, which Robert tells her is new, a newly opened renovation of an old railway station. Some of the paintings are famous. Even Shirley recognizes them. Van Gogh, Toulouse-Lautrec, Gauguin, Monet. She stands now in front of an unfamiliar Bonnard nude. The nude is lying flat on her back on an unmade bed, her legs spread, her hair dishevelled. Shirley shifts her weight from foot to foot. Her feet are killing her. And she is numbly sore, within, from the two nights and one evening of sexual intercourse. There is a dull ache in her lower back. A voluptuous, pleasant, womanly ache.

Is Shirley shocked by her own behaviour, is she surprised to find herself making love to a stranger in a strange city, less than a fortnight after her husband's death? She is not quite sure. On balance, she thinks not. Shirley's life may have seemed orderly, over the last twenty years, but it has not been quite as orderly as it has appeared. For example, Shirley, unlike Susie Enderby, has committed adultery several times, has earned her credentials as a member of the sinful and adulterous generation. It has nearly always been with the same man, it is true, but that does not make it more acceptable: in fact, as the man in question is her brother-in-law Steve, it makes it considerably less so. Steve, as a boy, had always fancied Shirley and she herself had been un-decided: there had been times when it had not been clear which of the brothers she would eventually favour. Her choice, over the years, had seemed to her increasingly arbitrary. Why Cliff, why not Steve? Steve himself had put this question to her one afternoon in the 1960s, at a cousin's wedding reception, inspired by champagne, and Shirley had found her heart beating, her lightly rouged cheeks burning, her whole body suddenly throbbing and melting under her new wide white-collared prim revealing low-cut floral summer dress: Steve had leant forward, touched her bare neck gently with his fingers, and they had wandered off together under the trees, away from the marquee and the wedding guests, had kissed and embraced, then had driven off recklessly to the old quarry, and spent twenty minutes fucking under the hot sun. 'I've wanted to fuck you for years, Shirley,' Steve had said, astonishingly, as he struggled with her tights and clutched at her bare buttocks, 'I've thought about fucking you for years.' Shirley had never heard this word used in earnest, and it thrilled her far more than Steve's revelation of persistence of amorous intent. It thrilled her so unmistakably that Steve got the message at once, and repeated it more and more insistently in her ear until he breathlessly collapsed on top of her. It was a word that reminded Shirley of the bad girl she had wanted to be, had believed herself to be, before she grew up and became a housewife and mother of two. Cliff's two. Did it remind Steve, too, of another self? Surely so, surely. They returned to the wedding party, wordless, before anyone had noticed they had gone, Shirley's stiff glazed cotton dress a little crumpled, but her hair demurely combed, her face retouched, relipsticked: Steve also a little crumpled, his tie loosened from the heat, but nobody saw save Shirley, for everybody was overheated, tipsy, merry, Bacchanalian, ungartered. (Well, almost everybody: Mrs Harper had been closely observant, but luckily Cliff, Steve and Shirley had not observed her observance.)

Shirley had never regretted this experiment, this recalling of a lost option. She and Steve had repeated it several times, when opportunity and mood coincided. It had not affected their social relations, or Shirley's respect for Steve's plain wife Dora, to whom, she was certain, Steve never used bad language, body language. It didn't seem to have anything to do with anything, it was neither right nor wrong, it had been what it was, a celebration of what might have been. It wasn't even an affair, and when it was over Shirley blotted it from her memory completely, and hoped Steve had too. It came to an end, an unspoken but recognized end, when Shirley decided to have another baby: she threw away her diaphragm, coerced her husband Cliff, went off to Paris on a Weekend Special, became pregnant with Celia, and announced her pregnancy to the world. Steve listened, as a member of that world, offered congratulations, and reverted to his old role of brother-in-law, friend, do-it-yourself adviser. He and Shirley continued to meet, frequently, at family events, in one another's houses. No *frisson* had passed between them for many years, but a fondness, perhaps, remained. Shirley, when she thought about it at all, hoped so. Steve was a decent chap, a kind man. She sometimes asked herself, a little jealously, if he had found another woman, into whose hot ear he could whisper bad words. Maybe he had: he looked reasonably content, more content than Cliff. Cliff had never known about her and Steve. Or so Steve and Shirley assumed. Although now, standing in the Museum, as shadowy remembrances of her past sexual self, her now resurrected self, flickered through Shirley's wheeling mind, she wondered, for a moment. Had Cliff known, all along? Known, and kept his mouth shut, and died silently? Had he smelled strange body odours, overseen illicit glances?

She dismisses these doubts, these questions from the past, and returns to the dizzy present.

And dizzy is the word for it. She is feeling odd, odder than she has felt since she first ran away from home. Insistent sexual activity (for Robert never seems to tire), unaccustomed food, and far more drink than usual have made her weightless, airy, wild: her eyes cannot focus on the statues, the paintings. Everything is at once heightened and fuzzy, bright and soft and explosive. She sails on a high erotic dream.

It is all magic. Robert has cast a spell upon her, or so she tells him. A spell would excuse all bad behaviour, condone all licence. The night before, she had felt slightly faint in the street, as they walked towards the little brasserie for their unassuming dinner: she had stumbled, and nearly fallen, and recovered herself, and had to stand and lean against the wall to catch her breath. Robert, all solicitude (for this was his role) had marched her into the pharmacy on the corner, and demanded a potion, a restorative potion, from the *pharmacien*. And the tall, thin, grey goat-bearded magician had gone off and mixed a pale green-grey chalky draught in a little conical medicine glass. 'What *is* it?' Shirley had wanted to know, giggling a little hysterically as it was pressed upon her. 'It's a French medicine. Never you mind what it is. It will do you good. Knock it back,' said Robert.

And Shirley had knocked it back. It was bitter, digestive, comforting. 'What on earth *was* it?' she asked again, as they wandered out to the street and on to their café.

'It was an aphrodisiac, of course,' said Robert. 'What else would you expect, from a man like that, in Paris?'

And they had both laughed, and staggered on, to their little Parisian supper of *jambon de Paris, salade de tomates et frites*, to Robert's friend Stukeley, who had become a regular in their lives – Neighbourhood Character, Witness, Wedding Guest.

And now here she was in the Musée d'Orsay, staring at Bonnard's *Femme assoupie*, and thinking of sex. It would be difficult to think about anything else in front of so blatantly erotic a painting. She wonders if she is 'in love' with Robert, or he with her. Probably not. No, he is using her as a bizarre revenge, to bury the corpse of Amélie, as she is using him to bury Cliff. Cliff and Amélie had been the prime movers in this affair, they had taken the initiative, and Shirley and Robert were obediently, helplessly potion-charmed, irresponsible, drifting and surging, directionless, in their wake.

The woman lies, exhausted, satisfied, her legs spread wide, one knee bent, forming a triangle, a theorem, a proposition. The dishevelled bed is like a map of the whole world.

Shirley experimentally takes off her shoes, and stands in stockinged feet on the cool flat rosy slabs. The sensation is delicious.

'Tired?' asks Robert. No, no, says Shirley, although she is, and he knows that she is. They move on, paying scanter attention to the paintings that solicit them, and descend through the lower galleries. And at the entrance to the Moreau room, Shirley sees someone that she knows. She turns away quickly, thinking she has not been seen.

The coincidence of this near-encounter is not as extreme as it might appear, for the woman she recognizes is an art historian, and where else should one expect to see art historians but in art galleries? She is Esther Breuer, friend of Shirley's sister Liz Headleand. Esther is accompanied by a man whom Shirley does not recognize, although Robert Holland does. Robert pretends not to see him. Everybody pretends not to see everybody. Shirley had once, on one of her rare rain-avoiding visits to the National Gallery, seen Esther give a lecture on Neapolitan art and the treatment of the subject of Judith and Holofernes. She cannot remember a word of the lecture, but she remembers the occasion well, and recalls it now.

Shirley and Robert move on, along the main concourse, towards the exit.

'Do you know who that was?' asks Robert.

'No, who?' says Shirley, guiltily, wondering how well Robert knows Esther, and whether he also by some disastrous misfortune knows Liz.

'That was Robert Oxenholme, Minister for Sponsorship,' says Robert Holland.

'Oh, really?' says Shirley, relieved. She has never heard of Robert Oxenholme. And they continue to make their way through the lofty halls, towards the taxi, the tomato salad, the steak and Stukeley, as Esther and her Robert linger in front of Moreau's ambiguous, quaintly obscene, well-endowed Jason, who is trampling on a small feathery monster. Jason's penis is tied up in a large pink silk ribbon, like a birthday present, and the sorceress Medea stands behind him with an expression of half-amused expectation.

Half an hour later, Esther Breuer and Robert Oxenholme settle into their little green basketwork chairs in the museum dining-room, in front of a reserved table covered with starched napery. Overhead, the chandeliers glitter. The waiters are attentive. Esther slips off her shoes, under the table: she too has Museum Foot, though not as badly as Shirley, for her shoes are soft and flat, not high and pinching.

'I think,' says Esther, as a waiter covers her diminutive lap with damask, 'that I saw Liz's sister, somewhere down there.'

'Really?' says Robert, without hesitation, as he reaches for the wine list.

'I *think* so,' says Esther. 'Rather surprising, really. One wouldn't expect to see her here. And she seemed to be with a strange man.'

'Then you'd better not tell Liz,' says Robert Oxenholme, pondering the vintages of white burgundies. He is not really interested in Liz or her sister. And neither, at this moment, much, is Esther. She has other things on her mind. One of them is Robert Oxenholme, who has just asked her to marry him, and the other is the museum itself, which she has just seen for the first time. What does she make of it, what does Robert make of it? Do they agree that the impressionists and post-impressionists are ill hung? Do they think there is too much junk, too much kitsch, too many multicoloured onyx and marble maidens? What do they make of the architectural conversion? What will they make of this restaurant and their approaching dinner? The view, they agree, is beyond reproach. The Seine flows beyond and beneath their repast.

'This restaurant is frightfully expensive, Robert,' says Esther, peering at the list.

'Is that a criticism or a complaint?' he asks.

'Well,' says Esther. 'I'll say one thing for this Museum. I haven't seen a single sponsorship advertisement. Not one. Nothing about Degas by courtesy of Dunlop tyres, or Maillol sponsored by Michelin, or Renoir by Renault, or any of that kind of stuff you have to pretend you're so keen on. The French spent government money on this. Is that right?'

'What about a Meursault, for a change?' asks Robert.

'Well, am I right or not?'

'There were many donations,' says Robert vaguely. 'In lieu of inheritance tax. It's a different system.'

'Donations,' says Esther. 'Yes. From artists and collectors. From the Redons, not the Renaults.'

'Those Redons are amazing,' says Robert, distracted. 'Amazing.'

And they talk, for a while, about the paintings. The meal proceeds, discreetly, smoothly. The lights of the city shimmer in the dark flowing water. Esther and Robert are both Italian Renaissance scholars, after their fashion: art nouveau, symbolism, the *fin de siècle* are not their field, but they enjoy wandering in a foreign land, and they are still under a strong enchantment. Robert talks well, about painting: he does not spend all his time discussing cost-effectiveness and subsidies and admission prices and lighting, although Esther teases him about these preoccupations. He likes the paintings, he understands them. He does not see them as walls of money. Esther wonders, if she marries Robert, will life proceed smoothly, well attended, into old age and the next century, the next millennium? With waiters and white burgundy at beck and call? It is a seductive prospect, and Robert knows it. But there are great gaps in their friendship, great holes and absences, subjects of which they never speak, cannot speak. Will it do? Can she have any faith in the fact that Robert seems to think it will do?

Now Robert is talking about the Puvis de Chavannes and Augustus John. The poor fisherman. It is a great painting, he says. The greatest portrait of poverty ever painted. He enthuses. The poor fisherman, with his sad rod at a sad angle. Impotence incarnate. The little boat, the flat water, the babe among the flowers on the shore. The discretion of the sacred, the high horizon. The resignation, the patience. He speaks of John's gypsies, of Gwen John's portraits of Dorelia, of Harold Harvey's Cornish fishwife.

Esther watches him. He is charming, he is rich, he is well connected, he is intelligent, he has a good job, he has a sort of title, he has curly hair, he shares her interests, and he is interested in marrying her. Why?

Esther has never been married. She cannot imagine what it would be like. The risk-taking part of her, the Bohemian freelance part of her, is attracted, perversely, to this gamble, to this gamble of security. She who has never covered her bets, never secured her interests or insured her life or possessions or committed herself to any one person – shall she not take the greatest risk of all?

She cannot decide whether marrying Robert would be taking a risk or throwing in the sponge. And if the sponge, *what* sponge? Is the sponge Elena Volpe, the woman with whom Esther has been living for the last year in Bologna?

Esther does not know. She does not wish to be moved by the fact that life with Elena in Bologna has been less than easy. She had looked upon Bologna as a forbidden dream, had succumbed to its temptations with a slight guilt, seduced by the architecture of the city and the gracious ardour of Elena's protestations. She had abandoned for Bologna and Elena her flat off Ladbroke Grove and a life of austere eccentricity, of solitude and concentration, of a narrow clear depth. But what she has embraced is neither soft nor simple. Or not, at least, for her. She is too old to learn new ways. Elena is young, still in her thirties, a fully paid-up, radical-feminist-lesbian-Marxist. It is easy for her. But for Esther it is impossible.

Had these options been available when she was young, Esther thinks she might have chosen them. Might have led a happier, richer, more 'normal' life. A less devious, more deviant life. But they were not available, and it is too late now, and Elena — well, yes, Elena *irritates* her.

Will Robert Oxenholme start to irritate her soon? Any minute now, perhaps? How can one tell?

He has assured her that they need not have a conventional marriage, a humdrum monogamous marriage. She will be free, he will be free.

Then why marry at all, she had asked. And he had answered, devastatingly, 'for fun'.

Esther, feeling for her shoes under the table, suddenly longs for her dark little London flat, with its red room, its blue room, its dying palm, its view over a dank unweeded garden, and its murderer upstairs. But it has gone, it has been demolished. She is homeless now, her boats are burned. She will have to wander on to the end of time. Of course she cannot marry Robert. Nor can she go on living with Elena. Where shall she go?

Robert is finishing off his pudding. He looks pleased with himself. He enjoys paintings, and he enjoys his food, and he enjoys the company of Esther Breuer. He has put himself on offer. There he is. Well polished, cultivated, not too heterosexual, *fin de siècle, fin de millennium* Man. He is on offer, but what is the price? There is no tag, no label. What will Esther have to pay for

187

this smiling bargain, if she takes it? What would it cost, to become the Honourable Mrs Robert Oxenholme?

Howard Beaver has told Alix that he has made her his literary executor, but he will not show her his will.

'I don't think that's fair,' said Alix. 'I refuse. You can't make me an executor without my consent. Can you?'

'I told my solicitor you were delighted,' said Beaver.

'Well, you can tell him different. Take my name off. I won't do it.'

'Don't be sulky, Bowen. You'll find it's to your advantage.'

'I don't want your money. Or your manuscripts. I've had enough of your manuscripts. I'm up to my ears in them. It just means more trouble. I bet you've left some ridiculous bequests that will mess up my declining years.'

'I'm going to live for ever, anyway, so the question is academic,' he says.

'Hma!' snorts Alix. She decides to take the offensive. The moment is ripe. 'Beaver,' she says, threateningly, putting down her thick white cup noisily in its chipped saucer.

'Yes?'

'I don't believe you *ever* worked on *transition*. I've looked through the complete run, and there's no mention of you at all. Anywhere.'

She stares at him. Does he look guilty? He stares back.

'I was only the tea boy,' he says after a while. 'They don't list tea boys, in the credits.'

'I thought you said you were assistant editor. In that interview you gave on Radio 3.'

'Did I?'

'According to the transcript.'

'All right,' he says. 'I was only there for a month or two. I admit it. So what?'

'And what *did* you do in Paris?'

'None of your business. I had a job. I worked.'

'But not on *transition*.'

'Not for long.'

Alix sighs. She can never get a straight answer from him about Paris. There is some mystery there, some deliberate obfuscation. She continues to open his post, using a hideous crudely carved wooden African paper knife. Given to Beaver by a fan. Or so he says. But how can one trust a word the old chap utters? He is looking ghastly today, his eyes are bloodshot, the lower lids droop to expose a yellow-white fleshy inner rim. He has been annoyed by a letter from a literary charity, begging for a manuscript or a legacy. Well, he is pretending he is annoyed. Really, he is flattered.

She lays aside various items of junk mail and attacks a more promising crisp white envelope with a handwritten address. It contains an invitation from Fanny Kettle. AT HOME, 7.30 ONWARDS, it says. She smiles at it, hands it over.

'Whoever are Ian and Fanny Kettle?' he wants to know.

'He's an archaeologist. She's a bit crazy, I think. But he's a proper archaeologist. He did those chariot burials at Eastwold. You've got his books. You may even have read them.'

'Have you been invited?'

'Yes. We got ours this morning too.'

'Will you go?'

'Maybe.'

'I think *I* will,' says Beaver. 'You and Brian can take me along. I could do with an outing. What do they drink, the Kettles?'

'Quite a lot, I should think.'

'Well, I'll come along with you.' Alix looks fierce. 'If you'll let me. Please,' he adds.

'Oh, all right,' says Alix. She gets up, puts the invitation on the mantelpiece, by the tea caddy.

'La Tène burials. *Viereckschanzen.* The only ones in the country,' meditates Beaver. 'Do you know what that chap Hardwick argues? He argues that there was a ritual element involved in the filling in of Iron Age wells with old bones and domestic rubbish. What do you say, Bowen?'

'I say, rubbish,' says Alix. 'No more ritual than the contents of your dustbin. Did Mrs Phillips come yesterday? No? I thought not. Why don't you get a proper home help? I do enough washing up at home.'

'I wonder if your friend's sister fell down a well,' says Beaver, provocatively. 'Still no news of her, you say?'

'Not a word,' says Alix, rather snappily. She cannot help feeling that others, perhaps even Liz, feel that she, Alix Bowen, is somehow responsible for Shirley Harper, somehow concerned in her fate, which seems to Alix absurd: just because they now live in the same city and have supped together once or twice, does that make Alix Shirley's keeper? Has she got to be *everybody's* keeper? She hardly knew the woman.

'Are you going to send anything to the begging authors?' she asks, to change the subject.

'We could send them a poem,' he said. 'Just one poem. We could send them the manuscript of that one you found the other day. "The Druid's Egg." I quite like that poem. It should be worth a few bob. First published in *Horizon*, I think.'

Alix shakes her head, but says nothing. It certainly didn't appear in *Horizon* — more likely *Penguin New Writing*, she thinks, but she hasn't tracked it down yet.

'And what was a Druid's egg?' she wants to know.

'Who knows? An oak apple? A dried puff ball? It's from Pliny. Story of a defendant in a lawsuit who was found to have a Druid's egg on his person in court.'

'What would he have that for?'

'Witchcraft. Didn't do him much good. They executed him.

And who was more superstitious, he that had it in his pocket, or they that chopped off his head?'

'So *that* was what your poem was about. Thanks for the gloss. I sometimes wonder why I bother to read poetry at all.'

'You haven't read your Pliny? It's charming stuff.'

Alix shrugged. 'Not really, no. Only bits and pieces. Here and there.'

'Nobody ever reads more than bits and pieces. No need to. A magpie mind, that's what you need to make poems. A bit here, a bit there. Little nests, little pickings. You don't want a world view. Just scraps.'

Alix and Beaver smile at each other. They enjoy such discussions. 'Of course,' pursues Beaver, provocatively, 'it's different if you're a novelist. Like your Brian. You need structure if you're a novelist. Narrative sequence. Solid chronology. All that kind of thing. How's Brian's novel coming along?'

Alix continues to smile and does not answer. No answer is expected. She rocks her chair back, puts her knees against the table, balances.

'Beaver,' says Alix, 'were you reading Lucan, in 1981? A little blue two-volume edition from the Lit and Phil? Translated into heroic couplets by Rowe?'

Beaver ponders.

'I can't remember,' he says. 'Would you like it to have been me?'

Alix gives the question some thought. 'I don't know,' she says, finally. 'If it *was* you, then that would be nice, because it would mean that it was a small world, and I know you, and you know me, and we both know Lucan, and here we are sitting talking about him though he's been dead two thousand years. That would be nice. But if it wasn't you, then there would be a third, somewhere. A third reader of Lucan. Whom we don't know. Or may not know. Or may know. And that would be nice too.'

191

'Maybe we'll meet him at Kettle's party,' says Beaver. 'We could go round Kettle's party, asking after Lucan.'

'Beaver, you *are* sexist,' says Alix.

'What do you mean? Explain.'

Alix explains.

Alix drives towards the evil Angela with even more reluctance than she felt when driving towards Paul's father. Paul's father had always been cast in her mind as a non-entity, and so he had proved to be. Nobody, at the trial or the post-mortems of the trial, had found anything much to say about Paul's father: butcher he may have been (and that had caused some speculation) but of cattle, not men. The defence had tried to make something of Paul's motherless boyhood, but neither Paul nor his father had co-operated very fully in this version of his evil genesis. Alix instinctively believed in it, but now she was about to put her theories to the test, she felt nervous, anxious. She was frightened of the prospect of Angela.

Paul was very unfrightening, and it was not only the top security of Porston Prison that made him seem so. His victims had not found him frightening either, until too late. He had killed quickly, quietly. Mercy killing. He had been much more turned on by the posthumous butchery. The revenge on a passive, silenced, uncomplaining sacrifice. The *tête coupée*, the augury, the slab. And the law in its wisdom had found him of sound mind. Paul was distressing rather than frightening. He instilled sorrow, not fear. Sorrow for human suffering, for human distress, for waste, for error.

All evil is error, some believe. Nobody knowingly chooses evil. This is not a wild theological heresy, it is a tenable philosophic position. As we have seen, it haunts Alix.

She drives north to Hartley Bridge by a route that is shorter and simpler, if less well planned, than the route that took her to

Toxetter. As it is a rural route, avoiding the great industrial conurbations that straddle the middle of upper England, she is not here provoked into much political thought about the nature of the north and How Britain Votes, and you may be spared her occasional reflections on these themes, for this is not a political novel, and anyway her reflections are repetitive and do not seem to be getting her anywhere very fast. Of more relevance to our present theme are her musings on butchers, Sir Thomas More, Bernard de Mandeville and vegetarianism, prompted by a bite of sesame-seed bar taken as she leaves the flat moor, passes the turning to Porston, and enters the northern dales. Had not More forbidden butchers in his Utopia, on the grounds that the butchering of animals brutalizes men? She thinks of the mild Bill Whitmore, the wax-pale Paul. Subdued to the trade we work in. Casual brutality taken for granted. Surgeons' jokes. Perhaps Paul really wanted to be a surgeon, and had just taken a wrong turning, by, as it were, mistake?

She could not recall how More had solved the problem of meat in his Utopia. He had not, she thought, been a vegetarian, a proto-Shavian. He had probably proposed the delegating of such tasks to slaves or criminals. Disappointing, really, the past, the way it kept begging questions. Give to those already outside the law the jobs that would otherwise drive them outside it. 'Athens Without Slaves': wasn't that a title she'd seen in a catalogue recently?

More's Solution did not seem quite fair, to Alix.

It came to Alix that More himself had had his head chopped off, and that his daughter had collected it from the spike where it had been exposed on London Bridge, and preserved it in spices until her death. Or so the history books said. But this could surely have nothing to do with anything, except to remind one that severed heads were a commonplace of history, of history much more recent than that of the Celts. Remember Madame

Tussaud's. A morbid fascination. These days, Alix sees severed heads wherever she looks. She collects them. Morbidly. They pop up like King Charles's head in the memoir of Dickens's Mr Dick.

No, not a political novel. More a pathological novel. A psychotic novel. Sorry about that. It won't happen again. Sorry.

Alix leaves the A64, turns on to a B road. The territory seems dimly familiar to her, from school outings of yesteryear. Memories are stirred, beneath the threshold of consciousness. Blackberry picking, wading in a stream, singing in a coach. But Alix is too agitated to allow these pleasant associations to surface from the past. She has reason to be nervous. Angela Whitmore Malkin is not expecting her, has not replied to her letter. Alix knows she will not. That she has no wish to be dug up. She will not be pleased to see Alix, to hear Alix speak of her son Paul. Alix has told nobody of her journey. She has not told Brian, or Sam, or Beaver, or Liz. This is a secret expedition. She can fail silently, if she judges it expedient to fail, and nobody will ever know she has lost her nerve at the last moment. This is only a reconnaissance trip, she tells herself. If she finds anything horrid, she can drive away and think again. Like Julius Caesar, returning from the conquest of Britain. She can recoup her forces, replan her attack.

Alix Bowen has got Roman Britain and severed heads on the brain. To the right of her lies Parisi country. Ahead of her, the heartland of the Brigantes. And Utopia, the Promised Land, where is that? Perhaps, she thinks, disconsolately changing gear as she approaches a steep bend, it would be wiser to scrap the whole human experiment. Let it blow up or die of the plague. That was what Stephen Cox had sometimes suggested. Stephen had seen Pol Pot's venture as a sort of final testing. A failed testing.

I feel sick, said Alix to herself, as she tried to dislodge bits of sesame seed from her ageing teeth and receding gums. I feel sick, and I am a coward.

She sings to herself, to keep her courage up. 'Now it is the brave man chooses, While the coward stands aside', she sings, loudly, from one of her favourite hymns from those long ago days when she and her schoolfriends picnicked in this pleasant pale-green dale. It is a lurid hymn: she is surprised they were allowed to sing anything quite so strong.

> By the light of burning martyrs,
> Christ, thy bleeding feet we track,
> Toiling up new Calvaries ever
> With the Cross that goes not back.

A very *odd* hymn really for nice little girls and boys to sing.

> Some great cause, God's new Messiah,
> Offering each the bloom or blight,
> And the choice goes by for ever
> 'Twixt that darkness and that light.

And the choice goes by for ever ... yes, she had liked that extremism, but of course it isn't quite so, the choice *keeps on beckoning*, the cross *keeps on beckoning*, one never knows if one has irrevocably chosen darkness or light, there is no relief, no remission, no luxury of despair or damnation, even Paul Whitmore struggles on in his darkness, after so many choices, so many damning choices, hoping for salvation, hoping for light, hoping for grace, hoping for explanation, hoping to rejoin the human race.

And here, suddenly, too soon, is Hartley Bridge, a little town – a village, really – huddled round a humpbacked bridge over the Hart, and there, half a mile up the hill on the other side, as the

195

Ordnance Survey map had promised, is the turning to Hartley Court. A white wooden board announces HARTLEY COURT in large lettering. The lettering was larger than one might expect for a private house. A cattle grid and a gravel drive wound back uphill from the road, through a copse of bare, straggling trees.

Alix sensed that the drive expected visitors: was Hartley Court perhaps an institution – a retirement home, a nursery garden, a prep school? If so, snooping would be a great deal easier. Alix's courage rose, slightly, and she drove on. Up the gravel, up to the forecourt of a rather imposing white-plastered early-nineteenth-century house, with little pillars and a curious first-floor balcony. There were two parked cars, but there was nobody about. The garden was large, adequately but not well kept: a patchy lawn dotted with not very well-grouped daffodils stretched down to a muddy pond, and high banks of shrubs backed the house and concealed what looked like acres of outbuildings. Alix sat in her car and stared around her. What next? Should she get out and bang on the door?

The front door was imposing. Painted white, studded, with a polished brass knocker in the shape of a woman's head with flowing locks, a gleaming brass letter-box, an octagonal brass knob of unusually large proportions. In the outdoor porch stood a boot-scraper and a tub planted with narcissi. Was Angela a housekeeper? A mistress? Both?

It was tea time. Alix decided to brave the door. Surely the place would not engulf her like Castle Despair, and never spew her out again? Though it was in some faint as yet indiscernible way sinister, and not only by association with the crimes of P. Whitmore. Alix could not work out what gave the scene a slight uneasiness until she opened her car door, and heard the barking. Had she provoked it, or had it been going on all the time? It was now unmistakable, growing louder and louder, a chorus of barking, from several directions, a barking and a rattling of chains, a scratching and a scrabbling, from within and around the house. Standing and looking now beyond the house, up the hillside at the steeply raked back garden, Alix spotted a huge cage. It was rattling with big dogs. They were leaping and throwing themselves at the wire. Mastiffs. Bulldogs. Something like that. Boxers. Huge, angry, hungry dogs.

Alix shivered, reasoned with herself. It is a kennels, a boarding-house for dogs. A dog breeder's. Of course, of course. She sniffed the air. The very air stank of dog.

Alix marched up to the front door, and rang the bell. The knocker, a female *tête coupée*, smiled gravely and impassively at her. It was a common design, the same design that Liz had had in Harley Street, had repeated at St John's Wood. Alix had never before thought of seeing it as a Medusa, as a Celtic offering. She thought of Jilly Fox's head, reposing upon her own car seat.

The door opened.

Paul Whitmore's mother Angela was unmistakable. She had a hairstyle of arranged carved red solid waves rising from her square brow. Only a professional could achieve such an effect. Alix blinked, stood her ground. Angela was wearing slacks – a word not much used these days, but slacks these were, in Alix's view. Mauve slacks. And a green large-knit large-stitch jersey over a mauve shirt. A cigarette burned in Angela's nail-varnished fingers. Alix tried to smile, and succeeded. Angela smiled, professionally.

'Mrs Simpson?' asked Angela. 'Come about the two-months bitch?'

Alix half nodded, half shook her head, and stepped slightly forward. She could see a fine entrance hall behind Angela, polished wood, large bowls of flowers, oak tables, oil paintings. No dogs.

'No,' said Alix, her foot well over the threshold, 'I've come about Paul.'

Angela looked away, very quickly, but did not slam the door or summon her hounds. Instead she froze. Her cigarette still burning.

'I'm not talking to you,' said Angela, eventually. 'I've nothing to say.'

Alix looked around at the solid furniture. On one of the dark gleaming tables stood a little vase of primroses. She took heart. From the back regions of the house, a dog began to mourn and wail.

'What a lovely house,' said Alix. 'The flowers are so lovely.'

'I'm not talking,' said Angela.

'Lovely primroses,' said Alix. 'We haven't had many yet, this year, over our way.'

Angela rose to the challenge.

'I don't do the flowers,' she said. 'The Colonel does the flowers.'

'But you do the dogs?'

'Me and Stanley, we do the dogs. And the Colonel. And Dr Everett.'

Right. Got it, thought Alix.

'But if you haven't come about the dogs –' counterattacked Angela. Angela was knocked off guard, unable to change her tack sharply enough, she was still geared for a servile welcome of Mrs Simpson.

'I'd like to *see* the dogs,' said Alix.

'The Colonel and Dr Everett are in London this week,' said Angela.

'But you could show me the dogs,' said Alix.

And Angela showed her the dogs. Well, what is bait, what is stupidity? Throw in a lump of poisoned meat, and you are over the wall.

Alix was appalled by the dogs, but smiled and did not say so. Bull mastiffs, they were, Angela told her, bred by the Colonel and the Doctor. There were cages at the back of the house, outbuildings, stables full of dogs, a warren of servants' quarters full of dogs, cellars full of dogs. The cellarage of the house, opening on garden level at one side, owing to the steep incline, was so vast and high roofed it could have taken in a row of double-decker buses or housed a legion of the Roman army. Instead, it bred dogs. There was a smell of dog and dog meat and dog shit and disinfectant and damp plaster, an overpowering, nauseating stench. Angela moved on, occasionally smiling as she showed off a squeaking blind litter, a prancing pup, a swollen-teated bitch, a slavering sabre-toothed dog. Not all the animals were pleased to see Angela. Some of them cowered in corners at her approach, as though recalling past encounters: others hurled themselves against tough wire mesh at her, ready to renew battle. At these, the unfavoured, she smiled grimly. She kicked one pup quite savagely as it tried to sneak past her into a corridor. They passed a room containing a huge wooden butcher's slab with cleavers. A bunch of unskinned rabbits dangled from a hook.

God's creatures, said atheist Alix to herself as she tried, diplomatically, to praise the dogs. But these were not God's creatures, they were Man's: thoroughbred, overbred, monstrosities. Hideous parodies. This is what Alix thought, as she sat down to tea in the kitchen with Angela Whitmore Malkin. The walls of the kitchen were adorned with portraits of dogs, with photographs and prizes and newspaper cuttings and calendars. China dogs stood on the large dresser, plates emblazoned with dogs hung from brackets, there was even an oil painting of a dog, the largest and most monstrous of all. He was called Axminster Ajax. Alix met his eye coldly.

Over tea, Alix persuaded Angela to talk about dogs and the

Colonel. Everything she said reinforced Alix's sense of having stumbled into a nightmare. These people lived and breathed dogs. It was crazy, it was ugly. What had Bill Whitmore said? 'You'll find it a queer place' — something like that. Yet presumably there were people in the outside world who thought the Colonel and the Doctor and Angela and Stanley quite normal. There was Mrs Simpson, for instance, who might have come, who yet might come about the two-months-old bitch. Alix shivered, as another sporadic burst of barking and howling broke out some-where in the nether regions. What if Angela suddenly went for her with a cleaver, then fed her to the dogs? Not a scrap of her would ever be seen again. She would have vanished utterly, without trace, not a scrap of skin or hair or bone would be left for the forensic scientists to identify.

'Yes, it's a big house,' Angela was saying. 'We keep the front rooms up, but it's hard work. Six years, the Colonel's been here. He's built it up beautifully.'

Angela's voice was harsh, high pitched, monotonous, yet at the same time overlaid and affected. Like the house and its grounds, she presented an uneasy combination of the kempt and the unkempt. Her hair was varnished into its high crown, and she was heavily made up, with green eye-shadow, false lashes, dark red lips, a false complexion imposed upon a natural uneven pallor. But her feet were clad in old scuffed jewelled high-heeled sandals and her slacks were stained. She wore large stud earrings of yellow metal, and a thick yellow metal choker necklace. Her varnished nails were very long — were they false too? A scar ran white and gleaming from her wrist up her inner arm, and vanished into the rolled-back cuff of her shirt.

All Alix Bowen's inherited social prejudices were revived into active play by the appearance of Angela Whitmore Malkin. She had, by Alix's standards, got just about everything wrong.

What on earth am I doing here, wondered Alix once more, as

she braced herself for one more attempt. She didn't even know how to address the woman. She'd tried and failed with Mrs Malkin on the letters. Now, accepting a second cup of tea, she went in on a new tack.

'Mrs Whitmore,' she said, 'I know you don't want to talk about Paul, but I do just want to say how very much he wants to hear from you. He doesn't even know where you are. He says he hasn't heard from you for many years.'

'And you're an interfering nosy little cow,' said Angela, standing up and turning away. 'You can tell that boy, tell him to keep off of me. Tell him to rot in hell. I wish he'd drop dead, I wish they'd do away with him. If you let on where I am, I'll make sure you don't get away with it.'

Angela walked over to the back door, stared out. Alix said nothing.

'I don't want to hear nothing, get it? Nothing. Not a word, not ever. Nobody knows here, and I'm keeping it that way. Who put you on to me? The old man, was it? Look, Mrs Nosy Parker, I've shown you the dogs, and I've given you a cup of tea, and now you get out of here, double-quick, scram, or you'll be sorry you ever set eyes on me.'

Alix finished her cup of tea. She knew this tone quite well, from her years of work with female offenders in the Garfield Centre: sometimes she could deal with it, sometimes she couldn't. She waited. Angela lit a cigarette.

'Look,' said Alix, 'I know it's upsetting for you, and it's not very nice for me either, but if you could just bring yourself to think about Paul, just a little . . .'

Angela turned back into the room. 'Think about that pig? Why should I? When did he ever give a thought to me? Nobody ever gave a thought to me. I've had to take care of myself, I have, I've had to fend for myself, and I'm not having the clock put back, not by anyone.' She glared at Alix, harsh, brittle, malevolent. 'Trying to involve me, aren't you?' she said. 'Well, don't. It's all over, it's all dead and rotten. And don't you try blaming me for anything. Been whining at you, have they, the old man and the pig?'

Alix shook her head. 'No,' she said, 'nobody whined. Paul would like a letter from you. That's all.'

'You go back and tell him I'm dead. That'll be the best day's work you've ever done, you interfering bitch. Tell him I'm dead.'

Alix sighed, pushed her cup away, stood up, reached in her shoulder bag for her driving glasses. 'Well, yes,' she said. 'In the circumstances, that might be the best thing.'

'You do that,' said Angela, pursuing Alix through long corridors to the front door. 'And don't you come back here again, madam. If you do, I'll set the dogs on you.'

Alix, who had been waiting for this phrase, was glad that it was not delivered until she was in sight of her car on the gravel drive. She looked back at the white house, at the caged deformities. She was rather sorry she hadn't been shown the front rooms: she'd have liked to have gleaned a little more about the Colonel and the Doctor.

'Thank you for the tea,' she said, politely.

'I'm warning you,' said Angela, on the threshold.

'I take the warning,' said Alix. 'I'll think about it. Ah, I wonder if this is Mrs Simpson?'

She put her key in the lock, opened her door, as another car pulled up, an estate car, with dog cage bars at the back. Mrs Simpson smiled, waved, as Alix started her engine and prepared to vacate her space: country civilities, middle-class smiles. Angela was obliged to smile too. Tall and fair and pleasant-faced was Mrs Simpson: whatever could she be wanting with a pedigree bull mastiff? Surely she would be happier with a Labrador, or a retriever, or a liver-spotted Dalmatian? But I've done enough interfering for one day, thought Alix, as she set off down the hill towards the cattle grid. Mrs Nosy Parker. Curiosity killed the cat. Alix smiled to herself, but a little shakily, as she turned on the car radio for company.

Charles, on the aeroplane to Baldai, tried to distract himself from fear by pondering the possibilities of a new electronic television game called Collage, which combined unlikely images with unlikely text. Or images with images, perhaps? The fun possibilities of superimposition had surely not yet been properly explored? He recalled the ancient woodland and the giant oak and the flowing Barle. He wondered what sort of television they had in Baldai. Then he moved on to the concept of the sinful and adulterous generation, and tried to count all the women with whom he had ever committed adultery. Should he include those Cambridge undergraduates and that Italian girl? They hadn't been classifiable as adultery, they'd been fornication. No, strictly, he should begin after his first marriage to Naomi. There was that Polish research assistant, and then a girl in Rome, and then – but no, that was later. And then there was Liz – did it qualify as adultery, sleeping with Liz after Naomi's death before he married Liz? And what about that time only last year, when he'd slept with Liz in a hotel in Northam, after divorcing Liz and marrying Henrietta? Was *that* adultery? There were some tricky theological points here. Somehow Charles did not think that this was the kind of thing that Jesus Christ had been speaking of, in Mark 8:35. 'Whosoever will save his life, shall lose it.' That was more to the point. Charles reached, moodily, for the in-flight magazine, for some kind of reassurance, but on flicking it open at random found himself confronted by the not-at-all reassuring image of Henrietta herself, dressed in a khaki shirt and sage-green shorts, with a yellow bandana round her head, posing with her wicked cousin Guy Hestercombe in front of a group of zebra. She appeared to be advertising safaris in Zambia – well, not directly, of course, not commercially, she was merely a decoration added to an article by a travel writer, but there were quotations from her adorning the travel writer's text. 'I've always adored Zambia,' says Lady Henrietta. 'No other African country has its wildlife, its majesty, its richness! And I just love K.K.!' Disquieted, Charles read on: Henrietta, it seemed, had been back here with a group of chums from her old, pre-Charles days, her old Latchett days. One of them was now running a safari business from an address in Princes Risborough. There were photographs of a sacred ibis, a lion, a bright-blue shoebill stork, a hippopotamus-infested lagoon. Henrietta had 'adored' it all! The hot showers! The obliging servants! Tea on the banks of the Zambesi!

Well, well, well. She probably had adored it, in her own way. She liked that kind of thing. She had dragged Charles out to Zambia, during their brief marriage, partly to visit her grand-daughter, partly to get some sun and see some game, and had trailed him round the marshes of Bangweulu and sat him in dug-out canoes and marched him after elusive rhino and, horror of horrors, made him fly in a one-propeller plane with a mad pilot who asked Charles to hold up the map and navigate. Charles had been terrified by the whole trip, terrified. And also slightly disapproving. He didn't much care for the odd upper-class throwback twitches of behaviour that the place brought out in Henrietta (twitches also deplored, he could see, by her daughter and son-in-law). Her manner, there, became even more offhand and dictatorial than it was at home, she shouted at servants and sneered at the food in a way that Charles found distressing, although no one could ever have called Charles a polite man. Her behaviour out in the bush had been acceptable, the straw huts and camp-fires suited her, but the way she carried on in Lusaka and at the Frenches' farm made Charles feel priggish and middle class, indeed it brought out a little of the long-buried egalitarian in him. She took him to watch a polo match (oh, the tedium!), and when that was over she took him to drinks in the clubhouse, where, leaning on the veranda, she inadvertently and drunkenly dropped her cigarette lighter into a thick prickly hedge. 'Shit,' said Henrietta, loudly, and then snapping her fingers, called, 'Here, you, piccaninny!' A small child materialized below the veranda wall. 'Fetch,' said Henrietta. And the small child scrabbled into the hedge, and searched, and eventually emerged, proud, smiling, dusty, scratched, triumphant. 'Catch!' said Henrietta, throwing down a small coin, after the child on tiptoe had reached up smiling and proudly delivered the lighter. The coin fell in the dust, under the prickly hedge, and the child scrabbled again.

And Henrietta laughed.

No, Henrietta in Zambia had not been endearing. Zambia had not endeared her. But there she was again, in her khaki shirt and green shorts, smiling in the sun with that old philanderer Guy Hestercombe. A worthless crowd. Yes, worthless. An adulterous, sinful generation.

Charles felt smug and serious, as he contemplated the frivolous and outmoded follies of his ex-wife and her cronies. He would have felt even more smug and serious had he known that at that moment the postman was delivering to his flat in Kentish Town an invitation which would let him off the hook of all his financial muddles and gambles, an invitation to a salaried post, a serious, acceptable and dignified post. But Charles did not know this, for he was five miles above the earth, spinning eastwards on his way to Baldai.

Mrs Nosy Parker, Angela had called her. On reflection, Alix found she did not like this form of address at all. It seemed undignified yet uncomfortably apposite. A schoolgirl's insult, not the name for an earnest seeker after truth, nor even for a bungling well-wisher trying to restore child to parent, parent to child. Angela had sent her packing with a flea in her ear. No, she had not liked Angela. Angela had been as unpleasant, more unpleasant than the more difficult inmates of the Garfield Centre. Angela seemed more like a hardened criminal than they did. Lacquer and varnish and cringing dogs. Despite herself, Alix continued to wonder about the Doctor and the Colonel.

Alix did not mention her visit to Brian and Sam, although it weighed upon her mind. She watched the television news silently, as policemen with tracker dogs hunted the moor for the buried corpses of long-dead murdered children, as the mothers of these children, prodded and goaded by the press, said they would never never forgive.

Nobody feels sorry for the victims, somebody said, predictably. But this, of course, was nonsense. Anyone with an ounce of imagination, or even without it, felt sorry for the victims, and the families of the victims. But however sorry one (or we) felt, the victims remained dead, buried high on the lonely moor, or burned to white ash in a north London crematorium. Whereas P. Whitmore was alive, in Porston Prison.

Of course Alix was sorry for Paul Whitmore's victims, for those who had had the ill luck to come his way at the wrong moment. That goes without saying. She did not think about them much because she could not bear to do so. Thinking about them served no purpose. One of these victims had been her friend Jilly Fox. Alix had seen Jilly Fox's parents appear on television to express their grief, their loss, their unwillingness ever to forgive. Jilly Fox's parents had refused to give her houseroom after her release from a prison sentence for drug charges. They had driven her back to the Harrow Road and dumped her there. Jilly Fox's parents had been away on a package tour holiday in Marrakesh when Jilly had been murdered, and they had not cut short their week in the sun. Jilly Fox's father was a narrow-minded sadist who had tormented his daughter into drugs, into prison, and to death. Well, that was one way of looking at the sequence of events. Jilly's way. He was the criminal, not Paul Whitmore. Paul Whitmore had been the executioner.

Alix sat and watched television.

That month, in England, a tramp had been burned to death 'for a laugh' by two youths as he sheltered in his cardboard hut.

A man in Hansborough had slept two nights in bed with his girlfriend without noticing she was dead. 'I suppose I must have been drunk,' he said.

A prisoner bullied his cell-mate in Wormwood Scrubs to commit suicide 'because he was a nutter'.

A man was tried for cutting off his girlfriend's mother's head and then murdering a passing stranger with a crossbow. He had put the head on his girlfriend's pillow and tucked the rest of the woman into the bedclothes: 'To give my girlfriend a fright,' he said. He said he did not know why he had killed the stranger on the pavement.

A skinhead 'rent collector' was remanded in custody for terrorizing fellow-squatters and torturing one to death by means of wire, glass and scalding water.

A mother was tried for killing her twelve-month-old baby by putting salt in his bottle. The baby had already been buggered by the forty-four-year-old husband. She admitted cruelty but denied a charge of unlawful killing.

A man was killed when his mates playfully thrust him into the back of a refuse truck: the Vulture beak got him.

A couple of youths attacked an old lady, tied her up, stuffed her in a broom cupboard, and set her house on fire: then they had run away, then they had run back to rescue her, at the risk of their own lives and in certain expectation of arrest and imprisonment. 'I don't know why we changed our minds,' one said.

A woman was raped in a field, then had her throat cut by a

207

gang of five. They slit her throat so that she would not be able to tell on them.

Lavinia, speechless, gushes blood, from mouth and stumps of arms.

Spot the one invented story, if you can. No prize offered.

Brian has never liked *Titus Andronicus*, has always considered it one of Shakespeare's lesser plays.

That night, Alix dreamed of a dog. Not a bull mastiff, but a mongrel dog, an ordinary brown-and-black dog-shaped dog. In her dream, Alix was in charge of it. She was waiting with it, in the vet's surgery. When her turn came, she went in, and a white-uniformed woman took hold of the dog, and before Alix could intervene, sliced off its tail. The dog did not even whimper. It turned to Alix and looked at her with terrible betrayed eyes and hid its head in her wide skirts. Alix comforted the poor sliced bleeding dog. It made no sound, no sound. She held it and held it, as the white-uniformed woman of her dream, the woman with the knife, began to bluff and bluster. And Alix heard herself begin to shout back, with the rage of years of courtesy: she began to shout abuse and condemnation at the monster woman on behalf of the silent, quivering, maimed dog, the poor dog sheltering in her skirts. The poor dog, the harmless poor dog. Alix wept. In her dream, angrily, she wept, and woke weeping.

'Anger is natural,' said Liz to her patient, in patient cliché. 'If you repress it, it manifests itself in these curious forms.'

Liz was paying little attention: his hour was nearly up, and anyway Mr Joby didn't really repay attention, he was a self-pitying bore. Or that is how Liz would have judged him had she met him socially, rather than professionally. She was trying to offload Joby. The sadness of dullness, the dullness of sadness.

Liz herself was still suffering from a bout of anger brought on the night before by a phone call from her eldest stepson

Jonathan. Jonathan had rung, ostensibly about Charles, but had then moved on to the equally dangerous topic of Liz's views on infantile sexuality. How had it come up? Liz, looking at her watch, easing out Joby, bidding him goodbye (or rather, alas, *au revoir*), couldn't quite remember. Had Jonathan heard her most recent radio broadcast? Yes, that had probably been it. And he'd dared to — well, not exactly to tick her off, but to imply that her interest in the topic was an embarrassment to him. To him, Jonathan, personally.

Liz snorted to herself as she began to go through the post on her desk. He had actually *said*, 'Of course, Liz, I know it's a fashionable subject, and you're always on to every new fashion, but I do think you might give this one a miss, when everyone else is making such a dog's dinner of it. You'll only upset yourself.'

'Darling,' said Liz, '*don't* talk to me as though I were a frail old granny with a weak heart. I'm not very easily upset.' And then, remembering that she was, although not frail, a granny, she had changed the subject by asking about Baby Cornelia's teeth.

Every new fashion. Liz pondered these words as she looked through her post. Fashion. Jonathan and Xanthe were fashionable, she supposed, they wore smart clothes, they always had a new car or two, they had a new baby, they had two personally designed bathrooms and curtains that matched their upholstery and they spent a lot of money on eating out and amusing themselves. This is the way people were, these days, and it seemed a little hard to be reproached by Jonathan for being fashionable when she was surely by now (she glanced down for confirmation at her old jersey dress) out of date?

Jonathan, the motherless babe whom she had courted and cajoled and seduced into loving her. Jonathan, who had taught her motherhood, whom she had taught to read. A is for Ant, B is for Bee. *The Lonely Unicorn*, his favourite picture book. (Ah, why, asks her other self. Ah, why?) She could no longer remember the warm softness of him, the butter-yellow scalp smell of his hair, his scuffed knees, his runny nose. He rounded on her now, and accused her.

Of fashion. Well, it was true, in an affluent society there is fashion in crimes and neuroses and diseases, as in clothes and cars and mustards and salad foliages, as in streets and furnishings and flowers and fabrics. And it was also true that child sex abuse had become suddenly, astonishingly fashionable, as a theme for indignation, moralizing, vindictiveness, sensational journalism. Liz herself had been taken by surprise by the violence of this new eruption of the nation's psyche. It was not a subject in which she had been particularly interested: adopted children rather than abused children had been more her line. Fancying herself fatherless, never having known her father, she had adopted adoption as a speciality. But of late, having, as she had thought, located her father, she had changed tack. And was it her fault that the whole nation had changed tack with her? Was she, as Jonathan seemed to allege, somehow guilty of *exploitation*? Because she had anticipated public interest by a few months, because her unfortunate father had anticipated this newly fashionable offence by fifty years?

She could understand Jonathan's resentment. It was not a happy subject, not a wholesome subject. 'Normal' people shied away from it, as they had (and do) from the revelations of Freud. Was Freud right, after all, in his initial assessments of the high incidence of abuse of children by parents? Was this what we were about to have to face? Jonathan certainly would not like it if he had to. And nor would she. She had had erotic dreams about Jonathan, when he was a boy. Had he of her? She had also had erotic dreams of Aaron and of Alan. Human nature. She wondered how Stephen Cox's inquiries into the matter were progressing.

We stare backwards into time, and continue to find new plots, new patterns.

Liz remembered wandering as a small child alone round Woolworth's in Northam, in the crowds, a child so small that she could hardly see what was on the glass-edged metal-jointed counters, in the smell of artificial ice-cream and harsh sugar and sawdust and cheap perfume, a metallic, dangerous, powdery smell which she had loved. Every now and then, as she wandered, she would feel a hand between her legs, tickling her bottom, pressing into her little cleft, and each time she would turn, sharply, to see who was there. And there was nobody there, as in that game of Grandmother's Footsteps, there was nobody there at all, only shabby old men gazing into space way above her head, intent, no doubt, on purchasing dull male commodities like electric plugs or screwdrivers or lengths of wire, ignorant of and indifferent to the little girl in cotton frock and cotton pants that struggled on ahead of them through the human flow. She had never managed to surprise anyone, to catch anyone, even to guess at anyone responsible for that fleeting (and yes, delightful) sensation, so often repeated – maybe, so often sought? Had she liked Woolworth's *because* of the dirty old men?

These thoughts now held no fears for her. They held no fears *because she had thought them.* It was as simple as that. She had woven her father into a plot, a pattern, and allowed him to emerge as harmless, inoffensive, suffering perhaps from some glandular abnormality: a timid man, sexually inadequate, with an unindulgent wife. Not a Horror. Not a Fiend. No, almost normal.

Lauritzen had found that the precipitating behaviour of the 'victim' played an important part in 48.4 per cent of cases of conviction for indecent exposure. (Though the sample, one had to admit, was small and, his critics argued, ill selected.)

Liz had come to terms with the possibilities of her own precipitating behaviour.

211

The thoughts that we have thought hold no fear. It is the unthought that holds us in thrall. Those burned papers, with their secret writing, emerging in the blackened ash, but stuffed down, tamped down, ignored, consumed in the Ideal Boiler. Letters of fire.

What we do not know is what we most know.

We pursue the known unknown, on and on, beyond the limits of the known world. What was that phrase Stephen had used? The fatal curiosity? When we see the Gorgon face to face, we die.

Liz, in her half-hour break before going down for lunch, brooded over these things. The meaning of symbols. The knowing of the unknown. She thought of Alix and the murderer. She thought of Stephen, vanished into Kampuchea. She thought of Cliff Harper, sitting slumped in his car in his garage full of fumes. She thought of her friend Esther Breuer, who had run away from England and the murderer's house of death, away from continuity and fear of continuity, into the unknown – away from, or towards, her destiny? She thought of Shirley, who had run from the face or threat of death, and had perhaps met her own Gorgon by now, at the bottom of a well, in a drowned car, at a cliff's foot. She thought of Charles, on his way to seek the dried husk, the flickering videotaped image of his old enemy, Dirk Davis. She tried to think of the whole human race, on its quest for its own self and its own destruction. The death instinct. For a moment, she encompassed it, she saw it for what it was, in its whole cycle, but then lost it again, her vision failed her, she shrank and sank back into her body, into her consulting room, into her contemplation of the letters on her desk.

Open before her lay a thick white Private and Confidential crested letter from a Lord Rothven, President of the National Child Care Trust, attempting to enlist her advice on how to cope with scandal. Her eyes skimmed once more over the text and subtext. '. . . hope you will not mind . . . enclosed papers relating to the case of ... long associated, now in paid employment of our organization ... you may recall, I had the pleasure of sitting next to you at the Annual Dinner of the Royal College of ... emboldened to approach you by one of our distinguished Vice-Patrons, your friend Hilda Stark ... subject of great delicacy ... perhaps your secretary could ring mine to make an appointment. Yours sincerely ...'

Jonathan would not like this at all. A scandal in high places, a child sex pornography scandal, involving the deputy director of one of our most respectable children's charities. Suspended on full pay. All publicity so far successfully avoided, said Rothven. 'Criminal proceedings inevitable ... your professional advice much valued ... suspected links with the UNICEF arrests connected with the Brussels Research and Information Centre of Childhood and Sexuality ...' And now Lord Rothven and Hilda Stark and all the other rubber-stamp patrons, all the royals and minor titles and captains of industry and television personalities, would have to run around in circles trying to pretend they couldn't possibly have known anything about it, that it wasn't their fault, that nobody ever told them anything.

Rothven's tone was perfectly decent, thought Liz. He wasn't prepared to ditch this guy without a struggle.

Suddenly into Liz's mind swims the image of the young man who had run the cub group Jonathan had once so keenly attended. A poor, virginal paedophile if ever there was one, utterly harmless, utterly recognizable to boys and mothers alike, recognizable to all save himself, and what harm had he done, teaching the children to tie their woggles and shine their badges and run races and fry eggs and light fires and wash their socks? A domestic young man, a devoted young man, with his thin neck and short hair and anxious eyes, a young man who believed in Christianity and clean living and team spirit and comradely communion. The most lonely young man in the world.

213

Maybe all the charities in Britain are staffed by delinquents, deviants, perverts. And what was Hilda Stark doing in this *galère*? Hilda had once been a patient of Liz's, a patient suffering from murderous impulses towards her baby daughter. An actress, a woman in the public eye, a showy woman who looked good on platforms, whose name adorned several fashionable charity appeals. Was it really wise of Hilda to have jumped on this particular bandwagon? Or had she jumped on it *because* of her own murky psychiatric past? After all, the baby daughter was now a strapping netball player with six O-Levels to her credit, and some expensive braces on her large front teeth. Let bygones be bygones.

Poor Lord Rothven, poor Hilda Stark, poor − . Poor all, poor everyone. Crazily pursuing what we most deplore. Who pushes us? Is it a mass psychosis, as Alix sometimes desperately suggests, a Hegelian supermadness that transcends the individual? Hippies at Stonehenge were its victims last year, child sex abusers and social workers this year, and who next? Long-distance coach drivers? Rural estate agents? Drinking housewives or drug-addicted surgeons? Hard not to believe, looking at the gutter press, that there must be *some* transcendent madness, for how could human beings who eat and sleep and shop in supermarkets and have children and use the lavatory ever be party to such persecutions, such witch hunts, now, in the late twentieth century? Is it the fault of Charles Headleand and his like? Have they let the genie out of the bottle, the genie that centuries of civilization and enlightenment had tried to imprison?

Publicity. Press. The new demons of democracy.

The week before, Liz had been seated at a gala dinner of the RIBA at the Goldsmiths' Hall next to a Law Lord who had been involved in the earlier stages of P. Whitmore's trial. She had endured his strong and ill-informed views on the Corbusier exhibition and the new Lloyd's building and the new Tate extension (none of which he had visited), and then had edged him on to P. Whitmore. Here, he had been illuminating. He had of course, he said, been of the opinion that Whitmore was as mad as a meat-axe (he glared at Liz as he said this, as though assuming she would dissent), and that he should not stand trial for murder, but the judge in the case had taken another view. Why? Liz had demurely inquired. 'Because,' said the red but shrivelled little walnut of a man, 'because he wanted his fortnight of glory. The limelight. The press. Oh yes, he wanted his name in the papers, he wanted the limelight.'

He spoke as one who understood this craving. A small old man who knew nothing about Corbusier, but who could distinguish the sane from the criminally insane, because that was his job. And who understood, moreover, the human frailties of his colleagues. The wigs and robes and medals and the ribbons and silver buckles. The headlines. Corruption and vanity. And people call *women* vain, reflected Liz, as she listened to the old lord. He did not ask her a single question throughout the meal. Liz did not mind, much: she was used to banal, self-obsessed monologues. She was a professional listener. Occasionally, as she listened, it had crossed her mind to interrupt him by claiming acquaintance with the infamous Whitmore, but she held her peace and let him talk.

Wigs and buckles. Leaders in the press. And thus it was that Paul Whitmore was incarcerated in Porston Prison, complaining about his vegetarian meals, rather than complaining about similar meals in Broadmoor or Rampton. It probably didn't make much difference where he was. To him. Though the decision had cost the state some money, as the old walnut knew.

The limelight. A curious word. Tidying up her letters, drifting towards lunch, she paused to look it up in her *Pocket Oxford*: 'Intense white light obtained by heating cylinder of lime in oxyhydrogen flame; (fig.) full glare of publicity.' Was that what

Hilda Stark bathed in daily? Was that what P. W. had wanted? And had got? She looked up quicklime. 'Unslaked lime.' No reference to Oscar Wilde or Reading Gaol.

She put the dictionary back on the shelf and stood for a moment irresolute. Into the silence, the telephone rang. Her secretary Vera spoke: there was a Mr Robert Holland on the line, wanting to speak to Liz about her sister, would she take the call? Liz found her mouth had gone dry. 'Yes,' she said. She had a very clearly transmitted picture of Shirley dead, lying in a shallow white outcast's grave.

Fanny Kettle was planning the finer details of her party. She was happy doing this, and her son Tony was happy for her. They sat together at the kitchen-table, surrounded by lists. He liked to see her innocently busy.

'I make it fifty-two acceptances, twelve refusals, and twenty who haven't replied,' said Tony.

'Well, I asked the caterers to do seventy-five, so I guess that's just about right,' said Fanny.

'Did we ever hear from the Duke?' asked Fanny, who knew quite well that we had, but who liked to dwell on such matters.

Tony searched through the pile and found the handsome crested papers. 'A very polite apology from the Duke, he's at a dinner in Manchester, he much regrets. Regrets too from the Marquis of Stocklinch. But Lady Joanna Hestercombe is coming or so she says.'

'Odd, that,' said Fanny. 'I wonder why?'

Tony stared at her thick grey headed missive, but it offered no clue. Lady Joanna Hestercombe, Aspin Court Farm, Stocklinch, it said. Telephone Stocklinch 329.

'I dunno,' said Tony. 'Maybe she likes parties?'

'I wouldn't have *thought* so, from the look of her. Horses are more her thing, I'm told. I wonder if we ought to order some more canapés?'

They checked numbers, the names of delicacies, poring over the glossy brochure of the smart catering firm recommended by one of Ian's television chaps. 'The bacon rolls stuffed with chicken livers sound good,' said Tony, hungrily, cutting himself another hunk of cheddar from the glistening ochre deeply fissured slab at his elbow, 'and the crab claws in garlic dip. Yummy.'

'What *I'm* planning,' said Fanny, 'is a really spectacular drink. It would be fun to start people off with a really exciting *coloured* drink. What do you think, Tony darling?'

He nodded, munching. He was wondering whether Alice Enderby, daughter of Janice and Edward Enderby, would come to the party with her parents. Should he make a point of making sure she was invited, or would Fanny tease him if he did?

'A vodka base, perhaps,' mused Fanny. 'With a little Angostura? Or grenadine? A pale-pink drink would be rather smart, don't you think? And we could give it a special name. Something exotic, something bewildering. Come on, think of something for me, Tony. Something wild and Celtic. Something primitive and primeval. Come on, you know all that archaeological stuff. Who was the Celtic goddess of parties?'

'I don't know if they had one,' said Tony, amused despite himself by his mother's frivolous misapplications of his father's mysteries: Fanny was so outrageous, what could one do but laugh and admire? 'There was a goddess of plenty,' he proffered. 'Would she do? Rosmerta, she was called.'

'Rosmerta.' Fanny tried out the name. 'Rosmerta. Rosmerta. No, I don't think she would do at all. Horrid word. A hurty smurty dirty word. But we're on the right lines. Who else is there?'

Tony ran through what he could recall of the Celtic pantheon: there was a Brigit, the goddess of the Brigantes? Or Sulis Minerva, from Bath? These Fanny rejected as wholly unfestive. Tony couldn't think of any more, so went off in search of

Graham Webster's *The British Celts and Their Gods under Rome*, and started thumbing through the index. Fanny didn't like the sound of any of the Celtic deities. The great Queen Rigatona sounded too like a kind of pasta, she said, and horse goddess Epona sounded bony and snooty. The glossary wasn't much help either. It listed only twenty-eight Celtic words, and none of them would do: *derna, deva, dubo, lem, leuca, maglis, matis* . . .

'Stop, stop,' cried Fanny, '*what* an ugly language, those won't do at all. Look up in the index for anything beginning with *p*. It's to be a pink drink, so something beginning with *p* would do.'

Patiently, Tony turned to the index. 'Pagan, paleolithic, *Pales*, pantheon,' he read. 'Hmm, pagan's not bad, Pagan Pink. Not bad.'

'But read on,' she urged him, 'read on.'

'Phallus,' he read, obligingly. 'Pharsalia.'

'That's it!' she cried. 'Pharsalian! Pharsalian Pink! Brilliant! I can just see it, a beautiful crystal bowl of Pharsalian Pink. A beautiful subtle misty pinky-bluey-smoky pink!'

Tony pointed out that Pharsalia didn't, strictly, phonetically, begin with a *p*. (He did not point out that Fanny's ideal drink colour strangely resembled that of methylated spirits.)

'Never mind,' said Fanny. 'It sounds wonderful. Pharsalian Pink! It's inspired. Clever boy. What does it mean?'

'I think it's the name of a poem,' said Tony, vaguely. His attention had been distracted by the entries for phallus: unobtrusively, furtively turning the pages, he had lit upon an alarming but intriguing drawing of a phallus with wings and legs from a sherd in the Colchester Castle Museum, and another drawing of a very rude frieze in which a pursuing youth spilled his seed upon the ground before reaching his destined maiden. The maiden's gesture in response to this copious premature ejaculation was ambiguous, but, either way, rude. He concealed the page from Fanny's gaze. It was not suitable for Fanny's eyes.

'Pharsalian Pink,' said Fanny. 'Yes, that should get them all going, don't you think?'

'Yes,' said Liz. 'Yes. Yes, I see. Yes. Of course. Yes. Thank you so much for ringing. Of course, yes, I understand. Thank you. Yes, thank you. Goodbye.'

Liz put the phone down. She had said she understood, but she did not understand at all. She could not take it all in. She looked down at what she had written on her note-pad. Robert Holland. Institute of English Studies. 188, rue de Vaugirard. 62 bis, rue de Saussure, 15è. A couple of telephone numbers. Robert Holland. Who on earth was Robert Holland? And what was he doing, in Paris, with her sister Shirley? The whole thing was quite impossible, and the most impossible part of it all was that Robert had sounded so normal, so ordinary, so like the kind of person one might know anyway, so like the kind of chap one has known all one's life. Liz felt dizzy. So Shirley wasn't lying in a shallow grave, she was hiding in a love nest in Paris. How could this be?

'What did she say?' asked Shirley. Shirley was lying back on the uncomfortable striped chaise longue with her feet up on a little pillow, sipping an Alka-Seltzer. She had decided she would have to go home and face the music. She was still feeling very odd – better, mentally, but physically she was coming to pieces. Her stomach was upset, she had a strange stinging bloody vaginal discharge, and a painful boil on her left buttock. She had confided some of these problems to Robert, but not all. She was surprised by how little they worried her. She had no intention of going to see a French doctor. She would go home, instead, and see Dr Peckham. And she needed a hot bath. It was impossible to get a hot bath in Robert's bathroom. She had failed to master the snake-like cantankerous system, and Robert admitted that it

219

was temperamental. She was beginning to yearn for her own well-appointed suburban bathroom. And what about the handle of the downstairs cloakroom lavatory? She hadn't got round to fixing it, had she? She had a dim idea that the handle of the door had killed Cliff. No, it was time she went home.

'She said everybody had been very worried about you. Of course,' said Robert.

Shirley smiled, irresponsibly.

'I bet she wasn't all *that* pleased to hear,' she said. 'I told you she wouldn't care, one way or the other.'

'I don't think that's quite true,' said Robert, cautiously. 'Of course she was relieved to hear you were alive. And well.'

'I'm not well,' said Shirley, shifting her bottom to ease the pressure on the boil. And she laughed.

'So all you have to do,' said Robert, 'is to make your mind up about your car. Whether you want to pick it up on the way or not. Or whether you want to come all the way back with me, to-morrow.'

'I suppose everybody will be very annoyed with me,' said Shirley. 'Whatever I do, they'll be annoyed with me. *You're* not annoyed with me, are you?'

'Of course not,' said Robert, and leant over and grasped her ankle reassuringly. He held her foot and stroked her toes. 'Why ever should *I* be annoyed with you?'

They smile at one another, a smile of complicity, ease, understanding. They are companions in crime, they have managed to avoid expectation, recrimination, commitment. They live in the present, they avoid tension. For the moment, there seems to be no problem in going back to Northam and a hot bath. Let the police and the lawyers and the coroner and her children and her sister mutter and fret and bluster. Who cares? None of it is important. Shirley stretches, yawns. She is perpetually tired. It is a delightful sensation, this tiredness. Her physical discomforts are delightful. Her body swims in a bloody flux, and Robert Holland companionably caresses her stockinged toes.

Some hours after receiving the phone call from Robert Holland, Liz received another phone call from Esther Breuer in Bologna. Esther wished to report that two evenings ago she had seen Shirley Harper in the Musée d'Orsay in Paris. At the time, she told Liz, she had thought this odd, but not very odd: she had now learned from Alix that Shirley had in theory disappeared, so perhaps Liz ought to know her whereabouts?

'Thanks awfully, Esther,' said Liz, 'but in fact I did have a phone call at lunch time today. From the man she's with. Saying she's coming home tomorrow. What a very odd affair. You say you actually *saw* her? Did she see you?'

'I don't know. I sort of think we pretended not to see one another.

'And in the Musée d'Orsay, you say? What on earth can she have been doing there? She's never been to an art gallery in her life. Well, hardly ever. Has she turned into a completely new person? If I hadn't had this phone call from this man, I'd have had to say that I thought you were mistaken. But a man is just as surprising as an art gallery. What did he look like?'

'Quite nice, really,' said Esther. 'Sort of middle aged and pleasant. Yes, pleasant. You know. Not a rapist or a murderer. The kind of person one might ask to dinner. If one asked people to dinner — which I don't.'

'I say,' said Liz, 'do you think Cliff committed suicide because he found out about Shirley and this man?'

'I didn't even know Cliff had committed suicide until Alix told me this morning,' said Esther.

'Well, it's not exactly headline news,' said Liz. 'How should you have known?' And then, a little suspiciously, 'And what *was* Alix phoning you about, anyway?'

'Oh, nothing much, she wanted me to translate some Italian phrases in a letter of Beaver's. And then we got chatting, and I told her she hadn't been able to get me earlier because I'd been in Paris, and then I told her about the Musée and happened to mention I'd seen Shirley . . .'

'And what *did* you make of the Musée?' asks Liz, temporarily distracted. Esther gives her impressions. They chatter on, moving from Moreau to Freud and the Oedipus complex and Vienna and whether or not Hoffmann is right to argue that Freud was wrong to revise his presentation of hysteria. They speak of Paul Whitmore, of Alix's obsession, of Esther's long-dead palm, of Paul Whitmore's curious sympathy for this palm, of what palm trees symbolized, if anything, of Saqui Farooqui's poem about a palm. 'Oh Esther,' says Liz, suddenly depressed, 'I wish you hadn't deserted us. With Alix up north and you in Italy, London's not what it was. And Stephen's still in Cambodia, and Charles is in Baldai, and all I have is my little tabby cat.'

'And Shirley, on her way, with her mysterious lover,' says Esther.

'Oh God, don't remind me of Shirley,' says Liz. 'But seriously, Est, are you ever thinking of coming back? It's not so bad here, you know. Or not for people like us.'

Esther hesitates. Shall she speak, shall she be silent? Where do her loyalties now lie? She does not know. Is it worth agreeing to marry Robert Oxenholme, just for the fun of shocking Liz out of her wits?

'Why don't you come and see me, Liz,' she retaliates. 'You and Alix, come out and see me. I'm sure you could find a pretext. If you need one. Think about it.'

'All right,' agrees Liz. As she puts down the phone, she suddenly feels not whimsically but deeply sad, alone and tired and old and sad. What next, she asks herself, and what is the point of what next? It is true that she misses Esther and Alix, and the irregularly regular little suppers that they used to share. She doesn't feel up to making any new friends. Why bother? She can hardly believe that Shirley has acquired a new man. Liz cannot imagine acquiring or wanting to acquire one. She had been happy, with Esther and Alix, with her growing children and stepchildren, with her share of Charles, and now they have all gone. Liz sits in her familiar armchair, gazing at her little inlaid table, at its fragile burden of scented jonquils in a glass vase, at a heap of unread new novels and a life of Melanie Klein and a book of photo-reportage about the Philippines. Her curiosity is at a low ebb. It occurs to her that not only may she die before she satisfies it, but that she may also lose it before she dies. Curiosity has kept her alive. What if she were to lose it now? She has not the energy to move. She is bored, lifeless. Her mind wanders to Shirley. Ought she to ring Steve and Dora Harper, ought she to try to contact Celia in Oxford, or Barry in Newcastle, or Bob in Australia, ought she to speak to Clive Enderby? She yawns. Paris. Paris and Shirley. The two do not go together. Paris. She remembers a wild weekend there with Charles, years and years ago, nearly thirty years ago, just before Sally was born . . . She nods, her eyes close, she dozes.

Alix, on her monthly visit to report to Paul Whitmore, thinks of Liz, and of Shirley, who will now be on her way home, and of Esther, and of the nature of curiosity, and of the nature of love. Sexual love, maternal love, sisterly love, friendship. She thinks of Angela Whitmore, and the dreadful dogs. Does Angela 'love' those dogs? Does Liz 'love' her tabby cat, or does she merely *pretend* to love her tabby cat? And Paul Whitmore, in Porston Prison, whom does he love, whom can he now love?

Alix is afraid that Paul Whitmore 'loves' her, Alix Bowen. Oh, not particularly, but just because she is there, because she is there and his mother is not. Can she possibly love Paul Whitmore? Is this what is asked of her?

223

Alix had received that morning a letter from her friend and admirer, from her husband's close friend, Otto Werner. A year or two ago she had fancied herself 'in love' with Otto, and he had declared himself to be 'in love' with her. They had done nothing about it, and Otto had gone off with his children and his wife Caroline to take up a post in Washington. Love, unstimulated, unsustained, had dwindled and faded. Could it be recovered, if Otto were to return and claim her? No, no, that was all over. His letter had been careful, courteous, rueful. He had written of American politics, of the Governor of Massachusetts's Employment and Training Choices Programme, of Workfare, of Brian's view that Britain was now a poor colony of the USA, a missile pad, a nuclear dump. He had not written of matters of the heart. He never did, he did not know how to. But he had signed himself 'Yours for ever, dearest Alix, your Otto'. Well, that would do. Nothing that Brian could not see, nothing that Brian could object to. A road not taken. An open letter.

Beaver's love letters were an extraordinary collection. Perversely, he seemed to have kept the most disagreeable, abusive ones – there must surely once have been some more tender notes, somewhere, from someone? Money featured in them frequently. Beaver had been a great borrower, and his women sometimes seemed to want their money back, as well as their hearts and minds. 'You owe me eleven thousand pounds,' one of them had written, in firm italic script, 'and a copy of *Paradise Lost*, and I think you may have got my translation of the *Divine Comedy*, to say nothing of four years of my life and Geoffrey's cashmere scarf.' Another had complained, more plangently, in stuttering typescript, 'How could you, H. B., after all I did for you in Birmingham? I really thought you meant to pay it back. Please, please, dear heart, I need that two hundred quid *now*, surely you could borrow it off Bertha? Or Sonya, if she's *so* devoted to you? Two hundred was all I had. My fond heart gave all. Give back to one who loved not wisely but too well. Please, try to get it over by Friday, before Jack gets home.'

Alix enjoyed reading these old letters, rustling of dead romance and forgotten betrayals. But she was also disturbed by them. How *upsetting* love affairs were. Why did people so *enjoy* being miserable? She herself had always preferred (she now could clearly see) safe men, undangerous men. She had not been attracted to the bastards and Beavers and Bohemians of this world. Her first husband Sebastian had been a happy man, cheerful, good-natured optimist, confident, friendly. He never had time to turn into anything worse. He had died too young to rot, to become a rotter. Brian was a good man, a strong man, a man who would never borrow a penny off anyone, a man who would lend his last fiver to a stranger. A man of honour. And Otto too was a good man, an honourable man, who had resisted the temptation of Alix's blue eyes, who had honourably removed himself from her mature Siren attractions, and taken himself off to the fleshpots of Reaganland. All honourable men. Is there something *wrong* with me, pondered Alix, that I only get off with honourable men, that only honourable men fancy me? Am I *afraid* of the bastard streak?

It's true that she quite enjoyed it, at a safe remove, in Beaver.

Love. Eros. Agape. The destroying angel. Angela Whitmore had not loved Paul Whitmore, and as a result he had killed several innocent strangers.

Alix's memory flicked, suddenly, to her one-time history teacher, Miss Fawcett. Miss Fawcett had preached love, in a curious and haunting manner, a manner which her pupils had found excessive and ridiculous. Miss Fawcett had – almost – been a figure of fun. She had been a representative eccentric, an eccentric of the kind that was often to be found in private boarding schools and may still, for all Alix knew, linger on there – a fierce, lonely, exalted spinster, whose life seemed to her young charges to exist on the edge of unbearable privation. Although the school was coeducational, and in theory at least espoused the equality and natural communion of the sexes, Miss Fawcett managed to bring to it a strange intensity of chosen virginity, an old-fashioned ardour.

Her room had been like a cell, an anchorite's cell. It was on the top corridor of School House, where in addition to her other duties she supervised the night-time ramblings of the fifth and sixth form girls. Alix, who was not a boarder, had been invited up there for tea, for a talking-to, a dressing-down, a putting-right. This was when Alix was in the upper fifth, and had taken up the cause of communism, partly to annoy her classmates.

'Sit down, Alix,' Miss Fawcett had said, nervously, severely.

And Alix sat, and looked around her, at the tall shiny cream-painted bare walls, at the narrow bed with its maroon woven bedspread and its little folding tartan rug, at the cheap wardrobe with cheap wood beading round its door, at the ill-fitting limp curtains, at the desk-bureau, at the bookcase. Nothing in the room matched, nothing fitted, everything had a temporary, impermanent, rickety look, and the room – carved out, partitioned out of a much larger room – was too high for its floor space, it was high and thin, with a high window, above eye level, through which one could never commune with anything but the sky. No photographs, no ornaments, no personal effects disturbed the room's austerity.

Miss Fawcett offered Alix a cup of tea, and a biscuit. She had a gas ring and kettle in the hearth, and a tin of biscuits on the table at her elbow. The biscuit was ceremonial. Alix nibbled it, as slowly as she could, as Miss Fawcett told her that she was distressed to hear Alix defending the Soviet Union and Joseph Stalin to her classmates. 'You're an intelligent girl, Alix,' she said, her grey face intent, quizzical, her corkscrew curls bobbing as she nodded in emphasis, 'an intelligent girl, I'm sure you are just trying out ideas, but these matters are too serious to play with, you know, too serious to make games of.'

'I'm not making games,' said Alix. 'I'm interested in communism. I think it's a good idea.'

'What is it that attracts you to it?' asked Miss Fawcett, sipping her pale tea.

And Alix had spoken of equality, of sharing, or her dislike of divisions of wealth and class. Her ideas were muddled, half-baked, she had no hope of defending them, she was acutely uncomfortable during this interrogation, for Miss Fawcett was a historian, she knew about the Soviet Union and the Second World War and the Treaty of Yalta and the show trials of the thirties and the death of Trotsky. She knew the god that failed. Alix knew next to nothing about any of this.

'Alix,' said Miss Fawcett, 'you speak of equality. But do you think that equality can be achieved by economic means, by redistribution, by taking from the rich and giving to the poor?'

'Well, yes, sort of,' said Alix.

'And are we born equal? Are we born to expect equality? Have we any natural right to equality?'

'I don't see why not,' said Alix, stubbornly.

'There is only one sense in which we are equal,' said Miss Fawcett.

'I know what you are trying to get me to say,' said Alix. 'That we are all equal in the eyes of God.'

Miss Fawcett nodded.

'But I'm afraid that doesn't really *mean* anything to me,' said Alix. Apologetically, not aggressively. 'I can't quite see what it *means*.'

But even as she said this, she could feel emanating from the dim bunched thin knitted figure of Miss Fawcett a wave of illumination, or conviction, that made the whole room surge and heave and flutter with light — or was it merely a distant ray of sun breaking through the high window, the high blind window?

'Alix,' said Miss Fawcett, 'we are all equal in the eyes of God because we are all loved by God. And our task on this earth is to emulate that love, by loving all. And if we achieve this, we achieve freedom, equality, brotherhood, sisterhood. Love is the answer. The highest love.'

Alix was deeply struck by this. It made good sense to her.

'But Miss Fawcett,' she said, 'how can you love everyone? Do *you* love everyone?' Her temerity amazed her, but Miss Fawcett was not amazed.

'Oh yes,' she said. 'I try. I fail, but I try. You see, in my position' — and she paused, deliberately, and looked around her small room, at her sparse possessions — 'it is easy to try.' Alix sat on the edge of her semi-hard institution chair, rigid with attention. Miss Fawcett was about to offer the key to the universe. 'Yes,' Miss Fawcett continued, 'for me, I make myself try. And occasionally, I succeed. And then you are all irradiated. All equally.'

She smiled serenely, severely.

'All?' Alix insisted.

'Yes, all.' Miss Fawcett sighed. 'You see, Alix, at my age, in my position — I see people come and go, you young people, you arrive at the age of eleven, twelve, thirteen, and pass through this school, and then on into the world, and another class comes, another year . . . why should I discriminate? Your faces are not individual faces, you are not girls and boys to me, as you are to yourselves, you are manifestations, waves, waves upon waves . . . I see the waves break on the shore. All equal, all equally. Yes,' Miss Fawcett smiled, forbiddingly, privately, mystically, 'I love all equally.'

Alix was silenced. Cautiously, she put her cup and saucer down in the hearth, on the crazed green tiles.

'My love, you see,' said Miss Fawcett, patiently, 'like the love of God, can make amends. If I am able to love the plain as well as the beautiful, the stupid as well as the clever, the mean as well as the good. It is love that redeems.'

Little motes of dust turned in the shaft of sunlight.

'So,' said Miss Fawcett, with an air of inexorable logic, 'you see that communism is not the answer. Love is the answer.'

'Yes,' said Alix. 'I see.'

'I don't suppose for a moment that you *do* see,' said Miss Fawcett, a little more briskly, 'you are far too young. But I thought I ought to speak to you just the same?'

'Thank you, Miss Fawcett,' said Alix, politely.

'You may go back to prep now,' said Miss Fawcett.

Alix rose to her feet and stood there for a moment, looking down at her scuffed brown sandals, her grey knee socks. She wanted to ask if Miss Fawcett needed to be loved by anyone else, or if she was content to do all the loving herself, but the question seemed impertinent – and anyway, she worked the answer out for herself as she slopped her way down the shallow stone stairs. Silly question, the answer was obvious, of course Miss Fawcett didn't need anyone to love her, because God loved her. And it was God's love of her that made her able to love everybody else, everybody in the world, equally, Alix Bowen, Tim Bowlby, Betty Sykes, Pinky Rowson, Kate Josephs, Joseph Stalin, Arthur Koestler, the lot, all of them, equally, all . . .

Alix, aged fifteen, puzzled at the way a system can provide its own answers, *none of which need have any relation at all to any outside system*, none of which could ever be checked. So religion had survived, so ideologies survived, in blatant defiance of *how things are*. Shuffling, then skipping, then running down a corridor (*Don't run, Bowen*, echoing vainly after her) and out, and across the autumnal lawn and down the conker avenue and home . . . and now, in her fifties, on her way to prison, Miss Fawcett (who had died the year before as sparsely as she had lived, in an old people's home) rose again to confront Alix Bowen, with that riddle, that old chestnut, of universal love. *L'amor, che muove il sol e l'altre stelle* ... Was it because of Miss Fawcett that she felt compelled to try to love Paul Whitmore? To *make* him lovable? To make *him* lovable?

Equal in the eyes of God.

Could Miss Fawcett have loved Paul? Abstractly, as a drop in a wave in the human ocean? As human stuff, despite all, as human matter?

Human matter. This week Alix had read in the paper of a delegation of women from a group of Pacific islands who were presenting a protest to the United Nations on the subject of radiation. They had given birth, they claimed, to monstrous deformities, to babies without heads, to babies with two heads, to babies like monkeys, to full-term lumps of human matter that looked like bunches of grapes.

Could one love a bunch of grapes? Alix shuddered. What will she say to Paul about Angela? She will await inspiration.

This week, Alix had made an experiment. She had been to have her hair done. For Alix, this was an event, an occasion, and it had not been vanity that inspired her, but curiosity. She had chosen a cheap hairdresser, on the Coalbright Road, in that long dreary ridge which houses a muddle of small neighbourhood shops, most of them bearing marks of doom. The more prosperous are not ethnic. The salon selected by Alix was not horrifyingly dismal – she was not prepared to martyr herself – but it was a little sad. A non-ethnic Monsieur Raoul presided, but not very visibly. He lurked in a back room. Alix allowed her hair to be washed, minimally trimmed, and dried by a nice girl with MANDY embroidered on the breast pocket of her pink overall. Mandy, confronted by Alix's fierce grey mane, suggested highlights, lowlights, conditioner. 'What kind of conditioner do you use, madame?' she inquired, kindly. 'I can tell it's not doing you any kind of good.' Alix did not like to admit that she did not use any conditioner.

She sat there, trying to reply to Mandy's small talk, while breathing in the salon atmosphere, while trying to imagine herself a small boy, twenty years ago. Curls of hair lay on the floor, old women sat around under old-fashioned dryers, Busy Lizzies and geraniums wilted on a windowsill, and old women's down-market magazines lay in a crumpled heap. Perhaps the Whitmore salon had been smarter than this?

And the smell. Had it smelled like this? It was the smell that seemed most pertinent. A hot, scorching, chemical smell. Poisonous, dangerous. Sickly sweet, yet acrid at the same time. The smell of deceit, of concealing, of repression. Layers on layers of smell. Alix sat back while the perfumed Mandy puffed hot air at her, and breathed it all in, hot air, perfume, poison and all. Yes, this could easily drive one mad. If lead fumes can poison one, then so could this. Hadn't Stephen Cox once thought he was going mad, when in the old days he lived over a dry cleaner's?

If I were in a detective story, thought Alix, as she pulled up outside Porston, I'd try to prove brain damage from hair lacquer. As a defence.

She was half serious.

She had brought Paul a bunch of grapes, some chocolate, and another book. Gates clanged behind her, keys turned.

Paul was waiting for her, at his table.

'You look different,' he said, accusingly.

'Yes,' she said. 'I had my hair done. It's not *very* different, is it?'

She had not expected him to be so observant. Would he guess why she had been to the hairdresser? That it had been, indeed, for him? She wondered what to say to him about Angela, as he described to her the disruption caused in the prison by the introduction of a new voluntary AIDS test. Very few had volunteered, and one who had and had been found positive was going through hell as a result. Paul thought this was not fair. Paul had volunteered, had been found negative. Or so he said.

The hour limped along. Time was running out, and she had not mentioned his mother. Neither had he. She found herself unable to refer to Angela. She hadn't yet told him that she had seen either of his parents. Of course, having seen *them*, she saw *him* differently. Could he *tell* that she had seen them, as he could tell that she had had her hair done?

They talked of Ian Kettle and his television series. Alix divulged that Ian and Fanny Kettle had invited her to a party. She often said things to Paul that she did not mean to say, simply to make conversation. Paul complained about the difficulties of signing on for parts of the education programme.

They wouldn't let him do archaeology and ancient history, he said, they couldn't get a tutor. He was thinking of pursuing his other interest, botany, instead. Alix spoke of the Open University. She would ask Brian about its courses, she said. And then Paul said, suddenly, 'I had a letter from my Dad. He said you'd been to see him.'

Alix felt herself, unaccountably, blushing. Her face burned. She put one hand up to touch it, to cover it.

'Yes,' she said. She should have told him at once, should have owned up.

'He said you were going to see my mother.'

'Yes,' said Alix. 'I'm going to try.'

The lie was out, now she would have to stand by it.

'My father sent me his love,' said Paul.

Alix felt the tears stand up in the rims of her eyes. She swallowed hard.

'Yes,' said Paul. 'He didn't have much to say. But he ended it with love, God bless.'

This is ridiculous, thought Alix. She was deeply moved. She sniffed. Her nose prickled.

'Thanks a lot,' said Paul.

'Oh, that's all right,' said Alix. The love of God. The indiscriminate love of God.

'It's a funny town, Toxetter,' she ventured, to fill in the silence. The moment had passed, the angel had flown. 'Yes, it's a dump,' said Paul Whitmore.

Charles Headleand and Nigel Bicester are sitting in the kitchen of the abandoned British Embassy in Baldai trying to tune in to the World Service of the BBC. Charles shakes his head. 'I don't get it,' he says. 'Could they be jamming the frequency?'

'Easily,' says Nigel, relieved that Charles has also failed to get the programme. 'In fact, probably.'

Charles switches off the strange, high-pitched whistle, and stirs another spoonful of sugar into his instant coffee.

'Christ, what a God-forsaken hole,' he says.

The embassy is not what he had expected. It is not smart. It is a dump. The old news photographs of the wall over which the video of the death of Dirk Davis had been thrown had made it look grander than it is. It is nothing like as smart as his apartment in New York, or as the house in Harley Street. Her Majesty's diplomats clearly do not live in the splendour to which they were once accustomed. Downhill all the way.

Charles is tired and irritable. He wants a drink, but there isn't anything to drink. This is a mad country. Baldai airport had been walled with liquor, jewelled marble halls of Duty Free had extended in every direction, an Aladdin's cave of booze, a mirage in the desert sands. But here, Bicester tells him, there's not a drop to be had.

'You must be going crazy out here,' says Charles, as a compliment, to young Bicester. 'However do you keep yourself occupied?'

'Oh, it's not so bad,' says Nigel Bicester. He is a pleasant, blond young man, public school, well spoken, deferential. 'I'm learning Arabic, it passes the time. And I have my music. And there are one or two chaps I see from time to time. Socially.'

'Brits, you mean?'

'Well, there's one Englishman, and a Scot. And a Canadian.'

'What are they doing out here?'

'Two of them are engineers. The Englishman's a writer. He teaches English. Odd sort of fellow, but he passes the time. He used to be out here with the British Council, and when they withdrew their presence he stayed on and privatized himself. He's gone a bit native.'

'What does he write?'

Bicester looked vague.

'I'm not quite clear. I think he said it was a prose epic.'

Charles got up, restlessly, and began to walk up and down the little kitchen, with its mementoes of England — jars of Nescafé, of Cooper's marmalade, of Marmite. Typhoo tea bags, Marvel milk powder.

'Ugly building, this,' he says.

'Yes, isn't it? Sixties Oriental Brutalism. I particularly dislike those tiles. If I do go mad, it will be the fault of those tiles.'

Charles smiles appreciatively at the offending floor with its crude geometry of cruel blue and green and black.

'And I'm not too keen on the light fittings either,' adds Bicester.

'No,' says Charles. 'Bit like a dentist's, aren't they?'

Nigel Bicester is pleased to have Charles Headland as his guest. As Charles has surmised, life in Baldai is dull. It is a mixture of dullness and fear and responsibility for things Nigel does not understand. Like the electricity generator. His departing superior had lectured him passionately about the generator, but Nigel knows he did not grasp the point.

Nigel hopes Charles will be a practical man. Although he had failed to get the World Service, he had showed impressive command of the fax and telex machinery, and had already sent messages buzzing round the globe. Although Nigel believes Dirk Davis is dead, he is hoping Charles will not establish this too easily. He wants him to hang around for a week or two. Maybe Charles plays chess. Nigel is bored with music and Arabic and his shabby prose writer.

So far, Charles has made no progress in his pursuit of Dirk Davis. He knows by now that he is on a wild goose chase, and that there is no point at all in trying to establish contact with those who claimed to have executed him. He has meetings arranged for the next day, with the doctor who is said to have certified the death, and with a dubious lawyer. He has already decided inwardly that he will accept whatever story they tell him. This may be cowardly, it may be undignified, but it is what he will do. Unless their accounts seem very suspicious. He hopes they will not. He hopes that by now they will have got their act together, even if they are not telling him the truth.

He does not like it in Baldai. There is nothing to see in the town but modern buildings of curious Texan structure, and a few palm trees that for all he knows may be made of plastic. Wide roads lead nowhere. The light is harsh. He cannot get the World Service, and Baldai TV, as he had feared, consists of long political and religious discourses in a foreign tongue, interspersed with Western commercials for soft drinks and soap and photo-copiers. At one point he feels a small sense of triumph as he finds a radio reading from the Koran in English: it seems like an old friend, and the passage chosen is more inspiring than most of those he managed to find on his own account. It enjoins men to honour their mothers who bore them with pain and reared them from helplessness, it speaks of the limitless knowledge of Allah, of his power to bring all things to light from their hidden places, even those things as small as grains of mustard seed. It tells

Charles that if all the trees on the earth were pens, and the sea, with seven more seas to replenish it, were ink, the writing of the words of Allah would never be finished. Allah created you as one soul, and as one soul he will bring you back to life. Charles listens, with interest. At whom is it aimed, this English rendering? There are no American tourists in Baldai.

The grain of mustard seed intrigues him. There are grains of mustard seed in biblical parables, he dimly recalls. He gets his stolen Gideon Bible out of his suitcase and tries to find them, but it is like looking for a needle in a haystack. A biblical Concordance would be useful, he thinks, but the embassy library does not rise to one. It had a selection of Wilbur Smith and James Clavell, but no scholarly apparatus to speak of, apart from a *Short English Dictionary* and a *Guide to the Birds of the Middle East*.

He is reduced to comparing the Koran's account of Joseph's dream with the Bible's. He is proud of himself for managing to find both.

As he fiddles with the knobs of the machine, and rummages through sacred texts, he finds his mind wandering to and wondering at the richness and variety of British television, and, more particularly, to the image of the old oak tree by the River Barle. Hundreds of years old, and bald, blasted, stag-crested; but alive, robust, deep-rooted, a grand old man, sire of a million acorns. Charles identifies with this oak. He thinks of his wives, and of his five children. He has not done too badly. He has done badly, but not too badly. He has sinned, but he has survived. The storms have raged about him, but he has weathered them. And the children should sing in his branches. Jonathan, Aaron, Alan, Sally and Stella. Is not his place with them, instead of here, chasing the ghosts of the dead?

Fanny's party is drawing near. It will be attended by as varied a gathering as Northam can afford, and by one or two uninvited guests, and the Dark Stranger. Susie Enderby has already bought some new pink beads to complement her new grey-pink silk dress. She does not yet know that Fanny Kettle is preparing a grey-pink drink, a Pharsalian Pink drink, but when she sees it she will perforce divine some charmed harmony in the match. The beads are mock-pearl, a three-string choker with a golden clasp, quite expensive for costume jewellery. She has shown them to Clive, a trifle guiltily, and has even gone so far as to show him the receipt from Lovell & Harris: £36.80.

She does not know about the pink drink, but she does know that Fanny has invited Blake Leith, as it were 'for' Susie. Fanny goes on and on, these days, about Blake Leith. The very name has become incantatory. Fanny is pushing Susie into the arms of Blake Leith. Why? As a whim, for fun, as a kindness? Susie does not know and cannot tell. Blake Leith is a ridiculous name, a seducer's name, a co-respondent's name, but Blake Leith, glimpsed once and briefly introduced as he was leaving and Susie was arriving at the Kettle household, had not looked ridiculous. Although he had looked like a seducer and a co-respondent. A tall, thin, shambling, greying figure, a casual villain in grey cord trousers and an old patched jacket. A journalist turned property developer, says Fanny. A wealthy man.

Alix Bowen has also bought a new dress for Fanny's party. Reluctantly, it is true, and of necessity. Her old blue ethnic party dress has finally perished. It met an honourable fate. She had worn it to dinner one cold night at their new friends', the Bells of the university English department, and had ruined it by helpfully clambering up into the loft to try to unblock a frozen pipe with a hair dryer. She had succeeded with the pipe, as various gurglings in the loft and cries of delight in the bathroom below testified, and had descended the stepladder dirty, triumphant and ripped. 'I told you it would work!' she was able to boast, as she dusted herself down, amidst the admiration of Brian,

Karen, Tim and another couple whose names Alix had never quite caught. 'I learned that in the big freeze of '62. Or was it '63?' Brian said that Alix was a genius with plumbing. 'I *understand* plumbing,' said Alix, settling herself down, the queen of the hour, to a brandy and soda. 'There's nothing mysterious or electrical about plumbing, plumbing's just like a human body, really. Intestines and blockages. It gets cold, it gets hot, it gets air in it. It's not like cars. I don't understand cars. Do I, Brian?' And they had discussed houses and cars, and whether houses were female and cars male, and Alix had remembered little Nicholas her son in that bitter bitter winter, a little boy with measles, hot and feverish, and in the end no water at all in the house despite her coaxing, for the pipes in the street had frozen solid, and she had had to queue at the water lorry with a plastic bucket . . .

She had treated herself to a new dress, a replacement dress, a new blue ethnic dress. While selecting it, she was not aware that she was repeating herself, imitating herself. She thought she was freely choosing, from an open mind, from the open rails, from a multiplicity of choice. It was only when she got it home, away from all the other dresses, that she began to see how familiar it was, how much it resembled the faithful faded tattered garment now bundled in a plastic bag in the bottom of a wardrobe. Oh well, never mind, she said to Brian, at least it shows I'm consistent. I like what I like. And why not?

Clive Enderby, you will not be surprised to hear, has not given a thought to what he will wear to Fanny Kettle's party. His mind is full of other things. Much of it is occupied with the affairs of the Hansborough Development Trust and Operation Pegasus and the sale of several acres of derelict land. If old Starbottom finds out what that land is potentially worth, he won't sell, but if he doesn't sell, it will continue to be worth nothing. Clive Enderby is still convinced that he can turn Hansborough Valley Road into Silicon Valley and tempt some real lively new businesses up here from the south. There is a lot of government money about to be made available, come the next election, when something surely will have to be seen to be done about inner-city blight and the decline of the manufacturing industries and the north–south rift. Clive Enderby and Hansborough Chamber of Commerce had got their maps and glossy brochures ready, displaying the charms and conveniences of the district. Clive has written some brilliant copy which has convinced even himself that Hansborough is the strategic centre of the new Britain. But he has heard rumours that Northam Council has rival plans to turn the Valley into the largest Shopping Mall and Funfare in Europe. Delegations have been sent off at the taxpayers' expense to admire shopping malls in Alberta and Texas and Florida and New South Wales. People speak of dolphins and cascades and giant animated polar bears and alligators lurking in palm-fringed grottoes.

Clive Enderby cannot think that this vision will ever materialize. How can one have a Shopping Mall and a Funfare when people are too poor to shop, too poor to have fun? We need jobs first, then fun. Clive is slightly shocked by the vulgarity of the vision, and cannot think that Perry Blinkhorn, well known as a puritan, can approve of it either. Clive feels slightly priggish about the notion of Britain as a Union Jacked tourist trap for rich Americans, and cannot work out whether or not his suspicions are properly right-wing. He has heard it said that the way ahead is to forget about real employment altogether, to encourage the manufacture of plastic policemen and the sale of candy-floss. Central London, he hears, has already turned into a replica of itself, a spitting image of itself. Is that success, or failure?

Clive is too much of a northerner, too much of a hard worker himself, he has too much in common with Perry Blinkhorn to want to turn Hansborough Valley Road into a dolphinarium. He sees clean factories, monorails, helicopters, landscaped estates, high salaries, the best of modern architecture, a prosperous revitalized community. Is that such a ridiculous concept? Is that an impossible Utopia?

Clive is sick of sentimental rubbish about the old days. The old days stank of filth and exploitation and incompetence. Let them sweat in the Pacific Basin, let the Koreans labour round the clock. Yorkshire does not want to go back to that kind of thing. It wants to go forward. Many of the factories that closed over the last few years deserved to go bust. Only last week Clive had been shown round the abandoned works of Cliff Harper by Cliff's brother Steve. It was enough to make a modern man weep. The mess, the muddle. A leaking roof, heaps of rusting spare parts, a dingy office deep in old invoices, unwashed mugs standing on work benches, green with mould. How could a man be expected to spend a working day in gloom like that? No wonder people prefer the dole. A pile of shavings, a mousetrap with a dead mouse still pinioned. A small dry grey husk of a mouse, in an old-fashioned, wooden mousetrap. Surely, there must be more up-to-date mousetrap models on the market, now, in the 1980s?

Driving back from Cliff's works, Clive had stopped his car on the crest of the hill and looked down the valley. That weekend, on the golf course, he had had a vision, a revelation. As he swung to the ninth green (rather brilliantly, for him) on a crisp spring morning, he had suddenly seen the answer to the scale of dereliction. The answer was grass. It was so simple, like all good solutions. Of course one could not rebuild all these abandoned acres, modern industry did not need such spaces, but the sight of them crumbling and decaying was a deterrent. So – grass them over. Why not? Grass over what you don't need, and rebuild the rest. Landscape it, and rebuild. A sea of green. It would cost money, but not all that much money. It had been tried, once, in the optimistic sixties – hadn't Stoke-on-Trent grassed over a few slag heaps, to the irritation of the locals, and made an industrial park in the centre of the conurbation?

Why had they stopped the programme?

Lack of money, lack of faith. Money is faith. Faith is money. Clive stared at the grey-brown-black acres, and willed them green. Grass. Astroturf. Clive saw an army of workers, laying grass. He determined to look into the economics of grass. Real grass, plastic grass, forced grass, false grass. Invest in grass. Grass over Cliff Harper, let Cliff Harper lie.

Shirley sits in Liz's drawing-room in St John's Wood and strokes the tabby cat. Now she is back in England, the craziness of her own behaviour begins to alarm her a little. Not much, or not yet much, but a little. Luckily, Liz is making herself useful for once by coming up with some explanatory phrases – 'hysterical fugue' seems to be the most plausible to Shirley.

Shirley nods at it, storing it away for future usage. Liz is being calm, practical, reassuring, big-sisterly, but, despite having deliberately, ostentatiously adopted this manner, she cannot resist the odd glint of sheer curiosity. She is, of course, particularly intrigued by Robert Holland, who had accompanied Shirley to Liz's house that afternoon and left her there, after refusing an offered cup of tea. She had guessed his appearance quite correctly from his telephone voice: he looked as Esther had told her, almost uncannily okay. So what on earth had he and Shirley been up to? What had they been playing at? How long had they known one another? Dare she ask?

Shirley shifts, carefully altering her position in her armchair, and smiles a little secret smile. She will stay the night at Liz's, go to Northam in the morning.

Liz has done her best to describe what has happened in Shirley's absence. She has spoken of Bob and Barry and of Celia, she has reported that the inquest on Cliff has been opened, the death certificate issued, but that the body has not yet been buried. 'People were waiting for you to come home,' she says,

241

feebly, and falls silent. She watches Shirley. Shirley must indeed, Liz considers, be in some kind of deep shock. What will happen when she emerges? Shirley is very thin, but a faint hectic flush lightens her pallor. She looks very attractive. Her eyes are dark, sunken, huge. Liz is fascinated by this new, unknown Shirley.

She is about to speak. Liz listens, intently. Shirley has all her attention.

'I've got this terrible boil on my bum,' says Shirley, in a kind of mock-plaintive tone. And smiles.

Liz is dumbfounded. 'What?' she says, playing for time.

'A boil on my bum,' explains Shirley, patiently, sweetly. 'You know. A boil. Bloody painful. Are you allowed to prescribe me anything for it? Or is that against the rules?'

'Oh, never mind the rules,' says Liz, rallying. 'I've got some antibiotics in the cabinet, you can have some.'

Surely Shirley will not ask her to look at the boil? The thought of looking at Shirley's bottom makes Liz feel quite faint. Liz shuts her eyes, momentarily. She opens them, the new Shirley is still sitting there, smiling enigmatically.

'I suppose you're wondering where I met Robert,' says the new Shirley. 'Well, it wasn't in Northam, you can be sure of that. I picked him up on the ferry. Or he picked me up. It comes to the same thing, I suppose. He's rather nice, don't you think?'

Liz wonders whether to pinch herself to see if she is awake.

'Yes,' she says feebly. *Rather nice?* Yes, those words did seem to describe her fleeting glimpse of Robert Holland.

'But I don't know,' says Shirley, 'if there's much future in him.'

Her voice is a little high and thin, meditative, caressing. Her words float in the large room.

'But then,' says Shirley, 'there may be. You never can tell.'

And she smiles, again, as her shocked, silenced sister staggers out of her chair, mumbles, and trudges off in search of antibiotics.

*

242

Consider Cliff Harper. This narrative has paid him no respect. It has used him as a ploy and a convenience, as a prop and a statistic. His story has not been told. His wife it would seem does not mourn him, his children it would seem do not mourn him, his mother reviles him, his father is too senile to know what has happened to him, and his partner curses his memory. Only his brother Steve and his sister-in-law Dora decently lament him. Or so it would seem.

This could have been the story of Cliff Harper, but it is not. That story will never be told. There are parts of Cliff Harper's life that are secret, known to none. Nobody knows them, not wife nor brother nor mother nor father nor children. He will take them to the grave. Already they are cold upon the slab.

If we could grieve for every sorrow and every life, we would never stop grieving. We would never be able to get up in the morning, we would never be able to feed the cat or water the pot plants. The air would be loud with lamentation. It is better not to know.

This story could tell you of Cliff's earliest financial transactions, of the rabbit he sold, and the old bicycle. He had worked on that bicycle, had done it up.

It could tell you of his difficulties at school. He was weak at maths.

It could tell you of how he fell in love with Shirley Ablewhite, when she was fifteen years old, and wild, raging with desire and demand beneath her school uniform.

It could tell you of his fears of never being able to satisfy that desire and that demand. It could tell of the defeat that filled him when Shirley turned away from him in their marriage bed, and sobbed quietly into her pillow, hoping he could not hear. He heard.

It could tell you of the woman he picked up in the Royal Hotel in Doncaster and of the infection he caught.

It could tell you of the panic that filled him when the V A T

243

inspector came to look at the accounts, of his resentment of the not-quite-respectful look on his bank manager's face.

It could tell you of his alarm when his eldest son Barry grew more and more stroppy, of his fights with Barry, of his shame when Barry went off to Newcastle and shacked up with a pig-tailed Irishman and became a day labourer. It could tell you of his relief when his second son Bob took himself off to Australia, out of reach, out of sight, almost out of mind. It could tell you of his fear of his close-lipped, hard-working daughter Celia, top-of-the-class Celia, whose expensive education had born strange fruit, who hardly spoke to or looked at her lumbering father.

It could tell you of the woman he picked up in the Three Horseshoes in Manchester.

It could tell you of his nightmares about his overdraft.

It could tell you of the pride he felt in the new car he bought in 1983. He was fond of this car. This was the car he died in.

It could tell you of his support for the Northam Rovers, and of his disappointment that Barry and Bob did not share his interest in soccer. Did he occasionally wonder, could it have been his own fault, for ramming it at them when they were infants, for making them play ball in the park on frosty Sunday mornings, as their little faces turned blue, and their noses ran, and their knees blazed and prickled and chafed, as he would shout at them for missing the ball? This story could not tell you, for it does not know.

But it could tell you of the woman he picked up in Birmingham, and of the infection he thought he caught from her, and of his fears of what, in these dangerous days, it might prove to be. It could note his conviction that he had sinned, that God had marked him out, that Shirley would be infected. It could tell you of his covert examinations of his own body, of his inability to make himself visit the doctor, of his decision to sleep with Shirley no more.

It could tell you of his plan to visit, secretly, an expensive clinic in London 'for a complete check-up', as so many stressed executives are driven to do, and of his hope that this check-up would reveal that he was not mortally ill. It could tell you of the way in which hope itself assumed a nightmare face, a mocking, high-coloured, painted face, a seducer's treacherous smile.

It could tell you of the dull thud in his body as he stared furtively at the tempting glossy brochure for the Corsham Clinic in Harley Street, with its tables of fees and its portraits of white-coated doctors and short-skirted nurses, of bowls of flowers on polished hardwood tables. Fear lurked in those pages, fear and a death sentence. How could he have himself tested, for £150, when a test could only confirm that he was a dying man? (The brochure had slightly misjudged its impact, you might say.)

Hope and fear grinned at him. In the end he could bear their mockery no longer, and gassed himself, without saying a word to anyone. He gassed himself with carbon monoxide in his garage in one of the nicer and newer suburbs of Northam.

It could tell you all these things. But you know them all. You may know more about them than this story is able to tell. Maybe you too have stared at glossy brochures, have read entries in medical dictionaries, have woken in the small hours with the knowledge of mortality.

Meanwhile, Celia reads Tacitus, and dwells on the colourful atrocities of an imperial past. Meanwhile, Barry lays bricks, smokes hash and eats pizza up in Newcastle, and Bob works on an Australian vineyard with a bunch of boring Eyeties, and Shirley and her sister Liz drive up the M1 in Shirley's rescued Mini towards the shell of the Harper home. Shirley is worrying about the soft, depressed, depressing, impotent lavatory handle in the downstairs cloakroom. She really should have wired it up before she ran away, she reflects.

This short story about Cliff could add a postscript, about Barry. Barry Harper has had even more of a bit part than Cliff, but that does not mean that he does not have a whole story of his own, still in the making. Barry, having no access even to the minimal explanations sketched in these paragraphs, blames himself for his father's death. In his view, if he had not cut up rough and buggered off to Newcastle, his father would still be alive. Barry reproaches himself, painfully, bitterly, pointlessly, and will so do for years to come. But what else could he have done? He and his father could not live under the same roof, they could not even eat at the same table.

Liz Headleand sat in Alix's spare room, trying on clothes. She was trying to find something to wear to Fanny Kettle's party. Alix had bullied her into going. 'I've *got* to go,' Alix explained, 'because of old Beaver,' and anyway, Alix had continued, Fanny Kettle herself was well worth a visit. 'She's the Madame Bovary of Northam,' Alix had said. 'Or maybe the Messalina, if rumour speaks true. So you see, you must come.'

'But who will be there?' Liz had asked.

'Oh, everybody,' said Alix. 'Town and gown, dukes and duchesses, rag, tag and bobtail.'

'Dukes and duchesses?'

'Well, not really. Sam says she asked them, but they didn't say they'd come.'

'Is Sam going?'

'Oh yes, of course. Everybody's going. Apart from the dukes and duchesses. Sam's a great friend of young Tony Kettle. And who knows, maybe her famous husband will be there. The famous Kettle. Iron Age Kettle might honour us.'

'It seems a bit much, going to a party,' Liz had murmured, 'what with Cliff still on ice, and Shirley gone dotty.'

'Sitting here won't help them,' said Alix, 'whereas going out will help me. So you might as well come.'

And thus Liz found herself, in Alix's spare room, going

through a heap of oddments pressed upon her by Alix, looking for party wear, and thinking of dukes and duchesses, and her dead mother, and Charles. She found to her dismay that she couldn't get into most of Alix's things. Have I really put on so much weight, she wondered, as she rejected a black skirt, a green slinky acetate evening dress from the sixties, and a Maltese lace blouse. Her mother had died fat. Shirley was very thin. Was there a moral in this?

But her mind was elsewhere. In Baldai, with Charles. Just before leaving London, she had received a mysterious phone call, from an unknown gentleman, wanting to know when Charles was expected home. He did not seem to realize that Liz was not Charles's wife, nor even his ex-wife, but his last ex-wife-but-one, and she had not disabused him. In the course of their brief conversation he had revealed to her that he was urgently expecting an answer to a letter he had written to Charles, inviting him to become the Director of the Royal Geographical Association. 'In confidence, you know,' he kept saying, in a fussy, prissy, storm-in-a-teacup voice, 'in confidence.' He needed a reply. The Queen needed a reply. The Prime Minister needed a reply. Where was Charles?

'He's staying in the embassy at Baldai, as far as I know,' Liz had said. 'You could try ringing him there,' said Liz. Incompetent old fool, she had said to herself, as she put down the phone. Can't even get hold of an up-to-date *Who's Who*. And what a bloody silly idea, asking Charles to be the Director of the RGA. Charles hated geography, hated travelling, his whole aim was to make travelling and geography redundant, through the satellite. Bloody fools.

But now in Alix's spare room, rejecting the too-tight Maltese blouse (a never-worn present from Alix's Auntie Flo) she stared at herself a little forlornly, reconsidering. Of course, in England, that was how things were done. The less you knew about something, the more likely you were to be asked to run it. That was how people got appointed in this country; at random, to run things about which they knew absolutely nothing. Charles was a manager, so let him manage the Royal Geographers. He probably retained the reputation for being a good manager. People didn't know of the crises through which Global International Network was staggering. And it came to her that the RGA had a reputation for being immensely wealthy. The salary there would be good, even by television standards. And the perks considerable. Sir Charles Headleand he could shortly be, at the very least. And she could have been Lady Headleand. If she had stuck to Charles, if he had stuck to her.

She sighed, and resolved to diet. Honours, stuffed shirts, the establishment. Charles had become the kind of person who liked that kind of thing. Banquets, toasts, speeches, receptions, trumpets. Charles would be delighted, she guessed, to become Sir Charles, and honourably to quit the field of profit and loss. He could escape from his flat in Kentish Town and live somewhere grand again.

But who would entertain for him? Who would arrange his geographical dinner parties? Maybe he would establish to his own satisfaction the demise of Dirk Davis, and would come back and marry Carla Davis, as his fourth wife. But surely Charles could see that Carla would never do? Even if money were heaped upon Carla, she would never do.

Liz almost found herself thinking that it was a pity that she and Charles had sold the house in Harley Street.

Charles had been like his old self, the last time she'd seen him. What was it he'd said about her mother? She couldn't quite remember, but she'd been much struck by it at the time. And by his interest, among other things. She was slightly surprised to find that he still bothered to think at all about herself, her mother, and Shirley.

Liz thought of Shirley.

Shirley had barricaded herself into her house, had locked herself in for the weekend. Would she be on the phone to that man, would she be swallowing sleeping pills, would she be reading Cliff's old love letters? Liz could not imagine. She did not really know Shirley very well. It occurred to her as she sat there on the spare bed in her underwear that the scene was now set for Shirley to repeat, in every detail, the withdrawal of their mother. Yes, Shirley could shut herself up, the widowed recluse, as old Mrs Ablewhite had done, and speak to no one, ever again. Was that how it would be? Was that how it had been?

No doubt about it, Shirley and I are both a bit mad, thought Liz, and not surprisingly. More surprising that for so long we have managed to appear to be viable.

The force of repetition is terrible, terrible. We assemble strangers at random gatherings, we shake off parents and lovers and husbands and wives and children. We miscegenate and emigrate, we fly to the uttermost parts of the earth, and yet the same face grins at us, the same hand beckons us. There is no escape.

And is that all there is to it? *All?*

Liz shook her head, as though to shake away these thoughts, and looked around at the familiar collection of undistinguished objects — the ill-matched furniture, the pewter candlesticks, the 1930s stained wood wardrobe, the rickety bookcase made by Brian in an evening class, the tapestry-seated chair embroidered decades ago by Alix's mother, the spotted cane bedside-table. A wave of love of Alix reached Liz, as she summoned her energy to struggle into the last possible item of party gear, an old bold purple Mexican tent-style cotton gown, and found to her relief that it fitted. Indeed, it looked quite good. Dare I wear this, wondered Liz, as she inspected the violent-green snake embroidery on the sleeves. After all, it's only Northam, who will notice? thought treacherous Liz.

Alix, already changed, was downstairs on her knees by the

249

bookcase, looking for the dictionary. She and Brian were trying to work out what a *Walpurgisnacht* was, and whether Fanny Kettle's party would be one. The dictionary had vanished. Over their heads they could hear the creaking of floorboards as Liz addressed herself to the mirror in borrowed garments. They had been discussing the supernatural. 'I think it's the wrong time of year,' said Alix. 'But I'm not sure. I think they happen in May. We're too early.'

Alix was wondering whether to tell Brian about the red marks on the front gate, on the pavement outside the house. It seemed he had not noticed them, and now they had almost disappeared, washed away by a light rain. Red hieroglyphs, written in some red greasy substance – lipstick perhaps? They had been faintly menacing, and had reminded Alix of Angela Malkin, and of Sam's story about the pig's trotters, and of the house where Jilly Fox had died. The walls of cities these days sprouted strange messages in unknown scripts. Other cultures live alongside our own. Perhaps these hieroglyphs were curses, the modern equivalent of the Roman *defixiones*, those leaden tablets that damned one's enemy in perpetuity. 'I curse Tretia Maria and her life and mind and memory and lungs and her words, thoughts and memory: thus may she be unable to speak the things that are concealed.' Thus a Roman Briton had cursed a woman long ago, and thus, perhaps, might Angela Malkin curse Alix Bowen.

Alix decided not to tell Brian about the red marks. It would only upset him. It did not occur to Alix that the symbols might have been directed at Brian, not at herself. She knew they were her own. But could not read them. Angela haunted her. She tries to put her from her mind.

'I like your new dress,' said Brian.

'Thank you,' said Alix. And in came Liz, in royal purple.

'What do you think?' said Liz. 'Do I look too grotesque?'

*

As the Bowens and Liz Headleand set off to pick up Howard Beaver, Shirley Harper lay in a deep hot orange-and-nasturtium scented bath, and stared at the repeating floral pattern of her bathroom wall. Since getting home, she has spent a lot of time in the bath, carelessly consuming electricity and oil and water, floating on a high timeless tide. The healing bath, the regression to the womb, the salve of the wounded. Her body drifted, almost weightless, her mind swam. Hysterical fugue. She repeated the words like an incantation. Her eyes moved over the repeating flowers, pale green, moss green and ivory, a pattern of lotus and leaf. She was very fond of this pattern. It soothed her. She thought of Cliff Harper and Steve Harper and Robert Holland, the three men of her life. She thought of her three children. She thought of her mother, and of Liz, and her unknown father. If she lay here long enough, if she poured in yet more hot and perfumed water, could she dissolve all ties, could she float free? What would be left? Should she subject her bones to this warm solution?

Many endings have occurred to Shirley, more, perhaps, than have occurred to you or me. She could open her veins now with a razor in this warm suburban tub, like Lucan in imperial Rome, and drift out of narrative and into the unknown. She could immure herself, as Liz has thought she might, she could shut herself up in her home, as her mother had done before her, and receive no callers, for the rest of time. She could abandon this house and all its associations, and gamble all on the goodwill of Robert Holland. She could enrol in one of Brian Bowen's evening classes on the Victorian novel, or she could try to get a job to keep herself busy, or she could make a pass at Steve Harper.

None of these endings seem very plausible, very likely. But then, Shirley's behaviour for the past month has been highly unlikely. It astonished me, it astonished her, and maybe it astonished you. What do *you* think will happen to her? Do *you* think our end is known in our beginning, that we are pre-determined, that we endlessly repeat? Perhaps you think it more than unlikely, perhaps you think it impossible that Shirley should have run away as she did, that she should have made even a month's bid for freedom. At her age, with her background, a respectable middle-aged Yorkshire housewife from Blackridge Green. Perhaps you wonder what she was doing in Paris at all? Perhaps, in short, you are even more of a determinist than I am? (And anyway, what *is* her age? I must say I have lost track of this a little myself. Is she forty-eight or nine now, as I had thought, or fifty, as others tell me? And if she *is* fifty, does that make her behaviour more or less implausible?)

The contrasting fates of those two sisters in Arnold Bennett's *Old Wives' Tale* has long exercised me. You will recall that the spirited Sophia runs off with a travelling salesman to Paris, where he abandons her and leaves her to a life of spirited and hard-working independence, while the quieter Constance stays at home, marries her father's assistant, and dies in the house she was born in. You will also remember that after her gay Paris period, Sophia in her old age returns home to the Five Towns and to Constance, a glamorous Frenchified figure – but old, old. Both die at the end of the novel, as sisters in real life die. Bennett makes no judgement on either life, but his friend, the rackety rake Frank Harris, complained that Bennett had given Sophia a muck-rake instead of a soul. She had run off to Paris, but had remained a housekeeper at heart. She had wasted Paris, wasted her mad escape, had enriched herself, like a dull bourgeoise, and returned a failure, a failed experiment. D. H. Lawrence had disliked Bennett's impassive narration, and wrote his own riposte in the form of *The Lost Girl*, a novel about a provincial draper's daughter who runs off to Italy with a travelling Italian entertainer and discovers sex, intensity, passion, landscape, what you will, in the freedom of the Apennines.

I don't know which of these stories you find most plausible. Shirley had not read either of them, though she had once heard some of an adaptation of *The Old Wives' Tale* on *Woman's Hour* on the radio. But although she had not read them, and therefore cannot reflect upon them, the issues they present are quite clear in her mind as she lies there in her hot bath.

She contemplates the reality of the suburban world to which she has returned. It is not really very convincing. Its hold is weak. True, the bath is excellent, far better than Robert's disastrous arrangement in Paris, and the cooker works well, and the bed is comfortable, and the television speaks to her in English. Moreover, somebody (it can only be Steve) has mended the handle of the downstairs cloakroom lavatory. But Shirley cannot help noticing how little difference her absence has made. Everything looks exactly the same, but not seriously so. It does not have the solid, terrible, grave sameness, the nightmare unchangingness of Abercorn Avenue. It is frivolous, arbitrary, random. There had been Joan Halliwell, walking her Airedale. There had been Mr Porter in his blue Honda Civic. There had been the newsagent's, with the overflowing litter bin. There had been an early ice-cream van, playing a ridiculous hollow sad tune. Nobody seems to notice she has been away, is back. Curtains do not twitch, faces do not appear at windows to watch the arrival of the delinquent Mrs Harper in her red Mini. It is not that kind of area. Tongues may wag, a little, discreetly, but even that she doubts. Even curiosity has died, here.

There had been post waiting for her, neatly stacked on the hall table. Bills, a reminder from the dentist, junk mail. Nothing.

Shall she resume her non-existence? Is that what you seriously expect?

But then of course, Robert Holland, like the Gerald Scales of Bennett's novel, like the Ciccio of D. H. Lawrence's, is not a very likely prospect either. What possible future could there be for him and Shirley? I have made him as plausible as I can, I have offered him motivation, but I have to admit that it doesn't seem probable that he and Shirley can continue to go on seeing one another. But then, extraordinary things do happen in life, and one cannot rule out Robert Holland.

I wonder if those of you who object to the turn that Shirley's life has taken are the same as those who objected to its monotony in the first place. If you are, you might reflect that it might be your task, not mine or hers, to offer her a satisfactory resolution.

Meanwhile Shirley, waiting for this resolution, turns on the hot tap once more, and lies back, and lets her hair float free, and her ears fill, as her lips taste the sweetly acrid oil.

Celia Harper has heard that her mother is back in England. She is appalled. Appalled by her own unwillingness ever to hear anything about it. 'Quite safe and sound,' the College Warden had said, offering Celia a sherry. Celia glowered at him as though the sherry were poisoned. She is angry with Liz, though she could not have said why. She sipped her poisoned sherry, balefully.

Janice and Edward Enderby are quarrelling on their way to Fanny Kettle's party. They are quarrelling about which of them forgot to set the video for the Channel 4 *Titus Andronicus*. Alice Enderby sits in the back of the car, listening to the old routine. If she were to video them, and play them back to themselves, would they be shocked, would they recognize themselves, would they try to stop this terrible bloody Jacobean marital farce? Alice Enderby abstracts herself from their circular nagging, and admires an enamel ring which adorns her middle finger, and surreptitiously strokes the hem of her new black lace slip. She has hopes of this party. She has hopes of Tony Kettle.

Fanny Kettle's witch's brew shimmered in a large crystal bowl, its mauve ice-cold spirit breath flickering in the high warm room. Its title, PHARSALIAN PINK, was propped up against it, inscribed in silver ink on a purple card designed by Tony. Ranged around the bowl were little shining glasses: reposing in it was a replica fourth-century Roman silver ladle adorned with a ram's head. Ian Kettle, who had mildly entered into the mood of the evening, had told Fanny that she ought to serve her drink from a Celtic wine bucket, but Fanny had stuck out for the crystal. Anachronistic it might be, but it was too pretty not to use, and whenever else did one have an opportunity? Ian Kettle was willing to humour his odd and faithless wife Fanny. He had long since given up all hope of trying to control her, had lost interest in her infidelities, and indeed had lost interest in sexual activity altogether. His emotional needs were adequately satisfied by the fan letters he received from admiring television viewers, and by the elevated devotion of a schoolmistress in Ilkley. Let Fanny play, while Ian worked. She didn't seem to be doing much harm. She was a nymphomaniac, a good old-fashioned nymphomaniac, but so what? That was Ian Kettle's view of his wife Fanny, at whom he now smiled quite proudly as she sipped and offered round her dangerous concoction.

Guests were already gathering, the room was filling, the conversational buzz was rising from subdued murmur to chatter and laughter and the odd excited recognizant shriek. Solid Northam academics (who thoroughly disapproved, in principle, of pretty Fanny's little ways) were all too ready to gather together and drink under her roof. They devoured small pastry parcels of chicken liver and tiny salmon and asparagus brown bread twirls, as they gazed around for more exciting faces than their own − was that big bearded chap over there Sigurd Sturllasson from Iceland and Yorkshire TV? − and told themselves that everything was perfectly O K because the Vice-Chancellor had turned up and moreover had gone quite pink in the face already. The Vice-Chancellor told himself that everything was perfectly OK because that old stick Martin Daintry was there eating a crab claw, and Sir Martin Daintry observed out of a corner of his dry eye that Joanna Hestercombe had condescended to a nibble of raw carrot and a tête-à-tête with, of all people, Perry Blinkhorn. Nobody was in a position to disapprove of anybody, so why not enjoy the party, and have another of those curious pink drinks?

Tony Kettle had deserted his position by the brew and had gone into a corner in the so-called library with Alice Enderby. Alice, wisely sipping orange juice, listened intently as he told her about his proposed refusal to embark, after his A-Levels, on any form of higher education. Alice Enderby had large staring brown eyes, a thyroid neck, irrepressibly curly hair (which she tried, unsuccessfully, to flatten with water and lacquer and gel), and a manic manner which she was saving for later in the evening. Alice Enderby had been through hell, this was her line, her parents were both as neurotic as hell, what could she do but laugh at them, and she rather admired Tony for being on such good terms with his obviously impossible mother. Alice could hardly speak to Janice and Edward Enderby. Home life was hell. Domesticity was hell, said Alice. Alice had vowed to commit suicide by the age of thirty, if she found herself in any way resembling her mother. But who would *tell* her when she was turning into her mother? Could she make Tony Kettle or some future Tony Kettle take a vow to alert her to growing signs of Janice-like behaviour? And if she *did* turn into Janice, would she still have the Alice-formed conviction that she ought to commit suicide, or would she be another person altogether? A Janice-person, a sadistic person? 'Yes,' said Tony, 'I'll stick it out till July, and then I'm off.' Alice nodded, and her eyes popped and her brown curls bounced as she twisted and twisted her enamel ring.

Alice's aunt Susie Enderby had not yet spoken to Blake Leith, but they had exchanged glances, a small recognition had passed between them. She had of course noticed the pale pink of the liquor and had wondered what kind of omen this might be. She was also discovering that her new pink and grey and white suede shoes were too tight: was she going to have to stand all evening, would the pain subside, would numbness succeed, should she have another drink to aid the anaesthesia? She had found herself talking to a chap called Len Wincobank, who said he was something to do with real estate: she dimly recognized his name, and seemed to recall that it had murky connotations, though of what nature she could not remember. Wincobank was making small talk about the beauties of the Peak District. Susie's eyes wandered, and met the wandering gaze of Blake Leith, stationed strategically on a diagonal at the other end of the room, by the French windows leading into the conservatory. She looked away quickly, and tried to concentrate on what Wincobank was saying. He had moved on from Chatsworth to the possibilities of developing the Hansborough Valley Road into an audio-visual tourist attraction. Her eyes wandered again, and this time lighted upon her husband Clive, who was talking intently to a large woman in a purple dress, a woman whom she had never seen before.

Clive Enderby was listening to Liz's account of Shirley's return with the mysterious stranger. The subject matter itself established intimacy, for they spoke to one another as fellow-citizens of the world, as unshocked adults. They discussed Shirley's plans for the future, the date of the inquest, the unpredictability of human behaviour. An undercurrent of sympathy, of mutual curiosity, flowed through their discussion of the affairs of others. They feel they are allies, although they do not know the cause.

The Bowen party had been here for some time, but Alix and Beaver were still bemused by the shock of finding themselves offered a drink called Pharsalian Pink. Does this mean that the third reader of Lucan's *Pharsalia* is here with them, in this very room, they ask one another? The Third Reader. The Third Man. Beaver, who does not care for vodka and has failed to find beer, has moved on to the wine, and is discussing spies and Cambridge of the 1930s with Alix. Beaver's old friend the classical scholar and translator, Philip Hoxton, had once been proposed in the pages of *The Times* as the Fourth Man of the Burgess–Maclean scandal: now *he*, says Beaver, would have appreciated Pharsalian Pink, but I can hardly think our hostess reads Latin, can you?

'Her husband's an archaeologist, I told you,' said Alix, reprovingly, wondering if she is going to have to spend the whole evening looking after Beaver, or whether she can foist him off on some young admirer. She looks around for young admirers, but the student age group (well, by now the post-grad age group), the age group that has rediscovered Beaver, seems to be missing. There are various teenagers, like Sam and Tony and Alice Enderby, but they are *too* young. She spots the Vice-Chancellor. He would surely be willing to pay his respects to a great man? After all, he'd given Beaver an honorary degree, rather belatedly, a couple of years ago. He could spare him five minutes. Not that he'd have heard of Lucan or the *Pharsalia*, for he was a scientist, as most vice-chancellors seemed to be these days, but he might be able to chat along about university politics, or the old days, or the sensational rise in bus fares . . . Or then again, perhaps not. The gap widens, even here, in the Socialist Republic of South Yorkshire, between those who take buses and those who do not. And vice-chancellors do not. Beaver is so rude, now he is old. Alix doesn't mind it, but many do. Beaver tells her another wartime partisan anecdote about old Hoxton in the Balkans. 'Maybe he was a spy, after all,' muses Beaver. 'I don't suppose it matters, one way or the other, do you? Get me another drink, Bowen, will you?'

'Are you sure you should?' asks Alix. He has already had two glasses of wine, as well as a preliminary snifter of the pink.

'Yes, I am,' says Beaver. 'Quite sure. I'll just wait here. Off you go.'

On her way to the drinks table, Alix passes Perry Blinkhorn, who interrupts his conversation with a tall, bony, middle-aged, horse-faced woman to salute her. Alix sees Brian, bending low over a very slightly lopsided dowager-humped old lady. Alix sees Liz, talking to Clive Enderby, and she sees her new friends the Bells, talking to another couple whom she uncertainly identifies as Janice and Edward Enderby. The Bells put out distress signals to her, they transmit hope of relief.

The evening wears on, the noise level mounts, and some of the elderly leave, but not Howard Beaver. He is sitting in a corner, and has found acolytes, in the form of a television researcher, her boyfriend, a journalist from the *Northam Star*, and radio reporter Tony Troughton. They are talking about making a programme about Beaver. This conversation suits Beaver very well. Elsewhere, other deals are being suggested or struck: property deals, political deals. Sexual transactions are also taking place, for the crystal bowl is empty, and the potion is at work. Tony Kettle has led Alice Enderby upstairs to bed, and they are already stripping off their clothes in reckless bravado, in wild abandon. His friend Sam has not been so lucky: Sam has been cornered by a young philosophy lecturer who wants to describe to Sam various versions of the Prisoner's Dilemma. Sam, who cannot follow this kind of thing even when he is sober, thinks he is going mad.

Blake Leith has wheedled Susie Enderby into the dank unlit unrestored conservatory, and they stand together by a row of withered geraniums, staring at the starlit April sky. He is talking in a low voice, urgently, as though time and life were running out, now, here, irrecoverably. He has one hand on her shoulder, and her dress has slipped slightly: his hot hand rests on her bare skin, lightly burning. He is talking of his own affairs, of his only son killed in a motorbike accident, of the emptiness of life, of his ruined hopes, of his envy of happy married couples, of his feeling that he is for ever excluded from peace and warmth and happiness, of his knowledge that he is outside, looking in, a ghost man, a shadow man, a straw man. He is very drunk, and so is Susie. He kneads her shoulder, her collarbone, his fingers sink towards her breast. Look, he says, look backwards, look at all those real people; and from the dark chill of the unused glass-house Susie looks back at the lighted party, where animated brightly coloured figures talk and laugh and gesture and eat and drink behind a solid pane. Look at them, he says, look. And she looks, then turns back to him, and he bends over her and kisses her and takes her in his arms. They stand there, locked in a Mills and Boon embrace. Susie, Susie, he whispers, and kisses her again, more deeply. There is nothing she can do about it, she is utterly convinced, her whole body trembles and blazes, and as he presses against her she is near orgasm inside her new thin silk dress. She has fallen helplessly, hopelessly in love with this smooth-talking, desperate second-rate small-town seducer, this self-condemned cad, this self-dramatizing worthless bastard. She has given herself up, and in a few days, in a few hours, in a few minutes, she will no longer be able to remember that she once knew him for what he was, that she once thought of him in these terms, for this knowledge of him is slipping from her and is being replaced, transfused, irradiated by a new knowledge, a new longing, a new and overwhelming desire. She hears herself groan in surrender as he searches for her under her clothes, as she presses her body towards him and offers its secrets, as she shakes and trembles to his fingers. This can never be undone, it is too late, she has left the real world of real people, and entered the dark world of passion, she has already forgotten where it was that she stood an hour ago, her old dry self, for now she is another person, she is this person, his person; and he, she can tell, is hers.

Where will this end? Neither of them knows. They have willed disaster, and they set out on its dark salted flood, burning, glorious, redeemed, transformed. Susie's feet bleed, one of her shoes is a white kid well of red blood, but she does not care, she is beyond care, in another kingdom.

Clive Enderby has not missed his wife, has not noticed her absence from the throng. He has been too busy talking about urban regeneration grants, while at the same time trying to keep half an eye on Liz Headland and half an eye on his sister-in-law Janice, who has been drinking far too heavily and looks as though she might say or even do something unforgivable at any moment. He can tell that Fanny Kettle could not care less if one of her guests were to rip off her clothes and dance naked on the table, indeed she would probably applaud loudly, but he has his professional reputation to consider as well as his poor brother's poor health. Clive is trying to keep a firm grip of things, but has a sense that he has already let go of one or two ends, and that bits of plot and machinery are beginning to speed up and unravel in an unintended way. Who could have predicted, for instance, that either Liz Headland or Joanna Hestercombe would be at this mad party? Does either of them have any idea who the other is? Bemused, as he chatters on about 420,000 square feet of industrial and commercial units, he wonders if his speculations are correct, and if he is guilty of criminal negligence in concealing them. 'I think the UDA should speak to the UDC more openly,' he hears himself saying, as Besserman nods sagely. Clive has no idea what he is talking about. He is mildly obsessed by the purple apparition of Liz Ablewhite. He senses drama, disaster, revelations.

Joanna Hestercombe is now talking to the Vice-Chancellor

about Simon Blessed and his paintings. She knows them well and indeed has loaned some to the exhibition. He is pretending to know them. Joanna is an unmarried, horse-riding, dog-owning woman, a woman happier in gumboots than in court shoes. Her steel-grey hair is scraped severely back from a high forehead and a central parting, and pinioned by a mother-of-pearl comb on either side, above the ear: below the combs, wiry tufts burst out vigorously, almost like a little girl's bunches. There is both innocence and worldliness in her face, her manner. She is thin, bony, finely drawn. Her teeth are prominent. She speaks of Simon Blessed's painting of one of her grandfather's horses, Archangel. The texture of the coat, the ripples of muscle under the chestnut skin are magnificently rendered, she says. Magnificently. She speaks precisely. She does not sound ridiculous. She knows what she is talking about.

Across the room a woman called Marcia Campbell (also, like Liz, a stranger to most of the gathering) is talking to Fanny Kettle about Ogham Abbey, the anchorite and Eastwold Grange. Fanny is telling Marcia what they got for the Grange, what they paid for this new Northam house, what they might have got for the Grange had it been in a less out-of-the-way part of the country. Marcia nods, smiles, encourages, volunteers that she has always liked that flat part of the country by the Humber, that she thinks it has its own desolate beauty. Too desolate by half, says Fanny. I was going mad, out there. Mad. And the damp, I can't tell you. It's under sea level, you know. Marcia nods again. Fanny prattles on. She has no idea who Marcia Campbell is, and has no recollection of having invited her, but as she arrived with Joanna Hestercombe of Stocklinch, she must be all right. So reasons Fanny, if reasoning it could be called. And Marcia is a good listener, patient, attentive. She does not let Fanny notice that her eyes keep straying towards that other uninvited guest, to Liz Headland in her purple dress.

It is easier now for Cliff and Marcia Campbell to keep an eye on Liz, for the party is thinning out a little. Groups of people are sitting on settees, perched on arms of chairs, leaning against bookshelves. The amorous glimmer of the Pharsalian Pink is beginning to dim, and Susie and Blake Leith have emerged from the conservatory. Fanny's guests are staider than they were in the old days, Ian Kettle notes with some relief: the only real troublemaker is Janice Enderby, who is having a boring high-pitched altercation with some unfortunate young academic from the polytechnic. 'Nelson Mandela House!' she cries, indignantly. 'Stuff Nelson Mandela!'

Ian Kettle himself is engaged in conversation with Perry Blinkhorn, Brian Bowen and old Beaver. They are talking about the Celts and the Romans, about imperialism and aggression, about the cults of Vercingetorix, Arminius and Boudicca. Do superior cultures really vanish without trace? Perry Blinkhorn argues that they may. Perry Blinkhorn, rightly suspected of being religious, has been reading Simone Weil, on the French Resistance, on the German war machine. But the Germans lost, Kettle points out. And who knows, the blood of the Parisi may still flow in your veins, in mine. We are both of local stock, you and I. What is defeat, what victory?

Blake Leith is talking to Liz about his home at the sea's edge. There is a strange look in his eyes, an exalted glitter, and a sea sex smell to him, a salt tang. On the red cliff's edge, he says. On the edge of the North Sea. He lights a French cigarette with trembling fingers. Liz has noticed that she herself is giving off a strange odour, an odour not her own: it must be the stale reactivated vegetable dye of the Mexican dress. She too smells, of fibre and fish. Of murex. Of magic. Of brew. And as she stands there, talking idly to this shabby handsome villain, she begins to feel a strange prickling in the back of her neck, a tingling, a premonition. Her scalp crawls, and she turns, a half second before Marcia Campbell touches her lightly on the shoulder.

'Hello,' says Marcia. 'Forgive my interrupting, may I introduce myself? I think you must be Elizabeth Headleand. And I think I am your half-sister Marcia Campbell.'

Liz's mouth drops open. She stares.

What she sees is a plump, smiling, pretty woman in her fifties in a loose black soft dress, with thick white hair in a bun held by a gold pin. She wears gold earrings, a gold necklace, and is carefully made up, with violet eyes, dark lashes, a dark-pink pencilled mouth, a fair clear skin. She holds out a hand, this smiling sociable apparition.

Liz holds out her own hand, uncertainly. The other woman grasps it, warmly, firmly. She smiles, encouragingly, and speaks again.

'Well, what I *mean* is,' she says, reasonably, 'I *know* I'm Marcia Campbell, well, in so far as I know anything, and for what *that* means, and I *think* I am your half-sister. If you see what I mean.'

This speech, despite its apparently hesitant qualifications, is entirely coherent and comprehensible to Liz, who manages to find a voice.

'Yes,' she says, rather faintly. 'I do see what you mean.'

They are left looking at one another. Blake Leith stares at them both for a moment, then mumbles excuses and melts away. He thinks they are playing some game with him. His mind is on other things.

'I wasn't sure, to begin with,' says Marcia. 'But then I did think it must be you. I mean, the you that I think you must be.'

'This is all very strange,' says Liz.

'Yes, isn't it?' says Marcia. 'Shall we sit down? It's even stranger than you think. Or than I thought, perhaps I mean. I don't *know* what you thought, do I? Shall we sit down?'

And slightly tranced, Liz follows her new half-sister to a small settee, a two-seater, where they sit side by side. They engage in conversation. Watching them from afar, Clive Enderby wonders what these two strangers can have found to talk about, that it should engross them so completely. They nod, fall silent, speak. They clasp and unclasp hands. Then, from afar, he sees Liz Headleand lift one hand, and gently, wonderingly, touch the other woman's brow, touch her white hair, touch her round cheek. The two women lean slowly towards one another, and slowly kiss one another on the cheek, slowly, ceremoniously. Then they fall once more to deep talk, earnestly, gravely, courteously.

And so might quietly have talked for hours, had not a diversion distracted and disrupted them and forced them into action. Howard Beaver, across the room, struggling to his feet from his armchair in order to potter off to the lavatory, let out a loud groan and fell gradually but heavily full length upon the floor. At first Liz and Marcia merely glanced in his direction and returned to their dialogue, assuming normal party drunkenness, but the ensuing panic made it clear that worse had befallen: 'Liz, Liz,' shouted Alix, who had made her way instantly to Beaver's side, and Liz, equally fast in her reactions, was there in seconds, pinching Beaver's mouth open, bending over him, breathing into him, massaging, pumping. 'Ring for an ambulance, quick,' she said, 'quick, quick,' as she pummelled and breathed, as Beaver let out low deep inhuman groans of struggle, of mortal combat, of pain.

'Oh God,' said Alix, 'oh God.'

'Is there another doctor here, a proper doctor?' cried Liz, as she paused dishevelled, from her task, and then resumed it, as Beaver groaned again. He was a big man and had fallen awkwardly, one leg crumpled beneath him: 'Pull him straight,' Liz, breathless, half weeping, said to Brian, 'help, pull him straight, has anyone rung for the ambulance?'

Beaver was still breathing when the ambulance arrived, breathing loudly, stertorously, terribly. 'I'd better go with him,' said Alix, who was pale with fear, with reluctance, with a kind of horror. No, no, I'll go. I'm more used to this kind of thing than you are, said Liz, bravely. The look of relief on Alix's face was undisguised. Yes, yes, that's O K, I'll be fine, said Liz, as she followed the stretcher out on to the dark street. Hop in, said the ambulance men, and Liz hopped in: as she settled herself on the blanket-covered bunk, she saw Marcia Campbell on the pavement, tapping at the closing door. I'll follow you, said Marcia. I've got my car here, I'll send Joanna home in a taxi, I'll follow you. Tell them to let me in, won't you? Liz nodded, and the door slammed shut, and the ambulance, bell ringing, accelerated down the silent dark streets past the twitching curtains towards the Royal Infirmary, where Liz and Shirley had been born, where Rita Ablewhite, mother of Liz Headleand and Shirley and of Marcia Campbell, had died.

After the disaster, Fanny Kettle's party broke up quite quickly. Even Janice Enderby fell silent and agreed to be led away. Alix burst into tears of shame, and cried all the way home, saying she had let down both Liz and Beaver, that it was all her fault for letting Beaver go to the party, for letting him have too much to drink, for not forcing him to leave earlier. She cried so much that Brian told her to shut up, which made her cry all the more bitterly. They were parking the car before they remembered they'd forgotten Sam: where the hell had *he* got to? Neither of them could remember having seen him for hours, not since the early pink phase of the party, and they were wondering whether to go back and look for him when he opened the front door and welcomed them home. Relief at finding him there cheered Alix, and they all sat down with a cup of tea to what they feared might prove to be literally a *post mortem.* 'But after all,' said Alix, recovering her spirits, 'he is over eighty. He's had a good innings. There'll be some good obituaries.' Then her face suddenly fell. 'Oh God,' she said. 'I've just remembered. He said he'd made me his literary executor. Let's all pray for a full recovery.'

Back at the house-warming, Ian Kettle wandered from room to room, collecting cold plates smeared with mayonnaise and ash and cream, salvaging cigarette butts from pot plants and bookshelves, retrieving half-empty wine bottles from behind armchairs. Beaver, in his falling, had brought down a small table and some glasses: the new beige carpet was stained wine-red. He dabbed at it, and gave up. He collected a pink plastic earring, a small red leather lady's evening bag, an address book, a cigarette lighter, and put them carefully on the mahogany sideboard. Pausing at the conservatory door, gazing into the darkness, he saw a faint white gleam on the paved floor: a lace handkerchief. He added it to his collection. Small, female, perishable relics. Party relics. Fanny would be in bed, fast asleep, dead to the world. The warmed house grew cold and quiet, it ticked quietly, and Ian Kettle quietly paced, thinking of rites and rituals, of ceremonies and drinking customs. Ian Kettle had been, was, a serious archaeologist, but he had been seduced by the television cameras, he had been talked into popularizing his mysteries. Was this wrong? He stooped, picked up the thin brown filter of a thin menthol cigarillo, sniffed it cautiously, and paced on. Howard Beaver had achieved eminence. Lasting eminence. Immortality, against all the odds. Dead or alive, he would live on. How had he managed that?

Up the stairs goes Ian Kettle, but when he opens his bedroom door, he sees that the bed is already fully occupied. A pair of black lace knickers hangs from one of the four poster's brass knobs, there are clothes strewn all over the floor, and the bedside light is still on, though the couple occupying the bed is fast asleep, way, way out, dead to the world. He smiles, slightly, a little ruefully, and makes his way, as he has done many times before, to the narrow bed in the study.

At home in Hansborough, Susie Enderby took off her new shoes, and gazed at the bright wet well of blood.

Liz and Marcia sat up through the night, in a dim waiting-room, waiting for news of Howard Beaver. He had had a stroke, he was in a deep coma, he might or might not recover. But for Liz's prompt action, he would have been dead. If he were to recover, Liz could foresee all sorts of difficulties for Alix, but these were not the matters that she and Marcia discussed.

They resumed the conversation of the two-seater settee. They had a lot of ground to cover, and they covered it fast.

Marcia was, and indeed always had been, the oldest daughter of Rita Ablewhite, born out of wedlock a year before Liz herself was born. Marcia had been adopted as a baby, and had always known she was adopted. Her parents ran theatrical digs in Sheffield, and it was only when her mother died that Marcia thought of tracing her 'real' parents. 'It seemed a bit disloyal when she was alive,' said Marcia, 'but I knew Dad wouldn't mind, he isn't the sort, and then that Bill was passed, you know, making it legal, and my psychotherapist said it would do no harm to ask. So I asked. And here I am.'

She laid a plump jewelled hand once more on Liz's.

'But this is *too* strange,' repeated Liz, peering at her half-sister's cheerful dimpled face. 'Whatever were *you* having psychotherapy *for*?'

Marcia shrugged her shoulders, spread her hands wide. 'Oh, an identity crisis, I suppose. Something along those lines. Depression caused by change of career, divorce, and Ma's death. Nothing much.'

They both laughed. Marcia had a low, musical, pleasant familiar laugh. Liz felt she had heard it many times before, as indeed she had, for Marcia had revealed herself to be a radio actress, whose voice and laugh were familiar to many. She had been, she now told Liz, a stage actress, but middle age and weight had put her out of the running for the *ingénue* parts in which she had anyway not been doing very well: she'd drifted towards radio, and was now regularly, comfortably employed. BBC rep you know, said Marcia.

'But how,' Liz asked, 'did you ever track me down?' Marcia made everything sound so normal, so unsurprising: and indeed her explanations continued in the same matter-of-fact vein.

'Oh, it was easy,' said Marcia. 'I asked my father, and he came clean. He knew it all, he'd got all the records, your mother – well, *our* mother's address, birth certificates, letters from the adoption agency, everything. But now I'll tell you something that really *is* odd, or at least I thought it was really odd when I found out about it, but now I see that it isn't – well, is anything *really* odd, I wonder? – when I first thought of going into therapy, guess who was recommended?'

Liz thought for a moment.

'Well, me, of course, I suppose,' she said.

'Quite right, my dear, quite right.' Marcia laughed, happily. 'I was told it was *quite* your line of business. And guess who told me?'

Liz frowned, puzzled, gave up.

'I'm not good at guessing games,' she said.

'Well, it was your old friend and my old friend, Hilda Stark.'

'Oh yes. Of course,' said Liz. 'Of course. And why didn't you come to me?'

'I don't know, really. I think I wanted to talk to a man. I don't know why. So I went to Jay Spenser.'

'Of course.'

'But you can imagine how intrigued I was, when I found the path led back to you anyway. Fascinating, isn't it?'

'Did you tell Jay about me?' asked Liz, suddenly worried on

some trivial level about her professional reputation amongst her colleagues.

'What *could I* tell about you? He knows you much better than I do. I've only just met you.'

'But you . . .' Liz shivered slightly, looked around the dim room, listened to a strange institutional hospital clicking that filled the silence, 'but you know all sorts of things about me that I don't know. That you exist, for example. I didn't know you existed until an hour ago.'

'Well, I certainly wasn't expecting to see you at that funny party,' said Marcia. 'I hope you didn't mind my coming up to you like that? A bit indiscreet of me, I mean you might have fainted with shock or turned on your heel and refused to speak (good phrase that, "turned on your heel", isn't it?). But I took a risk. It seemed to be *meant.* That we were both there. And frankly, the drink may have had something to do with it. Strong stuff, that pink, wasn't it?'

'So we were both at that party by accident,' said Liz.

'Uninvited guests,' said Marcia.

'And seriously,' pursued Marcia, 'you really had no idea I existed?'

'Well, no. I didn't. It seems now as though I'd known it all my life. But I hadn't. I thought there might be something odd in my mother — our mother's — early life, but I didn't dare look into it. How did you have the *courage* to make inquiries? You might have found *anything.*'

'Well, I couldn't see I'd anything to lose. And my father was quite an interesting old boy, you know. Old Percy Hestercombe. Not a bad chap, in his own ghastly way. There's blue blood in my veins, you know. The blood of Stocklinch. Pity he died before I could put in my claim.'

'And you went and made yourself known to *Joanna* Hestercombe? Just like that? Out of the blue?'

270

'Well, why not? She *is* my half-sister, after all. She didn't mind at all. We get on fine, Joanna and me. She's a dry old stick, but she's got a sense of humour. And she knows I'm not after her money. So why should she worry? As a matter of fact,' said Marcia, dropping her voice to a huskier, more conspiratorial tone, 'I'm not the only one, you know. There's another girl in Glasgow, and goodness knows, there might be *dozens* more all over the country. The aristocracy didn't worry about that kind of thing, you know, and Percy was a devil with the ladies. She's a nice girl, that girl in Glasgow. Married, two kids, keen on ballroom dancing. I didn't tell Joanna about her. I thought I'd gone far enough. Joanna's the only legitimate child, you know.'

Liz leaned her head back against the polystyrene-lined wall. She felt quite dizzy.

'Have a coffee,' said Marcia, solicitously, and jumped up and went over to the machine in the corner. KWIKDRINK, it said, and you could choose, she told Liz, between coffee with, coffee without, tea with, tea without, hot chocolate or hot orange.

'I'll have black coffee,' said Liz. Marcia peered, punched, pulled and finally managed to make the machine give up some hot dark water into a couple of cardboard cups. Marcia settled herself, delved in her large handbag.

'Here, Lizzy,' she said, 'have a drop of this,' and produced, with a discreet flourish, a silver hip flask of whisky. She topped up the coffees, and they sat for a moment in silence, sipping the fortified mixture.

'Never travel without,' said Marcia. 'Not even to a party. Golden rule.'

The room hummed.

'Can you hear that odd crackling?' said Liz.

A strange, prickling, electrical whine charged the air, irregularly.

'It's static, from this funny material,' said Marcia, stroking the

271

shiny chair seat. 'Or people's souls passing. You say our mother died in here?'

Liz nodded.

'Poor old thing,' said Marcia. 'I saw her once, you know. After Dad gave me her address, I came along to have a look. I didn't want to get in touch, Dad said she'd gone a bit loopy, by all accounts, but I just wanted to see where she lived and all. So I walked down Abercorn Avenue one day and peeped in. There didn't seem much point in knocking. She wouldn't have wanted to know.'

'And did you see her?'

'Yes, I saw her. Through the window. Poor old thing. Sitting in that front-room. Didn't have much of a life, did she? All my fault, I suppose. Must have hung over her. The disgrace. The fatal error. That was me!'

'Oh, there was more to it than that,' said Liz.

'Was there? Well, I don't feel too bad about it, I mean there wasn't much I could do about it, was there?'

'No, not really. There wasn't much anyone could do.'

'Poor old thing,' said Marcia, again, piously, lightly.

'So you're staying with Joanna Hestercombe, are you?' said Liz. 'And you get on with her well, you say?'

'Oh yes. Very well.'

'Why did you contact her before contacting me?'

'Oh, I don't know,' Marcia bridled, slightly. 'I was more *afraid* of you. Because of your reputation. And because you knew Jay Spenser. But I was going to *ask* if I could see you. Eventually. Truly. I promise. I was going to write to you. You're not jealous, are you?'

'*I* think Joanna Hestercombe looks terrifying,' said Liz. She sipped at her drink, puzzled, frowning. 'I can't work it out. Does this mean that I'm somehow related to my ex-husband Charles's ex-wife Henrietta? She was a Hestercombe, before she married Latchett.'

'No, it means that *I* am,' said Marcia. 'You aren't related to any of those people, I'm afraid. You're just related to me. *I'm* related to that lot. Though not officially, of course.'

Liz shook her head. 'I don't get it,' she said. 'I can't follow it. Are you related to my sister Shirley?'

'Yes, of course I am. She's just as much my half-sister as you are. I know all about Shirley Harper.'

'I bet you don't,' said Liz. 'Nobody does.'

And as they were beginning to dispute rights of possession over Shirley, and to disentangle Liz and Shirley's relationship with Marcia's daughters, a woman in a white coat came in and announced that Howard Beaver was dead.

Tony Kettle awoke the morning after the party with the worst hangover of his short life. He lay in bed as he touched consciousness, suffering simultaneously from the deepest instant depression, from a thumping headache, from confusion, from anxiety, and from a raging thirst. He lay there for some moments, gradually becoming aware of the fact that he was naked, and that he was in a strange bed, and that another naked person was in this strange bed with him.

Horror fills him. He remembers nothing. He dares not open his eyes. He hardly dares to breathe. Bacchanalian images of the night before float into his mind. Where is he? What has happened? Gradually he prises open his gummy lids, and notes that he is in his mother's bedroom, indeed he is in her bed. His heart stands still. He shuts his eyes, then peeps again. Some black lace knickers hang from the bed knob. A bottle of wine stands empty on the dressing-table. A heap of clothes lies on the floor.

The figure by his side is covered with the crumpled sheet. It is breathing, heavily. Despite his appalling physical condition and his state of mortal terror, Tony feels his flesh stir. He lies there, wishing he were dead.

273

Who is this by his side? Whose knickers are those? How did they get there? Whose idea of a joke was *that*?

Painfully, he once more opens his eyes, and carefully twitches at the corner of the sheet. Tousled hair, a bare shoulder, a naked breast. Dear God, thank God, of course it is Alice Enderby, sleeping heavily like a child. Dear God, thank God, of course those are Alice's knickers. He would know them anywhere. He remembers, now, hanging them there himself. They are old friends, those black knickers. He gazes from them to the sleeping Alice. His head begins to clear. He is reprieved. Her skin is soft, hot, smooth, cream, unblemished. He touches her hot shoulder. She mutters, and turns towards him. He takes her in his arms. He silently vows never to touch alcohol again.

Fanny Kettle wakes in Tony Kettle's bed, and also wonders how she got there. She yawns, stretches, shakes her head, and it all comes back. Of course. She'd found Tony and Alice Enderby asleep in her bed, like the babes in the wood. Well, passed out rather than asleep, more like. But they were young, they'd recover. She didn't grudge them a double bed. And Tony's bed is quite comfortable, although it's certainly time that somebody changed his sheets. He is a growing boy. A grown boy. And I am a grown woman, thinks Fanny, ungrudgingly. In the old days at Eastwold, she'd never have ended up after a party alone in a single bed. Does she mind? No, not really. She'd had half an eye on Len Wincobank, but had somehow forgotten all about him in the excitement.

Her mind roams back over the evening. How had it all gone? Quite zingingly, she thinks. Everybody seemed to have enjoyed themselves, except that poor old chap who died. And he was enjoying it until he snuffed it. There are worse ways to go, reflects Fanny, as she reaches for Tony's check dressing-gown and his down-at-heel schoolboy slippers, and prepares to shuffle down to the kitchen to make a pot of tea.

Edward and Janice Enderby greet the day with less fortitude. Each blames the other for having forgotten to bring Alice home. Each accuses the other of having been drunk. Edward accuses Janice of flirting with Len Wincobank. Janice accuses Edward of boring the Lady Joanna. They both revile Fanny Kettle for having had a party in the first place, and then accuse Howard Beaver of having ruined it by dying. They wrangle about when and whether to ring up the Kettles about Alice. They are still wrangling when Alice rings and tells them not to worry, she spent the night at a friend's. She does not say which friend. They shout at Alice for causing them so much anxiety, and then continue to shout at one another, as they will do for the rest of the morning, and intermittently for the rest of their lives. When Edward finally storms out of the house in a rage, saying he is going to buy a new giant Maccabee rhododendron at the garden centre (Janice loathes rhododendrons), Janice in revenge gets on the phone to Tony and Val Troughton, and asks them to dinner for Saturday week. Tony and Val are slightly under the weather from Fanny's party, and cannot think of an excuse, so they accept, unwillingly, although they are resentfully sure it's their turn to ask the Enderbys.

When Susie Enderby wakes up in the morning, she knows that her world has changed for ever. There will be no return. She is doomed to wait for the telephone, to sigh, to languish, to grieve, to lie, to sin. She is doomed to infidelity and joy. Is this what Fanny Kettle intended? No, it is far worse, far more serious than anything Fanny Kettle intended. Fanny had been playing. This is real.

*

Liz Headleand also woke to a new world, a shining, guiltless world. Howard Beaver was dead, but she was reborn. New waves of energy poured into her, her brain fizzed, her body leapt into action. The apparition of Marcia Campbell had had an extraordinarily exhilarating effect on Liz.

From the moment of revelation, she began to lose weight and to gain strength. It was as though she had emerged overnight, purged, from a long torpor. She was released into action. That morning she descended upon Shirley, forced her way into the barricaded house, and demanded to know what Shirley had done with the wine cooler from Abercorn Avenue, the wine cooler with its entwined monogram of Hestercombe, Oxenholme and Stocklinch. She assaulted Shirley with news of Marcia. The next day she rang Robert Holland and harangued him about Shirley. She accompanied Shirley, Steve and Dora to Cliff's inquest, and admired Shirley's brief cool performance in what she, perhaps rightly, thought of as the dock. (Took his own life while of unsound mind, said the fatherly coroner: possible cancer phobia was mentioned as a cause.) She drove up and down the M1, composing in her head a brilliantly original treatise on *Medusa: Our Hidden Knowledge.* She accepted, but then had to postpone, an invitation to tea with Joanna Hestercombe. She accused Clive Enderby of knowing more than he had let on. (Clive agreed that this was so.)

She rang the Vietnamese Embassy in London and demanded news of Stephen Cox and asked how to get a visa to visit Democratic Kampuchea. She rang Charles in Baldai and told him to come home at once and accept the Directorship of the RGA, as the Queen herself was pleading for him to do so daily. She bought an extravagant embroidered bedspread of many colours as a wedding present for Ivan Warner and Alicia Barnard. She asked all her children to supper and enthused to them about Marcia for as long as they would listen. She rang up Esther in Bologna to tell her about Marcia, and threatened to visit Esther with Alix in May. She told Alix she needed a holiday, and rang up a travel agency to book tickets. She bought some new lilies and a newt for her fishpond. She astonished everybody, as she herself had been astonished.

The only person she failed to astonish was, as we have seen, Clive Enderby, who had known part of the Plot all along, but who, at Fanny's party, had had his eye on the wrong half-sister. Clive at this late stage handed over the long-lost document to Liz, and together they stared at its quaint wording: stamped in faded blue and orange, sealed in dark-red wax, it covenanted to Rita Ablewhite ('the Annuitant') from Percy William Latchett de Percy Hestercombe ('the Grantor') a monthly sum of sixty-six pounds, six shillings and eightpence, provided that she agreed not to 'molest or annoy the Grantor or his wife or any of his relatives or friends', and provided that she continued 'to live in strict and chaste cohabitation with her husband, Alfred Ablewhite' at 'the address here named, of 8 Abercorn Avenue, Northam, Yorkshire.' On Ablewhite's death, should she remarry, 'the said monthly sum should be absolutely forfeited and cease to be payable.'

'This is a *monstrous* document,' said Liz, as she took in its implications. 'Do people make this kind of arrangement these days?'

'Not in my practice,' said Clive Enderby. 'But I bet old Percy had a few dotted around the countryside, by all accounts.'

'Well, it was bad luck for my poor mother,' said Liz. 'Do you think she took it quietly, or do you think she kicked up a fuss?'

'It would seem,' said Clive, 'wouldn't you think, that at some stage, she kicked up *quite* a fuss?'

'Good for her,' said Liz, warmly. 'I hope she gave them all some bad moments. The wife and the relatives and the friends.'

And she rang up Alix, to try to interest her in this interesting sociological and historical curiosity, but Alix had new worries of her own. The new Liz is rather exhausting, said Alix to Brian, as she put the phone down after one of Liz's more manic calls.

Alix herself was doubly preoccupied, with Howard Beaver's will, and with a poison-pen letter that she took to come from Angela Malkin.

Beaver's will was as annoying as he had threatened, and as ambiguous as Alix had feared. As literary executor, Alix was instructed to destroy all unpublished poems and correspondence 'except such material as should be deemed of legitimate interest to a biographer', and in reward for her fulfilment of this imprecise obligation she was to inherit the princely proceeds of Howard Beaver's share of Public Lending Right. Alix knows these proceeds to have amounted (over the few years of P L R's existence) to an average of some £80 per annum. She is also left with the option of editing Beaver's *Collected Letters*, should she so desire, in which case she could have the royalties (and the P L R) on the volume as well as any money she may be able to screw out of a publisher for a contract for this task. The copyright of the letters would, however, remain with the estate. Thus Alix is left in the ridiculous position of being free to burn or publish letters that do not belong to her, some of which are, she suspects, of considerable commercial value. If she burns them, nobody will be any the wiser. If she edits them, she will have a financial life interest in them. She is unable to work out what her moral obligations or her inclinations are. Brian advises her to wait, to let the dust settle. 'Dust!' exclaims Alix. 'Dust! There's so much dust settled already in that attic that it might as well stay where it is. Who cares about Beaver's correspondence? I'm sick of the stuff!'

Angela Malkin's letter was less ambiguous. It had no signature and no address, but it was posted in Thirsk, and read: 'Was that you snooping again late Saturday night. If you come near this place again, remember my warning.'

The message had, of course, the opposite effect. Alix received it as a challenge, a gauntlet. The fact that Angela had thought somebody was snooping around Hartley Court did not surprise her at all: it was the kind of place where one might expect snoopers. In retrospect, Alix had endowed the establishment with a criminal halo. It deserved snoopers. No good was going on there. Angela was clearly nervous that Alix would reveal her association with Paul to the sinister Colonel and his accomplice the Doctor. Alix had a hold over Angela, as this letter bore witness.

Alix thinks about Beaver and Paul. Beaver is dead now, she has attended his funeral and will attend his memorial service. She has seen him off, and she did not serve him badly, although she failed him at the last moment, when she let Liz take her place in the ambulance. She has a great deal of information about Beaver, she knows more about him than anyone alive, she certainly knows more about him than his fat, pompous, fifty-year-old son Frank, a jeweller from Bradford, or his ex-midwife daughter Lois from Canada. They know nothing of Beaver's amours, of his friendships with the great, of his working life. They do not seem ever to have read any of his poems. But all her knowledge of Beaver is now on paper. It is all literary. It belongs to the world of books. Beaver was her one living link with this mass of material. Now he has turned into a paper wilderness, a paper labyrinth to which she alone holds the clues. The Third Reader of Lucan was that silent scholar, Death.

With Paul, the reverse is true. She holds some clues to his history, because he has told her things that he has not told to others. But nothing is on paper. Nothing but two scraps from his father, and now this scrap from his mother, and the spare, sparse, better-punctuated letters she has received from Paul himself. There is no other documentation. This is not a paper case. It is real.

And, as a real case, it is more of a challenge. Alix in her life has read too many books, has pursued too many paper puzzles, has deciphered and decoded too many texts. The real, enigmatic, studious pallid Paul calls to her from Porston. The evil, ill-read Angela attracts her.

And so she made her plans to go again to Hartley Court, after Easter, in the last week of April. Again, she did not tell Brian and Sam where she was going. Uncharacteristically, she had kept quiet about her meeting with Angela. She had told nobody, not even Liz. But this time, she left a note on the kitchen-table, for Brian. In a sealed envelope. She expected to be back long before he had a chance to read it. It said: 'Darling B., I've gone to see my murderer's mother, at Hartley Court, Hartley Bridge, Phone No. H. B. 20320. If I never come back, come and collect my whitening bones tomorrow. See you for supper meanwhile. I'll be back about five. Love and kisses X X X A.'

She chose 'five' as an arbitrary symbol. She expected to be back long before five.

It was a strange, sultry morning. The sun broke through a mild thin cloud, and the air beat blue. There had been thunder the night before, and heavy rain, and now one could not tell whether the air had cleared or not. It was almost hot. She wound down the car windows, and took in the damp warm sappy breath of the day. To either side of her the ploughed fields smoked and exhaled. The earth gave up its moisture visibly. The hedgerow trees were a fresh newborn pale green, sprinkled with the white flowers of the blackthorn. Blackbirds and chaffinches sang, lambs bleated, and a bird that looked like a golden oriole or a bird of paradise flew over, hazardously and retrospectively identified by Alix as an azure and emerald-flashing magpie trailing a twig longer than itself. The crust of the world warmed and blossomed. The verges were yellow with dandelion, coltsfoot, celandine, primrose, daffodil. No more would Beaver see the greening of the year. He had written tenderly of the spring. 'You and I are both pantheists, Bowen,' he had said to her once. And she had laughed, and agreed that it might be so. Now he had returned to the great turning. I wish, thought Alix, a little enviously, that I had it in me to write just one little poem, just one little good poem, about the spring.

Meanwhile, more pressingly, what on earth was she going to say to Angela? She had not stood up to Angela very well last time. She had not been an eloquent advocate for Human Nature, or Human Matter, or whatever it was in Paul that she represented. She had allowed Angela to carry the day. But what could one say to a woman like Angela? Perhaps she merely wished to confirm the hopelessness of Angela. To carry to Paul a message to forget.

The day is really quite exceptional. She stops for petrol, and while a red-haired Celtic-looking young man in khaki overalls fills the tank she feels the sun on her face, on her bare neck, on the backs of her hands. Her skin softens, breathes. She takes off her cardigan and rolls down her pop sox and unbuttons her shirt. She drives on. Now there are white wind flowers on the banks, and she thinks she sees a cowslip. And yes, it was near here, surely, that forty years ago, on a school outing, she and her friends had found a place by the river, and had taken off their clothes and swum in their school knickers, innocent, flat-chested, transported. A day of paradise. Splashing in the shallows. Kingcups and lady's smocks.

She wishes she did not have to go to Hartley Court, but there is the little town, clustered in the valley, and there is the cattle grid, and the white board. Shall she pretend she has come to buy a dog? What shall she do if Angela abuses her?

But Angela is not there. Nobody is there. The house is shuttered, boarded. It looks eerie, forlorn. The clumps of daffodils are browning and withering, the grass is unmown. A few tulips stand, straggling, red, uncertainly attentive, feeble soldiers guarding nothing. Weeds smother the flowerbeds.

A notice is pinned to the fine front door, just below the Medusa head. Boldly, Alix gets out of her car, crosses the gravel,

281

reads it. It says BACK TOMORROW, but it looks old already, water-stained, fading.

Is she relieved, is she disappointed? She cannot tell. She stands, irresolute. And then she hears the whining and the barking.

The dogs, of course. There they are, in their cages up behind the house, greeting her, hurling themselves against their bars. They look hungry, but then they looked hungry last time. And they cannot get out. No, of course they cannot get out.

Alix wanders back to her car, kicking at the gravel with her grey plimsoll. She stands with her hand on the car door. It is an anti-climax. She was keyed for action. There is no action.

She looks up at the house, at the shuttered windows, at the drawn curtains of upper rooms, at the fluttering message. Then she begins to walk towards the rear of the house, listening as she goes to the changing tenor of the dogs, to a kind of frenzy of disappointment in their howling. Perhaps they are starving, perhaps they have been abandoned. Why does the house look so very, very shut? Are Angela and the Doctor and the Colonel lying dead in there, the victims of whoever was snooping on that Saturday night? Mass country house murders have been fashionable of late.

Alix proceeds, quietly, on her soft shoes, Mrs Nosy Parker herself. She reaches the back door, or one of the warren of several back doors. She tries it. Luckily it does not open. She peers through a window, but can see nothing. She moves on to another door, a door to a sort of cottage annexe, and pauses with her hand on its handle. From within, she can hear a terrible whimpering. Not a barking or a howling, but a small desperate high-pitched whimpering, a lone voice. It is a heart-rending sound. She tries the handle, and it gives, but she dares not open. She shuts it, keeping the knob in her hand. There is an appalling smell reeking at her from the crack that she has opened and closed. Within, the solitary brave whimpering continues, urgently.

There is a window, to the side of the door beneath a corrugated iron roof. She is too small to see through it. She looks around, and sees a heap of rubbish, an overflowing dustbin, a crate, an old enamel bucket, a cardboard box of tins of dog food. She builds herself an unsteady little platform, climbs up on it, and looks through the window.

She can see quite clearly into the room now. It is one of the dog-rooms that Angela showed her. Alix stares in horror. She can hardly believe her eyes.

Hanging from the ceiling, suspended from a beam, where earlier had hung a bunch of unskinned rabbits, is a horse's head. Beneath the horse's head lies a heap of dead and dying dogs. Some of them are dead, dead surely, skeletal, starved, collapsed, caved in, their ribs standing out, their lips drawn back in the grin of death. Others are still alive, still just alive, just stirring. One of them, hearing her, seeing her, sensing her, makes a dreadful effort, and rears itself up from the heap of corpses, only to collapse silently once more. Which is the one that is making this terrible, plaintive, persistent whimpering weeping sound? She cannot see it, it must be out of her line of vision, beneath her, just behind the door. The strongest survivor, the most pitifully hopeful, the last to die. It continues to call to her, with a terrible pleading.

Alix steps down from her rickety vantage point, and stands on the ground. She is shocked, disgusted, appalled. Those poor dogs, she says to herself, aloud. Those poor poor dogs. She had thought that the dogs themselves disgusted her, but seeing them like this, how can one feel anything but pity? How can *dogs* disgust?

What on earth has happened? Has Angela abandoned them? Is this *intentional*? What is that rotting maggoty horse's head doing, suspended out of their reach?

Alix knows she dare not open the door. She knows she must

go and look for help, tell someone, tell the police of Hartley Bridge, summon the RSPCA. The whining of the unseen dog pleads with her, calls her. It is a brave one, this unseen dog, it will not die quietly. She wishes that she dare open the door, rescue it, try to save it from the black hole. But she knows it is more sensible to get help.

She climbs back on to the box, for another look, and this time she sees the noisy young dog. It is still on its feet, unsteady, skinny, limping, but on its feet. It has backed away from the door, and is standing in the centre of the room, howling. Alix taps on the pane of glass. It looks up at her She waves at it. 'Hang on little dog,' she says. She climbs down again, and rips at the damp cardboard boxes of Pedigree Chum. There is enough meat here for all these dead and dying tormented creatures. But where is a tin opener? She dare not break into the house to look for one. What has she got in the car? Only her tool kit. She goes and gets her tool kit. She hammers at the tin with the screwdriver and spanner, has slowly made a deep jagged hole before she remembers that Sam's Swiss Army knife is in the car glove-pocket. She goes back for it, hacks away with it, succeeds in removing most of the lid of one of the tins. She climbs back on to her platform, breaks the glass of the window (it falls, crashing, splintering, and releases foul air) and drops the tin as gently as she can. The survivor dog goes for it, is still strong enough to go for it. Alix starts on another tin. She will throw this in too, she thinks, then go to the village for help.

This is what she thinks, but this is not what happens. For while she is hacking at the second tin, she hears the sound of a car on the gravel. Is she frightened, at eleven thirty on a spring morning, in broad daylight? Well, yes, she is. But she is also very angry. She stands, holding the jagged tin and the Swiss Army knife. Angela's car rounds the corner, comes to a halt. Angela is alone.

Angela gets out, stares at Alix. 'And just what do you think you're doing here?' she says, her hands on her hips, glowering, her red hair in a blazing crest.

'And just what do you think you're doing to these dogs?' says Alix, standing before the door of the dog house, the dog morgue.

'That's my business,' says Angela. 'I warned you. I warned you. Don't say I didn't warn you.'

The woman is mad, Alix realizes. She has always been mad.

'Get out of here,' says Angela.

'All right, all right,' says Alix. 'But only if you feed these dogs. Your dogs are dying. I'll report you. I'll get you for this.'

Angela advances upon Alix. Alix brandishes her tin and her knife. Angela continues to advance. A sort of hysterical laughter rises in Alix's throat, but she backs away from Angela, she cannot help it, she backs away and stands with her back against the door.

'Get away,' she says to Angela. In all her mild life she has never before been threatened with violence. 'Get away, don't touch me, get away.'

Angela advances. Alix throws the tin at her, not very hard, but at that range she cannot miss, and it hits Angela square in her cream-bloused chest. Angela grabs Alix's arm, Alix takes a step back, the door of the dog prison opens behind her, and she falls backwards into it on to her bum as Angela pushes her. But now her hesitations are over, she struggles up, gets back to her feet, punches back at Angela, hits out at her with her knife-hand. Angela backs off, she is frightened. 'Don't touch me,' yells Alix, 'you dreadful woman, you monster woman, you bitch you, don't touch me, keep away!'

Angela stands back, panting, bleeding, spattered with Pedigree Chum. The door behind Alix swings open, revealing the heap of dying flesh, the swinging head with its great dull white eyes, the staggering survivor dog trembling on its bowed legs. 'Look,' yells Alix, pointing at the dog, 'look what you've done! Haven't you done enough? Look what you've done!'

Angela has met her match in the mad-eyed Alix. She looks frightened. Alix knows she has won. Alix is still armed. She brandishes the small knife. She makes towards her car, backing away, taking care not to turn her back on Angela. 'I'll get you,' shouts Angela, as soon as Alix is out of close range. 'I'll get you!'

'No, you won't,' yells Alix, in a voice she didn't know she'd got. 'I've got *you*. You remember that. I've got *you*.' She gets into her car, fumbles desperately in her pocket for the car keys, switches on. 'I'm off to report you now, you sadistic bitch,' she shouts, through her lowered window, as she violently puts the car into reverse and then swings forward, and scrapes away across the drive.

She accelerates, triumphant, but has to stop, shaking, as she rejoins the road. She pulls in to one side, considers, and as she considers, notices how appallingly she smells. She is covered in dog shit and lumps of Chum and decomposing slime. Dog Matter. The back of her denim skirt, her shoes, her shirt are all filthy. Disgusting. Disgusting. She smells worse than a charnel house. Dog food has always struck her as one of the most disgusting substances on earth, worse even than dog shit, and now she is covered in it. Can she really present herself at the police station looking like this, smelling like this? No, she cannot. She considers her position, switches on, and drives slowly off, away from Hartley Bridge, and onwards, up the dale.

What she needs is a telephone box, but there are not so many telephone boxes in Upper Hartdale. The next village is Ossbury, will there be a box there, will it be empty, will she be able to use it unobtrusively? There is, it is, and she can. She has planned her statement. 999, she rings. Why waste time? Police, she says she wants. She says she wants to report an incident at Hartley Court. An assault. She rings off, and does not give her name. Then she drives on. She is a criminal. A self-confessed criminal. She had committed Bodily Harm. Maybe even Grievous Bodily Harm.

As she winds on, up the dale, stinking, the beauty of her position becomes clear to her. Angela cannot report her, as Angela does not want anybody to know where she is or who she is, and Alix is the only person who knows these things. Angela will have to suffer the dog food and the wound in silence. She will have to make up some story about her assailant. If Alix wishes to confess, that will be Alix's choice. And meanwhile, Alix will get on to the RSPCA, and get Angela locked up for maltreating the Colonel's dogs. It seems a satisfactory revenge. And if the Colonel and the Doctor have other secrets, well, that is their problem. Somehow Alix knows they have.

Alix the criminal feels light of heart. She has done a good deed. Maybe she has rescued the last tottering dog. And she has vindicated her theory about Paul Whitmore. He had been mothered by a mad woman, a fury, a harpy, a gorgon. He had been tormented, like the dogs, in a punishment block, with bloody treats hanging out of reach over his head. Poor Paul was exonerated. Angela is the guilty one. The finger points at Angela.

But now, she will have to get rid of this smell. She cannot stand it any longer. The moist warm sunny air aggravates the mingled odours. She will find water, and wash herself clean.

The road is mounting, now, away from the bed of the valley. She takes a small unsignposted turning, down to the right; it is little more than a cart track. She hopes it will lead her back to the river. And it does, or would, but it peters out by a five-barred gate tied up with orange-pink plastic string. Alix parks the car, and gets out, and leans on the gate. Yes, there will be the water, down beyond that curve, where the track leads onwards. She thinks she can hear it.

She examines herself, gingerly. Her clothes have had it. They are irrecoverable. She will have to throw them away. Has she got anything else to wear? In the back of the car are, as so often, Sam's swimming things, a damp stewed bundle in a plastic bag. The towel will be useful, but his trunks not. She rummages under the rubbish and finds a providential package destined for Oxfam or the Spastics. Hopefully, she opens it, and discovers that it contains the never-worn Maltese lace blouse rejected by Liz at the time of the Pink Party, and a long black slinky sequined evening skirt from *c.* 1969. She gazes at them in admiration. She is glad to have found a good use for the Maltese blouse, to be able to give the slinky skirt its last airing, its final fling. She puts them in the plastic bag with Sam's damp chlorine-perfumed towel, and climbs over the gate and sets off down the track towards what she hopes will be the water.

It is high noon, and the air shimmers. There is a little copse to one side, moorland to the other. Over the moorland, a black and white bird plays, tumbles and shrieks. The ground is dry yet spongy. There are purple, white and yellow flowers at her feet. The track winds down, and yes, she hears the sound of water, and there is the river, tumbling, flowing, sparkling, brown, vivid. It will be cold, she knows, but not *that* cold, to one who learned to swim in the cold waters of the North Sea. There is even a little beach for her, a brown mud beach, and a pool in the river's bend. She struggles out of her soiled garments, and stands there, naked, gazing upstream, her feet sinking into the mud. She sees a vivid flash of blue. A kingfisher. Her heart leaps with delight. She knows she is peculiarly blessed. The bank is spangled with wind flowers, their seven-petalled faces like mystic day-stars. Alder and oak in tiny bud lean over the water.

The water is cold, but she braves it. She splashes, immerses herself limb by limb, rolls in it, cleanses herself. Weeds tumble past her, she thinks she sees a fish. She rises, dripping, newly baptized, and clambers to the bank, and dries herself. She sits there, on Sam's towel, in the sun. She gazes at the trees, at the flowing water, at a branch bending low over the water, a branch of rubbed, smooth dark wood. A much used branch. The sacred grove, the sacred pool. It is an old friendly place. Others swim here. Here they hang their garments, while they swim.

She dresses herself, struggling into the Maltese blouse and the sequined skirt (she has put on a little weight since the 1960s, not as much as Liz, but a little) and bundles her old stuff into the bag. She will throw the bag away when she reaches civilization and its rubbish bins. She flings Sam's towel nonchalantly round her shoulders, and sticks a glossy kingcup behind her ear. Then she strides barefoot back up the track, toward her car.

Somebody is waiting for her. An old man leans on the gate, as he has leant for centuries. His face is gnarled and wrinkled. He is dark and small of stature, as his people were and are. He smiles at tall Alix, as she approaches up the track. His smile is broad, knowing, capacious, unsurprised. Ceremoniously, he unties the pink plastic string for her, and ceremoniously he swings open the gate for her. He holds it as she passes through.

'Thank you,' she says, in her foreign tongue, bowing her head slightly in gratitude. He says nothing, but he continues to smile. Their eyes meet. Her heart overflows. It is one of the most satisfactory, one of the most benign encounters of her life.

Brian was surprised and slightly disturbed by Alix's insistence upon revenge. She told him all now, belatedly: told him that evening, as she stirred the cheese sauce. She told him that she had already rung the RSPCA and reported Angela. This time she had given her name. 'They said they'd go at once,' said Alix. 'I hope they give her a good long sentence.'

'No you don't,' said Brian. 'And anyway, people don't get put in prison for ill-treating dogs.'

'Don't they?' said Alix, tossing her hair out of her eyes, and stirring busily as the sauce thickened. 'Don't they? Well, they should.'

'Now, you don't think that,' said Brian.

'You should have seen those dogs,' said Alix.

After a while, Alix calms down and agrees that Angela is clearly off her rocker and therefore not responsible. But that doesn't mean that Alix wasn't right to get in the RSPCA.

'Look,' said Alix, 'what else can I get her for?'

'You don't have to *get* her at all.'

'Yes, I do. I owe it to Paul.'

Brian hopes that this story is near its end. He has had enough of it. He does not like the new vindictive note in Alix's voice, the new glitter in her eye. He encourages her to describe, once more, Angela's attack upon Alix, Alix's retaliation.

'Look,' said Alix, 'I don't care what I did to her. She'll never dare bring a charge against me. She's in no position to.'

Brian has some vague idea that once an assault has been reported to the police, there is no way of a charge not being brought. He hopes he has got this wrong. But anyway, Alix is indifferent to this prospect. In a way, she might even relish it.

'I wouldn't mind,' said Alix, pouring the cheese sauce on to leeks and hard-boiled eggs and looking noisily for the paprika, 'I wouldn't at all mind appearing in the dock to explain precisely why I threw that tin at Angela Whitmore. I think I'd be able to make a few points to the general public. Don't you?'

Brian looked uncomfortable, and patted Alix's shoulder in a placating manner. He could only hope that Angela was as keen to hush things up as a normal person might be. But with two mad women, one of them sniffing martyrdom and casting herself as an apologist for murder, and the other a dog-torturer, clearly way beyond the call of reason, who could tell what to expect? Angela ought to put self-preservation first. But people don't always do what they ought, do they?

*

290

Shirley Harper is staying with Marcia Campbell in Marcia's London flat. She likes it much better at Marcia's than she ever liked it at Liz's. It is more her scale. It is more like home. She sits on Marcia's comfortable settee, her feet tucked up beneath her, and looks around approvingly. There are many reassuring features. Marcia has the same brass wall brackets as Shirley, she has the same John Lewis trolley, and the same Habitat coffee mugs. In the bathroom, miraculously, she even has the same green and ivory lotus wallpaper, with matching curtains. Shirley has commented on these coincidences, and Marcia has smiled and nodded, as though there is nothing surprising about them at all. Marcia does not comment on the fact that Liz's house also has echoes of her own. Marcia and Liz, Marcia had observed, seem to share a penchant for cut glass. Shirley does not like cut glass.

Marcia Campbell, sister *ex machina*, sits knitting a complicated pullover with a pattern of small red, grey and blue checks. As she has explained to Shirley, a lot of actresses knit, some of them rather well. It's the hanging around, the waiting, says Marcia. One has to do something.

Marcia has knitted her way through much of Shirley's life story. Shirley finds it surprisingly easy to tell all to Marcia. Marcia has proved an invaluable ally, in this last difficult fortnight. She even accompanied Shirley (with Liz, of course) to Cliff's inquest, and then to Cliff's funeral which was very decent of her, in view of the fact that they'd only just met. She was very nice to Celia and to Barry, and even the censorious Celia seemed to approve of Marcia. (Marcia believes that Celia has known of her existence all along, but has kept her mouth shut. Celia is still water and runs deep.) Marcia has proved an excellent mediator with Robert Holland, who increasingly will not do, who is increasingly suspected of being a middle-aged bore and a philandering neurotic, but whose interest in Shirley has been

much heightened by the Marcia factor. Marcia tacitly acknowledges that he will not do, while maintaining a perfectly friendly
attitude towards his manoeuvres. It is all very amicable.

Marcia's flat is in unfashionable Acton. It is small, and warm,
and richly patterned. It is cosy. Its furniture is soft and rounded
and mature, like its owner. It is full − too full, sighs Marcia − of
mementoes and keepsakes − framed photographs, saucers from
Harrogate and Hay-on-Wye, postcards from Venezuela and Korea
and New Zealand and Mali, beads and trinkets and bobbles and
souvenirs. People are always giving things and sending things to
Marcia, and, as she is a good-natured woman, she does not like
to part with these offerings. She seems to have friends in all
walks of life − bus drivers, knighted Thespians, managers of old
people's homes, schoolteachers, antique dealers, shopkeepers,
swimming-pool attendants. Her life is heterogeneous. A magpie
life. It's because my parents ran this boarding house, she explains
to Shirley. All sorts came through. Mainly theatrical, but lots of
others, people from all over the world. They all came to us, and
once they'd found us, they kept on coming back. It was like a
family.

Shirley is much taken with this diversity. There is room for
her here too, in the corner of this settee.

Marcia shares her flat with a black man. He is her live-in lover.
One day they may marry. Or they may not. His name is Oliver,
and he works at Bush House, for the World Service of the BBC.
He was born in Trinidad, he tells Shirley, but was educated in
Britain, and has worked here for thirty years. He is a very good-
looking man, with a wry smile and a small moustache. He and
Marcia have been together for three years now, he tells Shirley.
He is very pleased to meet Shirley, he says, as he too comes
from a large and complicated family and has many legitimate and
illegitimate siblings and half-siblings. They are scattered round
the globe, although concentrated mainly in the West Indies and

the Home Counties. Like Shirley, like Marcia, he discovered the identity of his own father late in life.

These mysteries seem natural to Marcia and Oliver. They do not seem fazed by them. They do not seem to think that the norm of suburban South Yorkshire is at all normal. It is only one of many patterns. They make all things seem possible. They are comfortingly unalarmed by the uncertainty of Shirley's finances, by her muddles over the defunct business, the mortgaged house. They know people who are in *much* worse muddles than Shirley, people without a bean, without a penny, without a prospect, who manage to rub along all right, and come out the other side. Look, they have muddled through themselves, through terrible risks, ridiculous uncertainties! Consider the lilies, says Marcia, that was my Mum's motto, when the milk ran out and the final notices came in. Consider the lilies.

Marcia knits, Oliver smokes a French cigarette, Shirley sits and watches and wonders. All three are half-listening to the Elgar cello concerto on Radio Three. The deep warm forgiving strains fill the small enormous room. The first tears rise to Shirley's eyes.

Carla Davis cannot believe what she hears. Charles Headleand has betrayed her. He has agreed to accept the word of those murderous assassins, those crazed fanatics. He has issued a statement, on his return to England. He has spoken of conciliation and understanding. He has betrayed her in public. Carla is dark with rage. She will have her revenge. She has always hated Charles. She pours herself another large Scotch, and plots vengeance.

Susie Enderby and Blake Leith make love in Blake's house, in Blake's bed, in Blake's bedroom overlooking the North Sea. High on the cliff, above a waste of grey water, they embrace and entwine and separate and converge. The waves dash white foam at the red cliff's foot. They are mad for one another, they are possessed, they writhe and moan and cry out. They are in deadly, deadly earnest. They had not meant this, but it has happened, it has overtaken them, it is impersonal, it sweeps them along. They cry out, the seagulls cry, their serpentine limbs coil and uncoil. When the paroxysms are over for a moment, when they are able to seize a moment's repose, they wander naked to the window, and gaze down at the raging water. Blake, his arm around Susie's bruised and savaged shoulders, quotes:

For the foam flowers endure where the rose blossoms wither,
And men that love lightly may die: but we?

Susie shudders, quails. But there is no returning, for Susie and Blake Leith. On they must go, on and on, until they are let drop. And then what, then what? Ah, do not ask. How can there be an ending for this most unsuitable of couples?

Fanny Kettle, shopping in Waitrose, catches sight of Alix Bowen. Alix waves, merrily, and they converge, their trollies interlocking. 'Hi,' says Alix, 'how are things?' Fanny and Alix have become quite friendly, brought together by the death of Beaver. Fanny had attended the funeral, resplendent in mink, with a dashing black felt hat and black rosetted shoes, and seamed black stockings. Alix has decided Fanny is simply a harmless well-meaning eccentric.

'I'm great, thanks,' says Fanny. 'Where did you find that asparagus? I didn't see any.'

'Oh, it's back there somewhere,' gestures Alix, vaguely, towards the rich international diversity of vegetables. 'In the pre-packed section, near the oyster mushrooms.' (She is slightly embarrassed to be caught with extravagant asparagus amongst her purchases, and hopes Fanny's eagle eyes have also noted the carrots, baby turnips and bumper packs of toilet tissue.)

'I say,' says Fanny, 'what a terrible thing about that woman and the dogs, in the paper. Tony told me all about it. You *were* brave. I think it's a scandal, only fining her £120. Will they close the place down?'

'I think so,' says Alix. She does not want to talk about it. She is sick of the whole thing. Revenge is not sweet after all. She has learned things about Angela Whitmore that she does not want to know. She has learned things about the Doctor and the Colonel that she does not want to know.

'And Tony tells me you're thinking of getting a dog yourselves?'

'Oh, does he?' says Alix. 'We'll see about that. Sam's always wanted a dog, but I'm not sure I can face one.'

'They are a terrible *tie*,' says Fanny.

And on this platitude, they part, Fanny towards the asparagus, Alix towards the butter.

Paul Whitmore sits in his solitary cell. He has been rereading and rereading Alix's letter. She has tried to explain him to himself, and he honours her attempt. She tells him that his mother is crazy. She alludes to the plight of the dogs. (Not all the dogs had been mistreated: some had been looked after with pride and care. Apparently this is a not unusual feature of cases of extreme abuse or neglect of animals.) She says his mother is in need of psychiatric treatment. She urges him not to think too much about his mother. She mentions the death of his twin sister.

Paul cannot remember his twin sister, however hard he tries. He can conjure up her photograph, framed on the mantelpiece, but he cannot remember her. He cannot recall that his mother ever spoke of her. So what has she got to do with it? Alix seems in some way to be blaming the death of the baby twin sister for the death of the dogs and the death of Jilly Fox. He cannot see the connection. He cannot follow the explanation. There seem to be too many explanations. Explanations recede and recede, down endless dark smelling corridors, down staircases and along walkways and round corners where victims lie in wait for him, up and on and down and round, round his confused brain and jumbled memory, walled in by grills and barbed wire and spiked barriers and iron gates, an endless prison of circularity.

Alix tells him that she will come to see him as soon as she gets back from Italy. Alix is a small light burning. She has not abandoned him. She forgives him. She loves him. His mother is mad and cannot forgive him and cannot love him, but Alix has been faithful to him. See, she signs herself, 'Love, Alix'. Would she write so if she did not love him? No, she would not. Paul touches her letter tenderly, then refolds it and puts it in its envelope. He will cherish it.

He puts the letter away in his drawer, with his other sparse possessions, and returns to his self-appointed task. He has taken up botany. He has not abandoned the Celts and the Druids, but has been finding them confusing of late. Did his favourite people really inhabit, as a recent source has told him, 'a world of gross meat-eaters, feasting round an open hearth, raising up whole limbs in both hands and biting off the meat'? A world of firedogs and roasting spits and great cauldrons and burning stewing flesh? He has turned to botany for comfort. He is drawing a cross-section of the stem of a woody plant. With care, he copies from the textbook. He is not allowed a real specimen. He is not allowed a razor blade for dissection. He labels the parts, in green fine-point pen, and then moves on to a cross-section of the globular capsule of a corn poppy.

Paul had always been fascinated by cross-sections. To slice through the meeting place, the joining point, the node itself, through the conductor, the connector, the conveyor of current. Through the many coloured wiring of life. If one slices neatly across the current, with Occam's razor, one will catch the mystery as it flows. This is a pure activity, clean, clinical, inquiring. Thus will he find the source of power.

Paul draws a circle. His method of drawing circles is curious. It is one he has used since primary school. He evolved it for himself. First of all, he draws a square, using a ruler, a lightly pencilled square. Then, within the square, he draws a circle. Then he rubs out the supporting framework. Thus he squares the circle. He has always thought this a good way of drawing circles. He draws, rubs, labels, perseveres. Like Alix, he perseveres. The poppy capsule is neatly divided, segmented into little compartments. Little pepper-pot compartments of oblivion. Botany is a pleasant pastime. Poppies are silk and scarlet, but this drawing is white and grey and flat.

It is Sunday in Northam, and Clive Enderby finds himself taking William and Victoria to the Hansborough Wildlife Park. Susie has vanished. He does not know where she is. She said she was going to see an old schoolfriend in Bradford, but he does not believe her. She does not expect him to believe her. When Susie and Clive look at one another these days, they stare, ashen, in disbelief. This is not possible, they silently agree, as they stagger on from terrible day to terrible day. They are nice people. This is not possible.

The wildlife park is a plot of derelict land, rescued from the demolition of the Pitts & Harley works. It is not Clive's kind of place at all, but the children begged to be taken, they had been once with their primary school, they had liked it there. To Clive's eye it is small, scruffy, shabby, overgrown with weeds. It is a mockery of his grandiose vision of green hills. Those who run it are grotesquely proud of it. A keen young woman in

World War II landgirl's dungarees points out features of interest and gives the children lists to tick. Sparrows, robins, starlings, magpies, kestrels, wrens, thrushes, mice, groundsel, dog's mercury, rocket, common mouse-ear, dandelions . . . weeds, nothing but vermin and weeds. A wooden hut houses more charts, diagrams, botanical information and cardboard cups of tea. Clive is bored out of his mind. The young woman explains that small is beautiful, and talks about the lungs of the city, the small breathing spaces that a city needs.

Clive watches the eager faces of William and Victoria. No, perhaps he is not exactly bored. It is more that he is in torment. He would like to believe that this small rescued space means something. But he cannot believe. Nor can he believe that he will go home, alone, with these children, at Sunday lunch time, and try to assemble for them a fun meal of baked beans, sausages, tomatoes, toast.

William is asking the name of a small purple flower growing in the scrubby verge. He has begun to develop a stammer, over the last few weeks. Clive's heart stands still whenever he hears it.

It is ground ivy, says the young woman. She shows him a picture in her book. William had guessed wrong from his chart, he had guessed self-heal. She explains the difference between the two plants, plants that look identical to Clive's impatient eye. It is a little too early in the year, anyway, she says, for self-heal.

Can one make oneself interested in such small things? For the sake of the children, perhaps?

'Now here,' says the young woman, 'is a real rarity.' Clive follows her pointing finger, as she indicates something that to his eye looks very like common-or-garden chickweed. But no, she explains, if you look carefully, you can see that it is an unusual variety of wood chickweed, which has no right to be growing here at all. She offers the children the use of her botanical lens. Then she offers the lens to Clive, and he finds himself gazing at the quiet unassuming little plant with something that almost approaches curiosity.

It is Sunday in London. Carla Davis waits for dusk, which comes late at this time of year. She walks over from Kentish Town to St John's Wood, muttering angrily to herself. There is Liz's house, next to the clinic. Its small front garden is in full bloom. A white magnolia, a pink cherry, a flowering currant. The colours are deep in the early evening. The lights are on, the curtains have not been drawn, she can see in. She sits on the crumbling garden wall, and stares at them. There they are, the Headleands: Liz and Charles, Aaron and Alan, and one of the girls, she does not know which. Charles is holding an open atlas, and they are all laughing. She cannot hear what they are saying, but they are laughing and laughing. Charles points at the atlas, speaks, and they all shake their heads and laugh the more. Charles looks puzzled, amused, bewildered. They are teasing him, he is taking it well.

Carla takes a lipstick from her bag, and draws a swastika on Liz's gate. She walks off, a little unsteadily, thinks better of it, returns, loosens a piece of mortar from the wall, and hurls it at the window. She knows they cannot see her, but she sees their astonished faces, silenced for a moment, as they swing grotesquely, in unison, towards the crash. The window does not break, but it splinters. She has a small amount of triumph. But then, bizarrely, they start to laugh again, and after a moment Aaron flings open the door and calls, 'Who's there?' His words echo into the dark street. He shrugs his shoulders. 'Be like that, then,' he calls, to nobody, and goes in and shuts the door.

Now the Headleands draw the curtains against the night, as Carla makes her way back to Kentish Town and the second half of the bottle.

It is Sunday in New Zealand, and as the Headleands draw the

curtains in St John's Wood, Stella Headland walks along a bright morning beach of black sand. The wind is in her hair, the sea crashes, the gulls swoop above her, the air is cold, crisp, pure. It is early morning and late autumn in New Zealand. Stella is happy. She has got away. She has gone to the other side of the world. She could go no further. She is free. She walks along the beach, in baggy trousers, in shapeless sweatshirt, with her hair loose and her feet bare, shedding weight, shedding history, shedding family. A rocky island rides the horizon, an empty island. There is no one here but the birds, but behind her, in the little town perching in the valley, she has friends, friends who have never heard of Liz and Charles Headleand, and a job teaching small children who have never been to England, and who look towards the shining Pacific.

Late May 1987

Esther, Liz and Alix sit at a little table beneath a vine trellis. They tell one another stories, as they watch the little boats put out upon the lake. It is mid-afternoon, and the day is just beginning to revive from its noontide swoon. Esther, Liz and Alix have lunched well. They have devoured varying kinds of pasta, and little mixed fried fishes of the lake and a sublime Gorgonzola, and a salad of green grasses, and they have drunk a litre of Bardolino and a litre or two of fizzy water. The wine was undated, but the water had been bottled in June 1986, the first anniversary of Esther's birthday picnic in Somerset, and the birth month of young Cornelia Headleand. They have commented on these not very near coincidences. Now they are sipping black coffee and deep-yellow Strega. The restaurant does not hurry them. There is no hurry here. They can sit here if they wish until night falls. They gaze across the mild dancing water, through a haze of midges, at a little island with a ruined tower, and at the far mountains with their snowy peaks. They are in a bowl of mountains. That evening, they have an appointment with Beaver's mistress in Pallanza. She has invited them for a drink. Meanwhile, they talk and talk. They all have so much to say, they do not know who should speak first, so their stories intermingle, as they have done for the last two days of their little Italian holiday.

Liz has told Esther the extraordinary story of the appearance of Marcia Campbell, and has updated Alix on the extraordinary rapport which has sprung up between Shirley and Marcia.

'I don't know,' says Liz, reverting to this theme, 'it seems to me to be nothing short of miraculous, the way those two get on. Well, what's really miraculous is the way Marcia gets on with *everybody*. She has this – this amazing *easiness*. She seems to find everything so easy. I don't understand it. Her parents must have been a remarkable couple. Well, they were, she says so. And Shirley and I always found things so – so hard. You should meet this man Oliver. I love him. He's perfect. Wherever did she find such a man? He's the most laid-back man in the Western world. How can they both be so nice to *everybody*?'

'She's an actress, you say,' says Esther.

'But it's not like that at *all*,' says Liz, shaking her head slowly. 'I mean, she does call people darling, and things like that. But that's not the point. There's more to it than that.'

Liz pauses, and watches a blue butterfly land upon the red check tablecloth.

'She calls me Lizzie,' says Liz, wonderingly.

She speaks of Joanna Hestercombe and her chestnut mare, and of Charles's response to the Marcia story.

'He tries to pretend he knew it all along, but if he did, why didn't he tell *me*?' says Liz.

'And what does Charles make of Marcia?' asks Alix.

'Oh, he loves her, of course,' says Liz. 'He thinks she's wonderful.'

301

And they discuss Charles, and his unfitness for the post he has of course accepted, and his abandoning of Carla Davis and her cause, and his new interest in playing the fatherly role. 'He's become positively patriarchal,' says Liz, 'it's amazing, he's always trying to organize little family evenings, he's bought Alan a new car, he's threatened to buy Aaron a piano, he takes Sally and her friend Jo to the theatre, he keeps on ringing Stella in New Zealand, he even came round to St John's Wood the other evening with a bunch of flowers. He's a changed man. He keeps talking about his responsibilities. He hasn't mentioned satellites for weeks. I don't know what's got into him.'

'Loneliness,' said Esther. 'That's what got into him. Loneliness in Baldai.'

The mention of loneliness brings them to Alix's murderer. Alix believes that she had unknotted and unravelled the strands of her murderer, that she has seen into him and known him. She presents Liz and Esther with her version of the murderer, and they have, by and large, accepted it. Yes, they concede, Paul Whitmore has clearly been unhinged by maternal neglect, by maternal hatred, by punitive discrimination in his early years. An abused child. Liz does not like to point out that by Alix's account, Paul's father is a perfectly normal, indeed quite kind-hearted chap, and that many children grow up fairly normal without any parental kindness at all. At least they do not grow up into mass murderers. She does not raise this objection as Alix is pleased with her explanation, and anyway, Liz has no better explanation to offer. She does not claim to understand the pathology of Paul Whitmore. Like Alix, she tends not to believe in evil. So Alix's version is as good as any, and it is certainly based on more information than anyone else has yet assembled about the poor Horror.

Alix has established, through more consultation with Paul's father, that Paul had a twin sister who died in infancy.

'I don't know how I missed it,' she repeats. 'There were the

302

photos, on the mantelpiece. I can see them now, but I didn't see them then. She died when she was eight months old. A cot death. No explanation, no reason.'

'And Angela blamed Paul?'

'So the old man says. He says she used to rant at him when he was a baby, saying he'd be better dead too, saying her life was over, saying she hated him for surviving. Paul can't remember any of this. Or so he says. But he must have been affected. How could one not be affected?'

'So,' said Esther. 'So, one feels sorry for Angela.'

'Well, sort of,' said Alix. She frowned. 'But it is *odd*, isn't it?' she repeats. 'That Paul should have turned out to fit so neatly the sort of explanation that I might be expected to find for him? Don't you think it's odd?'

'Well, not really,' said Esther. 'I mean, he's not just any old sort of murderer, he's *your* murderer. If he'd been a different kind of murderer, you'd have lost interest in him long ago. You only persevered because you knew he was going to turn out to be the kind of person he turns out to be. If he'd been a –' Esther gropes, desperately, for types alien to Alix's broad sympathies, 'a football hooligan murderer, or a racist murderer, or a City-scandal murderer, or a drug-pushing murderer, you mightn't have stuck with him. Or, come to that, he with you. Not all murderers are interested in Druids and Roman History and botany, you know.'

'I suppose so,' said Alix. 'Yes, I suppose so.' She is deep in thought. 'Actually he was a bit of a drug pusher,' she says, in parenthesis. 'He swears he never touched the stuff, but he used to carry it. He says it was a way of making friends and meeting people.' She reverts to her main theme. 'Yes, I suppose you're right,' she says, to Esther. 'So, I haven't proved anything. I've just confirmed my own prejudices about human nature. I've been travelling around a closed circuit. A closed system. Me and my murderer together. It wasn't a theorem, it was a circuit.'

'I wouldn't know,' says Esther. 'You're the social scientist, not me.'

Alix looks at Liz. Liz is polishing her sunglasses on a corner of her rather crumpled linen skirt, but after a moment she returns Alix's inquiring gaze.

'Put it this way,' says Liz. 'If you hadn't been on the same circuit, you wouldn't have been able to get anywhere with him at all. You'd never have been able to meet him at all.'

'That's not very satisfactory,' says Alix.

'No,' says Liz. 'One wants a theory that fits all occasions. A new theorem. But there isn't one. And look at the circularity of my own life. All the roads leading back to Marcia. Although I never even knew she was there.'

'Life sets us unfair puzzles,' says Alix. 'Puzzles with pieces missing. How I used to hate jigsaw puzzles with missing pieces. One got so far, and then could never finish them. Or not properly. Not quite properly.'

A silence falls. A leaf drops from the vine.

'And so,' repeats Esther, 'one feels sorry for Angela.'

'I don't feel guilty about Angela,' said Alix. 'Nor about the Doctor and the Colonel. It was time somebody got them. For something. And you should have seen those dogs. You should see our poor Bonzo.'

'I never thought you'd ever have a dog, Alix,' said Esther. 'Let alone a bull mastiff.'

'It's a *revolting* dog,' said Liz, severely.

'No, he isn't,' said Alix, defensively. 'He's coming on quite nicely. He's a very affectionate, intelligent dog. And anyway, Sam's always wanted a dog.'

'But not a bull mastiff,' repeated Esther.

'It can't help being a bull mastiff,' said Alix.

'Why ever did you call it Bonzo?' asked Esther.

'I don't know,' said Alix, watching the butterfly settle on the back of Esther's small brown cameo-ringed hand. 'I don't know. I think it was Brian's idea. It was a joke that stuck. Brian *likes* the dog. Brian's finished his novel, you know. I thought he'd never write another.'

Esther and Liz murmur congratulations. What will it be called, they ask. He hasn't got a title yet, says Alix, suggestions would be welcome. He wants something to do with hope arising out of disaster. It's a family chronicle of working-class life, a sort of celebration of tradition and change. It's jolly good, says Alix, loyally, but I haven't finished it yet. He says it ends in the year 2000, with a millenarian party on Houndsback Moor. And fireworks.

A waiter brings more coffee, and they spend a pleasant half hour inventing titles for Brian's novel. *The Rainbow*, Esther rather unkindly suggests. *Bright Sparks*, says Liz. *The Crucible? The Roman Candle? The Catherine Wheel? The Bengal Light?* says Alix, obscurely, her mind running on the first small feeble firework of the post-war years, a modest little coloured flame braving the end of black-out, celebrating the Beveridge Report and the Welfare State. A little coloured unspectacular glow.

'Catherine wheels never worked properly when we had them,' says Liz. 'They always got stuck. All that money, fizzling away. Stuck. Charles would get in such a rage. I've never really cared for fireworks.'

'Italian fireworks,' says Esther, 'are something else altogether. And very noisy too. Lots of bangs.'

'In Celtic mythology,' says Alix, 'wheels were believed to be apotropaic. It says so in one of Beaver's poems. I had to look the word up. Beaver used to do it on purpose. To obscure.'

'Beaver was a barbarian,' adds Alix, obscurely, thinking of Lucan, and the Roman legions, and Beaver's stubborn self-exile from the soft south. She has not yet decided whether or not to edit Beaver's letters. Her decision depends partly upon

what she makes of the Queen of Novara, whom she will meet
for the first time this evening. She is waiting for a sign, a
portent. Liz and Esther do not know whether to encourage her
to pursue the project or not. Would it be right for Alix to spend
more years of her life with Beaver's dusty old books and holiday
slides, with footnotes and dictionaries, looking up words like
'apotropaic' and discovering that it means 'warding off evil', and
worrying about what Beaver really did in Paris when he wasn't
working on a *transition*? They do not know, they cannot advise.
Part of Alix would be engaged and satisfied by this task. But
what of the other Alix? What of the stubborn mouse of Utah,
gnawing patiently away at the tangled knots of injustice, prefer-
ment, inequality, aggression? And what of the Alix, who lives
not in the past, but in the pale hour before dawn, dreaming of
that great festival which she glimpses now but in shadowy
images, that great festival to which all shall be invited, to which
all shall come in celebration? Liz Headleand, Esther Breuer,
Charles Headleand, Shirley Harper, Stephen Cox, Otto Werner,
Perry Blinkhorn, Marcia Campbell, Fanny Kettle, Steve and Dora,
Carla Davis, Dirk Davis, the Black Orchid, Paul Whitmore, Old
Uncle Tom Cobbleigh and *all*? It is already too late for Cliff
Harper and Howard Beaver, it may be too late for Dirk Davis,
time is running out for others on this list, and Alix wants this
party to take place in her lifetime, here on this earth. What help
from the letters of the dead?

'One would think,' says Esther, watching their friend the
butterfly, 'that at our age things would be *clearer*. That life, if you
like, would be even *more* circular than it is. That options would
have diminished to nothingness. Instead of opening up. As they
do. Odd, isn't it, the way new prospects continue to offer
themselves? One turns the corner, one climbs a little hill, and
there is a whole new vista. Or a vista that seems to be new.
How can this be?'

They gaze at the lake. Little boats with coloured sails skim lazily upon the water, a windsurfer tries the light breeze, a spluttering little orange chugger disturbs the peace. Esther raises her fresco-binoculars and watches them, then lifts her eyes up to the mountains. She focuses, stares, smiles. She hands the binoculars to Liz.

'Look,' she says, 'do look. I thought they were great silver eagles.'

And there, across the lake, beneath the steep mountain, hang great men-birds, hovering motionless in the bright air, against the falling forests of deep green. Liz watches, hands the glasses on to Alix, Alix watches.

'Icarus,' says Alix. 'The flights of Icarus.'

The afternoon wears itself away towards evening. They walk along the lake shore, the picturesque idyll to one side of them, and heaps of characteristic Italian speculative building rubble to the other. They pick their way over bricks, exposed pipes, unfinished draining systems, and a dry river bed, they walk past back gardens with rabbits in cages and nodding sunflowers, and find themselves in a small cemetery where the dead stare gravely at them from silver-framed photographs amongst bulbous dust-whitened plastic flowers. The blue butterfly is still with them. It settles on Esther's grey-blue hair.

'Amazing,' says Esther, staring with admiration at the tragic kitsch.

Esther has decided not to marry Robert Oxenholme. Well, she thinks she has decided not to marry him. She has not told him yet. She has not mentioned the proposal to Liz and Alix. She has decided that she is better on her own. She has decided to leave Elena Volpe. Now, standing there in the marble-chip-gleaming cemetery, she suddenly says: 'I'm coming back to London. I'm going to buy a flat. In London. That's the plan.'

Esther's parents have recently died, and have left her money.

She can now afford to buy a flat. Not a nice flat, in a nice district, but a flat.

Liz and Alix express their satisfaction at this decision. They all three wander back toward their hired Renault, talking of England and its prospects, of the approaching June election, of the way the wind blows.

'England's not a bad country,' says Liz, as they get into the car, to drive towards Pallanza.

'No,' says Alix. 'No.' The lake glitters, the mountains soar, the coloured sails catch the evening sun, and the shadows of the Lombard poplars are long. 'No,' says Alix, 'England's not a bad country. It's just a mean, cold, ugly, divided, tired, clapped-out post-imperial post-industrial slag-heap covered in polystyrene hamburger cartons. It's not a bad country at all. I love it.'

And they laugh – what else can they do? – as Liz drives off towards Pallanza, where an old woman waits for them on her terrace, amidst lichen-gilded baroque statues, and dark carved hedges. White peacocks stray on an emerald lawn beneath a spreading cedar. A fountain plays, its waters tumbling from an upheld shell. A frog croaks, the midges hum and lightly whine. The white azaleas and the white lilac cluster. The old woman's spectacles are folded before her on the wrought-iron table. She does not need them to gaze at her splendid view, her historic view of garden and lake. She is far-sighted now, she can see into the past and the future.

And the present she enjoys. She is looking forward to receiving her guests. She does not receive many visitors these days.

She is looking forward to the bottle of champagne that will be opened for them. She is looking forward to showing them her treasures. She is too old now to take them round the garden herself, but Robert Oxenholme will escort them. Robert Oxenholme will open the champagne. Dear Robert is good at these things. That is what he is for. There he sits, dear boy, at the far end of the terrace, reading the evening paper, smoking a little cigar to keep away the insects, as he waits to receive the three unknown women from England. He has been trying to persuade her to leave some of her treasures to the National Gallery. She has been elusive. She has been stringing him along. 'What has England done for me?' she has asked him. They are old friends, Robert Oxenholme and the Queen of Novara.

The old woman smiles and nods to herself. A blue butterfly settles on her folded spectacles. Life is still pleasant. She has wit and power and she owns beauty. The white peacocks strut and flaunt. The scent of lavender fills the evening air, blending with the blue smoke of the little cigar. She is filled with pleasurable anticipation as she hears the wheels of the hired Renault crunch along the gravel drive.